One-Way Trip . . .

Outside the little plane's window Sam saw the flames of a slash and burn operation in the jungle below. In seconds they would be over it. He hoped she wouldn't do what he feared she might.

She did. Leaning on the steering yoke, the White Angel put them into a dive . . . they were heading right for the flames!

Sam seized the yoke, overpowering her, putting the plane into a roll. When green jungle replaced flaming earth, he straightened the plane.

Cold steel poked into Sam's neck. He looked around into the barrel of a 9 mm Beretta.

"Hands off the controls, Mr. Borne."

The White Angel

E.B. Cross

St. Martin's Press
New York

THE WHITE ANGEL

Copyright © 1986 by E. B. Cross

Published by arrangement with the author.

ISBN: 0-312-90462-2   Can. ISBN: 0-312-90521-1

Printed in the United States of America

First St. Martin's Press mass market edition/November 1986

10 9 8 7 6 5 4 3 2 1

The characteristic of heroism is its
persistency.
—Ralph Waldo Emerson

1

PINNED

Reese had never killed a woman before, but this assignment, his latest from the Outfit, called for him to do so. It made him tight, uneasy, reluctant. He drained his pint of Guinness and placed it on the bar, watched the brown foam streak the sides of the empty glass, then glanced around the room. The Horseshoe Bar of the Shelbourne Hotel was full of tourists and businesspeople just off work. They stood two deep at the bar and crowded the tables along the walls. One woman directly across the bar from Reese made bedroom eyes at him, but there was nothing he could do about it now. He was on an assignment and it was time to deliver.

He slipped a pound note under his empty glass, then reached down and plucked his leather weekender from the floor. Nodding and smiling, he wriggled away from the bar and walked out into the lobby. To his left, the sitting room was full of people enjoying tea and snacks. As he passed the reception desk he nodded farewell to the clerk who'd checked him out of the hotel a half hour earlier, then pushed through the glass doors and walked out under the canopy. The

1

doorman at the foot of the stairs looked up and smiled.

"Would you be wanting a cab, sir?"

"No, thank you. I'm being picked up."

Reese looked across the street into the dark expanse of Saint Stephen's Green. That afternoon he'd had a nice stroll there, killing time; he'd even sat beside the small lake for half an hour and read the papers while small boys sailed boats under the watchful eyes of nannies. The light changed at the corner of Grafton Street and he watched the traffic race toward them. His caller had said he'd pick him up at six o'clock sharp and that he'd be driving a forest-green Jaguar XJ6. No Jaguar emerged from the stream of traffic. He checked his watch: a minute past six.

"Beautiful day today, wasn't it, sir?" the doorman remarked.

"Indeed it was."

"Is this your first trip to Dublin, sir?"

"No, I've been here many times."

The light at Grafton Street changed again and a new wave of traffic rolled toward them. Out of it emerged a forest-green Jaguar XJ6. Reese moved toward it quickly, grateful for its punctuality and relieved not to have to make any more small talk with the doorman, who shot in front of him and held the passenger door open. Reese ducked in and saw immediately that the backseat was occupied. The driver was a small man, no bigger than a jockey. He thrust out his hand and introduced himself.

"I'm Jenkins."

"Nice to meet you, Mr. Jenkins. I'm Warren Reese."

"That's what I figured."

Reese turned to the passenger in back. His heart

skipped. Even in the shadows it was possible to tell she was movie-star beautiful. Dressed in a beige riding outfit, complete with leather patched jodhpurs and gleaming boots, she wore a riding cap at a jaunty angle. It framed a perfect Aryan face the color of buttermilk, with pink cheeks and drop-dead blue eyes above a fine nose and a sensual mouth. On either side of her face blond tresses swept down and swirled before being pinned up at the back of her neck. She sat way back in the seat and made no effort to greet him. She was the woman, he was sure of it. The thought of killing so beautiful a creature redoubled his uneasiness.

Reese stuck out his hand. "And you're . . . ?"

She didn't take his hand. She only stared. Finally she touched his hand ever so briefly with hers and said, in a husky voice barely above a whisper, "I'm Wilda." She withdrew her hand and only stared.

"Would you like me to put your bag in back, Mr. Reese?" Jenkins asked.

"That's all right. I can do it." Reese started to swing his weekender over the seat into the passenger compartment beside the woman called Wilda. Jenkins grabbed it.

"Not there, Mr. Reese. Never there."

Jenkins took the bag and hopped out. While he put the bag in the trunk Reese turned back to Wilda.

"I didn't expect such a pleasant surprise as you to pick me up."

"Life is full of surprises, Mr. Reese."

"Yes, it is. Please call me Warren."

She ignored this. Reese felt the car bob on its springs as Jenkins slammed down the trunk lid. He was suddenly uncomfortable in the silence. This was

3

surely a bizarre couple. Right now his assignment didn't seem like a simple hit at all. All he had been instructed to do was to contact this man Jenkins, a prominent Kilkenny horse breeder, and offer him a deal on the stolen sperm of premier American Thoroughbreds. Through Jenkins he would contact the target, the blond woman in the backseat. How all this would work hadn't been explained to him. But the Company was sure that Jenkins would lead to the woman, and he had. On the surface it was an easy-access job. There were no complications, and no danger. He thought he'd never had an easier deal. But something wasn't right. The fit wasn't good.

Jenkins climbed in behind the wheel and they sped off without a word. The Dublin traffic was heavy, but they soon cleared it and raced through the suburbs, Jenkins tearing in and out of lanes of traffic. Reese attempted two or three times to make conversation, but Jenkins was the only one to reply on each occasion, and the attempts went nowhere. Soon they rode in silence, Reese noting the small towns they passed, the curious names, the small shops, the utter stillness of a provincial Catholic country after the sun goes down. The trip to Kilkenny, Reese estimated, would take about two hours. He knew only that Jenkins had a stud farm near there.

It was not long after Reese noted local signs for Kilkenny that Jenkins spun the Jaguar off the main road onto a local lane lined with hedges about eight feet high. The lane was narrow and dark. Only a thin curve of moon hung in the sky. Out of the blue Wilda spoke.

"You Americans are a foolish people, Mr. Reese."

He decided to be affable, though he'd heard this

kind of insult for years and hated it more now than ever. "I suppose so," he said, then added, "but I suppose all people are foolish now and again. It's what makes life so interesting."

"I disagree, Mr. Reese, emphatically. Americans are the most foolish people on earth."

He started to turn around in his seat to look at her, but she stopped him cold.

"Please don't turn around, Mr. Reese. I don't wish to debate this point. I only want you to remember it."

For some reason Reese felt impelled to obey. "I will," he said.

"That's good."

Jenkins slowed the Jaguar, and ahead Reese spotted a break in the hedge. Two stone pillars framed a wrought-iron gate. Jenkins reached up to the sun visor and pressed a switch. The Jaguar crept to a halt while the gate swung inward. Then they slowly moved through the gate and onto a gravel driveway stretching to a large courtyard before a stone farmhouse and garage. When they pulled into the courtyard, the woman called Wilda reached behind her and unpinned her hair. It cascaded down over her shoulders.

Jenkins stopped the car and rested his hand on his chest inside his hacking jacket. He left the engine running. It purred. Reese started to turn when he felt a piercing pain. Wilda jabbed her hairpin into his neck. She drove it about an inch deep, her index finger pressing it home steadily while her thumb and middle finger positioned it. Reese emitted a sound like a hiccup. His eyes widened. He looked toward Jenkins.

In the driver's seat Jenkins had turned partway around, like someone riding sidesaddle, his left leg hitched up on the seat. In his right hand he held a

Browning nine-millimeter automatic. He smiled and said, "Just sit nice now, Mr. Reese. It won't take but a minute."

Instinctively Reese reached for his gun, a twenty-two-caliber automatic he thought more than sufficient insurance for this job; he had planned to wait for the right moment and take the woman out with his bare hands. His body shook, betraying him. His arm jerked. His twitching hand found not his inside pocket but the buckle of his seat belt. Jenkins reached across and flicked his hand away from the buckle. "It's better to be buckled up for safety, Mr. Reese," he said, then laughed.

"That's enough, Jenkins," Wilda ordered. Jenkins immediately stopped laughing.

Reese heard them as though they were players on a far-off stage. They didn't seem immediate to him. They didn't seem real. He felt like he was underwater. He felt the way he had when he was six and his tonsils were taken out; he remembered the powerful drift, the relentless undertow of the ether. He felt the warm trickle of blood on his neck, though when he tried to reach up his arm didn't move.

Sweat beaded on his face. His chest ached. He thought how good an agent he'd always been, in Guatemala, in Honduras, in Cuba, in Iran, in Chile, everywhere. He'd been wounded, and commended; he'd been honored, and promoted. He was a top agent. And now this. He felt spittle stand out on his lips as he tried to speak. He felt it drool down his chin. His tongue weighed several tons.

"Don't try to speak, Mr. Reese. It is not your fault, Warren. All you Americans are trusting, and foolish. My hairpin was dipped in succinyl choline. You are already paralyzed. In seconds you will be dead. Per-

6

haps I am only telling you what you already know. I am aware you are a superior agent, but I am unbeatable and I must make this clear to everyone, no matter the cost. And you have paid the supreme price."

She leaned forward and took his face in her hands. Tenderly, very tenderly, she gazed at him. Then she reached into her pocket and extracted a linen handkerchief. She dabbed his forehead and blotted the spittle on his lips and chin. Then she leaned in and kissed him on the mouth. It was a long, erotic kiss.

It hurt Reese. It hurt him to die this way. It hurt him that she'd used his Christian name, that she'd made a point of it. It hurt his pride.

Wilda released him and Reese lost consciousness. His head lolled against his chest. Through a haze, vaguely, he heard Jenkins cut the purring engine.

Then he died.

2

SPADEWORK

Valhalla Ranch
October 4

It was hot in the big barn with the jungle sun beating down on it. Few places were hotter than the Amazon Basin. Occasionally a horse whinnied or shuffled around its stall. Flies buzzed. Tails flicked. In the beams of sunlight shooting from the open doors of the hayloft, insects whirled like motes. It was too hot to work. This didn't stop the broad-backed Indian bent over a spade in an empty stall in the middle of the room.

The Indian was digging into a rectangle outlined in the dirt floor of the stall. The rectangle was about four feet long and two feet wide. A man dressed like a cowboy had cut the outline in the floor with the barrel of the rifle he now cradled in his right arm as he leaned against the stall at the front. In his mouth he twirled a piece of straw. He wore expensive boots and seemed bored. He watched, the Indian worked.

The Indian dumped each spadeful of dirt into a wheelbarrow. He did not look up, even when the man dressed as a cowboy spoke; instead he kept his head down and stopped only briefly to wipe the sweat from his eyes. Sweat poured off him. It rolled down his arms and dropped off at the elbows and wrists. It ran in rivulets down his chest and back, soaking the tops of his pants, cut off and ragged at the bottom and cinched at the waist with a piece of rope. The crotch of his pants was wet where sweat had soaked through.

When the hooves of an approaching horse grew loud, the man dressed as a cowboy looked up. Entering the barn in a riding outfit was a spectacularly beautiful teenage girl leading a tall roan gelding. A smile lit the man's face. The girl led the gelding down the middle of the room and tried to pass the two men without acknowledging them. The gelding jerked to a stop, wrenching its neck around, and pulled the girl up short. The man had grabbed the reins.

"Aren't you even going to say hello, princess?" he said.

"I was merely attempting to pass. Do you have a problem with that?"

"No, no problem. It just didn't seem sociable, that's all."

He looked hard at the young girl, letting his eyes rake over her from head to toe. She was tall, about five feet eight, and had silvery blond hair and deep blue eyes. Her skin was pale, with naturally pink highlights in her cheeks, now flushed almost red from the heat and the exertion of riding. Her body was willowy but full, with high breasts, wide shoulders and long legs. She might have been an internationally celebrated model. With a delicate motion she reached up and wiped the sweat from her upper lip. She ignored the man's leer.

"Hello, Aldo," she said. "Will that do?"

"That will do nicely, but what is the hurry?"

9

"I'd like to rub Orfeo down, cool him out and wash him off, the way you showed me, remember?"

"Yes, I remember, and you are a very good student." He paused and smiled. "There are many other things I can teach you, now that you're older." He smiled again. He had a ruggedly handsome face, with a smooth olive complexion and a well-trimmed mustache, jet black like his hair. His forearms were laced with veins and muscles, and altogether he had the sturdy build typical of many Sicilians. His eyes were deep brown, large and penetrating. Above his left eye a white scar curled like a buttonhook.

"I think I've had enough lessons from you for one life, if you don't mind."

"I mind. Believe me, I mind."

The girl started to lead the gelding away, but the man yanked hard on the reins and the horse halted, its head swinging back hard. The girl sighed and took a deep breath.

"What *is* it, Aldo?"

"I wondered why you didn't ask me about the work here."

"I didn't think it was any of my business."

"It is part of all of our business. Your mother has ordered this hole dug for a purpose by my friend here, who tried recently to steal one of your mother's prized possessions."

"I assume this is the man who tired to steal Faust."

"That is correct."

"I wish he had succeeded," the girl said.

"Why?"

"Faust is a bad horse. I hate him."

"Faust is a good horse. You will see."

"I hope not."

"And you will see what your mother will do to those who try to take him from her."

"I will not. I take no interest in my mother's doings."

The man laughed. "You will take an interest in what happens here tomorrow, I know that. Your mother has told me."

"How? She's in Europe."

"She called. She will be back tonight, and tomorrow we will teach you why my friend here is so busy digging."

"It's another lesson I'll skip."

"Not this one, princess. Everybody on the ranch and in the town must watch, Mother's orders."

"I'm sure I'm not interested."

"You will be," Aldo said, then turned and looked at the Indian. The hole was about dug, the wheelbarrow full. Craning his neck, Aldo looked into the hole, checking its depth. Then he turned back to the girl. "Would you like a hint, a little preview maybe?"

"No."

"I will give you one anyway."

He turned back to the Indian and spoke rapidly to him in a strange dialect. The Indian put down the spade and stepped into the hole. It came up to just above his knees. He sat down in the hole like a man about to take a bath, then gazed up with a forlorn look on his glistening face. Sweat dripped off his chin. His head was positioned toward the back of the stall.

"That will do just fine," Aldo said. "Now we can rest, my friend." He turned back to the girl. "Can you guess what's in store for him tomorrow?"

"I have no interest."

"You will have. Believe me, you will have."

11

THE WHITE ANGEL

He dropped the reins and smacked the gelding on the neck. The horse started off, the girl in the lead. As she walked away, all the girl heard was Aldo's scornful laughter ringing off the rafters.

3

MANY RIVERS TO CROSS

Big Sur
October 5

Sam Borne was restless. For a month now he'd been recuperating from his last assignment, in Vietnam, where he'd put a stop to Doctor Sun Sun and his dream of flooding America with cheap heroin. Sam enjoyed the Ventana Inn, but it was not a place that could hold him for long. It was too slow. His arm had healed from the bullet wounds; he'd had a happy if brief relationship with a television producer named Wendy; he was having a longer and even better relationship with an accountant named Darlene; he'd swum a mile in the pool each day since his arm healed; he'd jogged up and down the majestic coast road for ten miles each day for the last two weeks; he'd read deeply in Emerson and in the Zen masters, trying as always to synthesize American transcendentalism with Oriental mysticism; and still he was restless.

"Excuse me, are you Mr. Borne?"

Sam looked up from the book he was reading. A young man about twenty years old stood over him in casual clothes. Sam recognized him. He was one of the young people who manned the reception desk in the

13

lounge. Under his arm was a packet. Sam sat up immediately.

"I'm Borne," he said, holding out his hand. He knew instantly that this was word from the Committee, that the packet would contain the dossier for his next assignment. While the young man explained that it was not hotel policy to disturb guests at the pool, Sam slipped his finger under the envelope and tore it open. As he pulled out its contents he murmured, "It's okay, don't worry about it."

The young man seemed relieved. "Well, sorry again. Take care," he said, then turned and left.

Sam scanned the all-important first page of his dossier. It called for him to be on the Rio flight from LAX tomorrow afternoon at two-thirty. That would put him into Rio at seven-thirty in the morning of the next day. He had time. The late-afternoon sun still topped the pines at the ocean end of the pool. There would be about another hour of good sunning weather.

"What is it, Sam?" Darlene asked. Darlene had replaced Wendy some five hours after Wendy departed to conquer the Nielsen ratings with the treatment for a men's adventure series Sam had worked out for her. Darlene was Sam's first Darlene; he never dreamed he'd actually encounter a woman named Darlene, but what was California for if not for fantasy fulfillment?

"It's just a notice from my company, nothing much," he lied.

"I thought you were on vacation."

"I am, but this is an emergency."

"What's wrong?"

"Nothing. I just have to make a couple calls and straighten something out."

"Oh, you just did this so I'd think you were important."

14

"You're right. Has it worked?"

Darlene turned over on her chaise, holding a towel in front of her. She was very young, twenty-three she'd told him, but he suspected she'd added a year or two. She had a smooth brown tan and deep dark eyes over a wide, inviting mouth. Across her nose lay a tiny cluster of freckles that wrinkled now as she squinted up at him. She was not tall, but she was sleek, and stacked. Her firm legs extended enticingly from the white line of her bikini bottom.

"Yes," she said, "it's worked. I believe you're important." She giggled. Sam winked at her. He wanted to be very careful here. He wanted not to hurt her at all.

"So can I go make my calls?"

"Yes, right after you put more lotion on my back and legs."

"Will do."

Sam picked up the suntan lotion, and Darlene lay back down on her stomach. He poured a little lotion onto his left palm, then worked it over the surface of both hands. Then he kneaded the oil into Darlene's neck and shoulder blades, then into her back and on down her legs. He swirled his hands as sensually as he could, penetrating with his fingertips from time to time, hoping to relax her and to please her. He felt a stinging sadness creep over him. This was always the worst part of any assignment, saying good-bye. And Darlene was much too young and wonderful for any but the gentlest of good-byes.

"Feel good?" he asked.

"Hmm."

"I'll give you thirty more seconds, then I'm off to Ma."

"Ma?"

"Ma Bell. I've got calls to make, remember?"

"How many?"

"Quite a few." He paused. "If I tell you some of them are overseas calls, will you think I'm even more important?"

"Sure. But how long will they take?"

"A good hour or so. You stay down here and then join me for drinks on the terrace, okay?"

"Sounds great."

"Good." Sam stopped massaging her and wiped his hands on a towel. He picked up his dossier and tucked it under his arm. Then he leaned down and kissed her softly on the cheek.

"Umm," she murmured.

"So long," he said. He stood up and walked rapidly down the length of the pool and on up the path toward their room. As he passed the main house and lounge he ducked in quickly and told the young man who'd brought him the dossier that he had an emergency and had to leave immediately. He would sign an open chit for his bill and that of Darlene Hanks and then he'd leave. She could stay as long as she wanted and he'd cover the bill, no problem. The young man gave him a big smile and stepped into the back room. He returned quickly with the credit-card chit. Sam signed it and departed.

Back in the room Sam called his old teacher at the Monterey Language Institute, Sergei Popovich. The phone was picked up on the fourth ring. It was Laura, Popovich's young daughter.

"Laura, hello, this is Sam Borne. Is Daddy there?"

"Yes."

"Put him on, honey, please."

"Okay."

Seconds later Sam heard the familiar deep voice and harsh accent of Sergei Popovich, the best teacher of Slavic languages, Sam believed, in this universe.

"Hello."

"Sergei, it's Sam. How are you?"

"Fine. Where are you?"

"Down the road. I'm in a hurry. How about dinner tonight?"

"Delighted. Where?"

"On the pier, where else? Just like the old days."

"You're on. I have class in an hour."

"What time do you finish?"

"Seven."

"Fine. I'll grab you at school. Still in the same old buildings, I assume."

"What else? Do you really think Uncle Sam will spring for new facilities for the most important languages taught at this school?"

"I don't guess so. See you at seven."

"Splendid."

Sam hung up and called the Stanford Court in San Francisco. They had a room at the top with a view. He was set for the night. He hung up, stripped off his swim trunks and pulled on a pair of tan slacks and a subtle blue-and-white-striped linen shirt by Stella. Then he packed his suitcase, holding out a sweater in case it got cool on the way up the coast or in Monterey.

Sam wrote Darlene a note, explaining that he had to leave and it couldn't be helped and thanking her for everything. Then he picked up his suitcase, tossed his sweater over his shoulder and left.

In the parking lot he threw his things into the Lamborghini and fired it up, hoping Darlene would not hear its distinctive deep-throated roar from the pool above him. Then he backed out and slowly wound his way down the lane leading to the coast highway, dipping under the big redwoods on his way.

Once out on the highway, he slipped a cassette into the tape deck. The sounds of Joe Cocker crooning the immortal words of Jimmy Cliff soon filled the air. It was "Many Rivers to Cross," one of his favorites. Sam felt the lightning rush he always got at the start of an assignment.

He was on his way to Rio, with many rivers to cross. He hoped, like the song said, it was his will that would keep him alive, and his pride that would help him survive.

4

BARNSTORM

Valhalla Ranch
October 5

People crowded every available space in the barn, leaving only an aisle down the center. They hung from rafters, stood precariously on the sides of stalls, filled the hayloft and spilled over into the yard. They were people of every kind and stripe. Some were black, some were Indian, some were a combination; some were pure European stock, many of them either Italian or Portuguese in descent; still others were a combination of Portuguese and Indian stock, called *mesticos.* Most of them were dressed poorly. They were either the hands who worked the vast ranch or inhabitants of the small village on the edge of the ranch's spread. All were there under orders of the woman known to them as Mother Beloved.

Armed men dressed as cowboys stood along the aisle. They were decidedly rough customers, with pistols hitched to their waists and rifles in their hands; many wore ammunition belts and some had bandoliers crisscrossed on their chests. They spoke to each other above the whispered comments of the spectators. In the wide entrance the man called Aldo stood with his hands on his hips, a cigarette dangling from

19

his lower lip. Fidgeting and frowning, he gazed into the sunlight over the crowd in the yard toward the main house some eighty yards away. Not a man to be kept waiting, he was annoyed. From time to time he turned and squinted back into the barn, making no effort to conceal his contempt for the spectators. With the guards he did not fraternize. He was clearly in charge.

Finally a woman dressed in the traditional gray and black of a maid appeared at the door of the big house and waved toward the barn. Aldo saw her and spat out orders to two guards on the fringe of the crowd in the yard. They turned and headed off toward one of the smaller buildings set off to the side. Minutes after disappearing into the building they emerged with the Indian who had dug the hole in the barn the previous day. They led him toward the barn at gunpoint. Bare-chested, he wore the same ragged pants as before and no shoes. His face showed no emotion. When they reached the crowd it parted and Aldo nodded impassively for the guards to hold their position. They waited.

After about five minutes the maid again appeared at the door of the big house. Aldo waved to her. She went back into the house. In seconds two women dressed in jeans and bush shirts came out of the house and started toward the barn. As they walked along they argued, gesturing and stopping from time to time. Finally the one spoke to the other with raised finger and they resumed their course toward the barn in silence.

Striking blondes, tall and willowy, the women were mother and daughter to even the dullest eye. As they drew into the yard the crowd stepped back for them. The older woman took no notice, while the younger woman shot sympathetic glances all around. No spectator dared return them.

"I'm glad you could make it, princess," Aldo said.

"That's enough from you," the mother snapped.

Aldo bit back a retort and said, "We're all set."

"Good. Let's proceed. I'll make a few remarks, and then you know what to do."

"Fine."

The older woman started into the barn and realized immediately that her daughter had stayed behind. She turned and glared at her.

"I'd like to stay here, Mother."

"You'll do nothing of the kind. Come here."

Sulking, the younger woman followed her mother into the barn. Inside, it was hot. And tense. Spectators and guards stopped wiping their faces on their sleeves. All whispering ceased and the guards stood at attention, only nodding at the woman as she walked past them and positioned herself in front of the stall where the Indian had dug the hole. Walking into the stall, she briefly inspected the hole, stepping off the distance from the front of the stall to the back of the hole. Satisfied, she walked back to the center of the aisle and stood, hands on hips, letting her cold gaze play over the crowd. Finally she spoke.

"You all know why I've called you here," she started, speaking perfect Portuguese slowly and deliberately for maximum effect. She paused. "This man tried to steal from me. He tried to deprive me of my property. He broke the rules, therefore he will be punished. I want each and every one of you to know that the same treatment will be meted out to you if you cross me in any way. I will not tolerate lawlessness among my people, is that clear?"

Everyone in the crowd nodded or murmured assent.

They had experienced this treatment before. They knew what was expected of them. They shuffled nervously. The woman paused again. Under her stern gaze the shuffling halted.

"Let no one here forget what they will now see. There is nothing I hate so much as a horse thief." She pointed to the entrance, where Aldo stood waiting. He nodded behind him, and the two guards led the Indian, still at gunpoint, into the barn and down the aisle. No one in the crowd dared look the Indian in the face. No one made a sound. When the Indian reached the stall where he'd dug the hole, he only glanced at it briefly, displaying no emotion. Aldo reached out and took from one of the guards a set of handcuffs. He snapped them on the Indian, then led him by the arm into the stall. Without having to be told, the Indian sat down in the hole, facing front. Aldo went to the front of the hole and stepped down into it. He reached out and a guard handed him a hank of rope. He grabbed the Indian by the ankle and looped the rope around it, then grabbed the Indian's other leg. Suddenly the Indian kicked him. Aldo snapped out orders to the guards above him. One guard walked forward and held his shotgun tight against the man's forehead. Aldo resumed. He tied the Indian's ankles tight, then dropped his legs into the hole and stepped out.

He spoke to another guard in a low voice. The guard handed Aldo his shotgun, then took the spade from its resting place against the side of the stall and started to shovel the dirt out of the wheelbarrow the Indian had loaded the day before. As he worked, the sound of the shovel biting into the pile atop the wheelbarrow was the only sound, followed each time by the swoosh and plop the dirt made as it landed in the hole. The guard worked quickly. When the wheelbarrow

22

was half empty, Aldo handed the shotgun to the older woman, walked back to the entrance, and disappeared. In the stony silence the work continued, the biting sound following rhythmically the swoosh and plop. In the crowd people mopped their faces and waited nervously, the tension mounting.

The guard finished filling the hole, then loudly tamped down the dirt with the back of the spade. A ruckus erupted from the yard. Loud whinnying followed shouts and cries, then came the sounds of hooves beating and scraping the earth, pawing frantically. The crowd in the barn stirred, all heads turning in the direction of the yard. The faces of the women reflected fright, those of the men revulsion.

In the yard, the crowd scrambled out of view. The sounds of a struggle continued, shouts and whinnying filling the air. Then, in a flash, a tremendous black stallion hove into view, held tight with lassos around its neck. Teams of two cowboys on each end pulled the lassos tight. The stallion reared magnificently, neighing and snorting, its front legs flailing the air, wheeling this way and that, Aldo managing to stay just clear of them as he yanked on a lasso pulled straight out front. Finally, after a long tussle, Aldo and the cowboys managed to control the stallion enough to lead him into the barn. The panicked crowd pushed and shoved, pressing themselves back as far as they could, widening the aisle.

The woman and her daughter stepped back against the row of stalls opposite the Indian, pressing back as far as they could. The mother hollered something to Aldo and he hollered something back. They spoke in German. Around them the crowd started to shout, some women screaming hysterically. The mother shouted again in German to Aldo, and he roared at the

23

top of his lungs in Portuguese that he would let the stallion go if the people did not shut up immediately. They quieted, though most of the women had to be restrained by the men, who in some cases had to clamp hands over mouths.

In the aisle, the stallion tried to rear again, but Aldo bore down hard on the lead lasso, and it only managed to hop before landing and holding its ground. Then it started to skid and paw the dirt floor like an obstinate mule. The two men on either side tightened their lassos. Then all five held the stallion fairly steady, though it continued to scrape its hooves and shift its flanks rapidly from side to side, canting its hind legs in a semicircle.

Aldo bore down harder, tightening the lasso hand over hand as he neared the stallion. When he got close enough, he gingerly reached out and stroked its snout while talking to it very softly. He was an accomplished horseman and it showed. Soon the stallion dipped its head, and Aldo reached higher on its snout. Still holding firmly to the rope, he moved in closer.

The mother crossed to the stallion. While Aldo and the men held firmly to their lassos, she took the stallion's head in both hands and cooed to it, stroking it all the while. Then she spoke to it in a whisper. "Faust, darling Faust, when will I get to ride you? When will you settle down, dear boy? You know I want to ride you like the wind. But I want you the way you are, not the way Aldo wants to make you. I want you intact, so please settle down." She leaned her head against the stallion's, then stepped back and cupped his chin while stroking the top of his snout. The crowd hushed. The daughter watched her mother in fascination. Then the mother turned to Aldo and said, "Put him in."

Aldo coaxed the stallion forward till it stood sideways in front of the stall. Then he pulled down hard on the lasso and pressed gently on its snout. The men on either side held firmly. The stallion started to back into the stall.

The crowd gasped. The daughter clasped her hands over her face and turned away. Whimpers escaped from some of the women. The mother walked calmly to the door of the stall and started to walk it closed.

The Indian's eyes widened as the stallion's hooves slowly moved closer, but he made not a sound. Sweat popped out on his forehead and ran into his eyes, causing him to blink. He clenched his mouth, then opened it quickly and sucked in a big breath. His Adam's apple bobbed just above where the dirt cut him off at the neck. The horse skidded sideways and dirt shot up into the Indian's face, sticking to the sweat. The bright steel horseshoes flashed as the stallion moved closer, until the hooves were only inches in front of the Indian's face.

Then they passed him by on either side. The Indian heard the stall door click shut, then he heard the woman softly whispering to the horse while its hooves danced to either side of his head. He strained to avoid them, instinctively ducking as they came nearer, craning his neck to one side, then the other. But it was only a matter of time. Dirt fanned over him. The crowd held its breath.

Then it happened. The stallion's right rear hoof glanced off the Indian's head, knocking it to the side and drawing blood from the temple. The Indian did not cry out or lose consciousness. The crowd cringed, the men wrapping the women in their arms. The blond woman stopped talking to the stallion and stepped back, looking for her daughter, who stood against the opposite stall clutching her face. She shouted a command to her and, when the daughter didn't respond, she snapped an order to Aldo, who left his spot beside her and crossed the aisle to the daughter. He grabbed her about the shoulders and manhandled her back to her mother. She kicked and elbowed at him, but to no avail. He merely pinned her arms against her sides and lifted her off the ground.

When Aldo got back to the stall, the mother roared at the daughter in German to preserve her dignity and that of their family. The daughter attempted to cover her face, but the mother ordered Aldo to pin her hands behind her back, and he did. As the mother cupped the daughter firmly under the chin and clamped her head in the direction of the stallion, it grew excited, sensing the alien presence in its stall. It pawed the earth with its hind feet, then kicked mightily, turning inward. A tremendous thud sounded, followed in quick succession by another, and another. The sound of bone crushing and flesh tearing could be heard above the moans and whimpers of the spectators. Then the stallion neighed loudly and kicked with both hind legs. A terrible snapping, tearing sound followed. The daughter squeezed her eyes tight, even as her mother shouted to the crowd in Portuguese that this is what would happen to anyone who stood in her way.

Aldo hopped along the side of the stall and worked his way to the back. Then, using a shotgun like a golf club, he pushed the severed head to the front. It rolled under the stall door and stopped at the feet of the women. The mother picked it up and held it aloft by the hair like a trophy. Crushed and mangled to a pulp, it dripped blood.

In the stall, the stallion kicked and snorted.

5

BY THE DOCK
OF THE BAY

Monterey
October 5

Sam Borne was no stranger to Monterey. He shot off
the expressway and threaded his way expertly to the
hill on the south side of town that held the world-
famous Defense Language Institute Foreign Language Center. To the Center he was no stranger either. Sam had been its most successful and least
acknowledged graduate. Of the six languages he'd
mastered there he'd got the nearly impossible score of
three-plus on all of them. The entire faculty was in awe
of him, except Sergei Popovich, the famous Russian
defector, once the deepest of deep moles, the man
Sam had pulled from behind the Iron Curtain just
when it was about to descend and crush him.

Sam slowed and entered the Institute grounds,
swinging right past the Public Relations building. He
glanced to his left and saw on the hill above him the
modern Chinese Language building. A class was just
letting out, and servicemen in the uniforms of all four
branches poured through the doors. They scattered
toward the dorms in the early-evening air, most to
spend the night in study. The Institute was nothing
if not intensive, whether you were taking a thirty-

two-week course in a Romance language or a forty-seven-week course in a Slavic language or something in between; they were all intensive, all challenging, all tough, even for a natural linguist like Sam.

He turned to the right and started down Private Bolio Road. From the top you got the full panorama of Monterey stretched below. It was breathtaking now, with the lights lining the bay twinkling in the hazy purple of early evening. Sam considered it the most Mediterranean sight in America. The bay swept in a majestic semicircle twenty-two miles wide from headland to headland. The town itself spread out on the shore and spilled upward onto the pine-clad hills ringing the entire bay, forming a natural amphitheater. In the bay, lights bobbed from the fishing craft and glittered from the long pier. It was a sight Sam knew and loved.

Ahead he saw the familiar old huts where Slavic languages were taught. They really were a disgrace, and should have been replaced long ago, but the rationale behind the national budget lay way beyond Sam, if not everybody else, and he put thoughts of it from his mind, deciding instead to taunt Sergei with it. Classes were just letting out, and servicemen exited from all doors. Sam pulled into the curb and waited. In moments Sergei appeared, and Sam waved. The stocky Russian started across the lawn to the Lamborghini, shaking his head in wonder as he came. When he was about twenty feet away, he said, "Now tell me, Borne, how does a fool like you get such a machine?"

"The secretary of defense gave it to me for helping get the new Chinese Language Building funded."

"Bastard," Sergei hissed, then walked around to the passenger side. When he settled in the sculpted bucket

28

seat, Sergei gave Sam a hard stare. "It's not the Chinese you have to worry about. It's the Russian bear that will claw you to death," he said. Sergei was a defector, but he was not free of Russian chauvinism, for which Sam liked him all the more.

"You see who got the big new building," Sam said.

"It is only so the Americans can suck up to the Chinese to keep the great bear occupied on his southern flank. And you had nothing to do with that building, you lying bastard." Sergei's face was mottled green from the dashboard lights. Sam looked at him and laughed. Sergei feigned indignation, then suddenly broke out in the deepest belly laugh in California. He reached over and hugged Sam around the shoulders.

"So what is the occasion? To what do I owe the honor of this dinner invitation?"

"You need an occasion to have dinner with me? I should have left you in Moscow."

"It would be the Gulag by now, dear boy. And I am grateful to you every minute of every day. Still, what is the occasion?"

"We're just two old friends having dinner, okay?"

"You are the most mysterious man alive, Sam. Just take care, please."

"Are you going sentimental on me?"

"We Russians are soulful, Sam. Just be careful, understand? You have that look in your eye. You are on assignment, I can tell."

"Let's get some pasta, huh?"

"Sounds good to me. Just be careful."

"With the pasta?"

Sergei grinned despite himself. "With the pasta, too," he said. "Let's go."

Sam put the Lamborghini in gear and wheeled down

the hill. At the bottom he turned left and headed out Stillwell Avenue and through the stone pillars and into the suburbs. In minutes they were through town and out to the pier. Sam pulled up in the big parking lot that was always crowded with tourist vehicles in the summer. Now it was half empty. When they got out a group of teenage boys came over and ogled the car, asking Sam lots of questions and peering inside, oohing and aahing. Sam let each in turn sit behind the wheel, then locked the car and headed with Sergei toward the dock.

As in the old days, they went directly to Domenico's. When they entered, Sam was delighted to learn that Sergei had called ahead and secured a table along the glass wall overlooking the bay. They settled in and glanced out toward the bobbing lights in the harbor. Sergei ordered a dry vodka martini and Sam followed suit. Sam asked after Sergei's daughter Laura. She was fine, and progressing well in school. He was doing his best to bring her up as both mother and father. It was difficult, and he had to have the nurse at school explain certain things to her. Sergei blushed. He was incapable of it, and Laura was eleven now. She seemed to have understood and to have taken things in stride. Still, one missed one's wife every day, so no doubt at age eleven one missed one's mother just as much. Sergei shrugged.

The waiter returned with the martinis and Sam proposed a toast to Sergei and his daughter. Sergei countered with one to Sam's health and safety. They took a sip. The vodka cooled Sam's tongue and throat, then fired his stomach. The waiter returned with menus and, waving them away, Sam suggested they start with cold antipasto. Sergei agreed. They were into an old ritual. Next Sam ordered linguine with clam sauce, followed by shrimp scampi for both. The waiter left and Sergei excused himself to make a call home to check that Laura was all right.

Sam gazed off over the water. On the north lip of the bay a jet with running lights flashing took off from the airport. A mood came over him. He felt contemplative, and nostalgic. Watching the reflections of the boat lights bob on the water, he cast his mind back to his first meeting with Sergei.

In the dead of winter in 1973 Sam Borne was called out of his Russian course at the Defense Language Institute Foreign Language Center. It was an emergency. Although to that point Sam had made only a few runs, there was no one else capable of pulling off the assignment the Committee had in mind. The CIA had flubbed the job of protecting a deep mole within the Russian GRU, the *Glavnoe Razvedyvatelnoe Upravlenie*, the Chief Intelligence Directorate of the General Staff. The man was a colonel in the Red Army named Sergei Popovich. He had been decorated heavily for heroism during the Great War, where at Stalingrad he had saved the lives of thousands of comrades; with daring, he had blocked a German offensive by disguising himself and a handful of men as a large fighting force protecting one of that beleaguered city's flanks.

But after the war the young lieutenant had been disillusioned with the turn the government had taken. Freedoms had not been restored. Martial law was in effect, as far as Sergei was concerned, all the time, and with his background in philosophy and his gift for languages, which permitted him to read smuggled magazines, journals and political accounts from the West, the colonel was already disenchanted with his homeland before bureaucratic bungling and unbelievable red tape cost him his first wife, Vera. She had contracted a curable form of cancer, but by the time Sergei was able to secure her the surgery and follow-up care she needed, Vera was too far gone. She died within the year, and Sergei Popovich was recruited by a CIA operative working out of the Moscow embassy as a commercial attaché.

Since then the attaché had run Sergei successfully, extracting from him key intelligence from GRU headquarters stashed behind the tight security surrounding the aircraft and rocket factories at the old Khodinka airfield in Moscow. Within this complex the Russian military establishment experiments with chemical warfare, breaks down and copies the latest Western technology in rocketry and aircraft, as well as in computers, and also indulges in the development and perfection of operational equipment essential to modern military spycraft, from hidden-camera technology to exploding pens to umbrellas the touch of whose point to flesh brings instant death; here methods of undetectable entry and of safecracking are taught by master criminals given a reprieve by a government only too willing to press their talents into service. To those in the GRU this complex is known as the Aquarium. It is virtually impenetrable.

Sam Borne was to penetrate it. Entering the country as a seaman on a freighter docking at Odessa, he jumped ship and connected with a CIA network long in operation on that city's waterfront. The network delivered him to a safe house in Moscow after a long and cold trip in the back of a produce truck under a pile of turnips. Sam used a straw to draw air, and survived the long trip by dint of will. At the safe house he was outfitted with the papers and uniform of a captain in the Red Army, on assignment to the center to investigate the latest computer smuggled from Italy, which despite NATO vigilance the GRU, working with a cell of Italian Communists, had managed to slip out of a base in Naples.

There would be only one shot. Sam would enter the Aquarium past the tightest security in Asia, find the GRU colonel, confined to quarters there, and quietly lead him out with false orders concealed on Sam's person in an indelicate place. Or he would fail. There would be no second chance, no margin for error.

The Moscow night wind slashed at the Russian captain's face, tearing his eyes. It knifed up his pants legs, chilling him to the bone, gusting against his chest, driving him back. He pushed on, hearing ahead the yapping of the dogs guarding the airfield. Soon he saw the ring of lights around the field, and the silhouettes of the sentries walking the dogs, even at this distance recognizable as German shepherds and Dobermans. They howled in the cold like wolves. He walked boldly, self-assuredly. It was not unusual for the Aquarium to have nocturnal activity, for an officer to call this late in the evening.

He approached the first checkpoint and stepped into the booth while the guards inspected his papers. They found them in order and returned them to him with some curt comments on the weather. The captain reciprocated, knowing that Muscovites were as obsessed with discussing the weather as were the Irish, but with much more reason. He left the booth and started into the complex. He knew the layout cold. In no time he reached the narrow lane that led to the Aquarium itself. He walked along it beside the thirty-foot walls of the Institute of Cosmic Biology. At the next checkpoint he nodded greetings and beat the

33

sentries to a comment on the frigid weather. Handing over his papers, he noted that the guards wore the special insignia on their uniforms that indicated they were members of the elite battalion charged with security at the complex. They passed him through. He walked on, stopped at one more checkpoint, then crossed a broad open area entirely surveilled by television cameras. Within the building ahead, the Aquarium itself, guards would be tracking his every movement on a bank of monitors.

He reached the doorway of the two-story outer building surrounding the nine-story main building, with its wide glass windows. He passed through the outer doors and stopped immediately. Two guards checked his papers and inquired what his business was. He replied to their satisfaction. They waved him down a short corridor, where another set repeated the papers check and the inquiry. Again he passed. Then they directed him to walk through a metal-detection hoop. He handed the one guard his watch, a clumsy Russian model, and stepped through the hoop. Like all personnel accustomed to the Aquarium, he wore no metal. He was not even wearing a metal belt buckle; suspenders held his pants up. The detector made no sound. He smiled as the guard holding his watch handed it back to him. Casually he asked directions to the lab where the computer from Italy was stored. He listened carefully and nodded understanding.

He left and followed directions until he was out of sight of the guards; then he walked calmly to a bank of elevators leading to a lab on the eighth floor. This was where the authorities had confined Colonel Popovich. When the elevator reached the eighth floor the captain stepped out and went directly to the lab. He was familiar with the place in every detail, even to the placement of the fire extinguishers.

The laboratories were large rooms, with wide double doors. He passed several before coming to number 88. It was double-locked. He knocked softly. He knew that guards patrolled the halls at fifteen-minute intervals. There was no answer. He knocked slightly harder. This time he heard shuffling feet. Soon a gruff voice from the other side said in Russian that he was fine and please leave him in peace till the morning. The captain ordered in perfect demotic Russian that the door be opened immediately.

It was. Beyond lay darkness. Tensed and ready, the captain stepped in and closed the door behind him. From the far corner of the room came a beam of light. It was from a tensor lamp at the head of a cot.

"What do you want?" Popovich snapped.

"Be quiet."

Popovich started to reply but heard footsteps in the corridor and stopped. The two strangers stood in the darkness while a guard tried the door. The locks snapped to and held. Neither man made a sound nor took a breath. The guard's footsteps continued on down the corridor. When they faded away, the captain said, "Listen." The single English word hung in the air like a five-volume declaration of independence.

The captain's explanation briefly elated Colonel Sergei Popovich, who knew that, with his cover blown, his fate was fixed, and grim. The authorities were only keeping him here till they had him thoroughly debriefed. In addition to being a philosopher and a linguist, Colonel Popovich was also one of the leading Soviet experts on the military use of computers. Once his store of knowledge had been completely transferred to younger officers at the center, he would be off to Lubyanka at best, Siberia if he was lucky, eternity if he wasn't. This was his one chance, and he was buoyed by it.

Popovich retreated to the corner of the room that contained the cot. The captain followed and noticed a copy of *Eugene Onegin* on the pillow. While Popovich changed rapidly into his formal uniform, replete with campaign ribbons and medals—the way he'd entered the complex as a form of silent protest—the captain excused himself and turned away. He took off his greatcoat and tunic, then dropped his pants, reached into the crotch of his thermal underwear, peeled back a layer of thin tape, extracted a narrow envelope and tucked it under his arm. He adjusted his underwear, pulled his pants back up and refastened his suspenders. He turned back to Popovich and, holding the envelope out to him, said, "Here're your papers."

Popovich took the envelope, slit it with his index finger, knelt down under the tensor light and shook out the contents. Several folded sheets of paper slid out. Popovich folded them back and read them. They were exact in every detail to official Red Army orders, even to the stock of paper used and the typeface. He looked up at the captain, awe starting to dominate his features. In the beam of light he looked like a saint in prayer in a medieval painting.

"We don't have much time," the captain said. "Everything is in order. Now we have to carry it off."

"We'll never do it. They'll never fall for it."

"The Lord hates a quitter."

"I'm an atheist."

"Okay, *I* hate a quitter."

"And you are . . . ?"

"Sam Borne."

"And you're with . . . ?"

"You."

"This is not a time for sarcasm."

"Or for resignation."

Popovich smiled. "So, what is the plan?"

Sam looked at his watch in the half-light from the tensor. "In about two minutes a guard will check this corridor again. When he finishes, he will be through for the night, as will all the personnel on duty when I entered. That means new crews will man the checkpoints between here and the street. We are going to give the personnel just time enough to settle in for a sleepy, cold night in Mother Russia. Then we are going to walk right out of here."

"And then?"

"You follow me."

"We'll never make it out of Moscow, assuming we clear the base."

"*Never*'s an addictive word. Try not to use it so much."

"I'll have lots of time to ponder that advice in the Gulag, I'm sure."

"Quiet."

From down the corridor came the sound of footsteps. They stopped every few paces while the guard checked the doors. Then he approached and tried their door, pulling the locks to with a snap. He walked on, checking doors, until he reached the end of the corridor. The sound of an elevator descending followed. Sam checked his watch again. "We wait ten minutes, then we go. Amuse yourself."

Popovich took Sam at his word. He went over to the cot, picked up his book and started to read. Sam went to the window and stood looking out at the base. He could see the hulks of some choppers down on the field, mostly Mi-8s with one long-legged Mi-10, and every once in a while a sentry with a Doberman or a German shepherd would pass his field of vision. Once a troop carrier rode by, empty except for the driver. When he looked back, Popovich had closed his book and sat with hands clasped around it, staring straight ahead into the darkened part of the lab. Sam checked his watch, then walked over and tapped Popovich on the shoulder. "Let's get our orders straight. It's time to move."

"Yes, it's time," Popovich said resignedly. He rose from the cot with the orders in his hand. Sam took them from him, sorted them and returned Popovich's to him. Sam put his in his inside pocket and pulled on his greatcoat. Popovich followed suit. When he started to button his greatcoat, Sam stopped him.

"Leave it open," Sam said. "You have enough glory on your chest for Hannibal. Let the guards see it till we reach the entrance."

"Is that all?"

"No. Buck up. What have you got to lose?"

"I will do my best, Mr. Borne," Popovich said, flashing Sam a false grin.

"Do better than that." Sam indicated the locks. Popovich released them and Sam stepped past him into the corridor. It was empty. Sam turned and winked. Popovich, taken aback, managed a smile. Sam started down the corridor, and Popovich fell into step beside him. In the elevator they were silent. On the ground floor Sam strode off the elevator and right over to the guards manning the inner checkpoint with the metal detector. Both guards looked up at his approach, surprise on their faces to see Popovich trailing this strange officer. Sam was impassive. So was Popovich.

Both guards seemed wary. Sam handed over his orders. Popovich took his out and stood waiting. The guard with Sam's orders handed them to his partner and took Popovich's. He was visibly relieved. When he vetted Popovich's orders, he was saddened as he looked at all the decorations on the colonel's chest. It was a grim thing to see such an honored warrior being transported to KGB headquarters on Dzerzhinsky Square. No doubt the brave colonel would be reduced there to a simpering idiot in the hellish cells of Lubyanka Prison. But it was none of the guard's business. He looked at his partner, showed him the destination written on Popovich's orders, and shook his head. The guards handed the orders back and wished them a good night.

Sam walked slightly ahead of Popovich down the corridor to the checkpoint at the entrance. The two sentries there watched them come, curiosity prominent on their features. Sam had kept his orders out and extended them as he approached. The first guard reached out and took them. After scanning them he handed them to his partner and took Popovich's. Then he handed Popovich's to his partner. He seemed skeptical. When his partner had checked the orders, the first guard conferred with him briefly in the room behind them with the bank of television monitors for surveillance. When they returned, the first guard asked, "Why were we not notified earlier that the colonel would be transferred tonight?"

"I was only notified myself an hour ago," Sam replied, promptly and surely.

"I take it, Captain, that you have done this kind of thing before?"

"Yes, but not here. I was for the last four years a section head in the German Democratic Republic, and

39

before that I was for three years assigned to the embassy in Mexico City." The Mexico City embassy had been a hotbed of KGB activity; to have served there conferred stature.

"I see. And you are taking the colonel into the city directly."

"Correct. My car is waiting."

"You may proceed."

"Good night, Corporal."

Sam led Popovich through the doors and out into the biting cold. Both men leaned against the wind as they walked to the waiting Chaika. Once they reached it, they climbed in quickly, Popovich first, and drove off at a respectable speed till they cleared the guards' field of vision from the entrance. Then the driver stepped on it as much as possible, allowing for the treachery of icy conditions. In no time they were streaming down the empty, cold night streets, heading for the safe house. As they drove, Popovich only turned to Sam once to say, "I don't see how we'll get out of the country. You realize of course that the guards will have registered our orders with Dzerzhinsky Square by now and that an alert will be out for us."

For Sam Borne this was his first taste of Russian paranoia. No matter how fierce or determined the external enemy might be, the Russians were up to resistance, they were capable of superhuman bravery in the face of the invader; but just take a brave Russian and oppose him to the system, and he crumbled. Russians were a people inured to secret police and repressive government for centuries. They were fearful of personal assertion, of dissidence, of defying or challenging accepted authority.

"We have a plan and a chance," Sam said in a tone

that discouraged further conversation. He turned away and gazed out the window at the bleak streets. Snow was piled on the sides, and few pedestrians were out. Occasionally they would pass another car or a public conveyance, but otherwise they had the city to themselves. It was spooky after southern California.

When they pulled up in front of the safe house, Sam got out and Popovich followed. The Chaika took off and disappeared around a corner. Sam led Popovich up the wide steps and through the door, which was opened for them. Sam said something to the man holding the door, then walked into the house and ascended the stairs, instructing Popovich over his shoulder to follow him. When they reached the second floor, Sam pushed open the door to a back bedroom and entered.

The bedroom looked like a star's dressing room, with a long vanity table against one wall under a large square mirror with light bulbs framing it on three sides. Jars and tubes, brushes and combs, lay on top of the table. On mannequin heads wigs reposed. Under the table on both sides were drawers. A small man rose from a stuffed sofa and nodded to Sam. "Here's your subject, Vasily, do your stuff," Sam said.

An hour later a standard Moscow taxi pulled up in front of the house, and two businessmen dressed impeccably in chesterfields with heavy mufflers and obviously new fur hats stepped out of the house and into it. They carried British passports and visas. They were taking the night flight to London. Both carried bags from Gum's department store as well as their luggage, and both had checkout slips and receipts from Intourist covering their five-day stay in Moscow. The younger man was tall and dark, handsome and assured. The older man had a well-manicured Commander Whitehead beard, salt and pepper and very distinguished, and a matching mustache. He seemed almost professorial. His shoulders were hunched, his posture stooped. Heavy gold spectacles with thick lenses slid down his nose. He appeared to be in his late sixties, while the younger man looked to be in his early twenties. The papers in their possession from their electrical supply firm listed them as senior researcher and research assistant, respectively.

At Sheremyetovo airport, security was heavy, even heavier than usual, and the two businessmen were taken aside into an examining room and questioned while their papers were vetted. They both told the same story. Theirs had been a consultation trip following up on a sales pitch made a week earlier by the president of their electronics firm. They had explained in detail the workings of the latest circuitry the company had developed. They were confident, the older man said in adequate if ungrammatical Russian, that they had sealed the deal. The younger man smiled and nodded at the security personnel after this exchange. They were allowed to pass through to the departure lounge, and three hours later they cleared Russian airspace.

At Heathrow Colonel Popovich was effusive with Sam, slapping his back and clasping him in bear hugs until a team from MI6 whisked him away. He didn't see Sam Borne again until a year later when Sam walked into the back of his classroom at Monterey and sat down.

The restaurant was nearly empty. Sam fingered his brandy snifter and listened as Sergei recounted the delightful times he and his first wife had had in their youth working on a collective farm one college summer in Soviet Georgia. Sergei, Sam knew, had never really recovered from the loss of his beloved Vera. And the fact that the woman with whom he'd fallen in love immediately upon arriving in America had left him for another woman didn't help. The second wife, Bonnie, had let nothing stand in her way, not Sergei, not Laura. She had been swept up in the women's movement in the late seventies and had eloped, not to be heard from for four years, to the Pacific Northwest with an account representative for an advertising firm in Seattle. Sergei had struggled on, hiring a woman to care for Laura while he taught. About none of this did Sam ever tease him. About everything else he always did.

"So, Sam, you see, I am a man who was blessed in his youth in a big way and who found no true happiness since, but what the hell, we're all stuck in one way or another, no?" Sergei leaned forward, his eyes gleaming. "For now we kill our brandy, and then I go. I have to see that the lady in my life has done her homework." He laughed. Sam grinned. "To your safety, Sam Borne, for I'm sure you're off on some wild-assed expedition." They clinked glasses and polished off their Rémy. Then they stood to leave.

On the way out, their waiter thanked them profusely. Out on the pier there were few strollers, and only the cries of gulls and the barking of seals broke the susurrus of the water lapping against the pilings.

In the car Sergei was quiet. Sam drove along, letting the silence drift, not wishing to intrude on his friend's thoughts. When they reached Sergei's white stucco house near the language center, they parted quickly, with Sergei showing his concern only by clasping Sam's outstretched hand in both of his for the briefest of moments.

43

THE WHITE ANGEL

"You pay next time," Sam said, and closed the door. He drove down to the corner and glanced into the rearview mirror before turning. Sergei stood rooted, looking after him. Sam waved and turned. In minutes he was back on the expressway, heading north, ninety miles from San Francisco.

6

NIGHT RAID

Amazon Basin
October 6

The jungle was quiet, the night dark and moonless. From time to time the night call of a bird pierced the stillness. More rarely, an animal cried out. Otherwise there was only the low hum of insects underpinning the quiet. In a clearing a building under construction sat with a string of lights winking from its superstructure. Off to the side was a bulldozer. Near the superstructure, cinder blocks and industrial piping were stacked in square piles. A Cyclone fence topped with barbed wire circled the clearing. On one side was a double gate and beside it a trailer. Light issued from the trailer's one window.

In the trailer two nightwatchmen played dominoes. Neither seemed intent on winning the game. They played at a snail's pace, taking time between each move. Theirs was a slow job, and a lonely one. They watched the compound each night from midnight till eight in the morning. Once the foreman, usually drunk, dropped them off at midnight, they were left absolutely to themselves. They had only to check the building and the equipment every hour on the hour. There had been a few attempted break-ins, but each had been thwarted. Theirs was an easy job, if you could stand the slow pace, so each night at this time they filled the hours with the clicking of dominoes.

The nightwatchmen were named Martim and Artur. They had grown up in the nearby village under the tutelage of the priest. They could barely read and write, having attended the church school for only two years each, but they were loyal and trustworthy men who attended church regularly with their families. When the Japanese businessmen, accompanied by government officials, came to their village and talked to the elders and the priest, Martim and Artur knew that good things would come of it, and now here was the factory going up and they were guarding it and they had both been promised by the Japanese that they would be trained in a government-sponsored program for high-paying technical jobs as soon as the factory was in full operation. They were happy men, content with the way things were going, and they didn't mind so much the long, lonely nights because they knew the outcome would be good.

"What was that?" Martim asked.

"Nothing."

"I thought I heard a horse."

"It was nothing," Artur said. "Your turn. Do something."

"Okay, but I thought I heard a horse."

"You are spooky tonight because I win so much."

Martim fondled a domino, then placed it down. Artur studied it briefly, picked up one of his own and placed it down. He made his decision much more quickly than Martim. He was on a roll and wanted to keep it going. He looked at Martim, a smile stealing into the corners of his mouth. Martim picked up another domino and deliberated. Just as he was about to place it down, the door opened suddenly and a man leaped in, brandishing a revolver.

"Good evening, gentlemen," the man said, waving the revolver at them.

Panic shot through Martim, followed quickly by guilt. He had let down the village, the Japanese, the government officials, the priest. He turned quickly to the wall behind him and reached out for the gun holstered there. His hand had grasped the butt when a bullet tore into his wrist, snapping it back and down. He grabbed it with his other hand. The bullet had bisected his wrist. Blood gushed out and down his arm. Artur stood up suddenly, knocking over his chair. The man with the gun fired once over his head. Artur cowered back against the wall, pleading with the man to be merciful, invoking the names of saints. Martim, clutching his arm, fell to his knees.

Two other men stuck their heads into the trailer. The man who'd shot Martim spoke to them rapidly. They climbed into the trailer. Both of them had revolvers drawn and ready. One immediately holstered his gun and walked over to where Martim writhed on his knees. He ordered him to stand and helped him roughly to his feet. Then he took a spool of rope from a hook on the wall and cut off a piece about three feet long. He wound this tightly around Martim's bicep, then twisted it into a tight knot. He said something sharply to the other man, who holstered his gun and took one of the chairs, held it over his head and smashed it down on the table. It broke apart. He picked up one of the legs and handed it to the man with Martim. The man jammed the chair leg into the knot and told Martim to twist it as tight as he could stand it. He did. The blood spouting from Martim's wrist stopped. The man who'd made the tourniquet

47

smiled back at the first man who'd entered and said, "I should have been a doctor, Aldo."

"You make a better fool," Aldo said. He told them to keep Artur and Martim under control and left the trailer. Outside, Martim and Artur could hear the sounds of hooves and a shrill woman's voice. Their stomachs tightened. The woman was shouting instructions to set charges. Then the door to the trailer opened again and Aldo stepped in, trailed by a remarkably beautiful gringo woman with blond hair falling from under a wide hat. She had eyes like a goddess, deep and blue, and an angular, cold face. Her mouth set, she seemed to look right through them. Fear paralyzed them. They had heard of such a woman.

Outside, the bulldozer's engine coughed and sputtered before kicking in with a roar. It rumbled a few yards before the sound of tearing steel rent the air above the diesel's roar. The trailer door opened and another man stuck his head in and told the woman all was ready. She said to wait. Then, after telling Aldo to tie Martim and Artur up and to bring them outside, she left.

While the other two men held them at gunpoint, Aldo set about tying Artur and Martim. He bound their hands behind their backs and tied their feet together at the ankles. The woman returned with a man carrying a five-gallon can of fuel for the bulldozer. The man started to spill the fuel over the floor of the trailer. Artur began to mumble the prayers he had learned from the priest at the school. Martim joined him. Then the woman shouted for them to be silent.

"Bring them out," she said to Aldo, and left. Aldo led them, hopping, out of the trailer. Outside, mounted horsemen ringed the trailer. Some held the reins of the empty horses for Aldo and the gringo woman and the other two men. The unmounted horses sidled to and fro. Artur and Martim had never seen such fine animals. The legends they had heard were true; there was such a woman after all. Deep despair ripped through them. Armed with rifles and pistols, all of the horsemen were dressed like cowboys. Some held burning torches. The blond woman nodded to the man called Aldo, and nooses fell over their heads. They would die by hanging, their necks snapped. Artur felt like collapsing. He looked balefully at Martim.

Then the man called Aldo loosened the nooses and slid the rope over their shoulders and under their arms. He cinched the ropes very tight, then knotted them hard. The rope bit into Artur's chest, making it difficult for him to breathe. He wanted to cry out, but restrained himself. Martim was in much worse shape, the tourniquet held by him now with great effort, pain contorting his face horribly.

The blond woman walked away from them and mounted the most beautiful of the animals, a large chestnut higher by two full hands than the other horses. She took the reins and nodded to Aldo. He said something quickly to the two men with him, and they each took the lead ropes for Artur and Martim. Aldo walked back to the trailer, struck a match and tossed it in, jumping back as he did so. The trailer ignited with a loud swoosh. In seconds tall flames licked its sides, roaring from the doorway, shooting from the window. Aldo walked back and mounted his horse, and the two men holding the lead ropes mounted theirs.

The blond gringo woman kneed the big chestnut slightly and it walked forward to where a box with a handle stood on the ground. Patting its neck, she whispered something to the horse. The chestnut picked up its foreleg and stamped down at the box. It missed the handle, knocking the box over. The man called Aldo leaped from his horse, went over and straightened the box. Then the woman whispered again and the chestnut carefully raised its foreleg and came down hard on the box, driving the handle down.

An earsplitting explosion erupted. Artur and Martim stumbled as the ground beneath them shifted and trembled. Above the flaming trailer they saw the superstructure of the factory collapse, the ironwork twisting even as it fell inward. Then there was the loud sound of iron tearing and banging against itself, a terrible screeching. Some of the horsemen cheered, but stopped when the gringo woman shouted for silence. Artur and Martim shot each other a fearful glance.

The woman led her beautiful horse back to the gate and the others followed, Aldo nodding finally to the horsemen holding the lead ropes on Artur and Martim. When the horsemen started toward the gate, Artur and Martim tried to keep up, hopping, but both pitched quickly forward on their faces and were dragged. At the gate the horsemen threw the ends of the ropes over the lintel pipe above the frame of the gate and pulled down on the loose end. Then they walked their horses away.

The ropes went tight, then pulled hard against Artur and Martim. Their feet pedaled on the ground briefly before they were hoisted into the air and hauled upward till they dangled some three feet off the ground. One of the other horsemen came forward and doused them with diesel fuel. Both started to pray aloud. The woman commanded them to be silent, but they continued to mumble. Aldo came forward and shouted for them to shut up. They managed to be quiet, but their lips continued to move.

The blond woman rode forward and stopped her horse in front of them. They swung slightly to and fro. She looked at them for a good thirty seconds, saying nothing, before leaning down and kissing first Artur, then Martim, slowly on the mouth. When she straightened up, she canted her horse back a few paces. Taking a match from her breast pocket, she struck it quickly with the long nail of her thumb, then tossed it against Artur. Instantly he turned into a human torch, flames engulfing him. He cried out and kicked, but the rope binding his feet held.

Martim broke out into a confiteor, but his words were lost in flames when the blond woman struck another match and tossed it against his soaked chest. He went up as quickly as Artur. Martim's screams rent the air briefly above the sucking sound of the two fires; then he stopped bucking and merely swung like Artur, a human torch beside a human torch.

The blond woman sat her horse and watched. When the flaming bodies were thoroughly burned, she gave an order and the horsemen holding the ropes walked over to the fence and tied the ends securely. Artur and Martim would swing, smoldering, till the singed ropes snapped and they dropped. Then the woman gave a signal and the entire band rode off into the night, the horsemen hooting as they spurred their mounts.

Behind them, from one burning body a flaming chair leg dropped.

7

IMPROVISATIONS

San Francisco
October 6

Sam Borne had a good seat. From where he sat at the small bar it was easy to see the performer on the tiny raised stage some thirty feet away. It was a stage Sam knew well. Back in the early seventies, when he was fresh out of the seven-term course at the Royal Academy of Dramatic Arts in London, and just starting in on the six languages he would study over a span of nearly four years at the Defense Language Institute Foreign Language Center in Monterey, his guidance officer at the Institute would drive him on Fridays and Saturdays the ninety miles up the coast to San Francisco so he could hone his skills as an actor, and, Sam secretly thought, learn more lessons in humility, for there was nothing harder in the world, not quantum physics, not brain surgery, not catching a double-header in Texas in August, there was nothing harder than standing before an audience and doing requested improvisations while filling the interstices with stand-up comic routines. In many ways it was the hardest assignment the Committee ever gave him in a life of hard assignments. That's why Sam secretly knew that comedian was the toughest vocation and thanked his stars he had escaped it as a way to earn his keep.

"Care for another one?" It was the bartender, a guy Sam had known for only thirty minutes, but one he liked.

"Yeah, thanks," Sam said. The bartender poured another glass of Black Bush neat. Black Bush, the top-end stuff from Bushmills, was now available in the States. This pleased Sam immensely.

"You're new around here, aren't you?" the bartender asked.

"This trip," Sam replied.

"You've been here before?"

"Many times. Years ago."

"It's okay as joints go."

"It's more than okay when you can sit back and watch with a good drink."

"I don't doubt that."

Someone down the bar hollered for a drink and the bartender left. The lights went down and a kid came out on the stage. He couldn't have been more than twenty-six or so. He was a bundle of nerves. His routine revolved around growing up in a house of all females, a mother and two sisters, all Jewish, all loving, all neurotic. When he was still in grade school, his father had abandoned him, and them, for a shiksa nurse who knew more tricks, his mother claimed, than Mata Hari; blond and wispy, she looked, in his mother's estimation, "like a boy." His father, a GYN man, had been all right until, according to his mother, he started to wear his hair long in the late sixties and took up smoking dope. His mother discounted the gene pool, he said, adding that his father was a direct descendant of Alice B. Toklas. The kid got a big laugh and Sam rooted for him, thinking back to his own days of training at RADA.

In the fall of 1969 Sam Borne arrived at 62-69 Gower Street in central London, the home of the Royal Academy of Dramatic Arts. Founded in 1904 by Sir Herbert Beerbohm Tree, the academy had for its original site the dome of Her Majesty's Theatre, but after only one year it was clear that more extensive facilities were called for and a large house in Gower Street was acquired, to which adjacent properties were later added to form the academy's present home, known the world over for the quality of its training and the prowess of its graduates, including such luminaries as Peter O'Toole, Albert Finney, John Hurt, Alan Bates, Susannah York, Charles Laughton, John Gielgud, Lisa Eichhorn, Anthony Hopkins and Glenda Jackson, to name a few. It is a selective institution, with only six percent of applicants accepted, and with only seventy-five students enrolled during any one term. There are three main courses of study: acting, stage management and specialist diploma courses. The physical plant includes a stage laboratory, a broadcasting studio, videotape facilities, a comprehensive theater laboratory, scenery and property workshops, a design office and a well-stocked wardrobe.

The academy's standards are high, its training rigorous. Students are not permitted to work, even though the tuition fees are high and the living expenses considerable. Twenty-five specialized teachers form the permanent staff, which is augmented by visiting directors. This gives a healthy student-to-teacher ratio of better than three to one and lessons are given in very small groups, where each student receives the maximum attention and the closest scrutiny. There are two fully equipped theaters, the Vanbrugh, with seating for over three hundred, and the Little, which accommodates about one hundred and twenty; in addition, there is a small studio theater providing experience of open-stage and in-the-round production.

It was into this academy atmosphere that the Committee launched Sam that fall of 1969. He had auditioned privately for Hugh Cruttwell, the school's principal, in a small theater on Manhattan's West Side that July on the morning of the day Neil Armstrong walked on the moon. He had been clumsy and raw, but Mr. Cruttwell was impressed with his potential and his energy. So he was in attendance when school opened a few weeks later. The workload was unbelievable. Like all RADA students, Sam attended classes each weekday from ten in the morning till five-thirty in the afternoon, with breaks for lunch and tea only. Before long he was into the grind, rehearsing two plays in the space of two days and taking the full complement of other courses in movement, costuming, makeup, action (the British term for improvisation), voice, stage fighting, singing and speech. Like all American students at RADA, he learned English dialects for consistency on stage and drilled each day to perfect speech patterns. He was an outstanding student from the start and an accomplished actor before long. His undoing was singing. No matter how hard he tried, there was no hope; he had a voice that couldn't carry a note in a bucket. That deficiency probably accounted in part for his admiration for Sinatra and Cocker, Randy Newman and Billie Holiday; how they could hold a note, roll it and caress it, he could never understand. It was magic. But for compensation he was a consummate mimic, able to pick up and deliver any accent or speech pattern almost instantly. There was no accounting for this talent; it was a gift, and an uncanny one.

At RADA the final term was devoted almost entirely to public performance. During his final term Sam had given two memorable performances, one as Mick in *The Caretaker* and one as Archie Rice in *The Entertainer*. He had been convincing, if not overwhelming, as Edward II in Marlowe's classic of that name, and he had rendered a wonderfully blithe Jacques in *As You Like It*. He had nearly got the central role in *Hamlet*, but had been relieved when it went to another student instead. Sam had problems with the prince of Denmark, finding him something of a whiner, although it would have been tremendously amusing to any number of aspiring actresses at the academy to watch him play a thirty-four-year-old virgin; despite the heavy workload, Sam had managed to establish himself as something of a Don Juan at the school. It was his first time spent relatively free of the jurisdiction of the Committee, since he had only a case officer who checked in on him from time to time, a Captain Anthony Wellings-Jones, who, Sam assumed, was affiliated with MI5 or 6. Altogether, the years at RADA were a happy time, capped magnificently when he won the Bancroft Gold Medal, the most esteemed of the awards and prizes given to RADA graduates.

Like the other American graduates of RADA, Sam was barred from working in British Equity, and therefore received none of the firm offers of professional representation heaped on his British classmates. Foreigners were restricted. But he still managed to get feelers from some prominent New York theatrical agents. These, of course, he had to ignore. For Sam it was on to Monterey and the Defense Language Institute Foreign Language Center and four years of grueling work, with many weekends spent on that very small stage in North Beach in San Francisco, doing improvisations, running routines, parrying hecklers, learning humility, honing skills learned at RADA.

On the stage the kid said he had written his congressman suggesting he propose legislation making it possible for any family member to divorce any other family member; if the bill passed, the kid said, he would file against both parents and each sister. He had had it. The audience gave him a big hand, and he stepped down from the small stage. Sam hoped he'd see the kid some night on Carson or Letterman. He had been that good.

"This one's from the lady in the green sweater," the bartender said, pouring Sam another Black Bush on ice. The bartender nodded in the direction of the lady. Sam looked over, smiled and nodded thanks. She was incredibly beautiful, with long red tresses falling on both sides of a spectacularly delicate face and ending in a flip just above her shoulders. She was wearing a bright green sweater and filled it superbly. She raised her cocktail glass to Sam and took a sip. The stool next to her was open.

Sam picked up his glass and walked over. "Thanks for the drink," he said, sticking out his hand. "I'm Sam Borne." She took his hand and shook it firmly. She had green eyes. Sam got lost in them.

"I'm Hannah Andersen," she said. "Glad to meet you." She had a slight accent overlying a husky voice. It was sexy.

THE WHITE ANGEL

"I enjoyed the show, did you?" Sam asked.

"I've seen it before. I come here often. But, yes, I enjoy this man's work, he's funny."

"You come here often. But you sound like you're from far away."

"I am. I'm from Sweden."

"The kid was good, but that's a long way to come for any act."

"I live in this neighborhood. I am originally from Sweden."

"What brought you to San Francisco?"

"You ask a lot of questions."

"I like answers. It's the only way I know to get them."

"The diplomatic service brought me. I work at the Swedish consulate."

"Do you like San Francisco?"

"Yes. And you?"

"I like the parts that don't look like de Sade's answer to Disneyland."

Hannah laughed. "And how about you?" she said. "You have that out-of-town look. Where are you from?"

"Everywhere and nowhere."

"For a man who likes answers, that is not an answer."

"I used to come here often too, years ago."

"What brought you?"

"I was a struggling entertainer. I used to work this joint."

"What happened?"

"I took up another line of work."

"By choice?"

"Not really."

"What line of work did you take up?"

"Accountancy."

She smiled. It was a private smile. Then she picked up her cocktail glass and drained it. "Would you like to hit another club I know for some great jazz?"

"Why not?"

8

BUSTED

Valhalla Ranch
October 6

The afternoon sun was hot and high. From the large barn came the sounds of a horse whinnying in protest. A number of cowboys emerged from a side entrance and scrambled onto the corral fence. Filled with an air of expectancy, they kept their eyes riveted on the opening from the barn into the empty corral. Hitching themselves onto the fence, they waited, swatting flies with their hats, passing a quick remark now and again, staring eagerly.

Soon Aldo emerged from the barn with a lead lasso. Leaning back, he was pulling on it like a man adjusting a kite. The whinnying grew louder. Then the black stallion emerged, bucking and hopping, planting its front feet and pulling back. There were several lassos around its neck. Aldo shouted and pulled hard, and the stallion came farther into the corral. It had a saddle on, and kept bucking and trying to shake it. Craning its neck around hard, it kept trying to get at the saddle with its teeth. Kicking and snorting, it forced the men behind it holding the other lassos to ease back. The men on the fence roared encouragement to Aldo, who responded by shouting louder to the men on the trailing lassos before turning and hurling curses at the fence jockeys. The veins in Aldo's neck started to pop out, his arms straining on the lead lasso. His washed-out denim shirt was stained with dark spots of perspiration on his back and chest and under his arms. The dark spots covered more of the shirt than the dry cloth.

Pulling and straining, cursing and shouting, Aldo got the stallion about twenty feet into the corral. The men with the trailing lassos stepped out of the barn and fanned off to the sides, pulling their lassos taut, offsetting each other and holding the animal roughly in the same spot. The stallion twisted its haunches from side to side, bucking and kicking out wildly with its hind legs before digging in with its forefeet and straining back against Aldo, who pulled down hard on the lead lasso, keeping the stallion's head straight, preventing it from turning and snapping its bared teeth at the saddle and the cinch.

Aldo shouted instructions, and a cowboy from the side broke off and came forward. Aldo handed him the lead lasso while shouting to one of the fence jockeys to man the side lasso vacated by the cowboy now on the lead. A short cowboy, younger than the others on the fence, leaped down, sprinted across the corral and grabbed the side lasso. Five men now pinned the big stallion, who still snorted and bucked. Putting his left hand on the lead lasso, Aldo bore down on it and started to walk toward the stallion, talking to the horse as he walked. The stallion tried to back up, but Aldo spat instructions to the men and they increased the pressure on the lassos. The stallion was pinned.

When Aldo reached the animal, continuing to talk, he stretched out his right hand and attempted to stroke its snout. The stallion flicked its head mightily

61

and backpedaled. Sensing what would happen, Aldo scurried back a few paces just as the stallion kicked out with its forefeet. Shouting and cursing, Aldo roared at the men to pin the stallion as hard as they could. It didn't matter. The big horse overpowered them and imposed its will. Gaining just enough slack, the stallion reared up and kicked out, forefeet wheeling dangerously in the air, whinnying as loud as it could. It was a fearsome and majestic sight.

Angered and defeated, Aldo wrenched down fiercely on the lead lasso. The stallion moved forward rapidly on its hind legs, trying to offset the pressure exerted on its head. Aldo shouted. The men on either side pulled as hard as they could, pinning the stallion with countervailing pressure. Then Aldo strained mightily on the lead lasso, ahead of the cowboy holding its end. Pushing down as hard as he could, he forced the stallion's head down. It's forefeet thundered onto the ground, forcing up a spray of dirt.

Immediately Aldo walked forward on the lead lasso, increasing his hold on the stallion. The fence jockeys shouted encouragement and Aldo flashed them a hateful look. He was not in control and he knew it. It would take much work to wear this stallion down, and he didn't have enough time. He had to deliver soon. It was an order from the boss; an order that was, of course, shit of the worst sort. As a great horseman, Aldo knew what was called for here. There was a simple remedy. A horse such as this one could be handled successfully only one way. You called the vet. The vet came. You overpowered the animal and, slash, you made it a gelding. That always worked, but not for this woman he worked for. She was stubborn, like all of her kind. She was also in love. She loved this filthy beast, this wild, uncontrollable stallion. There was no other explanation. She would not hear of gelding it. She wanted only one thing, and he, Aldo, was under orders to deliver it.

She wanted to ride this stallion and she wanted it fast. Enraged now, Aldo glanced up at the open hayloft. There she stood, watching, waiting, rooting for this fucking Faust even as she tightened the screws on him, Aldo, to break this mad beast for the saddle. And he would, just to show the wicked bitch who really ruled the roost here on this ranch. He would show her, just the way he would show her in bed, the way he rode her harder and harder, forced her higher and higher, and yet when she recovered from her ecstasy, and she recovered faster than any bitch he'd ever ridden, she would always make him feel small, inadequate. She always wanted more. Sometimes Aldo thought she couldn't be satisfied this side of the grave, but still he tried, and would try again and again, damn it, until one day he would make it, he would break this blond mare like the bitch she was, but for now he would break this fucking horse.

Sweat rolled down his face, stinging him, blinding him. His arms ached. His shirt was soaked through and clung to him. His dungarees were wet through the crotch, along the thighs. Still, he would prevail. He would prove again and forever that he was the best horseman in all the Amazon, in all Brazil; fuck it, in all South America and North America too. He wiped his brow and stared hard at the beast. The stallion stood coated with lather. It frothed along its neck, on its chest, on its shanks. It was tired, he was sure of it. It had to be tired. Aldo was tired. Now was the time.

Aldo walked down the lead lasso and reached out. The stallion flicked its head, then stopped. Aldo talked to the horse softly, then stroked its snout. The stallion bared its teeth, then snorted, but did not snap at Aldo's hand, as it had previously. Aldo felt the time was ripe. Gesturing to the men on the lines, he told them to hold firm. Then he worked his way around to the stallion's side, talking softly all the while, stroking the horse's lathered neck. Without any hasty movements or wasted motion, Aldo hitched his left foot in the stirrup and heaved himself up into the saddle. His right foot found the stirrup. He lashed the reins around his left fist and all was well. The fence jockeys clapped.

Then it happened. The stallion reared. Aldo reached out and grabbed the reins with his right hand and pulled back. The stallion twisted its head, whinnying, then came down quickly on its forefeet. When its forefeet hit the dirt, it reared again. Aldo shouted to the cowboys on the lassos to bear down. He nearly lost his seat. Rage energized him. He would not lose again to this fucking stallion. Today was the day. Today Faust learned what a rider on his back felt like, and he learned to like it or else.

The cowboys bore down and the stallion danced sideways and backward on its hind legs before coming down quickly on its forefeet. Aldo slammed forward; the ground leaped up. He was flung backward; the sky spun above him. He felt his feet slip in the stirrups and his legs thrust forward. The saddle shifted under him as the horse hopped sideways. Then the ground hurled up at him again and he pitched forward over the stallion's fetid neck. When the reins went slack, he reached out and grabbed the beast's slippery neck, his hands slewing along the slick flesh before he clasped them together at the front. Then he pitched forward as the ground shot up. The stallion had pirouetted on its forelegs and kicked out wildly with its hind legs, rotating them rapidly from side to side, abruptly shifting directions, bucking all the while. Aldo fell forward and planted his chest against the horse's neck. Under his chest he felt the wet mane, and he held on, fighting the tendency of his feet to come out of the stirrups by thrusting back hard with his legs. Below his face the stallion nickered and snorted.

Suddenly his chest came away from the mane as his weight flung rapidly backward. The stallion reared. Above him was sky, nothing but blue sky. He clenched the reins as tight as he could, shouting to the cowboys to bear down. He felt his legs slip in the saddle as the horse stood nearly vertical on its hind legs. Then it teetered. Aldo thought he was going over, but the horse's head above him jerked and he hurled forward, still in the saddle.

When its forefeet hit the ground, the stallion leaped on all four feet, landed and leaped rapidly again in the same way, propelling its whole body straight up, landing and almost immediately leaping up again. Aldo held on. This was a good sign. He had a chance today. The beast was finally succumbing to the inevitable, that he would be mastered by the great Aldo. This filthy animal was tired, beaten and ready to be dominated. Aldo glanced up to the open doors of the hayloft and saw the blond whore standing there with her hands on her hips. Now was the time.

He shouted to his men to drop their lassos. They did. The horse just leaped and landed in the same pattern, almost in the same spot. Aldo tightened his grip on the reins and prepared to administer lesson one in manners to this favored big bastard who had cost him so much time, so much aggravation, so much humiliation and frustration. He pushed into the stirrups.

This little movement was all it took. The great black stallion sensed the absence of the lassos restraining him and paused. Standing absolutely still, he flicked his neck rapidly from side to side. There was no pressure. He was free, except for the great unwanted weight on his back.

Confident, Aldo spurred the stallion. It tore off in a semicircle, then skidded to a stop and reared on its hind legs. Aldo felt panic lance through him, but ignored it. He would win this time. The stupid beast had to be tired, exhausted. The sky wheeled above him as the stallion reared, but it fell forward quickly and shot off, running rapidly along the fence, forcing the cowboys perched there to swing their legs clear. It threw its body against the fence, but Aldo had anticipated this move and lifted his leg in time to avoid having it crushed.

Quickly Aldo jerked the rein in the opposite direction. He would force the bit into the horse's mouth and force it back to the center of the corral, away from the fence. The stallion flexed its neck in the intended direction, then slammed back hard against the fence. Aldo lifted his leg again just in time, then wrenched hard on the reins. It worked. The big horse tore toward the center of the corral, skidded to a halt and reared on its hind legs, neighing as loud as it could. Aldo held his seat, gripping the reins as hard as he could. With the sky spinning above him, he felt again a stab of panic, but held on. The stallion hurled forward, then shot off again. It ran to the opposite fence and started to leap straight up and down on all four legs, banging its side off the fence. Like the accomplished horseman he was, Aldo shot his inside leg forward in the stirrup. The leg was clear as the stal-

66

lion's side thundered off the fence's planks. Aldo felt good. He had a chance, he would succeed.

The stallion banged once more off the fence, then bolted across the corral toward the cowboys, who shouted encouragement to Aldo as the big black stallion bore down on the fence again. Then it skidded to a halt and reared on its hind legs. It went nearly vertical. Aldo panicked. Lurching forward, he clasped both arms around the horse's neck.

The stallion felt the man's weight and shook its neck violently from side to side as it fell forward. Aldo clung to the neck, the reins clenched tight in his hands. When the stallion's forefeet hit the ground, it bucked backward, then catapulted onto its forefeet and shot its hind legs into the air, kicking both legs in one direction, then the other. Aldo pressed his arms against the neck, his shoulders and chest slipping to one side, his face forward. As soon as the stallion's hind legs hit the ground, it reached around and snapped its teeth at the rider's face. Aldo pushed hard against its neck, his hands sliding in the sweat lathered there. Just ahead of the stallion's snapping teeth, he righted himself in the saddle, panicked.

Whinnying, the stallion reared tremendously on its hind legs and twisted its whole body toward the fence. Aldo lost his grip in the stirrups and fell backward, clinging to the reins. The stallion felt Aldo's weight shift and rotated on its hind legs till its back was to the fence. Then it backpedaled.

Stretched out his full length, pinned between the fence and the stallion, Aldo screamed. The stallion pushed back, then shot forward. Aldo fell to the ground with a thud, unconscious. The stallion, snorting and neighing, spun around and reared above the fallen man. Two cowboys ran to the fence where Aldo lay and threw themselves on the ground. They grabbed the fallen ramrod by an arm and a leg and yanked him under the fence seconds before the angry stallion's hooves slammed into the earth where he had lain.

They rolled Aldo away from the fence and knelt beside him, stunned. They had never seen him so clearly bested, and they did not know whether his bones were broken, whether he would live or die. They looked up at each other, ignorant of what to do. Behind them the stallion snorted and whinnied in the corral.

"Step aside."

It was the mistress. The cowboys parted for her. Those kneeling stood up and stepped back. She stood over the fallen man, known to them as her lover, and looked down at him with more than the hint of a sneer. Then she kicked out with one of her shiny black boots. The boot tipped against Aldo's ribs. He stirred. She kicked him harder, then leaned down and slapped him hard on the face, first one cheek, then the other. He groaned. She slapped him again, harder, on each cheek.

He opened his eyes. Then he closed them again. With a painfully slow motion he brought one hand forward and rubbed his eyelids, then opened his eyes again. He took a deep breath, then sighed. "I will kill that fucking horse," he said in a low but emphatic voice.

"You'll do nothing of the kind."

"I hate that bastard."

"He's not a bastard. He comes from better stock than you."

"He's a stupid animal who needs the knife."

"Are you all right?"

"I think so."

"Then get to your feet and stop berating my prize."

Aldo sat up on an elbow and the cowboys stepped forward and helped him to his feet. He stood, testing himself, while two of his men started to knock the dust off him. It spread in clouds.

"Stop that," the blond woman snapped. The cowboys left off immediately. Aldo started to brush himself off gently.

"See that Faust is cooled out properly and washed down. Then feed him. I'll see you later." She started to walk away.

Aldo looked after her. "You care more about that fucking horse than you do about me."

"He's a better man."

9

FLYING DOWN TO RIO

Los Angeles–Rio de Janeiro
October 6–7

Sam Borne stretched out comfortably in the first-class cabin of the Varig 747. He was settling in for the twelve-hour flight to Rio de Janeiro. It was a few minutes before the scheduled takeoff time, and Sam knew that with the five-hour time difference he would not arrive in Rio till nearly eight the next morning. That gave him a lot of time to fill with thoughts of his latest assignment. He had never had one quite like this latest, but then again the Committee was always coming up with the craziest assignments for him. He felt cheated, of course, flying into Los Angeles only to fly out again. It was one of his favorite cities, LA, unlike any other in the world; it glittered and gleamed and offered a good time second in America only to New York. Maybe, if he got lucky, he'd get back there soon.

He picked up a magazine and started to read an article about Mel Gibson, the hottest new leading man in movies. He'd seen *The Year of Living Dangerously* and the incomparable *Road Warrior,* so he could appreciate what all the fuss was about. Gibson had real presence on the screen and projected a virility and vitality not seen often in modern movie stars. It all made Sam wonder if he could ever have enjoyed the life of an actor. He doubted it. No matter how hard he tried, unless something definite was on the line, like his life, he never got the charge from acting you were supposed to get.

There was a jolt as the big jet started to back from its berth. He fastened his seat belt. When the PA announced that the stewardesses would demonstrate the use of the oxygen masks and the life jackets, he looked up. The demonstrator for first class was first class herself, a tall woman with chocolate-brown hair swept back in a rolled bun. She had large eyes like a faun and high cheekbones framing a tiny nose above a wide, thin-lipped mouth. Her breasts were high and full, and she had the carriage of a princess. Her complexion was dusky. Sam pegged her for one of the triumphant racial mixtures you got in Brazil, responsible in great part for the legendary beauty of the girls of Rio. The PA announced that all personnel should take their seats for takeoff, and she walked down the aisle and was gone. As she passed, Sam noted a pair of legs worth killing for.

As they turned onto the takeoff runway Sam felt the brakes lock. The pilot revved the engines hard, then released the brakes. They raced down the runway and lifted off. From his window Sam saw the blue Pacific pass beneath them. The pilot banked hard left, and below them the outer islands loomed up and then, beyond, a lone tanker making its way south. Before they disappeared through the cloud bank Sam spotted a yacht under full sail tacking toward the coast.

He settled down and took up his magazine again. On planes and trains, he enjoyed light reading and thought there wasn't anything better when it came to light stuff than *People.* He turned to an article on Lee

Iacocca, a folk hero for politicians to conjure with. The man's comments made sense, but businessmen had traditionally not made good politicians, and Sam wondered what the outcome would be for this latest corporate messiah if, as rumored, he ran for president. It brought to mind Sam's one great political proposal, namely; that candidates for public office, including president, bid on the job the way building contractors did. The budget, that way, would be part of the platform, and things would be, at least theoretically, controllable. That and instant recall would solve a lot of political problems, but neither had a snowman's future in hell, so it was idle to speculate about them.

"Would you like something to drink?"

She was back. The Brazilian goddess stood over him, smiling. He smiled back.

"I'd like Bushmills if you have it."

"I'm sorry, we have only rye, bourbon and Scotch."

"In that case, I'll have a Scotch and soda on the rocks."

The name on her gold breast pin said Tiberia. She passed him his drink, reached into her pocket and pulled out a folded card. Handing it to him, she asked, "What would you like for dinner?"

Sam glanced at the card. He opted instantly for the chicken. Chicken was always the safest. He started to say something to Tiberia, but an aging tanghound across the aisle clamored for her attention, and Sam went back to his magazine.

An article predicting a big future for Kathleen Turner caught his eye. He didn't doubt she'd have a big future, having seen *Romancing the Stone* and *Body Heat*, but he scanned the piece quickly and skipped to an article on Sparky Anderson. The Tigers were the odds-on favorite to win the World Series, and Anderson was his usual homey self. It irked Sam that he would be out of the country during the series. Such luck was a hazard of his vocation; still, it was a pisser to track a whole season's worth of pennant races and then miss the big finale.

"Hello."

It was Tiberia back with his chicken. He ordered a glass of white wine and was pleasantly surprised when she brought a passably dry California chablis. While he picked at his chicken and a wilted salad, he read a feature piece on William Kennedy, the novelist who'd achieved acclaim in his fifties, winning a Pulitzer Prize, and had scripted the legendarily troubled *Cotton Club* for Francis Ford Coppola. Making a mental note to try one of the novels in Kennedy's Albany trilogy, Sam put the magazine aside and finished what he could of the chicken. Then he took up *Esquire* and read about the boom in screenplay writing. Everybody, according to the article, was writing a screenplay. All across America people were hitting the keys with INT and EXT preceding every new scene. According to *Esquire*, nobody wanted to write the Great American Novel anymore; now everybody wanted to write the Great American Movie. This was a heady aspiration, Sam thought, considering there were any number of Great American Movies already in the revival houses.

He finished the article on screenwriting and started a short story by Robert Stone, a writer whose work he liked enormously. Sipping a cup of strong Brazilian coffee, he finished the story, then flipped off his reading light and relaxed back into his chair, reviewing in his mind the essential facts about his latest target, Mother Beloved.

THE WHITE ANGEL

* * *

Mother Beloved was a study in treachery. A megalomaniac of the first rank, she was the absolute authority to the one hundred gunmen and women in her gang. The iron fist in the iron glove, she gave no quarter and asked for none in return. Some eighteen years back, she had penetrated the Amazon Basin with a handful of followers and through gargantuan treachery and wickedness had managed to gain absolute sway over a vast section of the Northeast, a territory larger than all Europe and so wild it lay beyond the reach of law and order, a situation the present Brazilian government was trying to remedy with the help of businessmen in Rio and São Paulo, as well as in the United States and Japan, all of whom wanted to develop the area.

Controversy raged in Brazil over this state of affairs. Many environmentalists rued the destruction of the great rain forest, but the government was determined to build the area up, viewing it as the nineteenth-century American government had viewed the American West. To the officials in Brasília and to the businessmen in Rio and São Paulo, the Northeast represented a golden opportunity to develop Brazil's natural resources. There were great opportunities in minerals, in forestry, in mining. On top of that, the huge native population offered a cheap labor pool. The area had already attracted American and Japanese firms, who were pouring in billions. Factories had been set up, and technical training was proving a great boon to the natives. Economic hope now existed in many communities.

This hope was precisely what Mother Beloved intended to stifle in the vast area under her control. She did not want progress. She wanted instead to maintain the primitive conditions which had allowed her to be-

come a virtual jungle empress. No matter how hard
the government tried, she had so far been successful
in keeping out any real progress. Under cover of night
she and her gang had raided and destroyed countless
factories and mining outposts. They had wrecked
more than one technical school, and more than one
instructor had disappeared through their agency.
They had tortured and hanged, they had terrorized,
they had left bloody corpses in their wake as object
lessons to the natives.

The government had tried everything to stop her.
They had sent special police units into the area, but
the jungle had conspired in their undoing, and Mother
Beloved had triumphed time and again. Then there
had been a special forces unit deployed by the Brazilian army. This had been briefly effective, calming the
natives and giving the illusion of stability. Illusion was
all it gave. Gradually, using every tactic available to
her, Mother Beloved had whittled this 250-man unit to
a scant cadre, a cadre the government had withdrawn
in frustration.

Defeated, the officials in Brasília had taken their
troubles to the American and Japanese businessmen
willing to invest in the area. Things had moved slowly,
but finally word had filtered to the right sources. The
Committee had been notified, and Sam Borne was
activated. He was to infiltrate Mother Beloved's redoubt impersonating an arms dealer; the Committee
had supplied entrée in the form of Mercedes Coozi, a
special friend of Mother Beloved herself. He was to
take out Mother Beloved quickly and escape. It would
not be easy. Mother Beloved controlled not only her
redoubt, a tremendous spread called the Valhalla
Ranch, but the town on its periphery as well as a network of spies throughout the entire area. She had eyes

and ears in every village and town once you hit her corner of the Northeast, and she knew what was happening the minute it happened. He would have to be convincing, he would have to be quick and, once he'd made the hit, he would have to flee immediately.

The ranch itself was a virtual fortress. It had up-to-the-minute surveillance equipment, including electronic devices of every kind. It had a guard unit on its borders. It had a command center in the ranch house itself, and it had the best kind of protection in its defenders, for the people Mother Beloved had taken into her gang looked upon her as a savior. Before she came, they had been dirt-poor, homeless and starving; since joining her forces, they had plenty to eat, good shelter, and a sense of power to go with their sense of belonging to a select community. All around them was still primitive and impoverished, and they, the gang members, were the elect; they had the goods and they had control. Every effort to bring progress to the area was a threat to them, as Mother Beloved never failed to emphasize. They were fanatical devotees, practically worshipers of the great blond goddess who had raised them from the mire and given them a sword. Their love for her was exceeded only by their fear of her.

Of course, Mother Beloved was no more an Aryan apparition in the Brazilian jungle than Sam Borne was an Eagle Scout. Her real name was Wilda von Hoffer; she had been briefly Mrs. Don José Carlos Álvarez, but this was only during her short marriage, the only lasting legacy of which was her daughter Erika, an eighteen-year-old beauty who was altogether too soft and weak-minded to suit her mother, a fact Wilda attributed to Erika's father, a minor member of the Bolivian landowning aristocracy she had married in a weak moment some twenty years back. Wilda never passed a day that she didn't silently congratulate herself on having had the dominant genes physically, for her daughter was a stunning replica of her, with no evidence of her father's Latin blood. Like her mother, Erika was a statuesque blonde with buttermilk skin and apple cheeks and eyes as blue as a clear Alpine lake; her legs were long and gently curved, with just a hint of muscle; they gave way to a torso fit for a Greek goddess. Both mother and daughter were world-class beauties, and they never stepped out together, whether in riding outfits or cocktail gowns or bathing suits, especially bathing suits, that Wilda did not cast long and serious looks at her daughter, appraising the competition, fearing time, jealous of youth.

Wilda von Hoffer had arrived in the South American jungle via the Vatican shuttle. Her father had been a prominent Prussian general in the Wehrmacht during the Second World War. He had served with distinction on the Eastern Front, but unlike many officers with his aristocratic bloodlines, he had been an avid Nazi; his uniform bore the special chevron of those who'd been members of the Nazi party prior to the 1933 takeover. When he was wounded during the early days of the retreat across Poland, he had been grateful to be shipped back to bomb-blasted Berlin. General Dieter von Hoffer had been no fool. Though not yet fully recovered, he had checked out of the military hospital in Berlin as soon as he was ambulatory and took the first ride he could commandeer to Munich, where his father-in-law had been an esteemed banker before the war. Fortunately for Dieter and his wife Ingrid, Ingrid's father still had good contacts with Eugenio Pacelli, now Pope Pius XII, and the Holy Father was a man to honor past favors and present passions, so Dieter and Ingrid were whisked through Switzerland and on into Italy under false identities. From Naples the couple departed on a steamer that landed them in Caracas two weeks later. From there they made their way into the Bolivian lowlands, where they established themselves on a plantation that was soon thriving. Ingrid had become pregnant en route just east of Gibraltar, and Wilda arrived eight months after they'd settled in their temporary housing on the plantation.

Dieter was a determined man. Over the years he built the plantation into a profit-making venture. His daughter and wife had a lovely life. When Wilda was eight, her horse-loving father gave her a pony, and she was smitten; riding and great horses became her lifelong passion. She received a good education in a convent school and a better one at home. It was while Wilda was finishing her education at the convent school that the men from Israel kidnapped her father and shanghaied him back to Tel Aviv, where justice was swift. Convicted by eyewitnesses of atrocities against the Jewish people in the Russian Pale, Dieter was quickly executed.

All this his daughter learned only by subjecting her delicate mother to extreme pressure. Under duress Ingrid broke down and informed Wilda what her father had done and what had happened to him. The daughter was not a von Hoffer for nothing. She swore no one, whether societies or people, would ever tame her, dominate her, or impose their will on her in any way; she would answer to no one, and no one would ever trap her. Hastily, she married Don José Carlos Álvarez, conscripted him in her deflowering, became pregnant, bore Erika, divorced Don José Carlos and, placing her infant daughter in the temporary care of her mother, hired a handful of mercenaries and set off across the border, scouting the location for the perfect stronghold. She found it several weeks later in the Amazon Basin.

Immediately she set about establishing her empire. She staked out a huge claim and soon had gangs of natives pressed into service. She knew from her father how to make the earth yield its bounty. She set about planting crops and soon had enough food harvested to feed herself, her mercs and the natives pressed into service. In the few instances where the natives gave her trouble, action was swift and sure. Most died at her own hand, blown away by a shotgun. They were tied to a post and then, bang, she executed them. In all instances she made certain there were witnesses to the executions so word would spread about her and her brand of administration. It worked. She was an absolute monarch in no time, the mercs having stayed on and formed a teaching cadre.

The one cabin erected by her was soon replaced by a large ranch house with a wide veranda and big rooms. The native huts built for the mercs gave way to bunkhouses, and then the first large barn was built. Wilda sent for her father's best horses and transported them to the ranch, where she started to breed them. Her obsession with horses increased; she was determined to breed championship Thoroughbreds. She had a mile racetrack built with its own small grandstand, and soon she was bringing in the semen of the best Thoroughbred studs in the world. She was not paying breeding fees for the semen, but was instead obtaining it clandestinely; she was in effect a renegade international breeder determined to falsify papers and bring her stable eventually to prominence through a linkup with an Irish breeder of Thoroughbreds with a big farm in Kilkenny. She was determined one day to stand at Churchill Downs or Epsom and know she'd bred the winner.

In the meantime, she enjoyed her majestic spread and its many outbuildings; now there were three barns in addition to four bunkhouses and a pair of bungalows for the domestic help. A recent addition, Wilda's pride and joy, was a small barn with a horse pool; she loved to watch her prize colts and fillies strengthen their legs by swimming in circles on a tether. And she loved having the track, where she would watch in the early mornings for hours as the native boys she'd had trained by an imported Panamanian jockey breezed their mounts.

And she maintained control of the towns and villages surrounding her ranch for miles on end. Her network reached everywhere. From the nucleus of the original mercs, her gang had grown till now it stood at a hundred strong. The mercs trained every member well. Each man and woman in the gang was an expert marksman; they all knew the basics in hand-to-hand combat and were completely at home with modern firearms and weapons of a wide range. They were all in excellent condition, having been driven in a tough physical regimen by one merc, Bruce Reilly, an obsessed Aussie with a mean streak wider than the Outback. Each bunkhouse was equipped with a Nautilus machine, and there were barbells and universal machines as well. Aldo, the debonair and macho ramrod of the ranch and head horse trainer, had schooled all of the gang in horsemanship; as a mounted force they could compare in competence and ferocity to a great nineteenth-century cavalry unit, only they were equipped with the best weapons the twentieth century had to offer and were lethal beyond description. When they rode down on a town or village, they were as terrifying to the inhabitants as the Cossacks had been to the Jews living on the steppes of Russia.

It was this well-trained force that Wilda von Hoffer, Mother Beloved to all she terrorized, wielded so effectively against the officials and businessmen trying to bring the benefits of progress and industry to the Northeast. That these government officials and businessmen would have made education and a decent environment available ultimately to hundreds of thousands of impoverished people counted for nothing with her, she wanted only to maintain suzerainty over this backward patch of a country struggling to achieve what it considered its manifest destiny.

For Mother Beloved, her own manifest destiny lay elsewhere; namely, back in Bolivia, where she had come to be known in certain circles as *el angel blanco*, the white angel. As soon as her mother passed on, leaving her the plantation Dieter von Hoffer had cultivated so carefully, she capitalized on the times. She started farming the coca plant, first on a modest basis, then as a big agribusiness. She was current, right in position to exploit the big explosion in cocaine use in the United States and Europe. Especially in Europe she had been successful, getting in ahead of many of the other South American suppliers by way of her background and education. In Germany and in France she had a tremendous network, with major tentacles stretching into Italy, the Low Countries and the United Kingdom. Though not as big as some, her operation was lucrative; she had more than enough money, and could have packed it all in, abandoning her Bolivian coca plantation and deserting her jungle ranch for a penthouse in Paris or a condo in Monaco, but that would never do for her. She had to be in control, the sole power, the empress, and only her current setup gave her that kind of power and position.

Few people held any interest for such a woman. Two types who did were horse breeders and arms dealers, and the only person as attractive to her as a superb horse breeder with no scruples was a top-shelf arms dealer with no scruples. Impersonating one, Sam Borne was scheduled to penetrate her organization and put a stop to the reign of terror Wilda von Hoffer had enjoyed in the depths of the Brazilian rain forest for eighteen long years.

"Excuse me, would you like some breakfast?" It was Tiberia. Sam had dozed off. He turned and lifted the plastic shade on the oval window. Outside, it was still dark.

"I'd like orange juice and some coffee, please."

"Of course." Tiberia took a container of prepoured orange juice from her serving tray and placed it before him. Then she balanced the tray in her left hand and poured him coffee.

"Would you like cream or sugar?"

"Cream, please."

She handed him a tiny container of cream. While he flipped off the top and poured the cream into the black coffee, Tiberia asked if he'd care for a croissant or some sweet pastry. He declined.

"When will we land?" he asked.

"In about an hour."

"Thank you."

The aging Romeo across the aisle clamored for her attention and Tiberia turned to him. Sam swallowed his orange juice in two big drafts, then sipped at his coffee. He sat back and closed his eyes. In moments he was in a mild meditation, freeing his mind of all concern, resting; it was rare for him to be able to sleep on a plane at all, and even though he had dozed off, he was still tired. That wrung-out feeling had stolen over him, jet lag. His neck felt stiff, his legs ached.

The next thing he knew, the PA system announced that all seat belts were to be fastened and all cigarettes extinguished. Sam opened his eyes and felt the engines cut back. His ears popped as the plane dropped down. They were in their approach pattern. He glanced out the window and saw the sky streaked with the purple and orange of dawn. Below, the green landscape was flecked with tract houses and an occasional tall apartment building. The plane banked, and he saw in the distance the distinctive bay of Rio.

It was time to go to work.

10

THE WOMAN IN WHITE

Valhalla Ranch
October 7

The young boy's name was Jesús. He had the broad features, straight black hair and bronze color of his Indian forebears, deepened slightly by his mulatto blood. He had a fine figure, with a broad hairless chest tapering to a narrow waist, and with rippling muscles in his arms and legs. His eyes were large and clear, and touched with apprehension. He did not like standing naked in this room in the big house. He had been forced to attend the *batuque* ceremony all the night before, and now in the early morning he was tired and he wanted more than anything to be transported back to the safety of his jungle village. All last night in the *terreiro* he had been frightened. He had heard of such ceremonies. He knew that the *terreiro* was the pavilion where the *batuque* rituals were played out. He knew that the *batuque*, sometimes called *candomble*, was primitive, based on the religions imported to the New World by African slaves. The peripatetic priest who visited his village had warned him never to have anything to do with it.

But he had had no choice. Two days ago the men rode into his village and hauled everyone into the

84

center at gunpoint. At first, like everyone else, he watched with his mother and his sisters as the men talked among themselves. Then they singled him out and made him fetch the family's donkey. They made him mount up. They were armed, and the head man fired his gun into the air to frighten everyone and to hold their attention. His mother cried and threw herself on him, but the head man fired two shots at her feet and his sisters managed to restrain her.

He left with the men and they rode through the dense jungle for two days until they reached the tiny village at the edge of this great ranch. There, in the village, he witnessed the *batuque* ceremony. He watched as the *pai de santo,* the spiritual leader, led the mediums in their dances, the drums beating, the gourds rattling, the metal pipes filled with lead shot shaking. He heard the songs and watched the mediums go into trance. Some shook violently, others whirled and spun, still others danced with unfocused eyes staring straight ahead. One man passed a lighted candle under his chin and along the underside of his arms. A woman broke into war whoops and fell, writhing, to the ground. At midnight a drummer leaped from the stage into the center of the room. After sprinkling gunpowder onto his hand, he lit it with a cigar. It exploded, sending a cloud of white smoke toward the ceiling but leaving the drummer unscathed.

Finally, toward dawn, the dancing stopped, the drumming and rattling ceased and the *pai de santo* led the mediums in a closing song. The boy stood off to the side, tired, but relieved to leave the big room with the spirit signs all around, on the walls and the ceiling. He was grateful that the dancing and singing were over, and that the people seemed to act normal again. They had frightened him; he understood why the good father had told him never to attend such ceremonies. But the other people present, as they filed out, only looked at him dolefully. He was puzzled, but before he could think why, the gunmen led him out. They took him beyond the locked gates of the ranch and up to the big house, where he was stripped, bathed and left standing in this room, naked, tired, apprehensive.

A door opened and a maid stuck her head into the room. He covered himself and blushed. She snapped off an order for him to leave the room through a door opposite, but he didn't move. It was not right to go about naked. He was ashamed, embarrassed. He would have to confess this to the priest, as well as his attendance at the *batuque* ceremony. If only he could wish himself back to his village, this would all seem like a nightmare. The maid shouted at him and whisked her hand in the direction of the door. He stood rooted. Angry now, the maid walked into the room and pushed him. He put his hand on the doorknob and looked back. The maid said she would call the gunman if he did not hurry. He turned the knob and entered the strangest room he'd ever seen.

It was all mirrored, walls, floor and ceiling. And everything was white. White was reflected everywhere. It came from a huge round bed covered with white satin that sat in the center of the room. He was disoriented, but he knew he was going to go to hell for being in such a room. It was the work of the devil. Out of the corner of his eye he saw something move and realized with a pounding in his chest that off to his left stood a woman dressed all in white like a bride. His hands flew to cover himself. Heat flooded his face. Tears blurred his vision.

"Welcome," the woman said. She smiled. She was

more beautiful than any woman he had ever seen. Her hair was blond, her skin fair, her eyes deep blue and her mouth painted red like a whore's. Her teeth were even and white, her dress shiny; it flared out from her waist to where it nearly touched the floor.

"The cat has your tongue, I see," she said. She waved a wand in her right hand and smiled again. "You seem to be trembling. Are you cold?"

He could not answer. It didn't matter. He noticed that the woman had something like a crown on her head, placed carefully on her hair. It shone with stones he thought were diamonds.

"Let me warm up the room," she whispered. Reaching behind her, she snapped something and the dress fell from her. Hearing him catch his breath, she smiled and winked as she stepped out of the dress, piled now at her feet. He dropped his eyes. And found a new horror. The mirrored floor reflected his naked body and seemed to make it larger. He looked up.

"I'm told none of the *encantados* entered you last night."

He didn't know what answer to make. He stared at the woman now, feeling changes come over his body that he couldn't control. She stood tall in white high heels with white stockings climbing her long legs. At the top of her thighs, the stockings were clipped to a little white sash with lace on it. Above, she wore a frilly white camisole, open in the middle, where her breasts pushed through, as they did at the top, spilling over. His blood started to rush, his heart to race. His groin tightened, pushing and throbbing against his cupped hands. He blinked rapidly, trying to free his mind of impure thoughts. The priest had told him this sometimes helped.

"If none of the spirits entered you, then none will

protect you," the beautiful woman said. She was right, he thought, none of the *encantados* had entered him. He was not of that belief. He believed instead in the Blessed Mother, and he prayed to her now, imploring her help to overcome what was happening to him. His lips trembled in prayer.

It was no use. The woman shrugged out of the camisole and stood with her breasts revealed. Instinctively he dropped his eyes, but recoiled at the reflection he saw in the mirrored floor. He had an inspiration. He looked away from the woman.

Again, it was no use. In the mirrored wall he watched as the woman walked across the room to him. When she was near enough she reached out with the wand and pried his hands away from his body. He recoiled from what he saw reflected and turned away, back to her.

Her face was near his. She smiled beautifully and he felt all willpower desert him, even as fear still caused him to tremble. Then the lady leaned forward and kissed him tenderly. The warmth of her lips flooded over him. He tasted the sticky paint on them. Its taste was pleasing. Her fingertips traced their way down his chest, then went lower till she held him. He fought to hold himself in, but her touch inflamed him.

"Ah, no patience, like all my young studs," the lady whispered. She stepped back and over to the bed. He didn't move. He couldn't keep his eyes off her. He knew what was happening. The older boys had spoken roughly of it, and now he had an idea of how magical it could be. It held him in its grip. His hands trembled on his thighs.

"I won't keep you waiting. I know how eager you are," she said, smiling. Her voice was low, and maddening. She took off her high heels, raising her thighs enticingly. Then she hitched her thumbs and forefingers within the sash and pushed it down her long legs, rolling her stockings off as she did. She was revealed to him.

"Come," she whispered. He walked across to her in two strides, eager, quivering, unsure of what he wanted but wanting something more than he'd ever wanted anything. Beckoning him with her eyes, she lay back on the big bed. He climbed onto it. He knelt over her, then on instinct reached out and touched her breast. She reached up and pulled him down, then positioned him and arched her back, guiding him into her.

"Ah, but you're eager," she whispered, rocking gently beneath him. He thrust into her, his eyes squeezed shut, every young muscle in his body taut. Soon his motion became hurried, frenzied. She felt his preliminary spasms and looped her arms behind him. With her left hand she grabbed the wand securely and pulled it apart. The cylinder came free, reflecting a flash of steel from all mirrored surfaces.

Above her he thrust forward and cried out, his whole body quaking, his eyes clenched tight, his teeth bared. His arms trembled, nearly giving out. He took a deep breath and expelled it slowly between his teeth. His eyes opened and he grinned at her, then mumbled his gratitude. He arched his back and felt the pinprick of cold steel. As he recoiled, she clenched him securely in her left arm and pulled him to her, at the same time driving her right arm straight down as hard as she could.

The stiletto skewered him in the back, chest high, slightly to the left of the spine. It could not have been placed more perfectly. Instinctively he fought against her, trying to raise himself. He succeeded only in impaling himself further. His eyes, staring wide, fixed on her, his mouth filling with blood.

The woman craned her head forward and kissed him.

11

COPACABANA

Rio de Janeiro
October 7

The phone rang before the bellhop opened the door. Once inside, Sam Borne ignored it and handed the man a generous tip. At the front desk, he'd changed one of the traveler's checks in his Committee packet to cruzeiros. The Meridien-Rio had given him the lousy hotel rate, so he planned to hit a bank that afternoon before they closed and change more money, but first he wanted a shower and a shave, followed by a good nap. The phone kept ringing. He walked across the room to the bedside table and picked it up.

"Welcome to Rio," the cheery voice said. Sam hated the cheerfulness of Committee contacts.

"Thanks. What's on your mind?"

"We just want to let you know there's time for a nice nap before you'll have company this afternoon." It was an annoying habit of many Committee contacts to use the royal "we." It was also annoying that they were always suggesting the obvious.

"What time can I expect this company?"

"You'll have visitors in the early afternoon. For now, relax and take that nap."

"Thanks, I will."

"Aside from that, everything is set."

"Terrific. So long." Sam hung up, feeling the vexation he always felt whenever the Committee, an organization he knew nothing about, demonstrated their niggling control of him. Although he'd been under their thumb since he was eleven years old, plucked off the streets of Tokyo in the early years of the sixties, he still resented their little instances of control, like calling him now, more than he resented their total control over his life. And control his life they certainly did, keeping him always on call, always in shape, always at a peak level of performance. In fact, the Committee had molded him completely, steering his education and training for these past twenty-odd years. They had been good to him in many ways, lavishing on him the best education and training the world had to offer, but he had seriously ambivalent feelings about them. One minute he loved them, the next he hated them. It was always one extreme or the other; he never hit any middle ground with the Committee. He doubted any intelligent person would have, given his situation and history. His was a story people would hardly be able to credit, not that they'd ever have the chance. The idea that he might try to sell his story to a magazine like *Life* or *M* or *Playboy* was amusing on several counts. First off, the Committee would never allow such a thing to happen, so it was a moot point; what's more, even if they did, no editor would consider such a story anything but the mad imaginings of a raving lunatic.

Sam Borne was named by the paratroopers of the Eleventh Airborne, nicknamed the Angels. In a way he was one of their own, having been fathered by a paratrooper killed in action at the drop at Munsan-Ni on

March 23, 1951. His mother had been a Japanese boatwoman, a river prostitute who'd sailed out of his life moments after he was born. Totally abandoned, he showed up, only hours old, in a handbasket on the United States air base at Mount Susshima on the second day of November in 1951. The paratroopers at the air base—called *rakkasans* by the Japanese, which translates literally as "falling-down umbrellas"—had named the infant Sam for his Uncle Sam and Borne because his father had been in the airborne division. For years, he lived on the base as a sort of mascot until the unit was transferred out of the country in the late fifties. At that time, some officers tried to take him back to Fort Campbell in Kentucky, where the Eleventh had its headquarters, but this was not feasible and Sam was left, like many children of war, to fend for himself.

By an indirect route he came to Tokyo. Once there, he wandered into San'ya, the neighborhood that after the war became the site of a large number of cheap lodging houses, rickety wooden structures where a bed for a night cost the same as a bowl of rice. At that time in San'ya there were three hundred or so hostels that twenty thousand people called home. Most of these residents were day laborers, called *nikoyon*. The one area of Tokyo that could be compared to the slums of Western cities, San'ya has a storied past, since, during the Edo period, it was the headquarters for Danzaemon, the legendary leader of the outcasts.

Edo, of course, was the name for Tokyo before 1868. In the Edo period, there were two types of outcasts. The *hinin* were the "nonpeople." These were the beggars and prostitutes, people who had fallen on hard times but who might be able to regain society by "washing their feet." The second class of outcasts were called *eta;* these unfortunates were permanently barred from society. The *eta* included twenty-eight professions, ranging from fortune-tellers to monkey-trainers to street entertainers, lion-dancers and pup-peteers. Many *eta* were involved in work considered unclean, such as slaughtering animals and tanning hides. Long ago in San'ya there had been an abattoir, but none existed at the time Sam Borne arrived, al-though there were, and still are, many enterprises dealing in hides and leather goods. In fact, the area is one of Japan's most important centers for wholesale footwear. There are many shops selling shoes, usually at very low prices, and in some of them one can even purchase traditional Japanese footwear such as *geta,* or wooden clogs, and *zori,* the simple sandals made from straw or other materials. Many of the successors of the outcasts still live in San'ya, and when the summer temperatures soar and the humidity is high, the police often find themselves engaged in running battles with them.

Into this neighborhood Sam Borne wandered in the late fifties and quickly established himself as a worthy heir to the fabled Danzaemon. In no time he had a gang following him everywhere. Its members, like Sam, were street urchins and orphans. When the sun went down, they would walk to the nearby subway station and head for the Ginza. There, amidst the neon lights and the rushing crowds, they singled out tourists or drunken GIs, sailors or soldiers still sta-tioned in Japan and out for a wild time, and pounced on them in a lightning strike, mugging them and strip-ping them of jewelry and wallets in a flash. Many of the tourists and GIs had to have medical attention. The problem grew serious, defeating the best efforts of the Tokyo police, so the MPs got involved. Eventually

Sam was caught. It was then he came to the attention of high-ranking officers, astounded that such a stripling had caused so much trouble.

At the request of the officers, he was taken to a center outside Tokyo and given a battery of tests, both mental and physical. He sat in a small stark room for hours taking test after test. He connected dots, recognized patterns, determined which direction a series of pulleys would exert its force in. He took perceptual tests. He took reflex tests. He put pegs of different shapes and sizes in holes cut for them in boards. His vision was tested, and his strength. A group of officers took him to an army base in the interior of the country and timed him over an obstacle course designed for grown men; he did it in record time, vaulting over fences, scaling walls, slithering under wires, shinnying up ropes, shooting hand over hand along a ladder suspended overhead. He ran on a measured track, he did the high hurdles. He was taken to an Olympic-sized swimming pool and swam laps in amazing times. He swam three miles without stopping.

Then doctors and technicians took over. They poked and prodded. They had Sam urinate in vials, they stuck him with needles, they extracted blood. They made him blow air in a glass tube and hold a plastic ball in the tube above a certain level for as long as he could. He could longer than anyone ever had; he had the lung power of a pearl diver. They took X rays. They clipped a sample of his hair.

Finally, they let him talk for what seemed like hours to a man who asked him about his earliest memories, and whether he'd rather be a tiger or a squirrel, a bird or an alligator, or whether he'd rather read or fish, or what he thought on rainy days, or whether he felt any guilt over hurting the people he'd mugged, or whether he'd rather play pinball or read to a sick friend. This man wanted to know what he thought of having no mother: he thought nothing of it; of what he thought of having no father: he thought nothing of it. The man wanted to know if he ever thought of going to Grandmother's house, or maybe talking to an aunt. He didn't understand this man, and answered the truth. This kind of stuff didn't matter to him. The man asked him what he thought of girls, and he answered honestly that he often went to Five Streets, the famous section in old Yoshiwara, near San'ya, where in the old times the licensed prostitutes worked in grand houses and where at that time some bordellos still operated; and he told the man that as he looked at the girls there with black stockings rolled on their lovely thighs he wanted to go at them, to do what the older guys talked about, and he knew it was true and couldn't wait because even now his body grew strange at the sight and it was like being hungry and not being able to eat. He couldn't wait. The man kept writing all that Sam said down on a pad he held on his lap. This went on for days and days, for hours at a stretch, and Sam grew intensely bored, and finally it ended.

One day soon thereafter he was taken to a different base, and there he went to school with service brats during the day and then at night he had his own special room in an officers' barracks. When he wasn't in school, there was always something new to learn, some new skill, some task he had to master. He learned all kinds of hand-to-hand combat; he learned to shoot on firing ranges, both indoor and out; he ran with men called rangers, challenging the obstacle courses they did; he went out on long marches, on forced marches; he underwent courses in survival in the jungle. He studied with the officers in a special advanced course on military tactics, on great battles, on startling strategies that led to surprising victories.

Then one day the officers at the base packed Sam's scant belongings and he bade farewell to those he'd gone to school with. The officers took him on a long journey into the mountains until they reached a four-hundred-year-old farmhouse about fifteen miles from Iga-Ueno in Nabari. The farmhouse was beautiful, nestled on a wooded mountainside in a glorious valley. It had many levels, wings having been added to it over the centuries, and the roofs were all uniformly tiled and all the walls were sturdy. Inside, it had plenty of space, with a large main room, a good-sized kitchen and many comfortable bedrooms. Upstairs, there was a large loft full of trays of silkworms. Many nights, Sam fell off to sleep thinking of the worms above him working away. The man who owned the house was a master ninja, and for several years Sam lived with him, studying everything the skilled man, whose name was Honzo Tenkatsu, had to teach. Honzo brought Sam along like a son, and Sam came to revere him like a father. The man taught him martial disciplines thousands of years old; he taught him all there was to know about ninjitsu.

Ninjitsu, the art of the ninja, is believed to have originated in China about five hundred years before the birth of Christ; it took its initial form as a treatise on spying in Sun-tse's classic on military science, *The Art of War*. The ninjas were originally trained to gain information about the enemy and to sabotage his operations. From the thirteenth to the seventeenth centuries, during Japan's turbulent feudal period, cloaked in black from head to toe and concealing on their persons a small arsenal of lethal weapons, ninjas flourished as masters of espionage, sabotage, arson and assassination. Mythological tales sprang up about them. Their daring feats became legendary. Then, in the seventeenth century, the powerful Tokugawa shogun banned the practice of ninjitsu, or even mention of the subject, on penalty of execution, and the tradition went underground, with only a handful of men willing to clandestinely practice its occult arts. Of course, ever since a Japanese film company produced a low-budget movie a few years ago about the ancient exploits of the ninja, ninjitsu and ninjas have been popularized into a vulgar cult, but at the bottom of this craze lies a very serious body of knowledge; it was this that Honzo Tenkatsu imparted to Sam, drilling him day in and day out.

Honzo Tenkatsu was a firm master, but a kind one. Not only did he school young Sam in all the physical arts of the ninja, but he undertook as well the spiritual and mental training that are the true hallmarks of the great ninja. During the day, the training was physical; at night, spiritual and mental. Sam was put through his paces more vigorously than any Olympic athlete. He learned the ancient martial arts so essential to the ninja, the very same arts that formed the basis for later systems like jujitsu, judo and karate. He learned to handle a sword; to throw dirks and the *shuriken*, the various-shaped throwing weapons with sharp points that killed on impact, some cross-shaped, others triangular, four-pointed, six-pointed, eight-pointed, ten-pointed or swastika-shaped; he learned to wield the *shuko*, a kind of medieval brass knuckles; he mastered archery; in the modern manner, he learned the fundamentals of boxing and of wrestling. He practiced long hours at running, jumping and swimming, especially at swimming underwater and holding his breath, an ability he built up to three minutes at a stretch. He spent hours climbing walls and trees, gaining ever-increasing speed at both. He took long, timed hikes, really forced marches in the great ninja tradition, which held that a true ninja, like a soldier under Alexander the Great, could cover seventy-five miles in a day. *Inpo,* the ancient art of hiding, was drilled into Sam by the hour, day after day, until he was a master at hiding in brush or in trees, in light or in shadow, in lofts or in attics, even in furniture; he became an acrobat at dissemblance, a magician at disguise.

During these years Honzo Tenkatsu tutored Sam exclusively. He would serve as Sam's opponent when one was called for, and never had Sam a more skilled, a more dangerous one. In his mid-forties, Honzo was a perfect physical specimen, a man who drove himself relentlessly to keep in top form. He also adhered in the ninja manner to a strict, high-protein diet, a trait he passed along by example to Sam. When Honzo had Sam ready in any phase of physical training, he would take him deeper into the mountains of the Iga-Ueno valley, the revered medieval hotbed of ninjas, and present his prize pupil at a *ryu,* a ninja school in a mountain stronghold. There Honzo would pit Sam against the best pupils of the other ninja masters, and eventually against the masters themselves, and always Sam would win. A legend started to spring up about him.

Soon Sam was besting Honzo himself, at least physically. Spiritually and mentally it was another matter. Honzo was a devout practitioner of *shugendo,* or mountain asceticism, and of *mikkyo,* esoteric Buddhism, and of *kuji kiri,* the art of meditation aided by patterning the fingers in the air and visualizing the pattern in the mind, sometimes used as a form of hypnosis. Honzo was as much a Buddhist as his forebears, the ninjas outlawed by the Tokugawa shogun for their religion.

THE WHITE ANGEL

He had connected with his *chi*, the power within everyone that can be marshaled to perform the will. He imparted the methodology and the philosophy of all three disciplines to Sam, who learned by daily practice; through driving determination and painstaking application, slowly but relentlessly, Sam mastered his breathing and gained control of his mind. He could fast for long periods, or endure discomfort, even pain, for long stretches. A side benefit of *kuji kiri* was that the practitioner developed instincts akin to those of primitive animals. Sam became incredibly attuned to his environment; he could read nature, sense weather, feel presences. And in the time-honored tradition of *kuji-kiri*, Sam acquired a healthy respect for the number nine, for its sacredness and its significance; ever since, at games of chance or when he felt like taking a flier at the track, he would put his money on that number.

In the long mountain evenings, in the harsh winter twilights or the lingering summer sunsets, after a rough day of physical exertion, before the religious sessions set in, Honzo would instruct Sam in all phases of strategy, both psychological and military. He would impart to Sam the wisdom of *gojo-goyoku*, the system of five feelings and five desires. He taught Sam to discern and to exploit an enemy's weakness, whether it was for sensual pleasures, idle amusements or total personal safety; whether it took the form of a soft heart or a short temper. Like the accomplished psychologist he was, Honzo passed along to Sam the wisdom of *satsu-jin-jitsu*, the art of having insight into man. Sam learned to read mankind like a simple map; no nuance of mood, no tic of face, no twitch of nerve escaped Sam's detection.

And they, master and student, discussed endlessly the elements of military strategy. Honzo stressed the importance of the first strike, the primacy of surprise, the benefits of the high ground, the dire consequences of being outflanked, the necessity for intelligence about the enemy, the essential nature of secrecy about one's plans. He told Sam tales from long ago about battles and coups, always stressing the quality that put the victor over the top, or the flaw that caused the vanquished their downfall. He discussed with Sam the strict requirements of good espionage, and recounted to him endless stories of agents not double-checking on fellow agents or trusting someone unnecessarily, all to their peril. He emphasized to Sam over and over again to rely on himself, to conserve his resources, to keep his own counsel, to draw upon himself and never, absolutely never, to panic or despair.

Then one day a car carrying two officers showed up at the farmhouse and Sam had to shed his black ninja outfit and head back to the base near Tokyo. There he put in another two years of compressed high school classes with a new set of service brats until the summer of 1969 when he traveled for the first time to the United States for his private audition for the Royal Academy of Dramatic Arts that led to his sojourn in London prior to his four years at Monterey at the Defense Language Institute Foreign Language Center. Of course, by this time Sam was well aware that his would be no ordinary life, for he had been sent on assignments, mostly straightforward hits like his trip into Saigon during the police action to take out a rogue CIA agent who'd used his clout with the Phoenix Program to eliminate competitors vying for the drug market among US GIs.

THE WHITE ANGEL

* * *

Sam stepped out of the bathroom, a large terry-cloth robe draped over his muscular frame. He felt that wrung-out enervation he always got after a long flight. His face felt heavy. He was glad he'd had the foresight to call down for a large orange juice and a bottle of Perrier before taking his shower. He went to his suitcase and took out a plastic jar of pills. From it he shook three multiple vitamins and a vitamin C pill. He crossed to the bedside table and swallowed the pills with a draft of orange juice, then washed it down with a sparkling, cold glass of Perrier.

He pulled back the green counterpane on his king-sized bed and, shucking the robe, climbed between the sheets. They felt cool and soothing, and when his head hit the cold pillow it was exhilarating and relaxing at the same time. Immediately his mind wandered. He wondered what Brazil, and the Amazon, held in store for him. He wondered how he would come to tangle with a character named Mother Beloved and her band of merry men, and women. He wondered, for the thousandth time, how the Committee managed to keep track of people like Mother Beloved. And he wondered who his company would be in a few hours.

Then he fell asleep.

12

CLOTHES MAKE
THE MAN

Rio de Janeiro
October 7

The bell rang and Sam came out punching. Right from the start, it was a tough fight. Worst of all, his opponent had no face. He jabbed. His opponent flicked his fist away. He threw a right cross. His opponent stepped back, craning his neck out of reach, smiling contemptuously. Sam pressed forward, unleashing a lightning-fast combination. His opponent sidestepped him as he flailed by, then pushed him contemptuously from behind with an open glove on the back of his neck. Sam stumbled. The bell rang again, too soon; the round couldn't be over yet. Then it rang again.

Sam woke with a start and grabbed the phone. He prided himself on being a light sleeper, yet everyone fell into REM sleep now and again. He had been deep in sleep, dreaming to beat the band. It was a familiar dream, the one where he was boxing for all he was worth and being embarrassed by an opponent with no face. He'd had it since he was a kid.

"Borne here," he muttered into the phone.

"Hello, Mr. Borne, I understand I'm expected. I'll be up in five minutes. Don't bother getting dressed."

"If you're half as sexy as your voice, that's the nicest thing anyone's ever said to me."

"Throw some cold water on your face. I'll be right up." She hung up. She had a voice sexy enough to melt Antarctica. Sam looked at the dead receiver and shrugged. Then he put the receiver on the cradle and took a deep breath, pulling his feet from beneath the bedclothes and sitting up on the side of the bed. A feeling shot through him that this particular Committee contact was going to be a live wire. Most contacts the Committee sent his way were straitlaced chaperons. This one sounded like the exception.

He stood up and walked across to the bathroom. His mouth felt woolly, the skin on his face tight. He threw cold water on his face and patted his cold, wet hands on the back of his neck. Then he inspected himself in the mirror. Before he could decide whether he was truly awake or not, there was a knock on the door. He put on the terry-cloth robe, walked out and opened the door.

The sight that greeted him woke him completely. A spectacular woman in a large sun hat stood with one hand hooked on her hip. Swept-back auburn hair peeked beneath the hat, with stray strands curling over her ears. She flashed him an atomic smile and said, "Hi, I'm Mercedes Coozi."

"I'm Sam Borne."

"Of course." She paused. "Aren't you going to invite us in?" Sam inspected the two men standing behind her, one middle-aged and one quite young. They had garment bags slung over their shoulders and boxes in their hands. Big and blue, the boxes were bound with string tied to little wooden handles on the top.

"Sure," he said, and stepped back. Mercedes strode

through regally, trailing the two men. Sam closed the door after them and looked at her. She was not a woman to hesitate.

"This is Mr. Charuto and his assistant Ramos," she said. The two men nodded deeply to Sam, who stuck out his hand and shook with both of them. "Mr. Charuto is a fine tailor here in Rio, and he and Ramos have put together a nice little wardrobe for you. You'll now try it on." The two men snipped the strings on the boxes and spread the garment bags on the bed. Sam stood rooted.

"Let's go, chop-chop," Mercedes said. "Get rid of that robe. We have to make sure everything fits right." She clapped for emphasis. Command was nothing new or daunting to her. A day or two in heaven and she was sure to make rearrangements, over anyone's protests, including God's. Sam was amused.

"I'll just be a minute," he said as he retreated to the bathroom, shagging a fresh set of underwear as he passed his suitcase. In the bathroom, he slipped into the underwear, then into the robe, and was back in the bedroom in minutes. Mr. Charuto and his assistant had spread the clothes from the garment bags on the bed; beside them, the boxes spilled out shoes, socks, shirts and underwear. Sam did not like what he saw.

"Let's go. I want to get this over with. We have a lot of ground to cover," Mercedes said. Sam gave her a look that said, "Lady, you're overdoing it," but she ignored this. He realized that he would have to try on the clothes and, out of territoriality, not modesty, he kept the robe on and fixed her with a stare.

"I'll see you later. Go down to the lobby and wait till we're through here," he said. She reacted to this like a stone wall to a stray breeze.

"Absolutely not. It's part of my brief to stick with

105

you and make sure all goes well. That includes seeing what you look like in these outfits." She gestured to the clothes spread on the bed. An old sergeant had once told Sam never to argue with a headstrong woman or a jackass. He took off the robe.

Mr. Charuto and his assistant leaped into action. They handed Sam trousers and suitcoats, one right after the other; they held shirts against the coats, matched ties, slipped shoes next to his bare feet, stuck hats on his head. All the while Mercedes Coozi kept up a rapid-fire commentary in Portuguese punctuated by sighs, groans and grunts. Sam could not see himself in a mirror; each time he asked, Mercedes vetoed the request in English and hastily instructed the tailor and his assistant in Portuguese to do something else. Sam understood Spanish perfectly and so caught enough of the Portuguese to get the gist of what she said. She thought the clothes were just right, like a master wardrobe mistress pleased with her Broadway production.

Even without a mirror, Sam knew the clothes were awful. He looked incredibly doughty, like a 1950s T-man. The suitcoats hung on him like grain sacks, the pants bagged, the shirts were roughly cut and made of cheap material, the ties were outdated, too wide and hideous. The shoes gave him the horrors; one was a pair of black plain-toed bluchers, the other a pair of mud-brown wing tips. The undershirts Ramos handed him were sleeveless; under the flimsy dress shirts they'd show, making him look like the ultimate schmo. Mr. Charuto capped the whole travesty when he pulled from a box a sporty straw hat like aging golfers wear. Sam could not have envisioned himself more ridiculous than this. He had a special horror of blue seersucker suits, and here he was in one; on top of that, insult to injury, they had brought him a brown seersucker suit. And, last but not least, there was a tan gabardine suit. None fit right.

Then there was the explorer wear. Ramos pulled off the bed two pairs of khaki trousers and a khaki safari jacket. There was even a pith helmet; this he would categorically refuse to wear. He had to draw the line somewhere. He tried the trousers and the jacket, but flicked the helmet away when Ramos handed it to him.

"Don't be difficult, Mr. Borne," Mercedes said. "We want you to look a certain way, you'll look a certain way." The use of "we" was not lost on him. He looked at her hard. "Go on, put it on," she said. "You have to come off in a certain mode, so you do what's necessary."

"Hold the homily," he said, taking the helmet in hand, holding it out like a wet, dead fish. He was sure this would make him look like Stanley looking for Livingston; or, worse, like Ramar of the Jungle. He looked at Mercedes with heat in his eyes.

"You're supposed to be the ultimate professional, Mr. Borne, so what's the big deal about this hat?"

"It's ridiculous."

"It's worn by the type of person you're going to be. Try it on."

Sam looked at Mr. Charuto and Ramos, pleading with his eyes for them not to laugh, letting them know he considered it all simpleminded too. From their blank looks during his exchanges with Mercedes, he knew they didn't understand English, but they couldn't fail to read his forlorn look. He put the hat on. Their faces remained expressionless.

"It's not so bad, Mr. Borne," Mercedes said.

"You don't have to wear it."

"That's true," she said.

There was a knock at the door. Mercedes walked

swiftly across the room and opened it. She said something quickly and turned to Mr. Charuto and Ramos and spoke rapidly in Portuguese. They scooped up the boxes and, nodding farewell to Sam, were gone in a flash. A man with a small kit under his arm entered the room. He was a short, mustachioed black man in a frayed, shiny blue serge suit. Wearing a tan porkpie hat with a tricolored band around it, he stood just within the door. Mercedes closed it behind him and, turning her attention back to Sam, walked past the short man.

"This is your barber, Mr. Borne. He's going to give you a nice haircut."

Sam's insides seized. He had a sudden and sure insight into the kind of haircut he was in for. It was the kind they specialized in at places like Camp Lejeune. Mercedes spoke to the little man in Portuguese, and he came forward. He stood just in front of Sam, looking up at the taller man. Then he flicked his hand in front of his forehead, and Sam realized that he still had the pith helmet on and that the man wanted him to remove it. He did. The little man smiled deferentially. Then he spoke to Mercedes.

"Mr. Amaro thinks it would be good if we went into the bathroom for your haircut," Mercedes said. "It will be easier." While she spoke Mr. Amaro opened his kit and took out a barber's cape and a pair of electric clippers. He didn't take out a comb or scissors, confirming Sam's worst suspicions.

Sam started for the bathroom but was brought up short by Mercedes. "It would be a good idea, Mr. Borne, to take off your trousers and the jacket. That way they won't get hair all over them." Sam had intended to do this in the bathroom; her suggestion he found overbearing. He turned away and strode to the bathroom, tossing over his shoulder, "I'll do just that in the bathroom."

"Fine."

Mercedes was the kind of woman, Sam realized, who'd always need to have the last word. In the bathroom he quickly shed his trousers and jacket and sat on the side of the tub. Mr. Amaro cinched the cape around his neck and plugged in the clippers. Then he started to shear Sam, running the clippers over his temples and nape, giving him the classic quasi-military cut so popular among American squareheads in the two decades following the Second World War. His hair fell in tufts and clumps onto the blue ticking of the cape. He reconciled himself to this grim fate just in time to look up and see Mercedes standing in the doorway, grinning. He bit back several pertinent remarks, figuring silence would give her less satisfaction. She pushed it.

"Don't worry, Mr. Borne, it will grow back."

"Is that a sadistic streak I detect, or are you just a born teaser?"

"I am anything but a sadistic tease, Mr. Borne."

"It's good to know."

Mr. Amaro chucked Sam under the chin, and he raised his head. Taking a steel comb from his kit and scooping the hair on top of Sam's head with it, Mr. Amaro sheared the hair off along the plane of the comb. Hair tumbled onto the cape, which was now fairly full, with a heavy pile accumulating in Sam's lap. In minutes it was over. The clippers ceased buzzing and Mr. Amaro ran the comb swiftly over Sam's scalp, raking the loose hairs onto his shoulders. Then he took a small whisk broom from his kit and dusted Sam's temples and nape, swirling it around his ears.

Sam sat there while Mr. Amaro replaced his instruments in his kit, the size of a fishing tackle box. Then the little man looked at him and nodded his good-bye. From the doorway Mercedes said, "I'll show Mr. Amaro out and meet you in the lobby in ten minutes. Wear one of the suits Mr. Charuto brought. Till then, ciao."

Sam had hoped he wouldn't have to wear these awful clothes so soon, but protest was futile, so he merely waved. When he heard the outside door shut, he stood and looked at himself in the mirror over the sink. He looked like a raw recruit, with that perpetually surprised look their exposed faces always had.

Christ, he thought, there isn't anything the Committee won't impose on me.

13

CHAPERONED

Rio de Janeiro
October 7

Beyond the glass, white spume from the breakers curled on the dark beach. Off in the distance Sugar Loaf hulked large against the night sky, lights sparkling on it all the way to the top. Out in the harbor running lights from yachts shone against the black water. On Avenida Atlantica, along the black-and-white-tiled promenade, lovers strolled, holding hands, stopping from time to time to embrace beneath a swaying palm. A stream of traffic along the avenida added its white and red lights to the pageantry as romantic Rio worked its magic. After only one day, Sam Borne knew why many experienced travelers considered Rio the most beautiful city in the world, just edging out Hong Kong and San Francisco in the splendor of its natural setting.

"I can see from your eyes that you like our city," Mercedes Coozi said. She smiled her big smile, and Sam Borne smiled back. Over the course of the last ten hours he had grown fond of her. That afternoon, once he joined her in the lobby, the wardrobe and haircut out of the way, she had relaxed. At that point, he had had no idea what was in store for him. She had quickly cleared matters up by telling him they had a nine-thirty flight the next morning to Manaus, and time to kill till then. What did he want to do? He wanted to see Rio and he was hungry. They combined the two, taking a taxi to Sugar Loaf and climbing by cable car to the restaurant halfway up Urca mountain. There, at a small table overlooking the blue waters of Guanabara Bay, Mercedes started the job of briefing Sam on what he'd be up against in Mother Beloved.

If till then Sam had been unconvinced of the ferocity of his target, Mercedes left him no room for doubt. She laid out in graphic detail just what Wilda von Hoffer was capable of, recounting incidents she'd seen, telling him of others she'd heard of and believed. The one that stuck in Sam's mind was incredible. Mother Beloved had taken a "rabble-rouser" out on the Amazon and thrown a side of beef into the water. It attracted hoards of piranhas. Then she set the man adrift on an inflatable raft, only to puncture it with bullet holes and watch it slowly deflate. The man had been determined to die with dignity, but Mercedes visibly shuddered remembering how he had screamed as soon as he slipped into the water.

There was more, much more. Naturally Sam wanted to know how Mercedes came to know so much. She confessed that she had a daughter about the age of Erika von Hoffer; that the two girls had become friendly at their convent school; that one thing led to another, and before she knew it, she and her daughter were invited to spend a spring break at the von Hoffer ranch. She loved to ride, and before long was practically in love with the ranch and its stables. Blushing, she said she was in fact in love, for a while, with Mother Beloved herself. Through questioning, Sam learned that Mercedes was the product of a marriage between an Italian immigrant father, who'd struck it rich, and a German mother. Both had been strict, but the father, in Italian style, had dominated the mother totally.

When Mercedes met Wilda von Hoffer, something happened inside her. Married off by her domineering father at an early age, Mercedes had never cared for her husband, and after her daughter Consuela was born, she left him and resumed her maiden name. Mother Beloved represented her first taste of power in a woman, and she had been seduced by it. She was not ashamed of having had an affair with a woman, she said, but she was deeply ashamed to have been involved with a monster like Mother Beloved. As time wore on she saw the woman for what she was, a murderess, an oppressor, a vandal maniacally holding progress and enlightenment hostage, depriving vast numbers of people of opportunity, knowledge, a chance at a better life. She had to be stopped. Mercedes was now dedicated to helping do so.

"I like your city very much," Sam said, then, after a pause, added, "and I like you enormously."

"It's mutual, Sam Borne," she replied, barely above a whisper. She picked up her cup of espresso and took a final sip. "I suppose it's time to call it a day."

"Or make it a night."

She let the invitation hang in the air. Then she said, "You know tomorrow will be a big day for us. We'll be on duty from here on out. My brief expressly forbids me from any personal involvement with you. It is good to follow orders."

"You don't strike me as a follower."

"I followed Mother Beloved."

"That was something you couldn't help."

She paused, looking at him swimmingly, her eyes

113

glistening. "So is this," she whispered. "Let's go to your room."

When Sam turned from the door, he noticed that Mercedes had crossed the room already. She stood against the glass wall, looking out. He went to her, stood slightly behind her and touched her softly on the shoulder. She looked off at the harbor, the waves foaming into the sandy beaches, the lights winking from the surrounding hills, from boats out on the dark waters. Above, stars filled the sky, a gibbous moon lending its faint light off on the horizon. Without saying a word, Sam opened the glass doors to the terrace and they stepped out onto it. Mercedes leaned against the wrought-iron railing and, in silence, he stood beside her. When she started to shiver, he put his arm around her and ran his hand up and down her forearm. She leaned into him, cradling her head against his shoulder.

"There are so many memories on that beach for me. We, my girlfriends and I, used to spend all our summer days there, perfecting our tans, talking of boys, longing for adventure, for travel, for something to happen to relieve the terrible boredom," she said softly, more to herself than to Sam. "I didn't know it then, but I was happy, at least better off than later." She fell silent, and he made no comment. It was a private moment, one he couldn't share. He pulled her gently to him, rubbing her arm.

"I'm sorry," she said.

"Don't be. There's nothing to be sorry for." He reached down, cupped her chin and raised her face. Then, slowly, very slowly, he bent down and kissed her softly on the lips. She shifted against him, turning from the rail, pressing into him, throwing both arms around his neck, standing on tiptoes. Her breasts swelled against his chest. They held the kiss for minutes, their breath growing short; then she pulled away and started to undo his tie, loosening it and opening the first two buttons of his shirt. Slowly, she kissed his chest, then his neck, all the while running her hands over his back. Behind her, he dipped his hands lower. She reached up, pulled his face to hers and kissed him hard. When she broke this time, he scooped her into his arms and carried her back into the room.

When he'd placed her down on the side of the bed, he knelt and slipped off her high heels. Immediately she leaned forward and wrapped her arms around his neck, drawing him into her. As she kissed him again, long and hard, he reached behind her and undid the zipper of her dress. As he slid the dress off her shoulders, he caressed her back. Then he stroked her breasts, running his hands firmly over the thin silk of her black bra. Beneath his palms he felt her nipples rise and stiffen to his touch. She moaned. He broke off the kiss and she stood, the dress falling to her ankles. Kissing her tenderly on the lips, he undid her bra. Then he slowly kissed her eyes, her lips, her neck. When he leaned down and kissed her breasts, teasing the nipples with his tongue, she sighed, fondling his head against her, running her fingers through his hair.

He slipped her panty hose down to midthigh, then caressed her slowly through the silk of her panties. She moaned, running her fingers more forcefully through his hair. When tremors shook her, her legs starting to tremble, he slipped her panties down and stripped her completely. Panting, she fumbled with the buttons on his shirt until he flicked her hand away and undid them himself. While he did she unfastened his belt and opened his trousers. She pushed them down, and he stepped out of them. Slipping to her knees, she worked off his socks, then stood. In the half-light, she was magnificent, the dark silhouette of a goddess in the soft gray light.

Urgent now, she climbed onto the bed and, taking Sam by both arms, pulled him down to her, her mouth hungry for his. He kissed her on the mouth; then, pinning her arms to the bed, he showered kisses on her face, lingering on her eyes, then trailing his mouth over her neck and down onto her breasts, all the while fondling her. She started to writhe and shift under him, but he took his time, teasing, prolonging her pleasure, coursing his mouth lower and lower until he had her nearly delirious.

"Please, now," she whispered.

He delayed, stroking her exquisitely, balancing her just on the point where she was about to break, then backing off and modulating her, building her ecstasy higher and higher, pointing for the ultimate. Her knees started to rise, she arched her back, she tugged on Sam's forearms all the while he stroked her breasts, caressing the nipples. She moaned loudly and whispered, her voice imploring, "Fuck me. Please, fuck me now."

A tremor shook her. Her whole body was alive and vibrant, eager and expectant. He had brought her to the brink. When she arched away from him, he rose on her and pressed himself home. Timing her just right, riding her, his every movement meshing with hers, yet controlling hers, he brought her to the apex of ecstasy, poised her there till, ready himself, he pushed her over the crest at precisely the right moment.

They were going to make a night of it.

14

FABULOUS CITIES

Brasília–Manaus
October 8

From the air, Brasília looked like outer space. Sam Borne peered hard out of the oval window of the 727 and saw below a city unlike any other on earth. Like everyone, he had heard of this fabulous city, of its futuristic skyline, of its wild architecture, of its unique layout; but you had to experience it from the air to realize just how unlike any other city it really is. Unreal, it holds within it all the contradictions of modern Brazil, the South American giant. Even from the air you could see the big modern high-rise apartments where the government officials lived flanking the spiraling, cantilevered marvels of the ministry buildings; and interspersed between them, shooting silver jets of water into the air, there were fountains everywhere. Yet, Sam knew, futuristic as this city was, in every way a spectacular technological achievement, not thirty miles away across the red plain, in the dense jungle, people didn't have enough water to boil an egg.

As they swung over the city on their approach pattern, Brasília looked like an ice sculpture set for a great science-fiction movie yet to be made, an epic of futurism. Carved whole, right from the heart of the jungle, it was a feat of civil engineering, a triumph of modern architecture. It was little wonder that, after seeing Brasília for the first time, the Russian cosmonaut Yuri Gagarin remarked, "I hadn't expected to reach Mars so soon." Sam was saddened to think he wouldn't have time to deplane and explore the city on foot. They would stop for forty minutes and then fly on to Manaus, another fabulous city, but one with its future in its past; it had had its moment as a paragon of futurism in the nineteenth century, and now time and technology had passed it by.

"So?" It was Mercedes Coozi leaning over Sam's shoulder.

"So what do you say when you look at something like this?" Sam said. "It's certainly a major accomplishment, unlike any other city I've ever seen, but it makes you uneasy. A city should have a history, a tradition, a lore to draw on. This whole thing is as sudden and unbelievable as the virgin birth, and probably left out as much fun along the way."

"It's a major statement, both politically and artistically. As a gringo, you're jealous."

"If you say so."

The plane dropped onto the runway with a thud and a tiny bounce, followed by a softer thud; then they were racing along the ground. In minutes they came to a stop, but they had to stay in their seats. There was only time for those passengers going to Brasília to deplane and for those heading for Manaus to board. Before Sam had read his copy of *The Wall Street Journal*, picked up at the airport in Rio, they were back on the runway, spooling up for the takeoff for Manaus. When the pilot starting racing down the runway, Mercedes clutched Sam's hand. She was the nervous type. Sam rarely experienced anxiety in an airplane; he was too overcome by the marvel of it ever to worry that he might bite the big one. Flight was an excitement for him, a thrill each time.

When the pilot leveled off, Mercedes released his hand and asked him yet again if he was prepared to face what would be expected of him, to confront Mother Beloved in the guise of an international arms dealer. She had gone from imperious bitch to nervous Nellie in the shortest span of time. He had assured her twice on the hop from Rio to Brasília that he knew what to do, that she shouldn't worry. His dossier had told him what background he'd have to use, and, as always, he had been thoroughly prepared by the Committee long ago for the identity he was to assume once they reached Mother Beloved's ranch.

This time out Sam was primed to impersonate an arms dealer, here to make a deal with Mother Beloved for a small arsenal. Thus his stodgy outfits, his square-head haircut; he was to match his appearance to a background that had him recruited out of Trinity College into the CIA in the early seventies, where he put in a decade before hitching his star to a legendary international arms dealer who'd been in the Outfit a generation before. This arms dealer, a Boston Irish-man named Patrick O'Shea, had started out in his twenties right out of Holy Cross College as a recruit in Wild Bill Donovan's OSS. With a perfect knowledge of German and French, Pat O'Shea had been dropped behind enemy lines, where he organized and directed resistance groups during the Allied invasion of Europe. As a charter member of the newly formed CIA, which replaced the OSS, he had eventually been stationed in Berlin during the initial days of the Cold War.

It was on vacations from this posting that he found his holy grail. Traveling with an overweight Red Cross nurse who would eventually become his wife, he toured Europe in an old prewar Renault. Passing through Italy, France, Belgium, the Netherlands, Germany and Denmark, he saw abandoned fields of weapons. An avid gun enthusiast since his father gave him a single-shot twenty-two when he was seven, a rare gift for a child of the Depression to receive, especially in South Boston, Pat O'Shea immediately spotted opportunity with a capital *O*. He knew that back in America there would be a ready market for the Luger pistols and Mauser rifles littering fields all over Western Europe. No one seemed to want them. On that first trip, he contented himself with taking a Schmeisser submachine gun, which, like all the many weapons he'd owned since that first twenty-two, he mastered quickly. He could break it down and reassemble it in lightning time.

When he was posted back to the States in late 1948, Pat O'Shea quickly contacted two of the arms companies whose catalogs he had pored over for years. Neither was interested in talking with him, let alone hiring him. Then he got a tip on a small-arms outfit in Phoenix, Arizona. Called Arizona Arms, this company was looking for someone to take it international. Pat took a few days' leave of absence from his CIA office, then located in downtown Washington, and flew to Arizona. He took in the Grand Canyon, and the president of Arizona Arms, Bob Carter, who, a gun collector and expert himself, had never met anyone with a knowledge so extensive as Pat O'Shea's. Not only did O'Shea know the history of American firearms cold, he also knew European weapons backward and forward, as well as the arms now being manufactured by the

Communist countries. He was a natural, and Bob Carter offered him the title of director of overseas marketing. Pat took it. Back in Washington, he resigned from the CIA and caught the shuttle to New York. Three days later, in Paris, he signed an agreement that called for him to clear the fields of France of leftover weapons and matériel. He had a year in which to do it. He was off and running.

Pat O'Shea had the model contract he needed. From Paris it was on to Brussels, Rome, Amsterdam, Copenhagen; in each capital he struck a similar deal. With the signed contracts under his arm, he rocketed across the Channel to London. There he used old Berlin contacts from MI6 to arrange meetings with high-ranking international financiers. When he showed them the contracts, he had no trouble arranging the funds he'd need to clear the fields and ship the equipment wherever he had found buyers for it. In the case of the small arms, this almost invariably meant shipping them back to the States, but Pat had made the deal for all the abandoned equipment as well, including tanks and troop carriers, machine guns and heavy artillery like the German eighty-eights, and much of it would have to be shipped halfway around the world, or farther, and often into remote areas.

A week later Pat O'Shea had dinner at the picturesque home of Bob Carter. After devouring steaks the size of hubcaps, thick as a baby's arm, with baked potatoes covered with sour cream and corn on the cob fresh off the stalk, Pat pulled out the contracts and handed them to Bob. Bob found a box of cheroots, offered one to O'Shea, and they both lit up. As Bob read the contracts, he smiled between puffs. Then, suddenly, his expression changed, his face flushed with anger. The contracts called for O'Shea to be

THE WHITE ANGEL

named an equal partner with Carter in a new company called Allarms, with an option for O'Shea to buy out Carter in five years. Between trembling lips, Carter asked his wife Lacey to leave the room. Then he fixed Pat O'Shea with a homicidal stare.

"Who the hell do you think you are?"

"I'm the guy who made all this happen. I'm the guy who knew where to find this stuff, who had the contacts to get into the government offices and draw up these contracts. I'm the guy who got the financial backers, and I'm the guy who can go elsewhere with this paper and get what I want," Pat replied, his freckled face impassive. "I'm also the guy who has the wherewithal to unload the heavy stuff in Latin America. In fact, I've already set up my itinerary down there, so what I need now is your cooperation. My first stop is Havana, where I'll be vacationing and negotiating for a week. You can send our contracts to me there. If that's not acceptable, I have a backup arrangement with a small firm in Dallas. The choice is yours."

"Get the hell out of my house."

"Okay, I will. But remember this. In five years, if you play ball with me, you'll have a settlement that is more than ten times the net worth of your current operation. Think about it. And you should know that I've talked to people with warehousing facilities on the East Coast, so with the one here in Arizona we'd be ready to double the size of the domestic operation this year alone."

Bob Carter looked hard across the table at him. "You're cocky, aren't you? You've got it all worked out. Except you don't have me where you want me." There was a long silence, during which Pat O'Shea stubbed out his cheroot, slowly rose from his chair and started out of the room. At the door, he paused.

"Think about it," he said. "I can be reached at the Nacional in Havana. I give you a week, then I close the deal with the Dallas people." He closed the door and left the house. A week later in Havana duplicate contracts arrived for a new firm called Allarms, which would supersede Arizona Arms and which would be for five years an equal partnership, at the end of which time one partner, said Patrick Aloysius O'Shea, would have the option to buy out the other partner, Robert Benton Carter.

In five years O'Shea did buy out Carter, and in seven years O'Shea shifted the company to Monte Carlo, favoring it over a move to Delaware: O'Shea wanted his company to be truly international, and he succeeded. From a one-room office in an apartment tower climbing the Monaco hills, he ran Allarms single-handedly. He sold to everyone, often to both sides in the same conflict. Without qualm or compunction, he sold to Castro and to Batista, to the IRA and to the Orangemen, to both sides in any number of Central American conflicts, to Iraq and to Iran, to Pakistan and to India; after each Arab-Israeli war, he bought the captured weapons of each side; since 1975, he had been angling to buy the whopping caches of American arms left behind in Vietnam, and he had a good chance of succeeding. Though not as notorious as Sir Basil Zaharoff, the merchant of death who had supplied both sides in the arms buildup that resulted in World War I, or as legendary as Sam Cummings, the man who built the modern arms empire called Interarms, Pat O'Shea had achieved his goal in becoming one of the richest arms dealers in the world.

One summer in the mid-seventies, a friend of a friend asked a favor of Patrick Aloysius O'Shea. It was the kind of favor O'Shea knew not to refuse if he wanted Allarms to stay in business. The result was that Sam Borne showed up in Monaco one stunning June morning, the Mediterranean shimmering blue, afloat with a small navy of private yachts, and took a cab to the apartment tower climbing the mountainside. There the door opened and Sam Borne introduced himself to O'Shea.

Over the next ten weeks Sam took the cram course in world arms and how they're brokered by men like O'Shea. Sam was privy to all calls O'Shea received on his phone, which had a scrambler on it; and when O'Shea took a meeting, no matter how private, no matter how important or clandestine the potential client, Sam sat in. Afterward, O'Shea drilled him to see if he'd understood everything that had been said. O'Shea also let Sam loose in his vast library, filled with expert books on firearms and weaponry, their history, features, development, everything. Then there was the centerpiece of O'Shea's life: his private collection. Here Sam saw weapons worth thousands, old muskets, rare revolvers, precious derringers; there were swords worn by emperors, personal sidearms of famous generals, rifles used by assassins; the entire collection was valued at over a million dollars, and O'Shea would not have sold it for twice that. By the time Sam left he had the equivalent of a Ph.D. in international arms dealing, not to mention another friend in the person of Patrick Aloysius O'Shea of South Boston and Monte Carlo, president and chief executive officer of Allarms.

So Sam Borne would have no trouble convincing Mother Beloved he was capable of fulfilling whatever orders for arms she might have. His knowledge acquired from O'Shea would stand him in good stead. The other key point in his new identity, the part before he became an international arms dealer, was taken up with the fabricated ten-year hitch in the CIA. This Sam could pull off easily. The Committee had seen to that as well.

One autumn in the mid-seventies, after completing his studies at the Defense Language Institute Foreign Language Center in Monterey, Sam had been shipped off to Virginia. There at Langley he joined a class of recruits for the CIA's Directorate of Operations, or clandestine services division. With them he toured the Langley complex, checking out the general quarters, plus the secret analysis rooms, the science and technology rooms, the tightly secure coding rooms and even the secret planning rooms. Then it had been off to do fieldwork. All of it was simple for Sam. By that time, with his training as a ninja and his commando training with the United States Army, he was more than a match for his instructors in hand-to-hand combat as well as in knowledge of all sorts of small arms. And as a marksman Sam left nothing to be desired, something that had endeared him immensely to Pat O'Shea when the two had traveled one steamy August day to the Tuscany estate of an Italian count, a great marksman, and Sam, backed by O'Shea's money, had won thousands from the angry count, a European clay pigeon champion and a sore loser. O'Shea, no slouch himself with a revolver or a rifle, had been no match for the count the several previous times they'd gambled, matched against each other, and even though the Irishman had not nearly recovered his previous losses against the arrogant count, he had the satisfaction that day of winning through Sam and of seeing the count humiliated.

During his accelerated hitch with the CIA, to ensure an accurate picture of what life was like as a CIA covert operative, Sam had gone out on assignment, connect-

ing with agents in Berlin, Lisbon, Luanda, Rangoon
and Singapore; he had posed as an aircraft salesman,
a free-lance writer, a management consultant and a
simple tourist. He had connected with consular officials, with professors, with executives of corporations
manning overseas offices, with journalists. On one assignment, a run to Stockholm, he had even par-
ticipated in wet work, forming one part of a hit team
when he could easily and more cleanly have eliminated
the target alone, but it gave him a feel for the CIA and
how it operated, one that he had needed countless
times since in his work for the Committee. It didn't,
however, give him a respect for the CIA, an organization he considered riddled with poseurs, dilettantes
and oafs.

He was ready. He had the arms business down pat.
He knew the CIA cold. It was only a question of meeting Mother Beloved, gaining her confidence, then dis-
patching her to eternity.

The seat-belt sign came on and Sam heard the tur-
bines cut back again as the 727 descended toward the
Manaus airport. It would be interesting to see this city,
so celebrated in the lore of the nineteenth century and
of Brazil itself. There were so many things about it that
were hard to believe. Just to think that Victorian set-
tlers, rich on rubber-plantation profits, had sent their
laundry by boat down the Amazon and then on to
London to have it done, to be returned by the same
route, was too stupendous to contemplate. There had
been tram lines here when the city was still just a
jungle outpost reachable only by water. The famous
opera house, the Teatro Amazonas, had hosted Jenny
Lind and the Ballet Russe. The Custom House and the
Lighthouse, famous landmarks, had been shipped

piece by piece from England and reassembled beside the floating dock, built especially to offset the yearly forty-foot rise of the Rio Negro.

Sam looked out the window. The green jungle canopy gave way to the high-rise apartment and office buildings of modern Manaus. Then, as they drew closer, descending all the while, he made out the red-tiled roofs of the old stucco buildings crowding the hills down to the dark river.

"So you're really in the jungle now," Mercedes said over his shoulder.

He turned and grinned at her. "I've been in them before."

"In the Amazon?"

"No."

"Then don't get too cocky."

15

PILLOW TALK

It started in his toes, rapidly climbed his legs, tripped along his spine, tingled in ripples across his scalp. Like a wave curling higher and higher, it held, not breaking. His arms quavered, his breath caught. He thrust harder, quicker, higher. Dipping lower, he arched his back, drove deeper. It built and built, subsided, then, in a rush, built higher. Gasping for air, his eyes squeezed shut, he bridled its rush, modulating it, savoring it, stretching it, holding it for the precise moment.

"Don't stop, don't stop," Mercedes implored.

He thrust rhythmically, steadily, again and again as she rotated against him, muttering in Portuguese, seeking the assistance of saints and angels, finally the Lord himself, while she pushed with both hands against his shoulders. She bucked, moaning and crying, rushing toward him and straining against him simultaneously, arching herself like a taut bow stretched to its limit. Suddenly she froze against him, mumbling and moaning, at the apex of her thrust, her back arched, stiff and tight. In a screech, she be-

seeched the Mother of God to help her, her head
rolling on the pillow from side to side.

Above her, he continued to thrust, faster and
faster, more furiously, reaching for the limit and beyond. Within him the tension built and built, wavering, mounting, then subsiding, only to build again.
The tingling increased. Then in a rush it crested. He
shook, spending himself, the ultimate satisfaction
rushing to every corner of his mind and body, tripping every nerve. Beneath him she fell away, and
slowly he lowered himself. Exhausted, they collapsed
against each other and the bed. For minutes, they lay
in silence, savoring the experience, each alone in the
afterwash of ecstasy. Finally Mercedes Coozi spoke,
piercing the mood.

"Sam Borne, I think I'm in love."

"It's the afterglow. See if it holds in the morning."

"It will hold for a lifetime, believe me."

"I'm flattered."

"So marry me."

Sam laughed. There was nothing so pleasing and
dangerous in a woman as boldness. If he let her, Mercedes Coozi would take him over in every department.
He'd end up a silly boulevardier in Rio, trailing kids
like a trestle set behind him. But her spunk was infec-
tious, and he liked her enormously.

Unamused, Mercedes reached up and slapped him.
It only served to increase his mirth. Laughing louder,
he rolled off her, to her side, and settled in, one arm
still thrown affectionately across her lovely chest. Next
to him, she immediately shifted and rose on one
elbow, her beautiful hair trailing down onto his chest,
soothing and stimulating him, her full breasts poised
above. With a long, sexy index finger, she swirled

patterns in the hairs on his chest, then said, nearly pouting, "Why do you laugh?"

"You're funny."

"Don't be curt."

"This is no time for talk of marriage. We have a job to do."

"Afterwards."

"Let's get to afterwards before we make any plans."

"I mean we should run away."

"*I* have a job to do."

Consternation suddenly flooded her face. She looked away, toward the glass wall and the glistening bay beyond. The mood was shot. It was as if an arctic wind had blown across the bed. Sam had a foreboding that what would follow would not be pleasant. He noticed that Mercedes's face was clouded now, her jaw set, her eyes fearful. Her finger no longer played in the hairs on his chest.

"Sam, listen to me, this is all a mistake. She will kill us both. She is a pure animal. Sick, completely sick. Let's call the whole thing off."

Had her face not been paralyzed with fear, Sam would have lost respect for her. But this was extraordinary. This was the kind of fear you saw on a human face the moment before the hood went on for an execution. It was as if Mercedes stood looking into her own open coffin, her corpse staring wide-eyed back at her.

"That's not possible," Sam said firmly, caressing her shoulder. "You know this woman has to be stopped. That's why I'm here."

"But, Sam," she said, anxiety cracking her voice, "you don't know what you're getting into. I have seen this woman kill as another might peel an apple. She is not human. She is never fooled. There have been

130

other attempts to stop her. They have all failed. She has killed all who have tried to stop her. Don't do this."

Sam took his hand from her shoulder and stroked her cheek. Then he pulled her head down against his chest. While he soothed the back of her neck, he talked to her softly. "You know that no one has been able to penetrate her organization before. You know that's where you come in. You have this woman's confidence. You have primed the pump for me. I have a clear path. I have entrée, I can get to her."

"She will see through us. She will kill us. I owed it to my daughter, if not to myself, to stay out of this."

"You will be out of it. All you have to do is take me up there tomorrow, then leave the next day. I'll take it from there."

Mercedes Coozi was the perfect defector. She still had the total confidence of the organization she was working against. No one, not even Mother Beloved herself, suspected that Mercedes had changed, that she was no longer infatuated with a woman so powerful, so ruthless. There had been an awakening of conscience in her. She had come to realize that Mother Beloved was out of control, that she was a detriment to herself and others, that she was a killer of the worst sort, cold-blooded and insatiable.

Over dinner, a few hours back, after Sam and she had toured Manaus, Mercedes had opened up to him, describing her disillusionment over seeing Mother Beloved in full flower. Without going into details, she had explained to Sam how she had gotten into some kinky scenes orchestrated by Mother Beloved, that things had gotten out of whack sexually. That had been one thing, their affair, but then Mercedes had learned something that was much darker: Mother Beloved had an insatiable appetite for sex mixed with murder. She liked to sacrifice young boys, obvious virgins, to a ritual that Mercedes had witnessed. She described to Sam the special room in Mother Beloved's house reserved for this ritual, and how it was carried out. Not the orgies, not the sadomasochism, not the bondage and degradation, not any of this had gotten to Mercedes. But the murder had. Once she had witnessed this from behind a two-way mirror, she could not accept herself, nor forgive herself.

Because of it, she had rethought her whole involvement with Mother Beloved, and with her organization. She had been ashamed to have ridden with Mother Beloved and her brigands into the night, only to raid and plunder, to vandalize and destroy. It had dawned on her how wrongheaded she'd been, how seduced she'd been in mind and body. Mercedes had realized that she was another aristocrat gone awry, that all the principles she'd learned as a child had been subverted, that she had enlisted in the crimes of a renegade.

Before dinner, earlier that evening, as twilight settled over the jungle capital, Sam and Mercedes had shared a drink in a sidewalk café facing the celebrated opera house, the Teatro Amazonas. An hour before, they had caught the last tour of the opera house, topping off an afternoon spent strolling the city, taking in the fish market, the Botanic Garden and the waterfront. Altogether it was a good day, since they had checked into the Novotel Hotel in the early afternoon, caught a quick lunch and followed it with a torrid session of lovemaking capped with a short, restorative nap.

When dusk had given way to night, they had left the café, strolled across the street and had a splendid dinner in Xodo, a good restaurant filled with American,

German and French tourists. There it was Mercedes had opened up. She told Sam how she had analyzed her situation, how she knew in an instant she had to take action. What she did was contact an old family friend, an influential businessman in São Paulo with interests in developing Amazonas. This old friend had put her eventually into contact with a coterie of other businessmen, friends of his. These men had taken Mercedes to a country estate for a weekend and grilled her thoroughly. She knew only that they were some of the most powerful men in Brazil, determined to develop the entire Amazon Basin, to open it the way the American capitalists, with government backing, had opened the American West in the nineteenth century.

Of course, Sam realized, as Mercedes did not, that these men had gotten word to the Committee. From what she said, Sam gathered that she knew nothing about him or the Committee. She was under the impression, which Sam would not correct, that he was a professional assassin hired by these influential São Paulo business magnates to put a stop to Mother Beloved and thus eliminate an impediment to their plans for the development of the Amazon. She was innocent of the existence of the Committee. She did not know that she was blindly acting on their behalf. Just as the Committee would have no official affiliation with the São Paulo business cartel, or with the Brazilian government, so they would have none with Mercedes and, if he was caught or failed, none with Sam. For, to Sam, it was eminently clear that behind all of this, thick as thieves with the Committee, was the Brazilian government. It was all tied in at the highest levels, but it operated, unacknowledged officially, at the lowest.

But here in bed, after midnight, in the afterglow of good sex, none of this larger theorizing mattered.

What mattered was ensuring that Mercedes would calm down, that she would not give Sam away. Hers was a simple task. Tomorrow she would make the introduction for Sam; then she would leave. All she had to do was stay in control, do a little acting, and exit.

The rest was up to him. He would have to win Mother Beloved's confidence, offer her good prices on the best arms, kill her at the first clean opportunity, and depart. His job now was to make sure Mercedes was up to her part. The São Paulo businessmen had told her all she need do was get Sam to Mother Beloved's ranch and then hightail it. That was all he expected, all he wanted, from her.

Against his chest, he felt her sob. He took her head in his hands and held her face up. "There is no reason for this fear," he said. "It is exaggerated. We can handle this. All you do is take me to her. You stay one day, riding and acting normal, then you depart. She can't read your mind. No one can read anyone's mind. That is all nonsense. Do you understand?"

A big tear rolled down Mercedes's cheek, dangled for a minute on her chin, then dropped warmly onto his chest. She was even more beautiful with her big brown eyes glistening with anxiety. "You told me this evening she had to be stopped, that she perverted everything she touched, didn't you?" he asked in a tone scarcely above a whisper.

She nodded.

"You know you can square yourself with yourself by doing this simple task, right?" he coaxed.

She nodded again.

"Then we're going to walk out of here tomorrow and do this thing, right?" he prompted, stroking her cheek gently.

"Yes, Sam, yes."

He took his thumb and wiped a tear from her cheek, then pulled her to him and kissed her hard on the mouth, his hands playing over the length of her body, lingering on her breasts, stroking them, teasing them. She moaned against his mouth, then climbed onto her knees, reaching down and stroking him, suddenly impatient, her anxiety behind her, desire overwhelming her. Sam felt the liquid warmth of her on him, her hair tenting his stomach and thighs. A sensation like a thousand trapped butterflies beat against him. His entire body thrilled to it. Then, when he could stand it no longer, he took her by the shoulders and, coaxing her up, guided her onto him. Her hands pushing against his chest, she straddled him, riding without worry or care, free and easy.

So far, he liked Brazil.

16

MAIL RUN

Manaus–Valhalla Ranch
October 9

Through the early-morning haze planes took off and landed, mostly commercial flights of Varig, Cruzeiro do Sul, Vasp and Trans-Brasil, the four major airlines of Brazil, which together covered the entire country, a country only slightly smaller than the United States, with not nearly so efficient a system of roads or railroads, making air travel the great civilizing influence on this gigantic, undeveloped young country. Air travel had been introduced in Brazil early on, in 1927, and it had been the main link ever since. There was no way, prior to its introduction, that people could get from one internal city to another, unless they undertook arduous expeditions, the kind the Europeans, especially the British, mounted with frequency and vigor in the nineteenth century, as they sought to catalog and classify a country where, in the jungles of the Amazon, in one square mile there could be as many as one hundred different species of ants, all unknown anywhere else in the world. Everything about Brazil was outsized, exaggerated, bizarre. No other country, Sam Borne thought, could have produced a monster like Mother Beloved.

From the observation deck, where Sam stood with Mercedes Coozi, there was a clear view of the entire airport, its runways and hangars. They watched in silence, Mercedes nervously smoking a cigarette. From time to time, Sam would touch her hand or arm, trying to soothe her, but mostly she pulled away, retreating into her own space, seeking to steel herself for what Sam had been unable to convince her would not be her deathwatch.

Interspersed among the commercial flights were a good number of private aircraft. These were flown by the ranchers settling Amazonas, and in most cases offered them their only quick means of obtaining mail, supplies or vital equipment.

Sam scanned the horizon, hoping to catch a glimpse of the plane that would bring him face to face with Wilda von Hoffer, aka Mother Beloved. Mercedes had been able to tell him only that she would come in a small plane, the one she always flew to gather her mail. Sam knew, though Mercedes probably didn't, that Mother Beloved also used these short hops to ferry her cocaine shipments. Since Mercedes knew nothing about aircraft, Sam had no clue to what type of plane he was scanning the skies for. Mercedes said only that she thought it was white.

All morning Sam had not been overly concerned with Mercedes. He considered that she merely had the kind of nervousness an athlete or an entertainer experienced right before game time or curtain up. Once Mother Beloved showed up, he had a sure feeling, somehow, that she would come through. So he had concentrated instead on preparing himself, setting himself, psyching himself, priming himself to kill the only woman he'd so far been assigned as a target. At first, he was not entirely comfortable with the idea of killing a woman. It had bothered him, but the more he learned of this woman, this Wilda von Hoffer, the easier the idea became. The dossier had spelled out her treachery clearly, yet it was the details he'd gotten from Mercedes that had convinced him she was unworthy of life. It took a special kind of animal, a truly twisted character, to revel in a mix of murder and sex, to take pleasure in subduing and oppressing vast numbers of people. When Sam heard Mercedes's descriptions of scenes of torture and mutilation, he ceased to have compassion for a woman so evil. He had never been able to convince himself, like some Pollyanna social worker, that all people were innately good, so it didn't strain his conscience now to focus on killing this woman. He would take out Mother Beloved coldbloodedly, as she had taken out so many innocent others.

From Zen, from the discipline drilled into him as a ninja, an actor, a commando, Sam knew that his will could enforce, through his body, what his mind could accept. He could clearly now accept executing Mother Beloved; it was only a case of biding his time, picking his spot, doing his stuff. He would convince her easily, dressed in his frumpy outfits, schooled in CIA lore and in international arms dealing moxie, that he was the genuine item. He would set her up and pounce. He had psyched himself well.

"I think that's her," Mercedes said, breaking into his reverie. Looking in the direction of her pointed finger, he saw a plane he took for a Rallye taxiing in from the runway, hitting the apron before a hangar at the extreme end of the field, past the big hangars of the commercial lines. It was painted white, with sporty red and blue trim. All small private aircraft were painted white for maximum visibility in the air, something many people didn't know, though it was true that lately some manufacturers had started to paint their craft tan. Sam thought the old universal white should be preserved. It was a safety feature, and any good pilot—and Sam was one—would tell you that you couldn't have enough safety features in the air.

"Yes, that's her plane, I'm sure of it," Mercedes said. "Let's go." She dropped her cigarette on the floor, then ground it with her foot a bit too hard. Sam took her by the arm to reassure her, saying as he did, "Everything will be fine, just relax." Hefting their luggage, they started through the terminal.

Outside, the torrid sun beat relentlessly down on the tarmac, making it slightly sticky underfoot. Sam followed behind Mercedes, allowing her to lead, to appear to be completely in charge of him, a mere business connection brought to Wilda von Hoffer at her request. As they approached the hangar, Sam saw that the white plane with the red and blue trim was one of several docked on the apron. It was a Rallye. If nothing else, Mother Beloved had good taste in airplanes.

"Hello, Wilda," Mercedes hollered, waving to a woman in white slacks and a black silk blouse emerging from a small office in the front of the hangar. The woman carried a small packet of mail in her left hand. She smiled and waved back. Sam had been unprepared for her, after all. As she walked toward them it was apparent that she was a world-class beauty. Tall, leggy, blond and fair, she was exciting to look at. She had the perfect carriage of a trained model, the vibrancy of all great beauties, and the poise of a princess. It occurred to Sam that killing such a gorgeous creature would be akin to slashing a great painting.

"Ciao, darling," she said, embracing Mercedes, kissing her affectionately on both cheeks. She stepped back, holding Mercedes's hands possessively in each of hers, looking at her fondly. Mercedes returned her gaze, staring intensely into her eyes, causing Sam a moment's uneasiness as he wondered if Mercedes would again fall completely under this woman's domination, to the point where she would betray him to her. He nicked the thought as paranoia, though paranoia in this instance would be somewhat warranted. He was stepping into a very hot matrix here.

It got quickly hotter. Stepping aside, Mercedes swept a hand in Sam's direction. Even before Mercedes could complete the introduction, Sam felt the heat of Mother Beloved's gaze. She raked her eyes over him from head to foot, taking in everything, letting her eyes bore into him, seeking to establish her dominance right from the start. Then she smiled the most devastating smile imaginable.

"I'm glad to meet you, Mr. Borne," she said, extending her hand. He shook it firmly, never letting his eyes stray from hers. It wouldn't do to let this woman know he felt the force of her character already. He summoned all the casualness he could muster, no longer doubting the power she had held over Mercedes, and yet, truth to tell, longing to fall under her sway, to take her in his arms and ravish her. The difficulty of this assignment rose exponentially now that he knew the opponent he was up against. He would have to use maximum care, and maximum self-control.

"The feeling is mutual, Ms. von Hoffer," he said, releasing her hand. "I've heard a lot about you from Mercedes, all of it impressive."

"Wonderful, but call me Wilda, please."

"Fine, and you call me Sam."

"Thank you. Now let's get under way." She walked off toward the Rallye. When she reached the ladder, she turned and said, "I suggest you ride in back, Sam, while Mercedes sits up front with me."

"Good enough," he said, and climbed the steps. At the top he tossed his luggage under the sliding canopy, reached back, took Mercedes's and tossed it in. Then he climbed in, stooped under the canopy and sat in the right-hand rear seat, the one that would afford the better view of the pilot. First Mercedes, then Mother Beloved followed. They settled in, adjusting their seat belts. Then Mother Beloved hit the ignition, and minutes later they taxied onto the runway. Traffic was light, and they were soon airborne. Looking over her shoulder, Sam noticed that Mother Beloved was an accomplished pilot. She handled the Rallye well, and ten minutes after takeoff they were cruising at 135 knots. Up front the two women fell into intense conversation, discussing the respective progress of their daughters, their latest wardrobe acquisitions, the personnel at the ranch, horses.

In the back Sam gazed out the canopy at the landscape passing below. It was an incredibly verdant green, with triple-cover jungle spreading endlessly, broken only occasionally by clearings holding ranch houses and outbuildings. From time to time they passed huge fires, flames leaping orange and red against the green, sending black smoke billowing into the clear sky. This was the slash-and-burn method of land clearance used everywhere in Brazil. It was the method that so upset the environmentalists and the agriculturists, who held that the earth would be destroyed by such ecological vandalism. Once the trees, plants and vines were removed, they claimed, the topsoil, which was only an inch or two thick, would blow off, leaving only hard-packed earth that would not support crops. This was not to mention the destruction of the entire ecosystem that supported the multifarious forms of jungle life dependent on those same trees, plants and vines. This controversy over clearing the great jungle raged fiercely, not only in Brazil but the world over. There were those who maintained that the earth's atmosphere was dependent on these jungle plants to cleanse it and purify it, to make it breathable by human beings. It was a big issue, one Sam wasn't clear on.

Interspersed among the greenery were brown ribbons, tributaries of the mighty Amazon, which mighty river itself Sam had glimpsed below in the early moments of the flight, but which they had left behind now. They were flying west-southwest from Manaus, toward Bolivia and Peru. Soon the landscape became almost solid green, with the occasional brown tributaries snaking through it, but with only rare clearings for ranches. They were now in the wildest sections of the great basin. It was only another half hour before Mother Beloved started to descend.

"We are coming up on the ranch," Mercedes said, speaking to Sam for only the second time on the entire two-hour flight. "It is just beyond that river." He followed her pointed finger and saw a brown river slithering through the jungle. As he watched, feeling the Rallye losing altitude, he saw the solid green canopy open up about three miles ahead. In a clearing stood a collection of buildings, some large and obviously barns, others long and clearly bunkhouses; off by itself sat a large, low ranch house. There was no airstrip per se, so Sam was not surprised when Mother Beloved guided the Rallye down onto an open field.

They came in smoothly. Mother Beloved impressed

Sam with her skill in setting the small plane gently on the field. With its fixed, heavy landing gear, the Rallye could—was in fact designed to—handle much rougher terrain. It was one of the premier short-field planes in the world, capable of taking off in four hundred feet and landing in less. The French could build a dandy plane. It was no wonder so many sportsmen, especially Europeans, preferred the Rallye to anything America had to offer. Sam had once flown one on a hunting trip in the Bohemian Forest, on another assignment. On that trip, he had used one of the plane's features so loved by sportsmen and aerial photographers, namely slowflight. The Rallye was one of the few planes in the world that could slow to sixty knots and not fall to the ground. On that trip, Sam's target, a count, had shot several deer from the air. Altogether, it was an impressive plane. Sam didn't wonder why Mother Beloved had chosen it for her ranch, considering the camouflage she wanted here—as well as, he would wager, in Bolivia at the coca plantation.

They taxied only a short distance before Mother Beloved turned the plane slowly and headed for the barn nearest the ranch house. As they moved closer, the doors of the barn swung open and they entered. When the plane was completely in, Mother Beloved cut the engine. Then she turned to Sam with a look on her face no man could mistake. Only it had more about it of command than of invitation.

"Welcome to my home, Sam," Wilda von Hoffer said. "May we get to know each other here."

"I have every confidence we will."

17

LUNCH ON THE GRASS

Valhalla Ranch
October 9

"Tell me, Sam, where did you grow up?"

The question came from Wilda von Hoffer. She sat across the redwood picnic table from Sam Borne and Mercedes Coozi. Beside her sat a vision, one Sam was taken with religiously: her daughter Erika. A younger version of her mother, blond and lithe, Erika was a blue-eyed masterpiece, a young woman who, as a model or an actress, could easily have made a name in New York or London, Los Angeles or Paris. She had the kind of perfection of face and feature, of figure and carriage, that made stunning young women fortunes each and every day in any of those world capitals of fashion and film. Dressed casually in black slacks and red blouse, wearing only a hint of makeup, she radiated glamour, combining sensuality and innocence in the way few beauties could, even beauties so young.

Since they had been introduced, Erika could not keep from stealing glances at Sam, who had returned them discreetly, aware he was as handicapped as a diamond cutter with DTs. Surrounded by three women, all interested in him, he was in a delicate, possibly explosive, position. It was best to temporize.

144

Erika was demure, her mother bold, Mercedes annoyed.

"I grew up all over," Sam lied. "My father was in the army and we lived all over."

"Who's we?"

"My mother, my sister and I."

"Where are they now?"

"They're all dead." Sam faked suitable solemnity.

"I'm sorry," Mother Beloved said, not convincing him for a minute. She was not at home with normal human emotions and was only following through for appearances. Sam knew what the next question would be.

"What happened to them?"

"They were all killed in a car crash." This was a great device for eliminating questions about his background. Sam had picked it up from a woman he'd once had a terrific fling with while between assignments in Jamaica. A fabulous redhead, she had been a New York–based editor of women's fiction, having cut her teeth on modern gothics, a form of novel in which the heroine is usually shorn of her parents at an early age by their death in a car crash. Sam loved it, and used it all the time. It put a cold stop to curiosity and got him off the hook. It also precluded the possibility, remote in this instance, that Mother Beloved would run a check on him. There was nothing to check. He was a singleton both in fact and in fiction, and couldn't be tripped up on his own invented story. But the device only worked if you told the car-crash story convincingly.

"It happened one summer while I was away at basketball camp," he added. "They were headed for my father's new posting at Fort Polk in Louisiana. They were almost there when a drunk driver hit them head-on, killing them all instantly." He dropped his voice. "They had to be cut out of the wreck."

"That's awful," Erika said. Sam shot a glance at her. She was genuinely touched. Beside him, Mercedes twitched on the bench. He didn't dare look at her for fear she would misinterpret this fabrication as an attempt to solicit pity from Wilda and Erika. None of their interest in him had been lost on her.

"I didn't know you were such an athlete, Sam," Mercedes said, changing the subject and, he was certain, twitting him.

"Sure," he said. "I played all the American games. Baseball, football and basketball."

"Were you any good at them?" Mother Beloved asked. Her tone was loaded.

"I made first team in all three sports in high school."

"I'm impressed."

Of course, this was not true. Sam had played all three sports, but he'd played them for base teams in Japan, not for regular high schools. He'd had no ordinary athletic opportunities in ordinary high schools. This deprivation grated on him. He loved sports, and was tremendously gifted at them, having been called by one base commander in Japan "our answer to Jim Thorpe." There was no doubt in Sam's mind that he would have made a fabulous college halfback and a good shooting guard, not to mention his baseball ability, which was tremendous, demonstrated amply in his performance in Japan against visiting collegiate teams from the U.S. He had hit, and hit with authority, several pitchers who later went on to glittering careers in the big leagues, so he knew he could hit a major-league fastball.

"Thank you," he said, playing Mother Beloved's heavyhandedness as lightly as possible.

"Would anyone like more wine?" Erika asked, lifting a bottle of Königsbacher Harle from a silver ice bucket on a stand beside her. Wrapping a towel around the bottle, she looked up. Sam smiled and said, "I'd like more." She smiled back and poured his crystal goblet half full. Her mother monitored this exchange carefully, then said, "I too would like more." Erika poured for her mother, then looked toward Mercedes. "Would you care for more, Mercedes?" she asked.

"Not until our entrée arrives," Mercedes answered.

"Then have some now," Mother Beloved said as the mosquito netting opened at one end of the pavilion and in walked the houseboy with a silver salver of Wiener schnitzel. A maid followed with a bowl of red potatoes and another of Brussels sprouts. Starting with Mercedes, the houseboy and the maid circled the table, filling each plate as they went. When they finished, Mother Beloved said, *"Bon appétit."* Everyone started to eat in silence. The veal was tender and delicious, the potatoes soft and tasty, the Brussels sprouts fresh. As always, Sam ate quickly, listening as Mother Beloved discussed horses with Mercedes. Without being obvious, whenever he could he cut a glance at Erika, who always returned it. Her eyes were nearly always fixed on him, a state of affairs he found warm and inviting.

When he finished his food, Sam sipped his wine and scanned the faces of the two women across the table from him. They were a remarkable sight, both stunning, one a younger replica of the other. Yet there were also great differences between them, differences

147

that went beyond genes and consanguinity. The one was an ice mistress, cold and hostile. She gave no quarter. She came first, you came last. She expected the world to shift on its axis at her whim. Other people were not human beings in their own right but merely adjuncts to her ego, pawns in a game of chess of which she was the only grand master. She was the empress of all, Her Imperial Highness, a woman capable of passing a death sentence while doing her nails. This was Wilda von Hoffer.

The other, the younger model, was different. Her blue eyes shone with warmth. Her smile radiated friendliness. Her manner spoke concern for others in every gesture. Kindness sat on her like a second skin. For her, other people were treasures enriching her own life. She was a willing comrade of all living creatures, great and small. To kill a fly would pain her. She was a bit player in the greatest production ever mounted, life. This was Erika Álvarez. Mother and daughter were as different as Jekyll and Hyde. There was no explaining life's simple ironies, Sam thought, no explaining them at all.

Upon arriving at the ranch, after only an hour in their company, Sam had come to one swift conclusion: Neither mother nor daughter cared for the other. After climbing out of the Rallye, Sam and Mercedes had been shown to the small guest house some fifty yards from the main house. There they stowed their luggage and freshened up in separate bedrooms; then, following instructions from Mother Beloved, they'd walked over to the main house for lunch on the lawn, in the tented pavilion protected by mosquito netting. While they were still in the house itself, Sam picked up on the nature of the relationship between the two women. As soon as Mother Beloved called to her

148

daughter to present herself for introductions and lunch, a shouting match in German erupted. Sam had not let on that he understood German, not even to Mercedes, who clearly did.

Mother and daughter had insulted each other roundly, with Erika refusing to come out of her bedroom and join the company. It had taken her mother a threat of restricting Erika to her room for a week to get her to join them. You didn't have to have a doctorate in psychology to know that the conflict between the women went beyond the typical antipathy of teenage daughter to authoritarian mother. Their dynamic went deeper. It was more than clinical casebook stuff. It was cosmic. It was hatred, full and deep. In a year it would be there, deeper still; in ten years, or forty, it would still be there, deeper still. They were ontological opposites. There would be no reconciliation, the twain would never meet.

"Tell me, Sam, have you ever killed anyone?"

It was Mother Beloved, snapping him out of his reverie and putting him on the spot. Under other circumstances, he would have viewed such a provocative question as outrageous, but with this woman it was evidently a test, probably the first of many. He met it cleanly, without a hitch in his swing.

"Yes," he said evenly.

Just then the houseboy returned with a silver bowl of strawberries, the maid trailing him with a smaller bowl of whipped cream. Without missing a beat, Mother Beloved asked, "Who and when?"

"These strawberries look delicious," he said, not so much to avoid her question as to show her, ever so slightly, that he wasn't at her beck and call, that he wasn't to be grilled about death like a schoolboy about grammar. He dipped a strawberry in cream and bit

149

into it slowly before deigning to look up at her, all the while feeling her eyes steady on him, burning into him, her antennae sensitive, like all autocrats', to any instance of insubordination or defiance.

"You didn't answer my question," she said, sharpness edging her voice.

"I'm aware. Why do you want to know such things?"

"I'm curious."

"Curiosity killed the cat."

"Satisfaction brought him back. So tell me."

"What exactly?"

"Who you killed. And when."

Sam stared at her hard. "There's more than one."

"Tell me one you remember."

"I remember them all."

"So tell me about one."

Sam glanced at Erika. She had a stricken look on her face, a look of disappointment. He would never have launched into this subject himself, but he felt, and he was sure he was right, that Mother Beloved set great store by such tests as she was now subjecting him to, and he could not afford at this point to alienate her, to have her find him weak, to think that he was unacceptable as a business partner. He needed to gain her confidence, or the job of killing her would be raised in difficulty exponentially. If he had to victimize Erika's sensibility to do so, so be it.

"I killed a man in Amsterdam."

"When?"

"August 28, 1982."

"You remember the exact date?"

"I have a mind for details that frightens me sometimes."

"Give me the details."

* * *

The fog rolled in off the North Sea and hung on the city like a cloak. Visibility was poor. A fine mist fell steadily, beading all surfaces with dew. In the early-morning hours of August 28 few people moved about. The streets and canals were mostly empty, except in the famous red-light district, where the whores still worked their windowed cribs, the porn shops still hawked their wares and lecherous drunks still prowled and staggered, unsure how to end their night.

In a small back room in a canal house on the Prinsengracht a man rose from his cot and dressed quickly. He stepped into black leather pants, matched them with a black silk shirt, open almost to his navel, then pulled on a pair of black engineer's boots, the kind favored by motorcyclists. After checking his face in the small mirror above the sink in the corner of the room, he left, tiptoeing quietly down the carpeted stairs, careful not to wake the tourists, mostly Americans, asleep in the rooms off the landing; careful at the foot of the stairs not to wake the proprietors, a pair of gentle homosexuals who looked after the comfort of their guests as though they were family. Holding the railing, the man tiptoed carefully down the steep set of stairs leading to the outside door, a double door at the bottom. When he reached it, using his handkerchief, he muffled the clicking sound of the locks opening. Then he swung the door open, stepped out and carefully, one hand pressing back to cushion the impact of the lock clicking shut, closed the door behind him.

On the front stoop he turned and paused, hearing the waters of the canal lap against the docked barges and against the stone walls of the canal itself. Turning left, he walked the few meters to the corner, where he saw the shuttered grocery store and the closed tobacconist across the Utrechtstraat. In front of a closed flower stand, he waited, listening to the lapping waters, alone in the fog.

Before he saw it he heard it: the clanging bell on the approaching number four trolley. Moving quickly to the middle of the bridge over the canal, he stood near the curb, waving his arm. The light on the trolley penetrated the fog. Through the wet windshield, the driver saw him and clanged to a stop. The man in black climbed on and paid with a strip of tickets. The driver greeted him in Dutch. He responded in English, a language almost universally spoken in Amsterdam. Switching to English, the driver commented on the lousy weather. The man in black commiserated, then moved far back in the nearly empty trolley. He did not want a conversation. He did not want to be remembered. He did not want to attract attention to himself.

In the back, he stared out the window. Water beaded on the window and trickled down in rivulets. They passed closed shops, almost all dark, and restaurants that were closed or closing, the last customers stepping out into the heavy weather. The trolley, the last of the night, reached the corner of Rembrandt-splein without taking on or discharging any other passengers.

As the trolley made its turn the man in black hit the indicator. The trolley stopped and discharged him. He stood in the middle of the street and surveyed the square quickly. Immediately he saw the lighted windows of the Wimpy's across the way. He walked directly to it, entered and spotted the man he sought, one of only two customers.

The man was tall, about six feet even, and had the angular good looks so common to the Dutch. His blond hair was long and straggly, and hung down his face on both sides; wet, it clung to his cheeks, matted and dirty. A goatee curled from the end of his pointed chin. His narrow mouth, when he opened it to talk, was clotted with crooked yellow teeth. He was dressed in a flannel American work shirt and torn, faded jeans. On his feet were dirty white running shoes with blue stripes. He scanned the man in black carefully, then spoke to him in English without preamble or pleasantry. "Let's get out of here. We can have a drink over there." He pointed to a row of cafés and restaurants lining the south side of the square.

When the two men settled themselves on the small awninged terrace of a café, the straggly Dutchman complimented his connection on the strictness with which he followed instructions. "You said to wear black, I wore black," the man said. "Yes, good," the Dutchman replied. Like all revolutionaries, he was sentential, and humorless. He paused for effect, then asked, "So, what is your name? I can't call you Mercury forever." Mercury had been the man's code name.

"My name is Yukio Yamaguchi." The man looked American, but he did have a slight Asian cast to his features. He knew what the Dutchman was thinking, and said, "My father was American, a serviceman, my mother Japanese. When he abandoned us, she gave me her name."

The Dutchman nodded. "And you have access to money and weapons that can help us in our historic struggle."

"Yes."

"You have trained with Fusako?"

"Yes." The Dutchman referred to Fusako Shigenobu, known as the Red Queen of Terror, the notorious leader of the Japanese Red Army.

153

"You have trained in Lebanon?"

"Yes."

A waiter came and said in Dutch that they must hurry. The café was closing in minutes. The Dutchman interpreted this for the man in black. Then he ordered an Amstel beer for himself. The man in black requested a Campari and soda. The waiter stalked off to get their drinks. The Dutchman sat in silence, his feet up on the iron rail fronting the terrace. The man in black said nothing. The waiter returned with the drinks and stood hovering over them. The Dutchman fished into his jeans and came up with a ten-guilder note. He gave the note to the waiter and told him to keep the change. The waiter moved away and started to stack the tables and chairs on the terrace.

"To the success of our collaboration," the Dutchman said, tipping the edge of his large beer glass against the smaller wine glass. The man in black smiled but said nothing. The Dutchman was confident that he was in control, that the man in black knew next to nothing about him, which wasn't so.

The man in black knew that his name was Hendrik Goltzius and that he had traveled and trained with the Baader-Meinhof in the late sixties and early seventies. With them he carried out numerous bank robberies, kidnapped and killed various West German businessmen and led an attack on a small United States military installation. When the original gang splintered in the seventies, he returned to his native Holland and organized a small gang that had not been very successful, nor active, until Goltzius himself connected with the South Moluccans and masterminded the terrorist campaigns carried out by them in late 1975 and early 1976. He conceived and planned the seizure of the train at Beilan and the takeover of the Indonesian

154

consulate in Amsterdam in December of 1975. Five months later, still behind the scenes, he organized and executed the train hijacking at Assen and the seizure of the school full of children at Bovinsmilde. Like all terrorists, Hendrik Goltzius had innocent blood on his hands; like all terrorists, he was therefore a moral, if not a physical, coward.

"To freedom," the man in black said, tipping his glass against the beer pilsner. The Dutchman smiled. He was sure the man in black referred to freedom in the peculiar grammar of terrorism. He tipped the tall pilsner back and took a huge swallow of beer, then put the glass down on the aluminum table and, after wiping his hand across his mouth, grinned conspiratorially at the man opposite.

"I am glad you are here to aid our cause," he said, clapping a hand on the man's shoulder. "We will triumph in my lifetime, I know it in my heart, in my soul. History is on our side." He drank another draft of beer, then pushed his grimy hair off his cheek, flicking it back. He stared off across the square, a man alone with fate, contemplating his own important role in the scheme of things. The waiter, finished stacking the tables and chairs, came over and asked politely that they leave. Goltzius drank off his remaining beer and rose. The man in black took a sip of his Campari, leaving half of it in the glass. He stood. The waiter thanked them and bade them good night. They walked out into the fog.

"Where is the packet?" Goltzius asked. He referred to the money the man in black was to deliver to him. It represented, he believed, contributions collected among the radical Japanese left. It was earmarked to buy plastique with which followers of Goltzius intended to annihilate the Van Gogh museum in two

155

days, when it was sure to be packed with tourists and art lovers.

"It's in my car. I'm parked nearby," the man in black said. He pointed to the southeast corner of the square, away from Utrechtstraat and away from the city center. They reached it quickly and walked down to the first canal, the Herengracht. As they mounted the humped bridge across the canal, the fog concealed them completely. The man in black glanced quickly behind him. Nothing. In front, nothing. There was only the gentle lapping sound of the canal water against the stone walls.

In the milky whiteness the man in black dropped half a step behind Goltzius, swung one arm around his neck, jammed the other against his nape. Pulling his foreward arm up, pressing his rear arm in and down, he snapped the Dutchman's neck, the crack of the bone like the sound a shelled walnut made. Instantly the dead man went limp, his weight pulling down hard. The man in black held the corpse up. It was then the first footsteps sounded, faint but growing louder, approaching. Quickly the man in black propped the dead man against the parapet, took him under each arm and straddled him closely, whispering endearments in audible German.

The footsteps came closer, punctuated with a rhythmic creaking. Then out of the whiteness emerged a man walking a bicycle. The man in black looked away, concentrating heavily on his lover. The man with the bicycle reached them and walked on, disappearing again into the fog. Not until the creaking and the footsteps faded did the man in black step back from the corpse.

Pushing the corpse backward onto the parapet, he snatched it by both feet and lifted. Slowly he slid it across the stone wall, then lowered it over the side, still holding it by the feet. Leaning over as far as he could, he let the corpse dangle above the lapping waters of the canal.

"To the success of our collaboration," he whispered, then let go. The corpse, invisible from the bridge in the thick fog, splashed into the canal. The man in black turned and walked off the bridge. His maroon Peugeot 504 was parked along the canal. He slipped behind the wheel and started the engine. Then he hit the fog lights.

Slowly he wound his way out of Amsterdam, creeping along the canals. When he hit the highway, heading south, he slipped a tape into the deck and listened to Handel's *Water Music* and Philip Glass's *Glassworks*. They went well with fog. The next morning he was securely ensconced on the Concorde for the early Paris to New York flight from Charles De Gaulle airport.

His American passport read Sam Borne.

His story finished, Sam looked up. Mother Beloved sat with a rapt expression on her face. He had risen in her estimation, which was why he'd deliberately embellished the details of the kill scene, sketching in every movement, describing every sound, creating feelings he hadn't experienced. For him it had been just another assignment from the Committee, an easy one for a change. He had dispatched Hendrik Goltzius without a flicker of emotion. To him, it was just another assignment. But for Mother Beloved it was more, much more. With her he had made his bones. He was a made man now, one she was fixated on. He felt the tension increase immediately between them, between him and Mother Beloved, and between her and Mer-

157

cedes. He looked at Erika only to find a mask of disgust on her fine features. He had fallen in her estimation: He was just another barbarian, the kind her mother loved and she loathed.

"You don't seem a violent man, Sam," Mother Beloved said. She was probing, looking for more information, for more details of his life. He would give her none. She was hooked. Now he would reel her in; her confidence in him, her infatuation with him, would serve better than any fishing tackle.

Sam glanced away, across the lawn stretching from the tented pavilion. He turned back, satisfied that his lunch on the grass would yield what he wanted.

"I have things to do," Erika said, standing.

"We all do," her mother countered, setting the record straight. "Mercedes and I will go to the stables. I'd like to show her how some of the horses are developing. I suggest you take a nap, Sam." She threw him a flirtatious look.

"Fine, it's just what I need," he said, glad of the opportunity to get off by himself, to think and evaluate.

Erika left without saying good-bye. The other two women rose and looked at Sam. "I'll just finish my coffee," he said.

"Sweet dreams," Mother Beloved said, leading Mercedes from the tent.

When Mercedes stole a backward glance, Sam noted the stricken look on her face.

To reassure her, he winked.

18

BIRDS OF A FEATHER

Valhalla Ranch
October 9

The lights of the Land-Rover pierced the darkness, scattering small animals, highlighting the puddles. An hour before, there had been a torrential downpour. The road was crude, just loose gravel, with deep grooves for the tires and lots of ruts. The Land-Rover bounced along, going too fast, overdriving its headlights, careening and fishtailing. At the wheel, Mother Beloved held the accelerator dangerously low. In the backseat, braced against the front seat and the sidewall, Sam Borne wondered just what she was trying to prove. Tough as the Land-Rover was, it wasn't designed to be driven so abusively; not to mention the discomfort such driving was causing the passengers, in this case Mercedes Coozi up front and him in back. They hit a particularly deep rut and Sam bounced up and struck his head on the roof.

"Christ," he hollered, "slow down."

"Don't be a pansy, Sam," Mother Beloved tossed back at him. "I know this road like the back of my hand, and I can handle anything that moves, especially this baby"—she patted the steering wheel with the heel of her hand—"so just relax and enjoy the ride."

There's nothing so aggravating as a directive that can't possibly be followed. Bouncing from one side of the road to the other, scraping the branches of the trees and shrubs on either side, they were only a hair's breadth away from going out of control, careening off the road and landing ass-up in a ditch.

In front, Mercedes, bracing herself on the dashboard, swiveled her head, half turning, flashing angry looks across at Mother Beloved and imploring looks back at Sam. Though frightened out of her wits, Sam noted, she wouldn't say anything. She was more than frightened of Mother Beloved, she was terrified of her, paralyzed by her, nullified by her. Sam had seen this happen before; tyrants were often able to frighten otherwise strong people into cowering submission.

Suddenly the lights splayed into an open area ahead and Mother Beloved jumped on the brakes. Skidding slightly, they slowed to a reasonable speed. Ahead, the road descended sharply. Below, the headlights illuminated a cluster of shacks sitting on either side of the road, which widened. Dogs, mangy and underfed, hovered around the shacks and strayed across the road. Scattered here and there, white chickens and reddish brown roosters pecked and scratched. At the sound of the approaching vehicle, children, dirty and dressed in rags, ran out of the shacks.

Riding the brakes, Mother Beloved jounced the Land-Rover down the slope and into the village. The children, excited, stood in the road, staring and waving. Behind them, the doors of the shacks opened, casting faint squares of light out into the road. In the doorways adults stood looking out. Once she hit level ground again, Mother Beloved stepped on the accelerator and the Land-Rover moved out quickly, splashing into the center of the village, the children jumping back to avoid the huge fans of water spraying out from its sides. Drenched, several dogs shied, then barked viciously, running beside the vehicle, only to be drenched again.

As they passed the shacks, Sam noticed that everyone started to move out, closing doors behind them, as if at some silent command. There was a quality, evident mainly in the children, that something was about to happen. Everyone followed the Land-Rover, the children running behind it, eager and expectant. From his seat in the back, Sam could see their faces clearly. Something was going to happen, something that had happened before, something they knew and apparently liked, if for no other reason than that it shattered the aching boredom of their lives in this hardscrabble village.

Mother Beloved hit the brakes and they stopped in front of a tar-paper shack with a corrugated tin roof, one much like all the others. She slapped the horn twice. The door opened. A grizzled man in a torn undershirt stood in the doorway, his belly flopping over his belt, his trousers hitched above his ankles, his feet bare. He wiped his eyes once, then held up his index finger. Behind him a woman appeared and tossed down a well-worn pair of boots. He bent and pulled them on, balancing himself against the doorjamb. When he straightened up, Mother Beloved flicked her index finger at him and he nodded understanding. She eased the Land-Rover forward, now trailing a line of children like the Pied Piper. At an opening between two shacks, she turned in and coasted down an incline, bouncing into and out of huge ruts. At the bottom the lights played on the sides of a wooden structure, three times as high as any of the shacks and ten times their size. It looked like a small barn. Mother

161

Beloved stopped before it and said, "Now you'll see something interesting, Sam, something I deeply love to watch." She climbed out, leaving Sam and Mercedes alone. Mercedes opened the door on her side and started to get out, then looked back and said, "Cockfighting."

Smoke hung above the crowd in blue layers. The crowd sat in bleachers along one wall, shouting bets to each other and encouragement to their birds. In front of the bleachers, on a wrought-iron bench, Mother Beloved sat between Sam and Mercedes. In front of them was the main pit, a sunken oval in the middle of the room, twelve feet wide and eighteen feet long; ringing it was a white wall nearly two feet high, most of it below the level of the floor. In the pit, the dirty sand floor was littered with feathers and spattered with blood. It reminded Sam that the word *arena* in Latin meant "sandy place," and that the Roman arena was the traditional setting for gladiatorial combat. The gladiators here were fighting cocks, most of them a mixture of red and brown, but some nearly all white, with only the odd red feather sticking out.

In front of them, across the pit, handlers cradled their birds in folded arms, like babies. They cooed to them, talked to them, stroked them. Part coach, part trainer, part parent, the handlers were passionate, each hoping his cock would be the champion, the one left standing when the matches ended. They stared into the pit, watching the elimination of bird after bird; watching the fat man in the torn undershirt, the referee, preside over the combat; watching the losers twitch in the sand, blinded, bleeding, dead or nearly dead. Above the pit hung hooded bulbs that shed an intense, cold light on it, flooding it with whiteness, setting it off from the dingy grayness in the rest of the building. Behind the handlers sat crates full of fresh cocks, their heads poking out between the slates, sometimes crowing.

"Isn't this the best?" Mother Beloved asked, throwing the question to Sam and Mercedes, not expecting or receiving an answer. She had sat enraptured for more than an hour, watching as bird after bird bit the dust, reveling in the agony, the passion, the triumph or disappointment of the handlers, alert to and enjoying the betting and the cheering of the people in the stands. To Sam it was all repulsive, lacking the true spirit of sport, devoid of the great human drama of, say, boxing; it was only a ritual, a cruel ritual, nothing more. He would as soon watch human beings knife each other to death as watch this senseless carnage; yet his face betrayed nothing; he was aware that his true feelings, revealed here, would jeopardize his position with Mother Beloved, would set her against him; this he couldn't afford. So he smiled at her when necessary, even shouted encouragement now and then, all the while controlling himself, thinking his thoughts, wondering when the opportunity to kill her would present itself, certain that he must do it swiftly, at the first opportunity; but patient, cautious, temporizing, knowing that the opportunity would present itself naturally, or, if it didn't, that he would create it; eager at all costs to do it professionally, with the least risk to himself and to Mercedes, and under the optimum conditions for them to make an easy escape.

In the pit a white cock lanced a red one. All the cocks wore pointed spurs made of surgical steel, about two and a half inches long. The referee in the torn undershirt, his hairy gut jutting out above his belt, stopped the match. Each handler grabbed his charge. The cocks were stuck together, unable to free themselves from the deep penetration of the spur, the red pinioned against the leg of the white. Like a man concerned to remove a thorn, the referee gently extracted the spur and the birds separated, the handlers snatching them back instantly. The handler of the red cuddled it, then, to revive it, stuck his finger down its throat and stretched out its neck.

Meanwhile, the handler of the white, a young man scarcely more than a boy, cradled his bird, cooing to it, stroking it, fluffing its feathers. He sensed victory. With this win he would be only one match away from the championship. The referee blew his whistle and indicated with a pointed finger the smaller pit, called a drag pit, perpendicular to the large one. The drag pit was used when one bird was no longer able to maneuver. The red, bleeding and dazed, its mobility shot, lay almost inert in its handler's arms.

The two handlers took their birds to opposite ends of the smaller pit and, at a blast from the whistle, released them. The red wobbled, unsteady on its claws. The white charged, attacking, and pecked out the red's remaining eye. Blind, beaten, the red, in a death panic, hopped and wobbled, ran in spurts, stopped. The white, tracking, attacked again, pecking the red relentlessly, clawing and thrusting. In a whirl of feathers, the red lost ground. Then, in an instant, the white scored with its spur, pinning the red dead still.

The referee stopped the match and the handlers grabbed their charges. When the referee extracted the spur, the red lay nearly lifeless in the fat hands of its handler, who, blowing on it, implored it not to die, then, knowing it was useless, wrung its neck. He tossed it disgustedly onto a pile of dead birds off to one side. The stage was set for the final match.

The crowd was abuzz, the backers lining up for this final match, the people wagering tiny amounts, sometimes not even currency, only objects, gambling reduced to barter; but they were avid, alive to the possibilities ahead, knowing the match could end in a matter of seconds or stretch on for minutes. There was an electric energy in the fetid air. The friends of the young man with the newly victorious white cock called encouragement to him, but he was busy with his charge, and limited his response to a few quick waves. He was stroking, caressing, rubbing and straightening his bird, blowing on its vent, pinching its neck, pulling on its yellow beak. And dreaming. He was dreaming of winning the pouch full of cruzeiros at Mother Beloved's feet, a leather pouch containing more money than he would earn in a month.

"Would you like to make a friendly bet on the outcome, Sam?" It was Mother Beloved. Sam turned and looked into her grinning face. She was alive to this in a way he never could be. She barely needed the added stimulation of a bet in order to achieve the fullest emotional jolt from the match, but it would not have been wise to turn her down.

"If you want to lose twenty-five thousand cruzeiros on the big red and brown, suit yourself," he said. It was worth the eighteen dollars to see Mother Beloved's face. She was ecstatic. "It's a deal," she said. "It's the choice I would have made if given one." Turning to Mercedes, she asked, "Would you like to get in on this, or not?"

Mercedes seemed for a moment not to know which choice to make. Sam was sure that, were he not there, she would have reacted quickly and naturally, but something held her back. She looked across Mother Beloved at him, and, knowing this was a mistake on her part, he hastened to lessen it. "Get in on it, Mercedes," he said. "We'll fleece her for the price of a good meal back in Rio." He laughed. Mercedes smiled and said, "Count me in for the same amount. I'm sure this big red bully will meet his match in our game little friend here, the white knight."

"You are both on. But it is I who will have a tremendous feast on you fools on my next trip to Rio, not the other way around," Mother Beloved said, her voice edged with more conviction than was called for. Sam was sure she thought Mercedes would side with her, against him, and she now had an intensified interest in winning.

The referee blasted his whistle, and all the hooting and hollering in the bleachers came to a halt. A deep quiet fell over the building. In the pit a man with a rake pushed the last bunch of pinfeathers between the comb of the rake and his hand and lifted it clear. The sand, stained with black spots from dried blood, was free of feathers, smooth, with only the swirls from the rake's tines forming tiny furrows. It reminded Sam in a flash of Kyoto, and he wished more than anything that he were there, meditating in the stone garden of Ryoan-ji, amidst the famous fifteen rocks, arranged in the serene five groups, with the sand all raked and symmetrical between. Instead he was here, about to watch a barbaric encounter between two fighting cocks, a useless perversion of nature, a pitting of nature against itself, something sure to fill any Zen master with horror. This was a peculiar rite he was about to witness, one that seemed so very Occidental, so raw and senseless, so without redeeming purpose.

In the pit the two handlers poised above their charges. The young man with the white cock, so recently victorious, showed the strain on his face. His counterpart was more relaxed, older, dressed in blue overalls with grease stains, a red kerchief knotted around his neck. He slowly stroked the huge red-and-brown fighting cock in his hands. His was the larger bird, and the more experienced, Sam would bet, just from looking at the face of the younger man across from him.

The referee blew his whistle again, and the handlers released the birds. They flew across the pit and hurled themselves at each other, both trying to score a quick kill, neither succeeding. They feinted, bobbed, hopped and flew. They pecked and clawed, clawed and pecked, hitting and missing, missing and hitting, neither able to gain the strong purchase on the other each sought. Finally they backed off, surveyed each other, the arena full of shouts and chants, the handlers roaring instructions at them, encouraging them, exhorting them. Then the red charged the white, who neatly flew at him, then hopped, leapfrogging him at the right moment, landing behind him, whirling around to see the angry red himself pivot and charge again. Again the white hopped him, skimming over him, crowing as he did. The crowd erupted.

To Sam it was gratifying to see this white bantam outwit his bigger, heavier, more experienced opponent. To Sam the white exemplified brains over brawn, one of the things he most liked to see in life. To Sam the white showed the best principles of a ninja, outthinking and outmaneuvering a more dangerous opponent. To Sam it was as though the white represented him in relation to the assignments the Committee always gave him; he was always going out against madmen, and madwomen, with the wherewithal to crush him effortlessly, and he had to outwit, outthink and outmaneuver them, and somehow triumph. No matter now that he had eighteen dollars riding on the white, he genuinely started to root for him, hoping he would once again demonstrate the superiority of the better prepared, the more thoughtful, the more resourceful warrior against a physically superior one.

Then the red nailed him. In a flash he moved on the white and pecked him swiftly, gouging out an eye. In a panic the white started to race around the pit, the red in hot pursuit. Sam wished then he could coach the white, talk to him, settle him. He was reacting, not thinking. He was stunned. The red caught him against the wooden wall of the pit and thrust his spur at him. The white twisted, dodging the spur. Again the red lunged, again the white whirled, narrowly escaping a spurring. Then the white scurried along the wall, the red pressing him relentlessly, wings beating against the white, trying to pin him. Finally the white broke through to one side and wisely, hopping and flying, propelled himself to the center of the pit, where he pivoted, backpedaling, and calculated right. The red came charging, high on his success, smelling the kill. The white waited, engaged him briefly in a whirlpool of feathers, then swung neatly to the side. The red lunged.

The white spurred him, impaling him savagely in the center of his heaving breast. They froze, welded together, the white starting to hop backward, dragging the heavier red, trying without success to free his leg. But the spur was much too deep, and the referee blew his whistle. The handlers leaped forward and cradled their birds as soon as the referee, almost gingerly, separated them. Each handler jostled his bird, the younger man wisely trying to settle the white, who sensed a kill and was overeager to consummate it; the older man trying to snap the big red back to alertness, hoping to accelerate his ability to shake off the daze he'd slumped into. The red had gone from top of the hill to bottom of the heap in a stroke. Now was the time the older man would find out whether his bird was a champion or not, whether he had the makings of a comeback in him. In Sam's credo, it was the measure of a boxer how many times he went down, the measure of a fighter how many times he got up. The same held for fighting cocks.

The referee blew his whistle, and the handlers brought their charges back to the center of the pit, holding them out at arm's length, ready to release them. The referee blew the whistle again, and the handlers released their birds. Immediately the white won Sam's heart. Standing stock-still, he let the red declare himself, which he did immediately, foolishly, predictably. Charging straight ahead, back on the aggressive, he shot at the white, headlong, unsteady, out of control. The white sideslipped him in a spin of feathers, then scurried backward, taking the red's measure, sidling out of his way as he charged again, pecking him, keeping him off balance. For a minute, maybe two, the white toyed with the red, wearing him down further, exasperating him, binding him tighter in his own rage. Then, with the red flustered and heaving, the white took his charge and parried it, spinning around him, planting himself behind him, greeting him when he turned with a spur right in the breast, pecking him simultaneously, taking an eye for an eye. And then another, rendering the big red blind and helpless, pinioning him. The crowd roared, those backing the white sensing their victory, the young handler holding his delirium in check, restraining himself, knowing that it was not unusual in a cockfight for a dying bird to mortally wound its opponent and score a victory.

In the bleachers everyone was on his feet, screaming, pounding each other on the shoulders and back, laughing. Sam looked directly at Mother Beloved, who, feeling his eyes on her, turned and scowled at him. He looked over at Mercedes. She was leaning forward, her fists balled, wailing. He looked back and saw the referee separate the birds, the handlers grabbing them instantly. The young man conducted himself magnificently, stroking the white, calming him, blowing on his vent. The older man stuck his finger down the throat of the big red, stretching out its neck, trying to bring it back. The red fluttered its wings, but it was listless, nearly inert.

As the tension mounted, the crowd whipping itself into full frenzy, the referee waited, allowing the handler of the red a chance. Then, finally, he blasted his whistle again and indicated the smaller drag pit at a right angle to the main pit. The handlers walked to opposite ends of the smaller pit, then stepped in, holding their birds, the white active, eager, the red motionless, dazed. The referee hit his whistle again, and the handlers released their birds. The white didn't hesitate. He charged the red and spurred him instantly, freezing him, casting both in a death tableau. The referee sounded his whistle and separated the birds. The white flapped triumphantly, in an access of energy, ready to fight again. The red collapsed into the hands of the older handler, bleeding, blind, listless and beaten. The handler put him down in the sand, and he keeled over. The crowd erupted, the younger handler all smiles; raising his arm above his head, he let loose an earsplitting whoop. The older handler retrieved the fallen red and wrung its neck before tossing it onto the heap of dead birds off to the side.

The referee raised the arm of the young handler above his head. Cradling the victorious white in the crook of his other arm, the young handler raised him shoulder high. They made a pretty picture, and Sam was happy for both.

When the crowd settled down, the referee walked the young man over to the bench and placed him directly in front of Mother Beloved. All smiles and grins, the young man kept bowing and nodding to her, his eyes leaping from time to time to the leather pouch full of cruzeiros. The crowd voiced its approval, clapping, whistling and shouting. Sam looked at the young handler and realized he couldn't be more than seventeen or eighteen. His face was flat, with high cheekbones and little beard; he was no doubt a *mestico* with a heavy dose of Indian blood. The white cock, Sam noticed, was still excited, flicking the reptilian inner eyelid of its remaining eye, the other a raw, empty red socket. It would be retired now, but retired a champion. The young handler would be able to charge a stud fee for its services. It would enter into the lore of the village, into the family lore of this deliriously happy young man.

Mother Beloved raised her arm, and the room silenced immediately. The young handler managed to stop grinning and stood before her like a new recruit before a general. She let the silence hang for a minute, then spoke sharply to the young man in Portuguese. From his Spanish, Sam could make out that she was asking him whether or not he thought he deserved the champion's purse. The young man hesitated, frozen with fear, uncertain what was expected of him, the capacity to think having abandoned him. His ecstasy could be washed away in a second, just like that. Ap-

171

prehension seized him. Then he said simply, "*Sim.*" He did not add another syllable. He let the one word speak volumes. He thought, and Sam agreed with him, that the simple word "yes" covered matters from A to Z.

Mother Beloved simply repeated his word, spitting it out contemptuously, then kicked the leather pouch full of cruzeiros at him. Some spilled out. The young man looked at her hard, winning Sam's further admiration, then stooped down and gathered up the money, pushing it into the pouch and, rising, holding the pouch aloft. The crowd erupted again, and the bleachers started to empty. The young handler stepped away from the bench and was soon hoisted aloft on the shoulders of friends. Still cradling the victorious cock in one hand, the pouch of money in the other, he rode the shoulders of his friends as they whooped and roared, writhing in a bulging conga line out of the building, everyone falling into line.

Mother Beloved sat with Sam and Mercedes until the building was empty, except for the referee and the man raking the pit. With only the scratching of the rake audible, she turned to Sam and said, "So I owe you twenty-five thousand cruzeiros. You can collect it when we reach the house." Turning to Mercedes, she said, "That goes for you too. And now," she continued, clapping her hands, "let's go to the house and enjoy a cool drink before retiring."

"That sounds like an excellent idea," Sam said, rising and stretching. The heat had been terrible, and his shirt stuck to his back. He would have liked to shower before drinks, but thought it best to go along with the program. Mercedes rose as well, as did Mother Beloved. While Sam and Mercedes walked outside,

Mother Beloved went over and said something to the fat referee in the torn undershirt.

Outdoors, the sky was carpeted with stars. Sam looked up and felt the majesty and wonder of creation again. Nature's magic never failed to exhilarate him. He only wished he could enjoy it under different circumstances. He wished he had the job over and were here in the jungle, like the Swedes and Germans and French who flocked to Manaus, to see this splendid side of nature free of care. Now that full night had descended, the air lacked the washed freshness it had had in the evening when they drove down, right after the downpour. The steamy heat was back; still, the night air was refreshing after the closed quarters of the pit building.

"She hates to lose," Mercedes whispered when they reached the Land-Rover.

"So do I."

"It's different with her. She makes people pay."

"Even over a little thing like a bet on a cockfight?"

"You'll see. She'll be in a mood now. I wish we'd lost."

"Bullshit."

Behind them they heard footsteps. They turned and saw Mother Beloved. Sam opened the door of the Land-Rover and climbed into the back. Mercedes got into the front and Mother Beloved slid behind the wheel. Before she hit the ignition, she turned in her seat and said, "So what were you two whispering about?"

Christ, Sam thought, on top of it all she's paranoid. It didn't surprise him. Most megalomaniacs were.

"You," he said, fighting fire with fire.

She hit the ignition, and the engine roared to life. She gunned it unnecessarily, dramatically.

"That's what I like about you, Sam, you're direct, like me," she said, slipping the Land-Rover into reverse. She turned to back away from the building and head out the way they'd come. Leaning over the seat, she looked right at him. "You might say we're birds of a feather."

"You might."

"So tell me, Sam, how do I know you're on the up-and-up?" Mother Beloved asked as they waited for the maid to bring them their drinks. She was sitting in one of the two stuffed armchairs flanking the big stone fireplace. Sam sat opposite her on one of the twin love seats separated from the armchairs by mahogany end tables. Mercedes sat across from him on the other.

"You don't," he answered, smiling. He was careful to look right at her as he said this.

"That's what I was afraid of."

"You don't really think I'd bring you someone who wasn't a respectable businessman, do you?" Mercedes said.

"I don't know what you'd do, Mercedes, and I wasn't asking you to join the conversation, that I recall." Mercedes's face colored. She looked down at her hands, in her lap, and Sam felt bad for her. She had ventured out and been burned. He was sure that was the last she'd be heard from tonight.

"Buying from an arms dealer isn't like shopping at a couturier," Sam said. "You don't operate in my business by spreading your name all over the place. You don't take ads in *Vanity Fair* or *Paris Match*. You try to keep your profile low. You trade instead on your reputation."

"Try not to belabor the obvious with me, Sam, and we'll get along much better." Mother Beloved paused as the maid brought in a large tray. On it was an ice bucket holding two splits of champagne, with champagne glasses turned upside down on the ice and with a bottle of cassis, a bottle of Chivas Regal and an Old-fashioned glass next to it. The maid took the champagne glasses out of the ice, popped each split and poured the champagne into each glass, then topped them with cassis. The champagne, tinged red, bubbled to the brim. Then the maid took the Chivas and poured it over ice into the old-fashioned glass. She handed the Kir Royales to each of the ladies and the Scotch to Sam. When she left through the swinging kitchen door, Mother Beloved spoke up. "I propose a toast to the successful conclusion of a mutually profitable business arrangement, Mr. Borne." She paused for effect as they raised their glasses before they actually drank. "Provided," she continued, "you meet with my approval tonight and tomorrow. Cheers."

They all drank, then sat in silence. Mother Beloved started to run her finger around the rim of her glass, setting up a beautiful humming sound. "You know, Mercedes," she said, "these glasses are the finest crystal, top-of-the-line Baccarat, given to me on the occasion of my unfortunate marriage by my loutish husband's maternal grandmother. She thought she'd got the perfect gift, and she had. I've always loved them. Like you, I love fine things, and this stemware gives me great pleasure. Paper thin, fragile, it's the best the world has to offer." She waited, letting the hum reverberate around the room, before turning to Sam. "Do you think, Mr. Borne, that you can deliver the world's finest merchandise?"

"If you can pay, I can deliver."

"Good. I like confidence in a man."

"What happened to your husband?" Sam asked, knowing perfectly well what had happened to him, but unable to control the urge to grill her as she grilled everyone else.

"He wasn't the best and I got rid of him."

"Short on confidence?"

"Short on a lot of things."

Wilda von Hoffer smiled at Sam over the rim of her glass, and his heart ached. As much as he'd grown to dislike this woman, there was no denying her beauty. With the fireplace behind her, sitting as though for a photographer, her long legs crossed sexily, she was stunning, a knockout. Though she misused it, her mouth was a masterpiece of sensuality, with thin lips, long and curved; and her face was mesmerizing, its fine bones showing through her tight skin the color of alabaster. Her blond tresses hung down on either side of her face, framing it perfectly, setting off the delicacy of her features, highlighting her deep blue eyes. Killing her would not be so easy after all.

"So tell me again, Mercedes, how you located this Mr. Sam Borne."

"I got his name from Geraldo. Then I cabled him in Monaco and he cabled back and now here he is, ready to do business."

"Geraldo's the colonel you're sleeping with?"

"Was."

"You've traded up?"

Mercedes blushed. Recovered, she said, "We're just friends now."

"You and Colonel Geraldo, you mean." Mercedes blushed again. Mother Beloved's meaning was clear. Sam could not risk intervening, though he wanted to; he would have loved to put this woman in her place, but the price would have been too high. He would put her in her place, permanently, soon enough.

"Yes," Mercedes said, her voice barely above a whisper.

"Well, it's time for me to hit the sack," Sam said, changing the subject.

"Good night, then, Sam, pleasant dreams," Mother Beloved said.

"Same to you."

"I think I'll retire as well. I'm exhausted," Mercedes said.

"No, you wait, I'd like a word with you," Mother Beloved said, her tone sharp and definite.

Sam rose and left. As he walked across the lawn to the guest house, he gazed at the stars blanketing the jungle sky. The fault was not in the stars but in ourselves, the Bard had written; yet it stumped him how nature could produce such exquisite beauty and then blight it as it had with Wilda von Hoffer, Mother Beloved.

19

HERE AND THERE

Sam Borne lay in bed, one hand curled under his head, the other holding a Gauloise. He was smoking slowly, letting the thick fumes wind above him, streaming toward the ceiling, where a large, old-fashioned fan with big, dark blades like sculling oars swirled them in its gentle breeze. He was thinking ahead, wondering what would happen in the morning. He had agreed, with Mercedes, to watch the morning workouts of the Thoroughbreds with Mother Beloved. This of course would be a pleasure for him. On many mornings, between assignments, he had haunted racetracks, watching the exercise boys work their mounts. There were few things like it, especially if you were lucky enough to be at Churchill Downs in May or at Saratoga in August. Here in the jungle, he was sure, Thoroughbreds would still work their magic.

It was the rest of the day he wondered about. What would he do? How would he occupy himself? It was clear that his best shot at Mother Beloved would come at night. During the day there was entirely too much activity around the ranch. There were too many people coming and going. There were the house servants.

There was the foreman, the guy named Aldo who functioned as the ranch's ramrod. He'd been introduced briefly to Sam earlier that evening before they went to the village for the cockfights. He struck Sam as a creep. From the start he'd given Sam hard looks, letting him know there was only one king of this roost, and he was it. Dark and handsome, well muscled and trim, he had gone to some lengths with body language to let Sam know he was more to Mother Beloved than another ranch hand. With pointed remarks, he established clearly, and clumsily, that he was her lover, before she cut him down to size, putting him in his place, not allowing him to come to the village, which he clearly wanted to do, making him instead stay behind and watch over things. When he skulked off, Sam was sure he had an enemy in him. No doubt Aldo would also prove an obstacle, if given half a chance, to a clean hit and a quick escape.

It all left no question in Sam's mind that the best time to hit Mother Beloved would be at night. Already he had calculated the distances from the main house to this guest house, from the main house to the stables, from the main house to the bunkhouses. In his mind he was sketching just how he could sneak from the guest house under cover of dark and use the shadows to his advantage. His ninja training had taught him the skillful use of darkness and shade, of shadow and light. He could sneak from the guest house to the main house undetected, he was sure, if there was anything less than a full moon, and the next full moon was not due for almost two weeks.

He had considered going in tonight, but he was hesitant. Another day of observation and reconnaissance would help immensely. He would concentrate all day tommorrow on how the ranch functioned, on how many people were where at any given time, on how much security the main house had. On the trip down to the village for the cockfights, he'd had an opportunity to see the security for the perimeter of the ranch firsthand, and it was extensive. There had been an electrified Cyclone fence all around the property, and when they left through the main gate, armed guards patrolled either side of it, each in his little kiosk, each with a control panel for releasing the main gate.

Mercedes had told him that armed guards with German shepherds also patrolled the perimeter, that the main house had a scanning room with a bank of television sets and a guard to monitor them twenty-four hours a day, that on the ranch's riverfront there was a double guard around the clock. This assignment would be no piece of cake. Assuming he could get to Mother Beloved, under cover of night, and kill her, he still had to consider his escape plans. Right away, he had seized on the idea of commandeering the Rallye and flying out of here. That idea might well work, but first he would have to know more about the night patrols. The Rallye was hangared in the barn very near the main house and within earshot of all the other central buildings. To spin its Lycoming's 235 horses in the dead of night would raise an enormous racket, arousing everyone on the ranch. Somehow he doubted the Rallye would be the best move. There was much to learn, much to discover, much to weigh and evaluate. He would have to be supersharp tomorrow, and he would have to pump Mercedes tonight for all the information he could get. All day he'd stored and filed questions for her. Now he was impatient to ask them.

He took a long pull on the Gauloise and wondered

what was keeping her. When he'd left, he noted the anxious look on her face. She was not comfortable around Mother Beloved, although so far he was certain she had behaved in a way not to arouse suspicions. But, with a character like Mother Beloved, you could never be sure just how much she was picking up without tipping her mitt. She had not risen to her present position without wiles and people-reading skills beyond the ordinary, and, though he wasn't paranoid about her, the longer he waited, the more uncomfortable he became.

He sat up and stubbed out his Gauloise in a Steuben ashtray on a teak night table beside the bed. Everything in the guest house, like everything in the main house, was top shelf. This drug business, whether you were in heroin or cocaine, was lucrative beyond imagining. The sitting-room furniture in the main house was ultrachic black Italian leather, the best Milano had to offer. On the white wall hung one of Jackson Pollock's more lyrical black-and-white paintings of the early fifties. The rugs were the purest white wool Sam had ever seen, and fluffy to the point where only the most uptight guest could resist slipping off his shoes and running his feet through it. Sam had not resisted.

He got out of bed, walked across the room to the window facing the main house, pushed back the curtain and looked across the lawn to the main house. In the darkness he could see only the lighted windows and the tawny squares of light they cast on the lawn. Then the door opened and Mercedes and Mother Beloved stood framed in the light. Before leaning over and kissing Mercedes on both cheeks, Mother Beloved shook her head firmly, denying her something. Mercedes stepped back slowly, as though making one last plea. Again Sam saw the taller woman in the doorway shake her head no, kiss her fingertips, flick them at Mercedes, then close the door in her face. Mercedes stood there a moment, then turned and headed toward the guest house. As she walked she kept her head down. Sam watched her all the way across the lawn. Then he heard her footsteps on the short porch, followed by the sound of the outside door opening and closing. She came into the narrow hallway in the center of the guest house, stood for a long moment before her door, then opened it and entered the room opposite his.

Sam was sure he'd heard a sniffle or two, and so did not go to her. He stepped away from the window, walked back to the bed and sat down. After a suitable interval he would go to her. But for now he would give her a minute. He considered lighting another cigarette, but resisted. He could not smoke nearly as much as he liked, so he rationed it. If he smoked as many Gauloises as he wanted, he'd be dead within the decade.

A knock on the door interrupted this thought. "Come in," he said. The door opened and Mercedes stepped in. In her left hand was a balled handkerchief. Her eyes were puffy and red-rimmed. As she looked at him tears welled in her eyes and she dipped her head. Sam went to her. Taking her in his arms, he cupped a hand behind her head and drew her to him. She rested her head on his chest, and he felt her sob. He stroked her hair slowly, then massaged her neck. He lowered his hand and stroked her back, murmuring softly against her ear, "It can't be that bad. Relax."

She loosed a big sob and blurted, "Oh, Sam, it is. It's worse than that. I'm terrified."

"Shhh," he whispered, "it'll be all right."

"No, no, it won't," she sobbed, then swiveled her

head on his chest and threw her arms around his neck. "I'm scared for you. You don't know what she's like."

"I have an idea."

"No, you don't."

Realizing this conversation would go nowhere, Sam changed tack. "What did she say to get you this upset?"

"She said she knew I was sleeping with you the minute she laid eyes on us at the airport. She is taking me away tomorrow, back to Manaus."

"So what? You were only intending to stay a day."

"I changed my mind. I wanted to stay, to help you. But she insisted I leave. She practically threw me out. She wants me out of here." She leaned back and looked up at him. Her face was stained with tears, her mascara had run. She looked as sad as a drowned clown.

"She's just jealous," he said.

"I know, but it's more than that. She wants you for herself. Don't think I didn't notice the way she looked at you." She sniffled and put her head back against his chest, digging her fingernails into his upper arms at the same time.

"Your imagination's running away with you." He wanted to soothe her, to calm her.

"I watched her look at you all day. I know that look. She had it for me. You're next."

"You're upset. You're not thinking clearly," he lied.

"I saw the whole picture just now. First she humiliated me. She made me feel the way the nuns in convent school used to. She made me feel like a whore, then she frightened me. I know she'll use you and discard you like so much Kleenex. I'm frightened for you."

If her obsession were not so deep, Sam would have

resented her low opinion of him. But he knew obsession, had studied it, even admired it; in art especially,
in literature most of all. Terror was just a form of
obsession. He would handle it, he would break it.
Right now he must bring her under control. This
upset, she was dangerous.

"Listen," he started, leading her by the arms over to
the bed and sitting her gently down on it, "everybody
is beatable. Nobody wins all the time. This Mother
Beloved is human, fallible. She'll trip up, like everybody else."

"You're wrong. She knows everything. She always
wins. She probably knows exactly what we're doing
now. She even said, 'Go sleep with him, he doesn't
strike me as the kind who waits well.' "

On that score, she's right, Sam thought, but he suppressed the comment. "That's ABC in human nature,
Mercedes. Everybody knows lovers are eager for each
other. What's new about that?" He hugged her. "Take
a deep breath, relax. It'll all work out, you'll see."

"No, I won't see. You're forgetting I have to leave
in the morning."

"You'll still know what happens. We'll still be in this
thing together."

"I know already what will happen. She will use you,
then kill you."

"I die hard. She won't kill me."

"She will. I know she will."

"Not if you help me."

"How? I won't be here."

"By answering my questions now. Can you do
that?"

"Yes."

"Okay. First, how many guards are out on the
grounds now, between here and the main house, be-

tween the main house and the bunkhouses and between the stables and the main house? How many are actually patrolling this central area?"

"None. That I know of."

"None at all?" From the window, Sam hadn't seen any either. Still, he found this hard to believe.

"She has guards on the gates, guards patrolling the fences and guards at the waterfront," Mercedes said.

"How about the house itself? Are there any guards inside?"

"No. None."

"What about the scanning room?"

"Oh, yeah. There's a guard on duty there all night. All day, too. All the time. Someone's always there."

That matched with what she'd told him earlier. He had to get Mercedes clearheaded, and fast. "So in the main house there is Mother Beloved, Erika, and the domestic staff, plus the guard on duty in the scanning room. Is that it?"

"Don't be silly. You saw Aldo. Most nights he's there too, although I'm sure he's about to be replaced."

That would be ideal. If in fact Sam got to sleep with Mother Beloved, conditions would be perfect for the hit. He could dispatch her easily. It was getting out afterward that he was concerned with now.

"How far is this waterfront?"

"About two kilometers."

"And you say there are two guards on it at all times?"

"Yes."

"What kinds of boats are docked there?"

"There's a launch and a runabout and a canoe or two."

"That's it?"

"Yes."

"How about the plane? Who besides her can fly it?"

"No one. She won't let anyone else touch it, though Aldo claims he can fly it. I think he's just bragging, though, strutting his machismo. I don't think he can actually fly it, but he can't stand the idea that she can and he can't, you understand."

"You've never seen anyone else fly it?"

"It would cost them their life."

"What is your relationship with Aldo like?" Sam asked.

"Why?"

"I need to know."

"It's all right."

This wasn't getting to the point. He would have to ask outright. "When you were involved with Wilda, what was Aldo like? Was he involved with her at the same time?"

Mercedes colored and dropped her head. "Yes."

"Yes, what?"

"Yes, he was involved with her at the same time."

"And he could handle it?"

"He didn't know."

"Know what?"

"That we were lovers. He didn't know we were involved with each other. Do we have to talk about this? I don't like to think about it, let alone discuss it."

"I'm sorry. I need to know."

"It was simple. We would make love in the afternoons, when he was forbidden the house. He would come at night. He thought all our time together was woman's time, just girlfriends. He never knew the other, the truth. Except . . ."

"Except what?" This kind of questioning was as awkward for Sam as it was painful to Mercedes. He

186

wanted an insight into Aldo, he wanted to know, even though he thought he already knew, how Aldo would react in the throes of sexual jealousy.

"Except . . ." Mercedes paused, dabbing her eyes, which again welled with tears. "Except one afternoon she invited Aldo and he took me while she watched, lying beside me, talking to me. He wore a goat's head, and lots of leather, but I'm sure it was Aldo." She cried, leaning against him. Then she whispered, "I'm so ashamed."

"Don't be."

"She made him leave immediately. Then she consoled me for hours, unknown to him, as a lover." She sobbed. "She had me completely under her power. She bewitched me. I couldn't say no to her."

"Shhh." He stroked her cheeks, pulling her tight against him.

"I'm so sorry."

"You don't have to be sorry on my account."

"But I am, I am. You're the best thing that ever happened to me."

"Shhh." Sam hooked his forefinger under her chin, raised her face and kissed her tenderly. She kissed him back with great passion. He caressed her, fondled her. Then he lowered her onto the bed and unbuttoned her blouse, kissing her all the while. As he leaned over her, bearing down on her, kissing her eyes, her neck, her throat, she suddenly pushed him away, both arms pressing against his shoulders. She sat up. He sat back. She looked at him for a long moment, then smiled.

She stood up slowly, walked to the switch on the wall, doused the overhead light. Then she moved to the bedside table and turned on a small brass lamp. Its red shade cast a ruby light. Silently she removed her blouse. Then she raised each leg and slipped off her low pumps. Winking at him, she loosened her belt, unhitched her slacks and let them fall to the floor. In her taupe bra and panties, she looked at him and smiled. Reaching behind her, she unclasped the bra and shucked it off. Her full breasts bobbed free. Hooking her thumbs in either side of her panties, she stepped out of them as gracefully as a ballerina. She was a vision in the red light, her hourglass figure tinged pink, her black hair hanging down on either side of her face, the ends falling on the swell of her breasts.

She stepped over to Sam and took his face in her hands. Kissing him softly, she reached down and unbuttoned his shirt. When she had the buttons undone, she slipped the shirt off his shoulders, then reached down and undid his belt. When the belt was free, she unhitched his pants and, taking his hands, guided him to his feet.

He attempted to kiss her, but she ducked away quickly, stooping to untie his shoes. When she had them free, she cradled his heels and pulled them off. Then she slid his pants down and off. Naked, he attempted to embrace her, but she pushed hard against his chest, forcing him back down on the bed. He reached out for her, but could touch no more than the tops of her shoulders. Her hair swaying above his flesh, just brushing it, sent waves of sensation shooting through him. But she wouldn't allow him to touch her, taking both his hands from her shoulders and pinning them against his legs.

He let his mind blank out. For what seemed like a short eternity, she ministered to him, the feeling like a thousand feathers brushing against him. Heaven could not be sweeter. When the tension verged near crescendo, she lightened her pace, extending his pleasure until finally his legs started to draw tight and quiver. Then, all in a rush, she climbed onto the bed and straddled him. The feathers were now angel wings, beating rapidly, carrying him higher, and higher still.

Through slitted eyes he saw her above him, riding with abandon, her eyes squeezed shut, her head thrown back. He stretched his hands out and caressed her breasts, the nipples taut against his palms. She moaned, leaning forward, rocking as far as she dared, moaning softly. Together they quickened their pace. Finally, when he could stand it no longer, he clutched her and ground her against him, arching himself hard into her.

"Oh, don't stop, Sam," she sighed, "don't stop."

He pulled her to him, driving into her, arching and thrusting. In moments she stiffened above him, her hands pressing against his chest. Under her he bowed his back, his body shaking, his release coming all in a wild rush. She let loose a long series of moans, then slumped down against his chest, curling into him, the tension gone from her, her mouth seeking his. For minutes she nestled against him, nibbling his jaw, his neck, his shoulder. She twisted a finger in his hair and curled it. She blew against his ear and twirled a finger around his lips. All the while, he stroked her, running his hands over her lovely hips, across her buttocks, around her back, over her shoulders. From time to time he leaned over and planted a peck on her cheek, her lips, her eyes.

"Can I stay the night with you?" she whispered, hugging his chest, her voice a little girl's. "Please?"

"Of course." He caressed the side of her face with the back of his hand, the knuckles gliding over her cheek, relaxing her. She buried her face in his shoulder. After a short while, he heard her breathing grow heavy. He pulled back the counterpane, lifted her gently and placed her under the covers. Drowsy, she whispered, "I love you," then subsided into sleep.

Sam lay beside her, his body emptied, his mind reeling.

An hour passed in the darkness, an hour during which Sam Borne's mind tumbled with thoughts of what the next day would bring. He reviewed a thousand times the various possibilities that could present themselves. He contemplated strategy, worked out scenarios, plotted courses of action. And still he was not tired, still his mind was not at rest. At times like these his Zen training saved him.

He rose and sat in the lotus position. His right foot resting on his left thigh, his left foot resting on his right thigh, he relaxed his shoulders, straightened his back, did not lean; placing his fists on either thigh, palms uppermost, he clicked his teeth together, lightly, at an even pace, thirty-six times, calming his heart. He would still his mind now, tempering it with good thoughts, priming it to enter meditation with pleasant thoughts peacefully contemplated. As was his habit, he cast his mind upon his most cherished memories. He thought of his days in ninja training with the great master Honzo Tenkatsu. They had been arduous years, but once his training was firmly in progress and on schedule, he had been able to bond closer with Tenkatsu, and the master had come to treat him like a son.

Before long they were taking holiday trips together, the old master showing him some of his favorite places, some of his most precious rituals. Together one April they followed the cherry blossoms north, hopping from town to town, staying in the best *ryokans*, the traditional wooden Japanese inns. Tenkatsu taught Sam the ineffable beauty of the cherry blossom; how to view it for hours, tuning in fully to its devastating intricacy; how to view its short life as a metaphor for his own; how to see its bloom as an emblem of nature's full possibility realizable within himself; how, like the cherry blossom, he too could bloom, however briefly, and thereby achieve all nature intended for him. In Japan this was a sacred ritual, viewing the cherry blossoms, and people would spend hours doing so; there was a word for it, *hanami*, and every April the Japanese would gather and view them together, sometimes by the thousands, such as in Ueno park in Tokyo, where often groups would drink and dance beneath the blossoms all day, laughing and reveling.

There were other trips. As Sam learned ninjitsu, he also became adept at Zen Buddhism. Tenkatsu instructed him well in this austere religion, with its emphasis on meditation, strict discipline and salvation through self-knowledge and self-reliance. Before long he took him for a visit to the temples at Kyoto. Ever since, it had been Sam's favorite city. There were those who extolled the virtues of Florence, especially in the late fall when the hordes of tourists receded and the city lay reposing under the slanting Tuscan sun, the Arno a fiery stream at sunset washing through the tawny hills. Sam had seen it then. He had seen Paris in May, and New York in October. He had seen San Francisco, Hong Kong, Rio. For him it was and always would be Kyoto; it was his favorite city, the one he revered above all others.

In his mind he returned there often, as now. He remembered the trips to see the famous festivals, es-

191

pecially the *aoi matsuri*, or Hollyhock Festival, held each year on May 15. Japan's oldest festival, and one of its most elegant, dating from the sixth century, it is famous for its procession, the centerpiece of which is a gaily decorated ox cart. On his first trip to see it, as the procession wound its way past, Sam had watched wide-eyed from the Kamigamo shrine, marveling at the bright colors and stunning patterns of the costumes, authentic re-creations of those worn centuries ago by noblemen and courtesans. He remembered particularly an imperial messenger and his retinue dressed in the style of the Heian period, from the eighth to the twelfth centuries, when Kyoto had been the center of turmoil, power and strife, when the arts had flourished, when such classics of Japanese literature as *The Pillow Book* and *The Tale of Genji* had been created. And he remembered the ox cart. In those earlier days, ox carts had been the principal means of transportation for the aristocracy. Decorated with hollyhocks, its huge wooden wheels intertwined with wisteria, drawn by a tremendous black ox garlanded with flowers, the festival cart was led by brightly costumed young girls, their red dresses matching the red silk tethers they guided the ox with, while a retinue of retainers, all dressed in white with black hats, walked on either side of them.

But most of all Sam remembered the horse racing. It was there his early addiction took hold. Standing at the Kamigamo shrine, he had thrilled to the races, the glorious horses decked in red silk bridles, large tassels depending from them, with matching saddle blankets; the jockeys dressed like ancient warriors, swords flapping from their sides. They had flashed past, the horses' hooves flying, their manes and tails whipping back in the air, the jockeys crouching forward. He had been captivated. The spectacle, the pageantry, the folk genius of the races had overwhelmed him. He had waited eagerly for the year to pass so he might see the festival again, and it had come around, and he had traveled with Tenkatsu and seen it.

And Tenkatsu had treated him to other delights of Kyoto. He had taken Sam to see the *gion matsuri*, another of Japan's big festivals, held in Kyoto each July. Famous for its parade of carts, this festival had thrilled Sam as well. He had watched the carts as they were dragged through the streets, towering and teetering, each with a history, each with a legend attached. And that had not been all. He and Tenkatsu had traveled to the city in August for the *daimonji okuribi*, or Great Bonfire Event. Because the Japanese visualize paradise at the tops of mountains, bonfires are lighted on the mountains surrounding the city to guide the souls of the dead safely there, instead of to hell. The dead souls who have visited during the eight days of the festival are those condemned to wander the surface of the earth; they are the ones the people are trying to light to paradise, relieving them of their suffering below. Knowing exactly what he was doing, Tenkatsu had taken Sam to the *ginkaku-ji*, or Silver Pavilion, directly in front of Mount Nyoigatake, the mountain on whose side the greatest bonfire is lighted, the fire in the shape of the Chinese character *daimonji*, which means "great." The origin of the Daimonji ritual is shrouded in mystery. The legend holds that when a temple which stood at the foot of the mountain burned down, the statue of Amida, the temple's chief object of worship, flew to the top of the mountain, shedding light along the way, guiding the dead souls to be reborn in Amida's Land of Bliss. The fire commemorates this miracle of the Buddha.

For Sam, it was all magical, Kyoto, from top to bottom, from the Shinto shrines to the Buddhist temples, from the perfect gardens to the majestic mountains, from the tranquil teahouses to the glorious rivers, on which one May Sunday Tenkatsu had shown him the *mifune matsuri*, or Boat Festival. In that festival, elaborately decorated boats had floated by on the river Oi, their prows supporting figureheads in the shape of dragons and phoenixes, while on their decks brightly costumed musicians played ancient instruments. The festival commemorated the boat excursions of the Heian court. Sam had reveled in all of it, would cherish all of it all of his days. Kyoto, mystical and beautiful, became the centerpiece of his personal mythology. He associated it with happy times, and with the highest expression of Japanese culture.

It was to that high culture that he harked back now, picturing in his mind's eye the beautiful *Kinkaku-ji*. This was the famous Temple of the Golden Pavilion immortalized in Yukio Mishima's novel of the same name. Built originally in 1397 by Shogun Ashikaga no Yoshimitsu to be turned into a Zen temple on his death, its walls entirely covered in gold leaf, it was burned to the ground in 1950 by a deranged monk, the hero of Mishima's novel. In 1955 it was restored exactly as before, and Tenkatsu had taken Sam there many times.

Sam pictured it now in sunlight, the golden phoenix atop its third tier glistening, bright and sharp, burnished by the sun's strong rays. In the lake beside which it sat he saw its reflection shimmering golden on the dark blue water, wavering, the red posts supporting its first tier undulating in the lake's steady current. In memory he entered and stood in the large room on the first floor, enjoying the outstanding examples of

Heian architecture and furniture. Then he climbed to the second floor and looked around at the open temple hall. Eager now, he climbed the final flight of stairs and entered the small, spare room that formed one of the greatest Zen cells ever.

He came forth, into the room, and assumed the lotus position, as he now sat on the bed next to Mercedes, and his mind went forth, tripping over happy memories, free of the tension of the assignment. He visualized himself walking the stone pathway between bamboo railings that led to the stunning tearoom at Koto-in, another masterpiece of Kyoto. He saw the pathway in autumn splendor, with the maples forming a red and orange canopy overhead. He remembered being there with Tenkatsu, taking tea, relaxing, speaking of noble things, dreaming big dreams, awaiting the fate life held in store for him, its joys and sorrows, its triumphs and failures. They sat, sipping luxurious green tea in gray cups, and spoke for hours. Mostly Tenkatsu spoke, Sam listened; mostly Tenkatsu taught, Sam learned.

Totally relaxed, Sam's mind suddenly shifted, flashing onto a black ink landscape by the great artist Sesshu, a master who flourished in the fifteenth century. He saw its blacks and grays against its white background. He saw the lines that represented a tree, the brush strokes that represented grass. He loved its economy, the severity of it. He loved the way it evoked rather than depicted. He loved its primacy of mood, its emphasis on control, its homage to tranquillity. He wished that he could disappear into that landscape, to embrace its spirit, to be subsumed in its aura, to feel fully and everlastingly at one with nature, part of the great design, in synchronicity with the grand scheme.

His breathing dropped. His heartbeat quelled. His

mind blanked. He was nearly there. His lips softly chanted the single word he loved above all others. *"Heiwa,"* he whispered. *"Heiwa."* It was the Japanese word for peace.

In a transport, he was there. Totally at rest, cosmically calm, he was in full meditation, in full *satori,* seeing the world unfold in its oneness, no dualism impeding him, no logic hampering him, just pure perception, pure oneness, himself one with all things, all things one with him.

"Heiwa."

20

RAILBIRDS

Mist rose off the jungle like burning incense. White and wispy, it hung in the air above the first layers of green, peeping through as the rays of the sun grew strong, burning into the mist, penetrating it, dissipating it, making it give way to the insufferable heat that would mount and mount through midday all the way to dusk; the jungle heat would grow, the sun baking into everything, replacing the mist with a haze that would sit on the skin like sopping gauze, wilting the spirit, tiring the body, stilling almost all action.

But now in the earliest hours of the day, dawn just gone, the air was pleasant, the heat bearable, the spirit buoyed. The beauty of the jungle, at daybreak and just after, was underrated. Or so Sam Borne thought as he leaned on the white rail and watched the exercise boys work the Thoroughbreds, leading them onto the track, trotting them slowly at first, then breezing them, then actually pushing them, galloping flat out under simulated race conditions.

It was the best time of day, the morning. In the morning everything seemed possible. In the morning the body was refreshed, the mind aquiver with possibilities, the setbacks of afternoon still hours away, the disappointments of evening only a lurking possibility. In the morning all achievement seemed imminent. It was clear to Sam what he wanted to achieve. He wanted to set Mother Beloved up, to gain her confidence, to consummate with her a phony arms deal; to have her present him, in her confidence, with the perfect opportunity to eliminate her and escape this jungle. He wanted to be done with this assignment, to have it behind him, not to have to think longer about what eliminating such a beautiful creature really entailed.

He looked at her now. She stood in a tower across the track from him, binoculars hung around her neck, wearing jodhpurs and riding boots, a quirt under her left arm, a stopwatch in her right hand. She stood all alone in the tower, at the finish line, a walkie-talkie resting on the ledge in front of her. From time to time she would pick it up and talk into it; then, from around the dirt track, at the head of the backstretch, Aldo would start the horse she wanted to time. The horse, exercise boy up, would tear down the backstretch, circle the far turn, hit the top of the stretch, then sprint down to the finish. Mother Beloved would thumb her stopwatch, check the time and talk again into the walkie-talkie. She would make notes and markings on a chart she held on a clipboard. Then she would pick up the walkie-talkie, and Aldo would start another horse. The process would repeat itself. It was a pleasant way to start a day, and Sam only wished he could have experienced it under different circumstances.

"I'm depressed."

It was Mercedes, at Sam's elbow. He turned and looked at her, then touched the collar of her blouse and pulled it up. He straightened a few strands of

198

straying hair, patting them very gently behind her ear. Then he smiled at her, checked to make sure no one was in earshot and said. "Don't be. This will all be over soon. Remember why you got into it in the first place."

"That's just it, I *can't* remember why I got into it in the first place."

"Sure you can. You wanted to put a stop to the madwoman across the way."

"It doesn't seem important now."

"Sure it does."

"No, what seems important is us. I never dreamed they'd send somebody like you to do the job. And I'm afraid you can't. I'm afraid you'll be killed, and I don't want to lose you." She dropped her eyes and studied her hands, nervously placing one on top of the other on the rail. Sam reached out and pinned her hands under his. When they were still, he withdrew his hand. She looked away, down the track, toward the top of the stretch. He shot a glance quickly over to the tower and was relieved to see Mother Beloved hunched over her clipboard. She hadn't been watching them. Sam did not want a scene. And anyone could read the kind of body language Mercedes was using. Without looking at her or touching her, without indicating concern or sympathy in any way, he said, "You can't do what you're about to do. You'll get yourself killed. You'll also get me killed. If you care the way you say you do, you'll rein in your emotions and play this thing like a pro. You can do it."

Behind him the sound of pounding hooves grew loud. He turned, not knowing what to expect. A vision greeted him. On a large roan gelding, Erika rode up to them, all in tans and browns, her hair pinned up under a riding cap set at a jaunty angle. She cantered up to them, then stopped a few yards off. Sam decided to wing it, hoping Mercedes would recover, overcome her mood, get a grip on herself.

"Good morning, Erika," he said, letting Mercedes know who had arrived.

"Good morning, Mr. Borne. Good morning, Aunt Mercedes."

"Good morning, Erika," Mercedes said, turning and, much to Sam's relief, smiling.

There was a moment of silence; then Erika said, "Was Mr. Borne regaling you with one of his murder stories?"

"That's not very funny, young lady," Mercedes said, her voice arch. "Apologize immediately for your rudeness."

"I don't like murder stories or people who tell them," Erika said, "and I don't see why I should apologize. I've had enough murder in my life without visitors adding their stories."

"You're entitled to your feelings, but you had no right to insult Mr. Borne for merely honoring a request from your mother. So an apology is in order."

"He could have resisted. He could have ignored her request."

"She is a hard woman to resist or ignore," Mercedes stated.

"Don't I know. Still, it could be done," Erika said.

Sam spoke up. "I'm sorry if it upset you so much, Erika. If I had known it would have this effect on you, I would have abstained," he lied. There was no way he could have allowed Erika's delicate sensibility to interfere with the relationship he had to establish with her mother, to set her up for the hit, but he didn't want to exacerbate Erika, he didn't want to alienate a creature so innocent, and one with reason and righteousness clearly on her side. It wasn't just that Erika was young, it wasn't just that she was unspeakably beautiful, even surpassing her mother, it was that she was right; she represented civilization and all that Sam held precious in life. She represented goodness in this corrupt setting, this environment dedicated to evil and its perpetration. "So I apologize for bad judgment," he added, "but not for the act itself. I hold no brief for terrorists."

"Then you shouldn't get in bed with my mother."

She had him. This was no ordinary teenager, inside or out. She was dead to center right. And Sam had painted himself into a very embarrassing corner. There was nothing to do but play along with her interesting choice of metaphor.

"Politics makes strange bedfellows of us all," he said, thinking that in time she would hark back to this answer and see its true significance.

"It's probably more a case of money than politics."

"The two are inseparable," he said. "You'll see that more clearly when you get older."

"It's clear enough now, thank you."

"*Basta,*" Mercedes snapped. "Enough debating. You owe Mr. Borne an apology, and I want to hear you give it to him now."

"I'm sorry, Mr. Borne," Erika said, softly but firmly. She was not. Sam realized the effort it took for her to make this false apology. He wanted to soften its sting as much as possible.

"I'm sorry, too," he said, "and I'll do my best to see that I don't offend you again." He looked at her as tenderly as he could, and to his delight she cut him a look of sympathy, not of contempt. There was a definite and heavy attraction between them, and he only wished he could capitalize on it immediately. She needed badly to be out from under her mother's noxious influence, to be set free in a world where her finer feelings and instincts would not be constantly violated.

The sound of thundering hooves rose behind them. They turned to see a gray colt tearing down the stretch, the exercise boy crouching in the stirrups, whipping the young colt's right shank, really pushing him. They drew nearer, then flashed past. Sam looked up and saw Mother Beloved press her stopwatch. Smiling, she picked up the walkie-talkie and said something excitedly into it. Then she leaned on the railing of the tower and shouted toward them, "That's the one I told you about, Mercedes. He's a future stakes winner, I assure you."

"That's Blitz, is it?"

"Yes. Isn't he marvelous?"

"Yes."

"Did you see him start?"

"Yes." Mercedes was lying. They had all been talking, backs turned, when Aldo started the colt. With Mother Beloved, Mercedes always took, Sam noted yet again, the path of least resistance. He would be relieved when she was out of the picture. When on an assignment, he liked to have as little to worry about as possible, and Mercedes was just not solid enough, not reliable enough, for him to feel comfortable with her as an ally, let alone a backup. She was a glorious woman, a wonderful woman, but somewhere along the line, in her home or in convent school, the core of her personality, her sense of self, had been too eroded, too vitiated for her to reconstitute herself fully, at least in time to be the kind of backup Sam liked to work with. So it was best that she was going. He only hoped nothing happened between now and the time she parted to jeopardize his mission.

"Do you know what his time was?" Mother Beloved shouted.

"No," Mercedes replied.

"It was one eleven and four-fifths. Not bad, eh?"

"Wonderful."

"And he's only going to be a three-year-old when I race him in the spring. Just watch out then."

"I can't wait."

"Now I have something special for you, in honor of our guest, Mr. Borne. A little match race."

Sam looked across the track and saw Aldo standing between two horses, both held by stable hands. He saw Aldo listen to the walkie-talkie. A quick glance at the tower showed Mother Beloved giving instructions into it. Then across the track Aldo nodded and spoke a word or two. He looked up and instructed the stable hands holding the two horses, then raised his arm, only to drop it quickly as the starter gun went off. The two horses roared away, streaking down the back-stretch. In the tower Mother Beloved watched, glancing at her stopwatch when the horses hit the far turn, then again when they reached the top of the home-stretch. It was a fairly even race, but in the stretch the horse on the rail, sorrel with a prominent blaze, started to pull ahead of the dark colt on the outside. By the time the inside colt hit the finish, he was a good length ahead of the other. In the tower Mother Beloved hit her stopwatch and looked at it quickly.

"That was not bad either," she shouted across to where they stood. "Not as good as Blitz, but not bad. One fourteen and a fifth. It will bring in a couple bucks next spring." She picked up the walkie-talkie and spoke briefly into it, then filled out her chart on the clipboard, climbed down and crossed to them. As she drew up to them on the track side of the rail, she had a smug look on her face. "Well, Sam, you see the pleasure I derive from watching beautiful animals perform at their best. They *are* beautiful, aren't they?"

"Yes, they are."

"I have always been fascinated by the results of breeding the best to the best. It's a shame it isn't regulated the same way among us humans, no?"

Not for nothing was she a Nazi. The question hung, awaiting an answer. Sam felt over his shoulder the pressure of Erika listening for his response.

"Natural selection has its attractions," he said.

"Ach, you Americans are all hopeless. If you're not democrats, you're romantics, sometimes, God help us both. Your failing is the world's tragedy."

"That's one way to look at it."

"That's the only way, Sam, only you Americans will never wake up to that simple fact in time to undo the damage you've already done."

"Fill me in on this later. I haven't had any breakfast."

"That's just what I'm talking about. No manners. No savoir faire. But fortunately I was about to suggest we all go over for breakfast."

"Good idea," Sam said, realizing that he would have to pull back. He had been dangerously close just now to entering into a real argument, one he couldn't afford to enter because there was no way he could win. Even if he won, he lost.

"Let's go," Mother Beloved said, and they all traipsed off toward the main house, Erika walking her horse behind them. When they reached the house and settled in the dining room, it wasn't long before Aldo joined them. He was, as usual, hostile. After discussing with Mother Beloved the various times the horses had achieved that morning, he lapsed into a sulk as she showered all her attention on Sam.

Finally, when they were finished, each sipping a final cup of rich Brazilian coffee, Mother Beloved said that she would meet Mercedes and Sam at the barn in ten minutes. Sam had not known till then that he would be flying to Manaus with them. He had assumed that Mother Beloved would fly down with Mercedes alone. This was not her intention. He hadn't figured on being invited. His pulse raced, his spirit soared. It was too good for words. This would be one of the easiest assignments he'd ever had. He would simply overpower Mother Beloved, kill her, take over the plane, fly him and Mercedes out of the jungle.

"Mother, please, I want to go," Erika said, a pout creeping into her voice.

"No, you cannot. Not this time."

"I want to be with Aunt Mercedes as long as possible. I want to fly today."

"I said no."

"Please."

"Do not disobey me. Act like a woman, not like a child," Mother Beloved exploded. She was angry, her color rising.

Erika was also angry. And embarrassed. Throughout the meal, she had been sneaking looks at Sam, some of which he had caught and returned. To be admonished now not to act like a child in front of him was more than she could bear. "I am not acting like a child. I would like to go. I want to fly with you."

"No. I forbid it. Now drop the subject."

"*Du hure. Du scheisshure.*" In German Erika called her mother a whore, then a shit whore.

Sam sipped his coffee, perfectly aware of what had

been said, trying like a gentleman to ignore the situation. In a sputtering stream of German, Mother Beloved berated her daughter, calling her much worse things than a whore. In a rage, she demanded that Erika apologize, then leave. Erika refused. Finally, frustrated, Mother Beloved rose from her place at the table and started around it to where Erika sat. Before she arrived there, Erika rose and started toward her.

Aldo leaped to his feet and interposed himself, grabbing Erika firmly about the torso, hauling her backward, pinning her arms and crossing his leg in front of hers in such a way to prevent her from kicking. Planting herself in front of her daughter, Mother Beloved slapped her several times, very hard, fanning her open palm across her face, catching her with a backhand on her return swing. The slaps reddened Erika's face, and when Mother Beloved finally stopped, a trickle of blood oozed from Erika's nose. Humiliated, Erika broke into tears, more from psychic than from physical pain, Sam was sure.

All his body aching to go to her aid, Sam managed to restrain himself. He wanted more than anything to rise and pull Aldo off her. His hands trembling slightly with the effort to cancel his natural impulses, Sam looked away. Glancing briefly at Mercedes, he saw her pain, but could not afford extended eye contact with her.

As Erika hung in Aldo's hands, her head down, ashamed, embarrassed, humiliated, Mother Beloved turned to the table and said, "Please leave. I will meet you in ten minutes' time in the barn. I am sorry you had to witness such a scene as this."

So am I, Sam thought as he rose and left with Mercedes, whose eyes, he now realized, were glassy with tears. It would be good to get airborne, to get Mother

Beloved away from the ranch, away from her personal army, up in the wild blue where he could kill her and stop her personal reign of terror. It would be good to get even with her for all the people she'd beaten, abused or murdered, not the least of whom was soft-hearted, steel-willed Erika.

21

ESCORT SERVICE

Amazon Basin–Manaus
October 10

Sam sat in the back right-hand seat of the Rallye. He had deliberately chosen the seat on the right-hand side so he might more easily observe Mother Beloved's flying technique. He wanted to see just how good a flier she was, and he wanted something to occupy his mind on the flight to Manaus, now that Aldo sat beside him. He had not figured on the ramrod being along, but when he and Mercedes had arrived at the barn, Aldo had been there, standing beside the Rallye, ready to go. Mother Beloved had smiled and said that Aldo was her escort service, supplemented today by him, Sam Borne. Thus were his plans of an easy takeout shattered.

They were cruising now at 7,500 feet, their heading 30 degrees. It never failed to make Sam feel that some cooperation was possible among all people when he considered the international laws governing the skies. No matter where you were in the world, if you were flying above three thousand feet on compass headings of 0–180 degrees, you were to fly on odd thousands plus 500 feet; on headings of 180–360, you were to fly on even thousands plus 500 feet. Simple. And it made for safety and order for everyone. Yet on any other issue, there was international chaos. Everyone was too busy trying to fuck over the next guy to think maybe everything could be worked out if people just put their cards on the table and behaved like civilized human beings with IQs in three figures. But that's the way it was, chaotic, and Sam wasn't about to hold his breath waiting for it to change.

They were flying in an almost cloudless sky, blue and clear as far as the eye could see. Below they passed over the same terrain Sam had observed the day before on the trip from Manaus to the ranch. The jungle cover was triple canopy, lush and thick, uninterrupted green everywhere except where the brown tributaries of the mighty Amazon snaked toward that monster river, still some distance ahead and to the west. They would pick up the Amazon a few miles from where its brown waters merged at Manaus with the black flow of the legendary Rio Negro. The day before, on his trip around Manaus with Mercedes, Sam had seen the confluence of the two rivers from the floating dock, and had marveled at how the different-colored waters merged but didn't mingle. He had been told that the Amazon flowed for hundreds of miles, almost to the sea, with the separate colors still distinct. It was only one of millions of marvels this renowned river embodied.

Every once in a while, he would see below the raging fires of the jungle, where ranchers were clearing land in the slash-and-burn Brazilian tradition. The orange flames would leap high above the jungle green, their black smoke billowing even higher still, drifting like low-lying thunderclouds for miles. It was an awesome sight, one that was oddly disconcerting.

Sam turned back from the canopy and looked at Mother Beloved. She was flying casually, her hands resting on the yoke, chatting in Portuguese with Mercedes. Sam could understand enough to tell that they were again discussing horses, that Mother Beloved had filled Mercedes in on some romantic adventure she'd had in Ireland, that she was recommending a new dress shop for her to try in Rio. Sam had noticed when Mother Beloved was describing her Irish escapade that Aldo, beside him in the back, had begun to fidget with his trousers, adjusting them in the crotch more than could be necessary short of a virulent case of jungle rot. He was angry, jealous, and unable to conceal it. It amused Sam.

Mercedes, Sam was relieved to note, had gotten herself completely under control. She and Sam had had a brief ten minutes together after breakfast. They had commiserated with each other over Erika's barbaric treatment, being slapped around like a slave, but then Sam had worked Mercedes for what parting information he could get. She had told him that Mother Beloved insisted that she check in for a night in Manaus at the Novotel Hotel. She was to take a pouch from Mother Beloved with her. She was to go out to dinner, and when she returned the pouch would be gone. Mercedes had done similar chores for Mother Beloved before; this time, she asked Sam directly to confirm her suspicions that Mother Beloved was involved in drugs. She said she had heard once from a mutual friend in Rio that Mother Beloved had a network that carried cocaine out of Manaus for her on the Air France flights to Europe. She knew no more than this.

Of course, Sam knew from his Committee dossier that this was accurate. He also knew that the cocaine left Manaus broken down into smaller, more easily concealed containers than the pouch Mercedes now carried in her suitcase. A network of Air France flight personnel, including pilots, concealed the coke in their specially designed flight luggage, the kind the airlines issued but which Mother Beloved had had carefully altered by clever Brazilian tailors in Rio. Their flight bags had the thinest of double linings, an inner wall, into which the coke was poured, then carefully smoothed down. It all worked like clockwork, and the carriers were raking in money nearly equal to their annual salaries from the airline, which ran the 747s into Manaus twice weekly, so Mother Beloved never had to worry about serious lapses in her distribution schedule. Once the coke was in France, it was picked up by her dealers, who spread it into every country in Western Europe, with a heavy concentration in West Germany, France and northern Italy.

Sam was struck again with wonder at the thoroughness of the Committee's information, how it seemed to know everything, worldwide. And its preparation was always just as thorough. This time, for instance, the Committee had provided him with Mercedes Coozi. She had been a big help so far, but he was glad he would soon be solo. Mercedes was a bit too nervous and jittery for this kind of work. Usually the Committee provided him with the best peripheral personnel, whether they were just escorts, such as those he'd had on his last assignment, the trip into Vietnam to knock off Doctor Sun Sun and his personal army, or whether, like Mercedes, they were more intimately involved, acting like her as agents provocateurs. Sam had never had, and wasn't eager to have, a full partner in his ventures. He'd never worked with anyone who'd had nearly the attention and training he'd had from the

Committee. As far as he knew, he was the only fully trained ninja, commando and actor the Committee had at its disposal.

The Committee was the shadowiest organization Sam had ever known. He had never met anyone who would admit to belonging to it, or even to knowing of its existence. When he was picked out in Japan, tested and trained, all during his ninja sojourn in the mountains with Honzo Tenkatsu, all during his years at the Royal Academy of Dramatic Arts, throughout his years at the Defense Language Institute Foreign Language Center, whenever he had been assigned to a base for training, whether it was Fort Gulick in the Canal Zone for jungle fighting and survival training, or Pensacola Naval Air Station for flight training in jets, no matter if it was Fort Leavenworth for cavalry duty or Fort Wolters for helicopter training, no matter where Sam was, no matter who was entrusted with his training, no one would admit to him the existence of any controlling organization, not even his beloved mentor Tenkatsu.

He had no proof of the Committee's existence until he was sent on assignment, when he'd always receive a dossier with a detailed profile of the target and all the facts necessary to understand the target and his or her operation. That was all. No corroboration. No proof. Just the dossier, the airline tickets he'd need to get to wherever the target operated, and always, always, there would be the simple phrase at the end of the dossier, after the standard complimentary closing of "Gratefully yours": THE COMMITTEE. That was all.

Not that Sam hadn't asked about the Committee time and again. In each place he'd been assigned, there had been someone charged with overseeing him. On all the bases he'd had a commanding officer, a sort of case officer, to whom he would report and who would take special charge of him, checking on his progress, seeing that all training would have the desired results. Sam didn't mind so much, just so long as the case officer didn't single him out for special treatment or privileges the other guys in the training program didn't get. Whenever Sam confronted these special officers about the Committee, they would always give him the standard treatment, always act as though his imagination had run away with him. "What committee?" was always the stone wall they threw at him.

He had grown quite fond of some of the people who'd trained him along the way. Not, for sure, as fond as he'd become of Honzo Tenkatsu, but still very fond. There had been an old sergeant at West Point one summer when Sam was sent there to take some basic computer courses and to get a feel for the campus, should he ever need that background available to him for an assignment, and that old sergeant, named Kelly, had taught him in long hours in the gym the more advanced techniques of boxing. They had worked for hours on the heavy bag, the speed bag, the medicine ball, and Sam had excelled at all of it, being superbly conditioned and with the quickness and reflexes of a cat, until Kelly had worked him in the ring, sparring with him for hours. This had been a severe challenge, for Kelly had been the Golden Gloves champion of New York before entering the service, ignoring offers to turn pro, and Sam had had to scramble at first to keep clear of all the old sergeant's tricks, like thumbing, but he learned much about fistfighting.

When he'd gotten better, toward the end of summer, the old sergeant had packed him into an olive-green Ford and driven him down to New York City, a place that always made Sam's heart jump, and there he'd worked him against serious middleweights, light heavies and heavies in Gleason's gym on West Thirtieth Street. It was an experience Sam had cherished. He had fought guys who'd later been ranked, and, in the case of one light heavy, even a champion. But he'd always held his own, even as he learned from these more experienced boxers. Of course, during these bouts Sam had martial arts moves available to him that would have stopped all these boxers dead, literally, but it wouldn't have been sporting to use them and, anyway, he wanted to learn the manly art and that's what the Committee, through Kelly, was trying to teach him.

That's how the Committee had always worked, through people, and by indirection. For instance, while he learned computers that summer at West Point, he also learned boxing. While he mastered the art, philosophy and techniques of the ninja with Honzo Tenkatsu, he also absorbed the tenets of Zen Buddhism. While he studied acting for years in London, he also took trips to the Continent on school holidays, learning his way around Paris, Berlin, Rome, Lisbon, Amsterdam, Madrid and countless other European cities. Often on these trips he'd have a fellow student with him, usually an actress, and it would always turn out that she couldn't wait to show him the Goyas in the Prado, the Botticellis in the Uffizi, the Rembrandts in the Rijksmuseum or the Cézannes in the Jeu de Paume. There had been one memorable trip through Ireland with a red-haired Irish actress who'd insisted on reading Yeats aloud and on visiting the great man's grave in Drumcliff churchyard. And there'd been the time he'd met the art student from Temple University's Tyler School studying in Rome for a year and she'd taught Sam the finer points of classical architecture up and down the Italian boot.

All of this amazed Sam. The Committee had educated and trained him to a fine point. Always they had functioned like an unseen hand. At Monterey there had been Sergei. He had taught Sam all about European history, and all the while he'd done it, Sam had learned Russian and enjoyed himself. Sergei had also directed his reading while he studied other languages at Monterey; he'd read almost all the classics of European literature and history. Indirection again. And while at Monterey there had been the trips up the coast on Fridays to polish his improvisational skills at that small nightclub, little more than a boîte, in North Beach. Every minute had been utilized, every opportunity maximized. It was all a grand design, all a planned existence. Sam was a made man, not a self-made man; he was a finished product, a finely tuned machine. And so far as he knew he was unique. Never had he come across anyone approximating his life experience, and he was fairly certain he never would.

Yet his life was an enigma. He wanted to settle down in the Midwest teaching literature and raising a family, bringing up a son he hoped would be a world-beater at shortstop, yet he inwardly distrusted this dream existence, even as the Committee never let him realize it. He had written letters to case officers, importuning them to deliver the letters to the Committee; pleading letters, letters in which he begged to be allowed to retire, to live this idyllic life, and always they had been silent. Only once, in a dossier, had the Committee commented on his request, saying merely, IT'S NOT FOR YOU.

In his heart Sam knew what they meant. He knew it as surely as he knew he couldn't give up Gauloises completely, only moderate their use; he knew it as surely as he suspected, in his heart, that he wasn't a one-woman man, or, for that matter, cut out to be a father. From experience he knew that between assignments he grew restless, bored, irritable; he needed the surge action offered, the rush danger gave him. Still, he felt entitled to at least try this Midwestern fantasy, and when between assignments once he exchanged his airline ticket to a resort in Sardinia for one to Chicago, from which base he intended to light out for the heartland, the Committee had come down on him. He had been subjected to all kinds of trouble getting into the country at passport control, and then in the customs office he had been quarantined until some military officers showed up and took him to a hotel room, where a man representing the Committee had spoken to him on the phone. That voice was the nearest he'd ever come to direct contact with a ranking Committee member.

It had been unnerving. The man had told him coldly that within twenty-four hours of being released from Committee control, he would be extradited and indicted on any number of assassination and murder charges. It was a double whammy; he was in the middle, jeopardy ahead, jeopardy behind, no place to hide. Sam's blood ran cold. Of course, with all the hits he'd put on people, he could easily be put away or executed on real charges. Nothing would have to be trumped up. He'd done it all. But that was the thing. The Committee had had him do it.

But, truth to tell, no one he'd bumped off for the Committee was someone he wouldn't have killed for himself. All of the targets were malevolent in one way or another. Just plain bastards. Killers and exploiters. Profiteers and dictators. All of his targets held the interests of the free world hostage. And Sam regretted not a single one. In fact, if he had a trophy room—if he had any kind of permanent place—he'd put up pictures of the bastards he'd eliminated the way hunters hung antlered heads, or fishermen hung swordfish. But he didn't have a permanent place, so what the hell. He'd be content with the good feeling it gave him to know he'd done something beneficial and right. In truth, he liked the Committee for giving him the opportunity.

In fact, in a lot of ways, he liked the Committee. It seemed to have the best instincts to go with its impeccable systems. Sam never ceased to be amazed at the way it monitored everything going on in the world, no matter where it happened, no matter when, no matter who was involved. It had better information than the CIA, the NSA, MI6, the FBI, Mossad, the KGB, whoever. More often than not, when the Committee got involved, it was the CIA, for whom Sam had no love, that had fucked up. Or the FBI. Or MI6, Mossad, the KGB, whoever. Sometimes two or three of them combined for a double or triple fuckup. And always the Committee stepped in. Sam got assigned. Things got straightened out.

And through it all, all twenty-some years of total control, Sam never knew who the Committee were. They trained him, they educated him. They sent him on assignments. Between assignments they stationed him in resorts, where he cooled out, lived it up and, if it went too long, grew edgy, restless, irascible. So

217

they sent him for refresher courses. They put him back on army bases, in rigorous training regimens. They sent him to Edwards Air Force Base and strapped him into experimental jets. They put him on the boards somewhere in a community theater, or in summer stock. They had him work an obscure nightclub. They shipped him back to Monterey for some brushup work on Chinese or Russian, French or Spanish, Italian or German. They came up with something, every time; they were the unseen hand.

Always, they controlled him, they refined him. They were the shadowiest organization ever. That was all.

"You've been very quiet, Sam. Is anything wrong?"

It was Mother Beloved, looking back over her shoulder. Ahead Sam saw the muddy waters of the Amazon, brown in all the jungle green. Way off, on the horizon, he saw what he took to be the hodgepodge of high-rise apartment and office buildings sprouting from Manaus.

"No, nothing's wrong. I was just enjoying the scenery. Isn't that Manaus ahead?"

"Yes. We will land in minutes."

"Good."

"Why good? We will be there less than half an hour, while I check the mail and refuel."

"It's good because it's better than not being there, if you follow."

Mother Beloved frowned, then smiled. "Yes, I see your point."

Sam looked back out and down, and saw some scattered buildings on the outskirts of the city. He heard Mother Beloved talk with the tower, and felt them start their descent. Looking ahead again, he saw the high rises shooting white amid the red tile roofs of the older buildings. He was eager now to dump Mercedes and let the chips fall where they might. He was set, poised in mind and body, ready to execute his assignment at the first opportunity and bid adieu to the jungle.

"I'll miss you, Sam," Mercedes said. She was half turned in her seat, looking over her left shoulder at him.

"None of that," Mother Beloved snapped, between exchanges with the tower. They were over the suburbs now, flying very low, the Rallye's shadow slithering over the ground, leapfrogging buildings below. Ahead Sam saw the light stanchions for the airport, painted red, set in a line for the runway.

"I'll miss you too," he said, knowing he was lying, but determined to let Mother Beloved stew a little.

22

LOOP DE LOOP

Manaus–Valhalla Ranch
October 10

They taxied out onto the runway, having got final clearance. Beside Sam Borne, Mother Beloved looked imperious in her aviator sunglasses, her hands holding firmly to the yoke. She revved the Lycoming's 235 horses and they shot down the runway. When they reached speed, she pulled back on the yoke and they lifted into the sky. They climbed steeply, quickly passing the airport's outbuildings; then they glided over the suburban sprawl around the airport and were on their way. They would be back at the Valhalla ranch in about two hours, the cocaine on its way to Europe, and Mercedes Coozi conveniently out of the way—both for Mother Beloved and for Sam.

Now the final phase would play itself out. Sam did not want to delay any longer than he had to. It vexed him that Aldo was along, sitting now behind Mother Beloved in the back left-hand seat. Without him there, it would be easy to take her out. He could simply commandeer the Rallye's controls and kill her, a well-placed hand vising the life from her as the other steadily flew the plane. But this was not to be.

In the brief time they'd spent at the airport, Sam

confirmed what he suspected on the flight down when, sitting next to Aldo, he thought he detected the bulge of a handgun under his windbreaker. At the airport, waiting near the fuel pumps, he had seen clearly the butt of an automatic stuck in Aldo's belt when he pushed back his jacket to get his cigarettes. Mother Beloved left little to chance. She was too smart to fly a plane alone with a stranger. All of which meant Sam would have to bide a little time and look for his opening back at the ranch.

They leveled off at 6,500 feet on a heading of 210. Glancing over to the left, Sam saw that they were cruising again at 130 knots. He hoped for a quiet ride, and thought it was a distinct possibility when Mother Beloved launched into a conversation in Portuguese with Aldo. They were discussing the possibilities of opening a cattle ranch in Pará. Aldo, as a horseman, was against it. But Mother Beloved seemed determined to do it. Over breakfast she had filled in Sam and Mercedes on her plan, explaining how she wanted to diversify and find new outlets for her drive to breed the perfect specimen, whether it was horses or cattle. To Sam, looking across the breakfast table at Erika, it appeared she had succeeded in the human sphere.

From what Sam could make out, Aldo was arguing against the cattle ranch as a serious security risk. The Valhalla ranch was a veritable jungle redoubt, nearly impregnable. But to open a cattle ranch in Pará presented different problems. There they would be deeper into vulnerable territory, territory where the government forces had easier access, where it would not be possible to maintain their complete hold over the surrounding area and its people. Mother Beloved brushed this aside as so much stupidity. She would own the ranch in a dummy situation, only sneaking in

221

for visits, checking. She would hire someone to run it and simply use it as a money-laundering operation, one she could have fun with. If she opened another string of dry cleaners in Rio or São Paulo, what fun could she have with that? No, she would look into it. She would breed her cattle. Aldo, Sam could tell without looking back at him, was fuming, his objections ignored.

"So tell me, Sam, what do you think I should order from you?" Mother Beloved asked, looking across at him, her eyes unreadable behind the aviator glasses. Sam himself was wearing a pair; in sunglasses he favored aviator's, and wore them even on the ground. He could tell she was serious. It was time to do business.

"What do you want to use the weapons for?"

"I want to use them for night raids mostly. I want them to be accurate. And to have lots of firepower."

"Night, you say."

"Yes. How about Armalites? Someone told me they'd be perfect for what I want."

"They would be good. I'll give you a good price on M-16s."

"Are they as good?"

"Yes. The M-16 grew out of the Armalite. It's the same thing, the M-16 being the military designation for the Armalite AR-15." This was true. Both rifles had been developed from the work of the great inventor of small arms, Eugene Stoner. The Armalite AR-15 had been produced in the late 1950s while Stoner was employed by the Fairchild Engine and Airplane Company.

"Are there better rifles I should consider? I don't want to spare expenses and get shoddy goods."

"I don't sell shoddy goods, and the M-16 will do just

fine for what you want. It's light. You can carry it and a lot else besides. It has a rapid rate of fire. It's got a thirty-round magazine. You can't go wrong. And since you want it for night work, I'll give you a good deal on infrared sniperscopes. You'll be able to make out a man at five hundred yards in starlight. You can't go wrong." Sam raised an index finger and flicked it at her to emphasize his point.

"And how about grenade launchers?" she asked.

"I'll give you a nice price on M-79s. You can work them accurately up to four hundred yards. No problem."

"I'll also need about fifty shotguns."

"For that I'll give you another great price, again on Vietnam surplus. You won't be able to do better than the price I'll lay on you for Remington 870s. They fire like hell and at short range they're devastating."

"What about machine guns?"

"Depends what you want them for."

"For raids some, for my personal protection more."

"You mean submachine guns."

"Whatever."

"I'll make you a nice price on Uzis."

"No. I prefer another weapon. Not Uzis." Sam thought of the dossier, and how her father had been apprehended and executed by the Israelis. He briefly considered reassuring her that the Uzis he'd sell would all be made in Belgium, but on second thought he knew this would not be appreciated.

"How about Heckler and Koch MP5A3s?"

"Wonderful." Let it not be said he didn't know the way to a Valkyrie's heart.

"You'll have to place a minimum order of twenty-five."

"Fine. Over lunch we'll work out the quantities and

the prices for everything. I'm delighted with the way you do business, Mr. Borne."

"Wait till you sign the order," Sam said, then laughed. Mother Beloved joined in, but Aldo did not. Glancing quickly over his shoulder, Sam saw that the ramrod had a stern expression on his face. He was staring intently forward, at Sam. No doubt he felt left out. Good, Sam thought, let his anger marinate. When the time was right, Sam would put a fire under it and cook him good.

"I like the European touch of Heckler and Koch," Mother Beloved said. "I like things European, don't you, Sam?"

"Many of them. I like this plane."

"So do I. I adore the Rallye. I couldn't wait to own one."

"A lot of sportsmen feel the same."

"Yes, they do. And so do photographers." Sam knew why photographers loved the Rallye, but, sensing her need to tell him, he decided to humor her. So he asked why.

"They love the shots they get from these. You throw the plane into slowflight and you get marvelous photos, crisp and clear, very distinct, with the highest resolution. It's simply incredible."

"I hadn't thought of that."

"Do you know, I have a friend, Hellmuth, and he puts skis on his Rallye and flies it into the high Alps. He lands on snowfields and then skis slopes no one else ever reaches. He does it all alone."

"He has iron nerves or is completely insane."

"Both, I think, but I admire it, don't you?"

"Marginally."

"Marginally," she mimicked. "You Americans are so conservative where true courage is concerned."

"It can't be helped." From the back there came a snort. Sam looked around at Aldo, who glared at him. He turned forward again and looked to his right at the scenery below. It was beautiful, verdant and lush. But treacherous, he knew.

"Tell me, Sam, have you ever wanted to fly?" Mother Beloved asked. Much of the time it was all he wanted to do. He loved flight more than an eagle.

"Yes," he said. It was the truth, though deviously incomplete. He could fly almost anything, and had. His flight training had been extensive. He had logged countless hours in the air in everything from T-34 Bravos at Pensacola to the most advanced jets at Edwards Air Force Base, not to mention all types of helicopters at Forts Wolters in Texas and Rucker in Alabama. And sometimes, between assignments, he had flown formation with the Blue Angels. He had even on occasion between assignments been able to fly various domestic light planes, even some old biplanes, most notably a Tiger Moth. And while at RADA one sunny English day in late spring of 1970 he'd flown over the Sussex countryside in a Spitfire. He'd flown almost everything: an old Japanese Zero, an old Mustang, a still-in-service DC-3 once in Africa, just about everything.

"Perhaps someday you'll get a chance."

"Perhaps."

Sam looked over and saw an amused smile on her face, the smile someone had when they knew something you didn't. She turned back, still smiling, and pulled the yoke toward her. The nose swung up, the sky wheeling above them, the centrifugal force pinning them in their seats. Up they went, then over. The sky hung briefly below them, around them, then disappeared, replaced by the jungle green, far below; then

225

quickly the nose came up again and ahead lay the horizon and the line where the blue sky met the green earth.

"Still with us, Sam?" Mother Beloved asked, laughing, hoping that the simple inside loop she'd done would have shaken him up. She was about to have more fun. "Make sure your harness is fastened," she said, not making an effort to regain the four hundred or five hundred feet they had lost to the loop. Sam did not have to fasten his harness. He always flew with his harness fastened, no matter how long or short the trip, no matter what; even on commercial flights, he kept his seat belt fastened. He took every edge he could get. Even in a car, he always fastened his seat belt.

"How about you, Aldo, are you buttoned in?" she asked.

"Yes, but don't do it, please. *Meu Deus!*" he pleaded, though God was unlikely to save him from what she planned.

Laughing, Mother Beloved pushed the yoke forward. The nose dipped and the ground came up; then the centripetal force hurled them forward, throwing them against their harnesses. The ground slid by under them; then sky appeared at its end, upside down, rushing at them; then suddenly it was behind and above them all at once. Then the nose came down, leveling off, and ahead the horizon rolled up again. They had made an outside loop, one of the most excruciatingly unpleasant sensations flight had to offer. Dizziness and nausea flooded over Sam. In the back Aldo moaned. Mother Beloved laughed.

"Don't be sick, Aldo, I don't want it," she snapped, serious. "You've been through this enough times. I thought you wanted to be a flier too."

"I do. I watch carefully. I could fly this plane," he said, machismo lacing his tone.

"You won't get a chance till you stop moaning like a cow in heat every time we do a little acrobatics."

"Okay," he said, before he dry-heaved, retching. Mother Beloved laughed.

"And how are you, Sam?" she wanted to know.

"Fine."

"Good. I like a man with a stomach for flight." She looked over at him and winked, jerking her head in Aldo's direction. She smirked, then turned back. She made no attempt to regain lost altitude, and Sam had a feeling she wasn't through yet. Below and slightly ahead he saw the flames of a slash-and-burn operation leaping toward the sky. In seconds they would be over it. He hoped she wouldn't do what he feared she might.

She did.

Leaning in on the yoke, she put them into a dive and held it there. They were heading right for the flames, which seemed to leap higher every second.

"No, stop, please," Aldo implored from behind, his voice cracking.

Mother Beloved cackled. She held them in a dive, the flames all they could see, coming nearer and nearer.

Sam was not afraid, but angry. Mother Beloved was showing off recklessly. A real pilot would not fool around over a raging fire. It was pointless. Holding his anger in, containing himself, he hoped she would cease her little game and pull up. But she didn't. Still, he waited, slowly counting off three seconds.

Then he acted. Seizing the yoke, he pulled up on it hard, wrenching control of the plane from her, overpowering her. The nose came up level, the horizon directly in front of them. Sam estimated they still had a good seven or eight hundred feet between the fuselage and the flames. Flicking his wrists to the right, he put them in an aileron roll, then held. They rolled again and again, the sky and the flaming earth whirling in front of them, topsy-turvy, spinning in full circles. When the flaming earth was replaced by green jungle, Sam straightened his wrists. The plane leveled off, away from the flames. He looked hard at Mother Beloved.

"Aldo," she hissed. "Aldo."

Cold steel poked into Sam's neck. He looked around into the barrel of a nine-millimeter Beretta. Aldo, looking faint and flushed, held it in his wavering right hand. In his left hand he held a red kerchief to his mouth. He moved the barrel of the Beretta closer to Sam. It was inches from his face.

"Hands off the controls, Mr. Borne," Mother Beloved managed to sputter, anger cracking her voice. Her face was flushed with rage, her lips trembling. On the yoke, her knuckles were perfectly white. "Don't ever do anything like that again. Not ever. I'm the boss. I'm in charge around here, and I don't like insubordination. I'll let it go this one time. If it ever happens again, I won't be responsible for the consequences. Is that clear?"

"Yes."

"Good."

"Now will you tell him to get that gun barrel out of my face?"

"You're sure you understand me?"

"Yes."

Mother Beloved let a long pause hang in the air,

then said slowly, "Take the gun down, Aldo, but keep
it handy."

Aldo took the gun back. He rested it on his thigh.

After another long pause, Mother Beloved spoke.
"What did you think you were doing?"

"Showing you an aileron roll," Sam deadpanned.

"I've seen aileron rolls. I've even done them."

"Congratulations."

"I don't like your tone. I don't like the way things
are going."

"Sorry."

"Why didn't you tell me you flew?"

"You didn't ask."

"Yes I did."

"No. You asked if I ever wanted to fly, not if I flew."

"You're splitting hairs. You were less than forth-
coming."

"I answered the question asked."

"Then answer this. Where did you learn to handle
a plane like that?"

"Around."

"Where?"

"First in the service. Then with friends."

"You handled it well."

"I handle a lot of things well."

"We shall see."

"I hope so."

In the back Aldo grunted. "How are you with
horses, Mister Borne?" he asked.

"I'll ask the questions here, Aldo," Mother Beloved
snapped. She paused, then, a grin stealing across her
face, said, "As a matter of fact, Mr. Borne, Aldo has a
point. How are you with horses?"

"I can handle them."

"We shall see."

Mother Beloved laughed, and Aldo joined in. Sam sat still, his eyes ahead, on the horizon.

"After lunch, Sam, I have a horse I want you to handle. His name is Faust, and I think the experience will prove interesting." Aldo chuckled. Sam looked across at Mother Beloved hard. She smiled the smile she had that said she knew something you didn't.

"I hope so," Sam said, then went back to looking at the horizon.

23

DUSTUP

In the heat of the afternoon Sam Borne followed
Mother Beloved across the lawn and entered the barn.
Inside it was cooler, and dark. From down the line of
stalls they could hear, even before their eyes adjusted
to the reduced light, the shouts and grunts of the
cowboys working at one stall toward the end. Out of
the glare of the sun, his eyes adjusted, Sam noticed
that Aldo stood in the middle of the center aisle, his
hands on his hips, arms akimbo, a big grin lighting his
face. Around him three cowboys stood with ropes taut.
The ends of the ropes, Sam could see as they drew
nearer, were strung around the neck of a tremendous
black horse whose head jerked from side to side
against the restraint of the lassos. The horse's hooves
sent up a constant shuffling, digging sound as it pulled
and pushed against the ropes. Finally it whinnied, bar-
ing its teeth. It was angry and riled. Sam did not like
at all the way things were starting to shape up, especially looking at Aldo and his silly, fuck-you grin.

"We got the saddle on him," Aldo said; "now all we
have to do is get him out in the corral and watch Borne
here ride him." He laughed, and the cowboys holding

the ropes laughed too. Mother Beloved only smiled and looked at Sam. "No one," she said, "has yet been able to stay on Faust. In fact, we haven't succeeded fully in putting someone up on him at all. He fights us every which way. He's the most spirited stallion I've ever had, and Aldo is all for gelding him, but I don't want to. He represents something pure to me, something almost holy, and I'd like to keep him intact as long as I can. He's beautiful, isn't he?"

"Yes, he is. He looks like an exceptional animal."

"Oh, he is. He most certainly is. I bred him from one of the finest stallions in the world. He's got better bloodlines than a Hapsburg, but all Aldo can see is an animal he can't handle." She gave Aldo a withering look. He sulked and, hawking loudly, spat on the ground. Scratching his groin, he said, "Nobody can handle this animal. He's out of his head."

Sam looked toward the stall and saw that the neck and breast of the stallion were flecked with foam. It stood out in white lines against the glistening black flesh. In its eyes, wide with anger, there was a defiant look, a look wild with energy, radiating willfulness. The stallion nickered and rolled its head, shaking its mane, trying to free itself from the lassos. "He's got lovely spirit," Sam said. "He's ready to take on the world."

"Yes, and to win," Mother Beloved said, exaltation in her voice. "I want more than anything to ride him. To streak across a field with him, to watch one of the boys gallop him around the track. But so far no luck. He's too much his own man."

The stallion pulled hard against the lassos, dragging the cowboys toward his stall, their heels making runnels in the sandy floor of the barn. Then he reared on his hind legs, his front hooves beating a loud, rapid tattoo off the slats of the stall's gate, a high, loud whinny rending the air. Sam knew that this was hopeless, that this horse had never been approached correctly, and wasn't being approached correctly now.

As if to confirm this, Aldo leaped forward and seized the middle lasso about a foot above where the cowboy in the center held it. Pulling down hard, jerking and wrenching, he forced the stallion to fight him harder, its neck straining, its hooves lashing out, thundering off the slats. Aldo briefly won, and the stallion crashed down on his forefeet. When he did, Aldo lunged at him and struck him on the snout. Just then the stallion reared again, kicking mightily, snapping its neck against the lassos, backing into the stall on its hind legs as hard as it could, slipping and sliding against the tension of the lassos, kicking up sand and dust, whinnying defiantly. Pulling hard, inching his way up the lasso, Aldo managed again, with the help of the other cowboys, to pull the stallion down. But only temporarily.

No sooner did the stallion's forefeet hit the ground than he reared mightily again. He was a tremendous fighter, and would go on like this, Sam knew, for hours. The situation was hopeless. Sam could only wonder at Aldo's reputation as a handler of horseflesh if this was his best show. Beginning to feel disgust and anger, Sam was tempted to interfere, but held himself back. He would not attempt to break this horse under these conditions, after such obvious riling.

As Sam watched, Aldo and the cowboys managed again to get the stallion down on all fours, briefly. When it reared again, Aldo stepped back on the rope and looked over his shoulder. "Do you think you can handle this beast, Borne? Are you ready to break your neck trying?" He spat on the ground at Sam's feet.

"The horse knows he's being taunted by a jackass. There's no way I'm going to get up on him after watching this three-ring circus."

Aldo looked like a man who'd watched his mother raped by a full platoon. His hands knotted, his mouth tightened, his eyes narrowed. He dropped the rope and walked the three paces back to where Sam stood next to Mother Beloved.

In Sam the thing he dimly understood had taken over. Though he was not in danger of jeopardizing the assignment, he knew he was about to make a move that might complicate it endlessly. He had stood by and watched this magnificent beast taunted and abused for as long as he could. Unable to restrain himself longer, he didn't really care to. To watch nature abused this way was painful to him. To see an animal as glorious as this black stallion being wrenched and pulled like a stupid mule, its energy being misdirected and misused, was painful beyond description. It was like watching a Stradivarius used like a ukulele. Withdrawing deep within himself, coiled and poised, Sam drew upon an endless supply of raw energy, harnessed and focused like none other the world had ever seen; disciplined, trained, perfected, honed for twenty-odd years. And now on ready alert.

"Who did you call a jackass?" Aldo asked, stepping closer to Sam, puffing his chest, trying for every menacing nuance his body could yield.

"You."

Aldo swung a roundhouse right. Sam snared it with his left hand, just beyond Aldo's wrist, and, allowing Aldo's momentum to carry him forward, merely crouched under it and hurled the ramrod up and over his back, flipping him against the stall gate opposite, where he thudded off the slats and slumped to the ground. Grinning maniacally, he pushed off with both hands and charged. Sidestepping, Sam drove his right leg under Aldo's charging feet and chopped him across the neck with an open left hand. Aldo sprawled facedown in the dust, quivering. When he turned over and pushed himself upright, he didn't smile, only got to his feet and took two rapid steps toward Sam before kicking out mightily with his right foot. Sam caught his boot in both hands and, twisting it sharply to the right, spun him full circle and sent him crashing to the dirt again.

"I think you've had enough, Aldo," Mother Beloved said.

"Quiet, woman. This is none of your affair."

"Everything on this ranch is my affair. And you remember who you're talking to."

"Shut up," Aldo snapped, then broke into a stream of Portuguese. The three cowboys holding the lassos dropped them and stood ready, hesitant, a look of consternation on their faces. Mother Beloved spoke to them rapidly in Portuguese; then Aldo started to talk over her, louder, bitterly, his voice a growl. They looked from Aldo to Mother Beloved and back, then back and forth again. Finally Sam spoke up, looking right at Mother Beloved. "Please move out of the way. Everything will be all right." She looked at him, then away. She walked down the aisle until she was well out of the way, then turned, an amused look on her face, and stood, her eyes darting quickly from Sam to Aldo and the three cowboys.

The cowboys took this for permission. The one closest to Sam, a tall man with a thick mustache, positioned himself around to Sam's left, trying to get an advantage by flanking him. The middle one, a short man, moved over closer to Aldo, but still to Sam's right. Aldo was directly ahead. To Sam's extreme right the third cowboy, stocky and wearing leather chaps, sidled farther to the right, flanking Sam, spreading their attack, making it more difficult for him to cover all of them. In Portuguese Aldo told them to charge when he did.

Sam set himself.

Aldo charged. The cowboys charged. Sam leaped quickly to his right and caught the short cowboy with a tremendous kick to the groin. His eyes bulged and his hands clasped his crotch as he sank to his knees. Spinning farther to his right, Sam kicked out again and caught the stocky cowboy in the head, sending him sprawling in the dirt, knocked out cold, twisting as he went down into the side of the charging Aldo, who compensated to his right, colliding with the tall cowboy. They bounced off each other and toward Sam.

Shifting again to his right, Sam grabbed Aldo's outthrust arm even as Aldo inadvertently shielded the tall cowboy from him. Pulling Aldo by the arm, Sam delivered a thundering right cross to his jaw, dropping him like a sack of flour. He collapsed in the dust, unconscious. The short cowboy had by this time regained his feet. Backpedaling by him, Sam cut an arcing right hand horizontally into his throat. He went toppling into the dirt again.

That left the tall cowboy, who vaulted past the splayed body of Aldo and lunged at Sam as he delivered the throat chop to the short cowboy. Sam pivoted to his left, around and behind the smaller cowboy, but not in time. The tall cowboy cuffed him a hard shot on the jaw, knocking him to his knees. Maintaining himself, Sam thrust out his left arm and intercepted two more right-hand blows. Then the tall cowboy kicked at him. Swiveling to his right, Sam avoided the kick, which sailed past him to his left, then hurled himself to his feet and dove into the cowboy's midsection, driving him across the aisle and slamming him off a stall gate. Gripping him on both upper arms, pinning him, Sam drove the top of his head into the man's chin. There was a sharp crack as the man's jaws collided, his teeth mashing. Quickly Sam drove his left fist, then his right, into the man's solar plexus. Backing off, he threw an uppercutting left-right-left combination off the man's face, striking his chin, mouth and nose, the cartilage of which collapsed with a crunching sound. Spouting blood from his nose and mouth, the tall cowboy quivered, equipoised momentarily, then, his legs folding under him, collapsed in a heap. In the dirt he lay perfectly still.

Stepping farther back, out of the way of the toppling cowboy, Sam checked the other three. Aldo was out cold in the dirt, saliva and blood drooling from the side of his mouth, forming a dark little puddle beside his head. The short cowboy tried to regain his knees, but keeled over in the dirt again. The stocky cowboy sat up, rubbing his eyes, leaning on an arm, still dazed. Sam rubbed his jaw, dusted his knees, and looked down the barn toward Mother Beloved.

Her eyes were fixed on the four men sprawled in the dirt. On her face was a look of sheer ecstasy. She was in some kind of transport, as though all her chimes had chimed just right, together, in cosmic harmony.

She looked up at Sam, smiled, then clapped.

24

IN THE SADDLE

"Saddle me a horse," Sam said.

Mother Beloved looked at him with a quizzical, disbelieving expression on her face. She was not used to taking orders, but something about the way Sam had dispatched four of her best men had made a deep impression on her. She looked around and saw that the stocky cowboy had managed to gain his feet and was leaning against a stall, his thumb and forefinger rubbing his nose and the corners of his eyes. She left Sam, walked to the cowboy and spoke to him harshly. He nodded and walked off, nearly staggering.

In minutes he was back, trailing two other ranch hands carrying buckets. They walked up to Mother Beloved, who gave them quick instructions. The ranch hands stood above the prostrate cowboys and dumped the buckets on them, splashing them awake with a stream of cold water. They writhed and groaned, unable at first to move. Mother Beloved crossed to Aldo and kicked him hard in the ribs. Then she spoke sharply in Portuguese, and the ranch hands helped Aldo and the other two cowboys to their feet. Mother Beloved spoke to the stocky cowboy, and he disappeared into a room at the end of the barn. When he reappeared, carrying a bridle and halter, he went to one stall down the line and climbed up to fix the bridle on the head of a big chestnut. Then he opened the stall and led the big gelding out.

Dusting themselves off, partially supported by the ranch hands, Aldo and the others all started to leave. On their way, when Aldo drew abreast of Sam, he stopped and glared at him, then said slowly in his heavy English, "I have a long memory, Borne."

"Congratulations."

"You'll remember this with regret before long."

"Idle threats rate with me right behind counterfeit promises."

"You'll see, my friend."

"I'm all eyes."

Mother Beloved shouted in Portuguese, and Aldo and the others moved on. In their wake, the stocky cowboy led the big chestnut gelding down the aisle. When he reached Sam, the cowboy handed him the halter, nodded respectfully, and started to walk off after the others. Mother Beloved sauntered over to Sam, smiling coquettishly. "Now tell me, Mr. Borne, what do you plan next? Do you really think you can do anything with Faust?"

"Let's say I can't do any worse than what I've seen."

"Well, he was okay till an Indian stole him. Before that, he was just a normally spirited stallion, but when the Indian was caught and I got him back, he was impossible. You'll no doubt find that out."

"Maybe."

"Just remember. No rough stuff. No tied rowels, no spade bits. And no striking him between the ears with the butt of a loaded quirt."

"I intend to break him, not butcher him."

"Is there anything I can do?"

"Yes. Tell that cowboy to stay here."

She turned and spoke rapidly in Portuguese to the stocky cowboy. He halted in the barn's doorway. Sam said, "Tell him to saddle a horse for himself and to wait for me outside the barn. What's his name anyway?"

"His name's Zico. He's a good man."

"I noticed. He took a good shot."

"Is there anything else I can do?"

"Yes. Leave."

"Well, that's easy enough." She started to leave, tossing off over her shoulder, "Be careful. Faust is as devilishly clever as his namesake."

Sam gave his standard answer. "I'm always careful," he said. When he was alone with the two horses, after Zico had saddled a big gray mare and walked it out of the barn, he tied the chestnut to the front of Faust's stall and went to the tack room. He wanted to let the chestnut have a calming effect on Faust, and he wanted to check over the gear in the tack room. He had a good idea of what he'd need if his hunch about Faust was at all correct. When he found a good hackamore, he went back to the barn and climbed up on the side of Faust's stall. There he worked his way slowly, talking all the while to the big stallion, to the point where Faust would allow him to stroke his mane, to pat his neck, to run his hand down his face.

Sam had a few very important things going for him. He knew that he could place himself in harmony with nature. In his ninja training with Honzo Tenkatsu, he had mastered the art of *kuji-kiri*, one of the most startling psychic and mystical arts of ninjitsu. It consisted of making magical in-signs in the air, many based on patterns of four vertical and five horizontal lines, giving the magical number of nine, the most important number in *shugendo,* or mountain asceticism, and in *mikkyo,* or esoteric Buddhism. He knew how to use the magical finger exercises to hypnotize an enemy into inaction or temporary paralysis; but, more important, as a sideline to these exercises, he had sharpened and developed his perception extraordinarily, in the great ninja tradition, so that it gave him psychological insight into all living things, to the point where he tuned in to their very spirit. This he now used with Faust.

On a more practical level, Sam had spent a number of weeks one summer at Fort Leavenworth, undergoing the traditional horse training given to the cavalry. It was rigorous in the extreme, and he had learned all sorts of things about horses, from breaking them to caring for them to riding them as though he had been born on one. Since that summer, he had been placed at times between assignments by the Committee on dude ranches, generally on the Lazy L in Arizona. So he knew horseflesh, and how to handle it.

After about half an hour, when the big stallion was calm, Sam mounted the chestnut and, using the reins on the bridle Aldo's men had put on Faust, led him out of the barn. Sam nodded to Zico as he emerged, and the startled cowboy fell in behind them. As Sam led Faust calmly away from the central buildings of the ranch, he noted the shocked looks on the faces of the help. Many stared wide-eyed, their jaws slack.

Sam led the way down past the racetrack to a clearing behind it with a small stand of trees in its center. The ground was sandy, and wouldn't give Faust good footholds. He dismounted there and indicated for Zico to sit his horse. He did. Sam had a hunch about Faust, since he had let Aldo and his men get the saddle on him, and he wanted now to test it, but not too precipitately. He stroked the big stallion's neck and head, relaxing him, talking to him, leading him in small circles. He seemed okay. He followed. He didn't kick or cut up. Early on, Sam had noted that Faust didn't have a spur scar on him, so he hadn't been chewed into and brutalized by Aldo or his men, or by this Indian horse thief who'd got his hands on him.

After a good while, Sam gestured to Zico that he was going to try to mount. He gingerly put his foot in the left stirrup. Faust held still. Sam bounced his weight in the stirrup. Still no reaction. Then he swung up and over.

It took maybe two seconds. Faust didn't drop his head and buck. He didn't twist and kick. He reared straight up and fell over backward. From what Mother Beloved had said about not hitting him with a quirt, Sam half expected this. So he slid clear before being crushed. Backpedaling, he watched as Faust scrambled to his feet and just stood there, shaking briefly, flicking his mane before settling in.

Sam looked at Zico, who shrugged, shaking his head no, indicating it was hopeless. In return Sam smiled and walked to the chestnut. From his saddle he took the hackamore. Then he walked back and patted Faust. He held out his hand, and Faust snuffled at it. This was not a naturally mean animal. Now Sam knew what he wanted to know. He reached up and stripped the saddle, took off the bridle and eased on the hackamore. Stepping back, he indicated to Zico to come and hold the hackamore. In Spanish, slowly, Sam told him to let go of the hackamore and step back as soon as he straddled Faust. Zico frowned, shaking his hands in front of him, trying to convey to Sam his fears for him. Sam nodded his thanks.

Carefully Sam wrapped the hackamore reins in his left hand, made a fist, then twisted it into Faust's mane. Grabbing a handful of black mane with his right hand, he swung himself aboard. The stallion went right up, rearing straight toward the sky, his forelegs kicking. As the big horse fell backward Sam leaped clear. As he did he threw all his weight on the reins and cracked Faust's head hard off the ground. It made a tremendous thud, leaving an impress on the sand. When Faust staggered up, his legs were not so steady. Really stung, he swayed, then stumbled.

That was lesson one, and just the beginning. Sam had to put him through it four more times. Talking to him, soothing him, Sam bore down on him, disciplining him, teaching him, making him pay the price each time. After bouncing off the earth five times, Faust got the message. Dazed and exhausted, he finally quit. After a brief rest, he'd stand perfectly still while Sam mounted, then stand still till Sam kicked him in the ribs. After a short while, he'd go forward or back, he'd swing sideways or go in a circle, following leads when Sam swung his hands in either direction. Somebody, as Sam had suspected, had really abused Faust. And Faust had learned to retaliate. He had learned, probably as the result of being pulled over accidentally by someone using a spade bit, how to get rid of a rider. Ever since, he'd used this knowledge. Now he'd been broken of it.

For fun Sam rode him over to the track, Zico trailing, holding the lead on the chestnut. Leaning down, Sam opened the track gate and led him out onto its smooth surface. Kicking him, Sam got Faust into a full gallop. They tore down the track. Faust had speed to burn, and stamina. He would be an exciting horse to watch run competitively, and Sam, flying down the backstretch on him, his black mane whipping back into his face, regretted that he'd never get to see him race. When they hit the top of the homestretch, Zico waved to Sam with his hat, a wide smile lighting his face. Sam raced Faust past the finish pole, then eased up on him. Faust had worked up a good lather, but even so, considering the ordeal Sam had put him through in breaking him, he was an exceptional horse. Speed like his was indeed rare.

Slowly he walked Faust back to the gate. Zico beamed at him, then extended his hat toward the big house. Sam followed his gesture with his eyes. On the veranda of the big house, Mother Beloved stood looking down at them through binoculars. When she saw Sam looking in her direction, she started to wave frantically. He waved back. Then he noticed that all around the main house, among the barns and outbuildings, work had come to a standstill. All of the cowboys and other help, the exercise boys and jockeys, the maids, stood looking down at the track too. He turned and saw that Zico was waving his hat at all of them, feeling part of the triumph.

Sam led Faust through the gate, and Zico closed it behind them. Then they made the slow walk back to the barn. As they drew near it Mother Beloved walked over and intercepted them. "That was marvelous, Sam, just marvelous." She was smiling fit to burst. She walked over to Faust and patted his neck. Sam climbed down. "This is just extraordinary," she continued, "extraordinary. Where did you learn such horsemanship? You must tell me."

"Everybody's entitled to some secrets," Sam said, then walked off in the direction of the guest house.

"Drinks at six, Sam."

"I'll be there." That left enough time for a hot bath and a short nap. And some time to think.

As Sam passed the cowboys' bunkhouse he noticed Aldo standing on its short porch. Crooking his left arm, Aldo crossed it with his right, then jerked the left fist toward his chest.

In return Sam gave him the high sign.

25

CHAMPAGNE AND CAVIAR

Valhalla Ranch
October 10

Sam Borne sat in a stuffed armchair, thinking. A thick terry-cloth towel wrapped around his waist, his feet propped before him on the end of the bed, he reviewed in his mind all that had taken place since his arrival at Valhalla Ranch, and all he had still to do. With the breaking of Faust, he was in clover as far as Mother Beloved was concerned. There was no mistaking the sexual tension that had built between them. Sam had her right where he wanted her. He needed only an opening. He suspected that opening would present itself tonight. And he wanted to be mentally prepared to capitalize on it.

His reverie was broken by the sound of the outside door to the guest house opening and closing. Footsteps in the hallway followed. Then came a light knock on the door to his room.

"Who is it?"

"It's me, Erika. May I come in?"

"In a minute."

Sam rose and walked across the room to a closet. From it he pulled a pair of slacks. He slipped into these

246

and threw on a clean shirt. Then he opened the door. In his bare feet, he was scarcely taller than Erika. She was so beautiful, dressed in a deep blue blouse and white slacks that hugged her hips, that he was temporarily unable to do anything but stare at her.

"May I come in?"

Catching himself, realizing his paralysis could be interpreted as rudeness, he said, "Of course," stepping back as he did so and extending his arm in a welcoming gesture. Erika stepped into the small room. There were only two armchairs, the bed and a night table.

"Please have a seat," he said, indicating the chair opposite the one he'd been sitting in. Erika walked over and sat down. Right away she spoke up. "I have no right to ask you this, but I will anyway," she said, then hesitated. She was afraid of what she was about to ask, afraid that it would bounce back on her in some way. She looked at her feet. Sam looked too. They were encased in blue pumps with low heels. They matched the blouse. Here in the jungle she was as chic and sophisticated as any fashion-conscious model in Paris or New York.

"Ask anything," Sam said, trying to put her at ease.

All in a rush she said, "Would you take me with you when you leave?" It came out so fast it sounded like one long word.

Sam would have liked nothing more than to take her with him, everywhere. But her request put him in a tight spot. He couldn't afford to alienate what he'd so carefully built up with her mother. He had to keep the ball rolling, and involvement with Erika could halt it. Yet turning her down, after witnessing the slapping scene at breakfast that morning, was difficult. Her treatment at the hands of Aldo and her mother still bothered him. He would have liked to free her from them.

But then there was the Committee to consider. Sam was always getting himself into trouble with his "do-gooder side," as the Committee referred to it. They wanted him only to carry out the assignments they gave him, not to undertake more than that. They didn't want him adding responsibilities to his tasks, which were already difficult enough. They wanted him to keep the job clean. To go in, do it, and get out. If he undertook to spring Erika, he could be letting himself in for a reprimand. Or more than that. When he undertook added responsibilities or took added risks in any way, the Committee often came down on him hard, sometimes stationing him between assignments on army bases or at Camp Lejeune or Parris Island, making him undergo the raw physical-training regimen of teenage recruits. Or they might assign him to the tracking station in Keflavík, Iceland, for a month. Or to the one in Adak, in the Aleutians. They could always find ways to make their displeasure known. It was only when an assignment went smoothly and he followed instructions to the letter that he got a sojourn in a resort with all the amenities, including a casino. Blackjack was a large passion with him. Anyway, taking on Erika now would not please the Committee. She was none of their affair, they'd figure, and thereby none of his.

But looking at her it was hard to remember that. And Sam had a natural aversion, something deep in his gut, against seeing anyone subjected to the kind of bullying Erika had been victimized by that very morning.

"That's not possible, Erika," he said. "I'm a businessman, like any other, here to take an order. I can't become involved with domestic matters between my client and members of her family." This hurt, but there it was.

As he spoke, Erika's face was a blank. Then she slowly raised her hand to her chin and cupped it. Suddenly her face started to quiver as she fought back tears. The tears won. They squeezed out of her eyes and coursed down her cheeks.

Sam's heart went into full meltdown. He wanted to go to her, to hold her, to tell her all would be right. Yet he didn't. He stayed put, propped on the foot of the bed, fighting himself. As the first sobs broke from Erika, she bent over, as though to hide somewhat the strength of her emotions. Her shoulders shook. Sam slid along the end of the bed and touched her upper arm.

"You don't know what it's like," she managed between sobs. "I hate her more than you can know."

"All teenagers hate their parents." As soon as he said it he realized how dumb it was. And how inappropriate.

"That's not what I'm talking about. She's evil. This place is evil. I'd kill her if I could."

That's exactly what *I'm* going to do, Sam thought. He could pursue any conversational tack but this one. So he continued in the avuncular, false tone he'd already started with. "That's just a manner of speech, you don't mean it."

"Oh, but I do, you don't know how I mean it. I'd shoot her without batting an eyelash." Erika had gained more control now. The sobs were not racking her as hard. She looked up, squeegeeing tears off her cheeks with an index finger. Her eyes were red-rimmed. In her lap her hands worked their way into

249

tight knots, only to come undone and be reworked again. She took a deep breath and continued. "Please just consider what I've asked. I know you're a cool-headed businessman, but can't you consider taking me with you when you go? Can't you help me in some way?"

Sam had an easy out here, the one he'd always had. "You know I'm dependent on your mother to get out of here, like anyone else who visits this ranch. How do you think I can take you with me when I'll be dependent on her for a flight out, just like anybody else?"

"I could wheedle a trip down to Manaus with you, and we could work out a plan. I'd get conveniently lost, you'd know where to find me, you'd have a ticket for me. In minutes I'd be on a plane, out of this hell. Simple."

"And your mother would never suspect me, and never cancel the order I'm here to take. Be realistic, Erika. This is not feasible."

"I think a lot's feasible where you're concerned." She sniffled. Sam reached into his pocket, pulled out his handkerchief and handed it to her. She blew her nose, then folded the handkerchief and dabbed her eyes. "There's something special about you. I knew it the minute I laid eyes on you." Hearing this was as frustrating as cornering the market the day before a Communist takeover. Sam felt that lightness of head he always got when his blood rushed south.

"Thank you. I think there is something very special about you, too, and I knew it the minute I laid eyes on you." He paused. "However, I still can't interfere in a domestic matter between a client and a member of her family."

Balling the handkerchief in one hand, then the other, Erika looked at him with the world's warmest eyes. Then she stood. "I'm sorry to have bothered you," she said, "and I'm especially sorry to have lost my composure."

"It's quite all right. It's good to lose your composure every now and again."

"Mother would be furious."

"She'll never know unless you tell her."

"I won't, for sure."

"I wouldn't be surprised if you're not shipped out of here to school in a year or so."

"No. Mother says my schooling stopped at convent school. I wanted to go to the Sorbonne, but she won't hear of it. She says I'll fall under the wrong influences and have my values corrupted."

"Of course she means her values." Like a true dictator, he thought, Wilda von Hoffer is opposed to intellectual freedom. Patterns in the power mad always hold true.

"Of course, her values," Erika said softly. "I must go now. I'll see you in an hour or so for drinks, I understand."

"Yes. And I think it would be a good idea, if you don't mind my saying so, for you to go in and douse your face with water. No one has to know you've been upset."

"Thank you. I will, if you don't mind."

"Not at all."

Sam walked over and opened the door to the bathroom. Erika walked silently in and closed the door. Sam sat in one armchair and felt like hell. In a few minutes she emerged, radiant as the sun, all smiles.

"Thank you," she said. "I'll see you in a little while."

"Till then," Sam said, closing the door behind her. He crossed to the bed and stretched out on it. He had the ability to fall quickly into short, rejuvenating naps, and now was the perfect time to take one. He couldn't afford to dwell on his anger at having to treat Erika so coldly. He couldn't tell what the night held in store for him, but he had a strong feeling that it held a lot, and he wanted to be rested and ready for it.

"To the swift and sure conclusion of our deal," Mother Beloved said, holding her champagne glass aloft and tipping it in Sam's direction. She smiled and took a deep sip. Sam did the same. As did Aldo and Erika. They were all standing in the main room of the ranch house, before a big stone fireplace that, Sam suspected, was rarely used. Sam was dressed in his khaki outfit, with the safari jacket over a white oxford shirt. He had the bluchers on, and had laughed at himself in the full-length mirror in his room before coming over to the main house. He looked like a 1950s schmuck all dressed up for a weekend in the woods.

Mother Beloved, on the other hand, was dressed in a chic hostess outfit of clinging silk. It was green and yellow, intermingled in large swatches that swirled into each other. On her feet were white sandals. She looked like any internationally rich hostess. Her daughter, by contrast, was dressed demurely, as she had been earlier when she visited Sam. She still wore the blue blouse over the white slacks with the blue pumps on her feet. Both women were unbearably beautiful, twin Teutonic goddesses, one slightly older than the other, yet they might as easily have passed for sisters as for mother and daughter. Aldo was dressed in a clean red sports shirt and gray slacks over black boots. He was disgruntled.

For half an hour before this toast, Mother Beloved had gone over with Sam the order she wished to place for weapons. In the end the order Sam had convinced her to take exceeded the bounds of what Aldo wanted to do. She had ordered a small arsenal, with ammunition to keep it in working trim for a long time, and she was feeling euphoric. Sam himself was projecting the image of the businessman who'd struck a jackpot. Of course, he would never deliver on this order. It was all trumpery. But he would have been a liar and a greater actor than he was if he had denied the pleasure he'd got from watching Aldo's advice ignored in favor of his salesmanship. He had convinced Mother Beloved on each and every issue, and if he had been a legitimate arms dealer, he would have spent two very profitable days here in the jungle.

"The conclusion of our deal will be swift and sure," Sam said, smiling over his glass, playing his part. "As soon as you deposit the money to my account in Monaco, I will put the wheels in motion. In a matter of weeks the arms will be delivered here in Manaus, the best goods the world has to offer. I guarantee it." He tipped his glass, and he and Mother Beloved continued the sexual pas de deux they had been dancing since the dustup in the barn and the breaking of Faust. She was enchanted with Sam, playing to him. Their eyes were singing a silent roundelay, long stares serving for the refrains. Aldo was in full eclipse, a situation that could prove dangerous if Sam did not play it just right.

"I'm sure we will have no problems, Sam," Mother Beloved said. "I'm absolutely sure. You're a man of character, that is clear. And now we will continue our little celebration with some beluga caviar." She rang a small silver bell on an end table, and a maid appeared with a large silver tray. On the tray was a crystal bowl filled with ice on which beluga caviar sat in a lovely cairn, shiny gray against the clear ice. On another tray melba toast was arranged in a circle. This was Sam's favorite way to enjoy caviar, a food about which he could be reverential. Mother Beloved, he thought, was not all bad, not that that would save her. He crossed to the coffee table on which the maid set the tray and prepared a piece of toast slavered with the sturgeon roe for Mother Beloved and Erika. Then he asked Aldo if he'd like one. Aldo grunted no, and Mother Beloved snorted dismissively at him. Sam simply made another melba toast with caviar and dug in. It was salty and sharp, a tad too much so. Sam squeezed a few drops of lemon on it and tasted again. Just right, perfection. He took a sip of champagne, holding the bubbling Dom Perignon on his palate. Life could be so sweet.

"Tell me, Sam," Mother Beloved said, "is a hundred-odd thousand a good enough payday for you on such a short trip?"

"Exhilarating."

"Good. I don't want a man who broke Faust to feel he has wasted his time here at Valhalla."

"I certainly don't feel that at all."

Aldo grunted, poured himself more champagne and quaffed it like beer. Mother Beloved shot a look at him that said he should consider himself on notice.

"In the morning I am going to take Faust for a little gallop myself," Mother Beloved said. "I've waited so long to ride him I can't believe it will actually be possible. You do think I'll have no problems, don't you, Sam?"

"I guarantee it."

"Wonderful. And then afterward I'll have one of the jockeys work him over the track. I'm dying to time him in six furlongs. I bet with a little work he comes in under one twelve."

"I hope so," Sam said.

"Then maybe come spring I'll run him in some races for three-year-olds, starting him slowly, bringing him along carefully. I know in my heart he has the makings of a champion."

"I think you may be right on this one," Sam said. He shot her a big smile. "How about some more caviar?"

"I'd love some."

"And you, Erika?"

"Yes, please."

"Aldo?"

Aldo said nothing. Bent over the caviar tray, Sam looked up at him. Slowly, very slowly, Aldo shook his head from side to side.

Sam prepared the melba toasts and passed them around.

"We mustn't fill up on this caviar," Mother Beloved said. "I've had the cook lay on something very special tonight, which will be a very special night, if I have anything to say."

"You usually do," Aldo said. He had hit the champagne hard, and it was starting to show.

"Don't be a boor," Mother Beloved said, casting him a stare cold enough to freeze hell. "And ease up on the champagne. You don't drink Dom Perignon like beer, like a peasant."

Looking right at her, Aldo took a big swallow. Mother Beloved chose to ignore him. Instead she looked at Sam and said, "I've had one of my favorite dishes prepared, with the best Brazilian beef. We are having Tournedos Rossini."

"Terrific," Sam said, "it's one of my favorites as

255

well. And I haven't had it in a long while. You're a woman after my own heart."

"Maybe more," Mother Beloved said, laughing. She was getting loose. The champagne and the excitement of the day had gone to her head. Sam saw Erika frown disgustedly at her mother's obvious bawdiness.

"You never know on a very special night," Aldo said. His words were slightly slurred. His eyes were glassy, his face flushed. He scratched the hairs on his chest, which was as close to swaggering as he could come without moving.

"Go to the bunkhouse, Aldo," Mother Beloved said. "You're entirely too boring for this kind of evening."

"I was just on my way," he said, putting his glass down hard on the coffee table and casting a lecherous look from head to toe over Erika, undressing her mentally, throwing sand in her mother's face as best he could under the circumstances.

"Good night," Mother Beloved said, her tone definite. Aldo cast her a sneer, then turned and walked slowly from the room. His boots sounded on the boards of the veranda; then his footsteps trailed off, blurred by the night sounds of the jungle.

"After dinner," Mother Beloved said, "I've arranged something special for you down in the village, Sam. Have you ever seen an authentic Brazilian voodoo ritual?"

"No."

"Well, you won't be able to say that after tonight."

26

BLACK MAGIC

Valhalla Ranch
October 10

They heard the drums before they saw them. The crowd outside the concrete building parted for Mother Beloved and Sam Borne. The building sat in a small hollow behind the houses clustered in a group that formed the main village. It was the village next to the ranch, the one where much of the ranch help lived, where Sam had watched the cockfights the previous evening. This time they had come in search of black magic, the ancient rites of voodoo. For some reason Mother Beloved was determined to treat Sam to a quintessentially Brazilian evening. Or so she claimed. As excited as she was, Sam felt sure there was some big payoff in it for her.

They entered the large concrete building. It was different from the simple shacks in the village, built of tar paper with corrugated tin roofs, that huddled on either side of the main road. With concrete sides, open windows in the walls and a high, pitched tile roof, it stood out from all the others. Judging from the abysmal poverty of the village, Sam was sure that this building had been constructed with help from Mother Beloved. It stood out in grandeur like the churches

257

one saw in dusty Spanish villages, clearly a focal point of some kind, and an object of pride for the inhabitants of the village. Sam had heard of these buildings, better than all the others in the poorest of villages; called *terreiros*, they were built for voodoo rites.

Inside was a large room ringed on three sides with bleachers. In the front was a small stage; above it crude murals decorated the wall. In front of the stage was a simple railing, and behind it sat a group of drummers and two boys, one with a set of gourd rattles, the other shaking lead pipes filled with shot. They set up a steady rhythm that pounded out into the room. In front of the railing was a large open space that stretched to the bleachers on the other three sides. In the front row of bleachers directly opposite the stage a space was left open for Mother Beloved and company.

Sam followed her there now. As he moved behind her he nodded at the villagers already gathered for the ceremony. They were sweating profusely, even the children, since the heat in the building was stifling. Their excitement level was apparent. It seemed to Sam that Mother Beloved kept these people constantly agitated for her own amusement. The children especially were charged.

To all that would happen Sam was no stranger. He had seen voodoo rites in Haiti and other parts of the Caribbean, not to mention in the southern states of America. He had viewed these rites with interest, but they had done nothing special for him, so he could only wonder at Mother Beloved's devotion to them. Looking at her now, he realized that she was every bit as charged as the children. Her face glistened with perspiration, and a glint shone from her eyes.

Feeling Sam's eyes on her, she turned to him and

smiled, flashing her perfect white teeth. "I find these rites unbelievably stimulating, Sam, and I know you will too. Once the natives get properly motivated, you won't be able to bear it."

He doubted this, but kept his own counsel.

"I have found over the years," Mother Beloved continued, "that few things have satisfied me as have these pagan rituals. They are free, unfettered, not complicated like the Christian service. Here people just get to the essentials. They live in connection with the primal drives that propel all of us. I believe a man of your broad sophistication will be greatly touched and motivated by this service, as I always am."

"I'm looking forward to it," he said, and gave her a big smile. He knew that the ritual would not touch him, that nothing substantial would happen to him, but it was good to keep Mother Beloved on the track she had already started down, to keep her running smoothly toward the rendezvous he planned for her tonight.

Beside him, she clapped. At the far side of the room, next to the stage, a curtain parted and a line of women came out. Dressed in white skirts and blouses ringed with red and blue designs at the edges, they streamed into the large room, formed two lines and started to dance to the music. Sam saw that the designs on the skirts and blouses were of spirit symbols; they were similar to those painted in garish murals on the wall above the stage and around the other three walls in a frieze.

As the women danced some of them began to gyrate wildly, whipping themselves into states of excitation akin to hysteria. Shaking and shimmying, they threw themselves with abandon in one direction, then the other. Joining hands, they whipped themselves around the room in pairs. Then they formed themselves into a circle and moved around the perimeter of the room in a counterclockwise motion.

When the line was flowing smoothly, the music pounding out rhythmically, the curtain beside the stage parted again and a tall man stepped out. Dressed in white pants and a bright green shirt, beads dangling from his neck, he moved quickly into the center of the moving circle. He had an air of mastery about him. He was clearly in charge. He was a tall man, about six feet two, with angular features and dark skin. He was no doubt descended from African slaves. Many African slaves here in Brazil had fled their harsh plantation masters and formed small jungle communities, called *quilombos*. Here, in the jungle, in these communities, they had preserved their African religions. In most cases in the New World, these African religions had mixed with Catholicism, and the result was voodoo. Here in Brazil it was often called *candomble* or *batuque*. No matter what it was called, it provided a spectacle. But not being a superstitious man, Sam did not find it stimulating after one or two viewings.

"The man in the middle is the *pai de santo*," Mother Beloved whispered to Sam, elbowing him for his attention. "That is the name given to the male leaders. He will orchestrate the ceremony."

Sam nodded. Mother Beloved went back to directing her attention at the circle of moving women. The leader strolled about casually in the middle of the circle, watching the women move, gyrating and writhing in some form of mental transport. When one woman appeared to convulse, the *pai de santo* gave her a shawl that a young boy brought to him. He wrapped this about the transported woman and she writhed and chanted, lost to the world.

"She is in contact with a spirit," Mother Beloved explained to Sam. "In another realm of being now. I find it fascinating beyond words." Sam looked at her and nodded, hoping his gesture conveyed at least interest, if not enthusiasm. She didn't take time to register his reaction, but returned her attention instead to what was happening in the center of the room.

From behind the curtain at the front came a table on wheels. About the size of a hospital gurney, it had a full white skirt draped from it. When the table was in place in front of the railing behind which the musicians sat, the *pai de santo* bowed to two young boys who immediately went behind the curtain again and emerged with portraits in gilt frames. They were of Catholic saints. The *pai de santo* took these and set them up on either side of the table. Then he nodded at the two boys. They went behind the curtain again and emerged in seconds with a gleaming candelabrum holding seven lighted candles. This the *pai de santo* set in the center of the table. Then the boys came out with two statues, one of the Madonna and Child, the other of the Sacred Heart, the heart exposed and dripping blood, a flame shooting from its top. These the *pai de santo* placed at either end of the table, beyond the portraits of the saints. Then he turned and accepted two vases full of orchids from two young girls dressed in white skirts and blouses with the same spirit symbols designed on them as on the outfits of the women dancing.

The leader now walked over to the woman possessed and led her by the shoulders to a place directly before the altar. There, attended by two other women, she knelt and prayed, shaking and chanting. Meanwhile the circle of women continued to gyrate around the room in a counterclockwise direction. After a short while, another of the dancers was stricken with a spirit. She too was given a shawl and led by the *pai de santo* to a position beside the other possessed woman. The two prostrated themselves before the makeshift altar while the music and dancing went on around them.

After a while, the *pai de santo* clapped, and the circling women formed themselves into two lines. They danced opposite each other while the music played, the two possessed women writhed in prayer, and the audience stared. Then the *pai de santo* clapped, and the two possessed women stood and faced the room, their backs to the altar, wrapped in the shawls. Many of the people in the bleachers climbed down. They entered the open area and walked between the two lines of women to the two possessed women in front. There they knelt and kissed the ground, greeting the spirit gods in possession of the women formally, hoping to gain their good graces. Then the possessed women laid their hands on the heads of the supplicants while the supplicants made their silent requests. The possessed women chanted all the while, their voices discernible above the music. When the supplicants had made a silent prayer, they rose and left and others replaced them on their knees before the possessed.

This lasted for nearly an hour. Sam tried to maintain his interest, but it was difficult. He focused instead on what he had to do that night. He wanted to be ready for the hit. He was sure the opportunity for it would present itself, and he suddenly wanted desperately to get it over with, to get out of Brazil, to cool out. This was always a dangerous phase to enter in any assignment, the moment where you could feel it, taste it, know it as yours, the accomplishment of it, yet know that you had to temporize or it would all be lost. Sam had steeled himself for years to resist impulses at this juncture, to bide his time, to assess and reassess his plans, to retain a cool head and an even pulse and to move only when the moment was completely ripe.

In the room the *pai de santo* walked into the center and clapped. The line of supplicants from the bleachers had dwindled until now there were only the last two. Hearing the clap, they rose and returned to their seats in the bleachers, leaving the two possessed women at the front of the room with their attendants. The *pai de santo* flicked his wrists at the lines of women in white, and they stepped back against the bleachers on either side.

The *pai de santo* turned to the musicians and silenced them with a gesture, then he shot an index finger in the direction of the room's entrance and the lights were doused. All was suddenly plunged into darkness except for the halo cast by the candlelight on the altar. In the dim glow Sam could just see the expectant looks on the faces of the adults and children in the bleachers. Then from behind the curtain at the front of the room came a procession of men bearing torches. The torches appeared to be made of gasoline-soaked rags tied to tree branches. The torchbearers circled the room, then took up positions on either side of the altar. There were ten of them, stretched in a line down the room from the altar.

The *pai de santo* clapped, and from behind the curtain came the bleating of what Sam was sure was a goat. There followed the crowing of chickens. Then into the room came two boys leading a goat on a tether, followed by two girls, each bearing in her arms a flapping chicken. They circled the room, then walked down the aisle formed by the torchbearers. At the head of the aisle stood the *pai de santo* with the two possessed women before the altar. The boys controlled the goat, choking it on its tether, and the girls stood behind, holding the chickens.

The drums started a slow beat, joined after a while sedately by the gourd rattles and the pipes lined with shot. The *pai de santo* clapped again, and a young boy emerged from behind the curtain carrying a large butcher knife and a golden salver. The blade of the knife shone in the light from the candles and torches. Behind him came a girl with a large golden bowl. Both the salver and the bowl gleamed in the light. The boy presented the salver and the butcher's knife to the *pai de santo*. He took them and raised them above his head, breaking into a wild chant, and the women in white joined him. Then he fell silent, and they followed suit. Only the low beat of the music could be heard.

The *pai de santo* motioned to the boys holding the goat, and they brought it over to him. Two men came out from behind the curtain and moved to the goat. They held it steady on either side. Then the *pai de santo* grabbed it roughly by the head and slit its throat. The girl with the golden bowl immediately rushed forward and pushed the bowl beneath the goat's rupturing arteries. The men holding it bore down on it hard. In its death panic the goat kicked and thrashed, trying to free itself from fate. In moments it was over. The goat collapsed. The young girl withdrew the golden bowl. The *pai de santo* raised the dripping knife blade and intoned a chant. Then he reached down and severed the goat's head. Holding it aloft, he placed it on the golden salver and put it on the altar. He raised the blade once more over his head and intoned a chant that the women in white picked up and amplified.

The two men dragged the carcass of the goat out of the room through the curtained entrance beside the stage. The *pai de santo* lowered the blade, and the two girls with the chickens automatically stepped forward. As if sensing their fate, the chickens started to crow. The girls held them out at arm's length, their wings flapping. The *pai de santo* let out a high-pitched chant, then descended on the chickens in a rush. The blade flashed twice as he cut their throats. The girl with the golden bowl rushed from one chicken to the next, catching as much blood as she could, the birds still flapping their wings, their blood spurting out. When the wings stilled, the girl stood back. The *pai de santo* led the women in white in an antiphonal chorus, then he motioned for the girl with the bowl to bring it to him.

In the torchlight, the *pai de santo* raised the bowl above his head, intoning a chant. Then he lowered it, paused dramatically, and took a big draft. He turned to the altar, placed the bowl beside the salver with the severed goat's head, and stepped back. He indicated for the musicians to raise their music, then swept an arm toward one line of women in white, then the other. The lines started forward. Alternating from one line to the other, the women stepped up to the altar, raised the bowl to their lips and drank. When they had finished, the *pai de santo* took the bowl to the two possessed women. With the help of their attendants, each of them took a deep drink. Finally the *pai de santo* offered the bowl to the torchbearers. When they were finished, he placed the bowl beside the salver with the severed head and stepped back. In a loud voice, he led the women in white in a chant, then he swept an arm toward the musicians. They increased their tempo even further. The loud music beat rhythmically around the room.

"They've offered their propitiations to the African gods," Mother Beloved whispered to Sam. "Now the lively part of the ceremony can be carried out with their blessing. Spirits have come and been welcomed. All is well." Sam looked at her in the light reflected from the torches and knew she was mad. "What you'll see next will never leave you," she continued. "Twenty, thirty years from now you will think of it, as will I. It will endure in memory like a living, breathing thing. It is more stark than a bullfight, more lurid than a cockfight. It is simply unforgettable."

Twenty years from now you'll be long dead, Sam thought to himself. And if he remembered this night, it would be because he remembered almost everything about his assignments. He hoped he'd be around, still in one piece, twenty years from now. At the rate the Committee employed him, he took it one day at a time.

In the center of the room the *pai de santo* moved down the aisle formed by the torchbearers until he stood directly in front of Mother Beloved. Silently he bowed to her. She nodded back. The *pai de santo* smiled and turned. He clapped and the curtain at the front of the room parted and two men entered the room. Black, they were stripped to the waist. Their chests glistened with sweat in the torchlight. They both wore white pants cut below the knees like clam-diggers. Both were barefoot. They came down the room until they stood directly in front of the *pai de santo*. He spoke briefly to both of them, then stepped aside as they moved closer to Mother Beloved. She spoke to them in Portuguese, then slowly and deliber-ately blew each a kiss.

The *pai de santo* clapped again and the women in white filed down to the front, where they took up places on either side of the altar. The torchbearers spread themselves at intervals around the room. The large area in the center was now open. The curtain at the front parted again, and two young boys emerged carrying blades in each hand. The blades glinted in the light. As the boys moved down the room to the *pai de santo,* Sam noticed that the blades had leather straps attached to them. The two black men walked to either side of the room and sat on the earthen floor. The *pai de santo* inspected the blades in each boy's hands, then spoke to them rapidly. They moved to the black men stationed on either side of the room. The boys showed the men the blades, then the men reached down and started to fix the blades to their feet, strapping them tight around their ankles, yanking on them hard, making certain they were secure. The boys helped them, adjusting and pulling, then testing the blades gently in the earthen floor. The blades were firm. The boys rose and walked to the far side of the room.

The *pai de santo* bowed again to Mother Beloved, then moved to the center of the room, equidistant between the two combatants. He waved a hand at each and they shimmied forward on their buttocks. When the *pai de santo* held up his hand, both men stopped. They sat watching as the *pai de santo* walked off a few yards and motioned to one of the two boys at the front of the room. The boy automatically went to the altar, grabbed the butcher's knife and walked it over to the *pai de santo.* He took it and started to cut a circle around the two combatants. When he completed the ring, he stepped back and held up a hand. The music stopped. In a loud voice, the *pai de santo* intoned a verse, then pointed the knife first toward one combatant, then the other. The men shimmied to the perimeter of the circle cut in the dirt, and poised. The *pai de santo* raised his arm. The music started.

"This is called *capoeira,*" Mother Beloved whispered to Sam. "It was developed by the slaves from dancing to fool their masters. Disguised as a revel, it would lull the masters, then suddenly the blades would flash and the masters would lie slain. For years it was an effective weapon of the oppressed, but is now nearly extinct. It is pure. You will see only its combat phase."

Sam looked at her dispassionately. She was disgusting. He felt nothing for her but loathing. Seeing her in this light made his task easier. Like a poinsettia, she was beautiful but deadly. She reveled in carnage, in bestial behavior, in bloodletting of one kind or another. Not content with the disgusting spectacle of gamecocks gouging the life from one another, she needed more. She needed to see human beings act out this deadly duel. Sam noticed that her face was enraptured. She was into this in a way no normal person could be, and, realizing as he did that what would follow was nothing short of a command performance for her benefit, a performance in which one man and possibly two would be maimed or killed, he felt revulsion for her course through every nerve and tissue of his body.

Sam turned back to the room. The *pai de santo* extended one arm to each combatant in turn. They nodded and rose, their hands and feet supporting them, each with his back arched off the earth, his chest and stomach toward the ceiling. They rested on their heels, their feet canted out at an angle so the blades would not snag in the earth. They had great strength and conditioning to do this. Sam admired them.

The *pai de santo* dropped his arm, and the drumbeat stepped up immediately, joined in loud counterpoint by the gourd rattles and the pipes filled with shot. The crowd released a collective sigh. The fight was on. Both men scrambled one way and then the other, offsetting each other's moves and countermoves. They crabbed sideways on their heels, their hands scurrying along the ground. They stayed within the circle. For nearly a minute they oscillated. Then one man got a bead on the other and sliced him hard.

Instantly a red line appeared on the stricken man's leg from knee to ankle. The blood gleamed against his dark flesh. His face was a mask of indifference, the pain registering not one iota. The stricken man was apparently not impaired in motion. He quickly wheeled away from the other man, covering half the circle in one direction before reversing himself and shooting back the way he'd come, bypassing his opponent, who reversed himself and pressed his attack. Then in a flash the stricken man thrust a bladed foot at the other and cut him viciously across the calf. Blood stood out immediately on the man's leg, a red stream that coursed diagonally down to his ankle. The man tried to move out of his opponent's way, but his wound was deeper, his mobility more severely impaired. He stumbled backward, the blood now spurting from his sliced artery in a bright red stream. The man who'd been wounded first realized his advantage and pressed the man with the deep calf wound.

In a flash he cut off the other's escape route, forcing him to shift suddenly in the opposite direction, forcing his weight onto the leg with the sliced artery in the calf. He faltered. The other was on him. Instantly he shot forward on his hands and ankles, raised his right leg and kicked powerfully toward his opponent's chest. The blade sank in until the sole of the man's foot jammed against his opponent's chest. The dying man struck out quickly, hoping to take his murderer with him. But he was unsuccessful, the victor flicking a knee at his good leg, parrying it, while with his other leg he pinned the dying man's wounded leg to the ground. Briefly they stared at each other.

This, Sam thought, is what it must have been like for ancient gladiators: opponents in a duel to the death, one lost, the other won to fight another day. The dying man grinned nobly, then his body went slack against the victor's foot. His torso heaved forward, his arms hanging slack. A sickly rattle issued from his throat, just audible above the music from where Sam sat. Then his head lolled forward, his chin on his still chest.

The crowd sat silent. Then the *pai de santo* clapped and the crowd followed suit, none more eagerly than Mother Beloved. Sam applauded, but reluctantly. While the crowd still clapped, the *pai de santo* stepped into the circle and grabbed the dead man about the shoulders. The victor heaved his leg back as hard as he could, rotating it, shaking it from side to side. Finally the blade jerked free, dripping blood. The *pai de santo* let the corpse fall back against the earth, then stepped to the victor and raised his arm. The boy who'd acted as the victor's second came forward and helped him take off the blades, undoing the straps rapidly. Then the victor stood, shining with sweat, his wounded leg still dripping blood, a large smile spread wide on his face. The *pai de santo* raised his arm, then led the man over to Mother Beloved. She congratulated him in rapid Portuguese, shook his hand, then dismissed him. He walked, still trailing blood, the length of the room, the crowd cheering him all the way, then exited through the curtain at the front and was gone. Two men dragged the corpse of the dead combatant across the room and through the curtain.

Just then a drummer leaped from behind his conga

270

and raced to the center of the room. Writhing and spinning, he was in full possession, a spirit having taken him over completely. The *pai de santo* observed him briefly, then gestured to one of the young boys by the altar. The boy disappeared behind the curtain, then reappeared again, holding a small vessel in one hand. This he brought rapidly to the *pai de santo,* who took it and stepped over to the possessed drummer. Grabbing the drummer's hand, he sprinkled powder onto its open palm. Then he turned. The young boy had quickly gone to the candelabrum on the altar and plucked a lighted candle from it. The *pai de santo* took the candle from the boy and held it over the possessed man's open hand. The powder exploded, the possessed man undisturbed by it, protected as he was by the powerful Exu demons of African lore. A cloud of smoke rose from the man's hand, the loud pop of its ignition ringing clearly over the music. Then the *pai de santo* reached out and grabbed the possessed man's other hand. He put the lighted candle in it. The man took it and passed it close along his underarms, then pressed it within inches of his chin. His face impassive, he registered no reaction. The Exu demons were exercising their powers in full. As the possessed drummer glided about the room, the *pai de santo* whirled his hand and the torchbearers and women in white fell in behind him. Gyrating, hips swinging, they sashayed behind him, wheeling about the room, raising their voices in a loud chorus, the drums beating a steady rhythm behind them, the gourds rattling, the pipes lined with shot shaking, filling the air with their high tempo. In the center stood the *pai de santo,* proud as any spiritual leader could possibly be.

Sam felt a hand on his shoulder and turned to face Mother Beloved. She had a feral look in her eye. Her lips were trembling. She was fairly possessed herself. "Now is the time to feel the spirit oneself, Sam. There is nothing like it." Without another word, she rose and stepped down from the bleachers. Seeing her join the whirling mob, the *pai de santo* quickstepped to the altar and took the golden salver with the goat's head from it. He stepped back and waited till Mother Beloved came around in the circling mob. Then he handed it to her. She stepped into the center of the room and traced a smaller circle within the larger one whirling beside her. She raced around the room, her face wild, her hair flying behind her.

Who would believe it? Sam thought. Sitting rooted to his seat, he watched, amazed more than amused. Madness was everywhere. He suppressed an urge to get up and leave, knowing it would be his assignment's undoing, if not his own. Before he could assimilate fully the madness swirling all around him, Mother Beloved was waving wildly with one arm for him to join her, the other balancing the salver with the severed goat's head.

He knew this was no casual invitation. Everything hung in the balance. He rose and descended. Immediately he was swept up in the spinning mob. As he spun along, Mother Beloved hastened to his side and, handing him one side of the salver, pulled him into the orbit of her smaller circle. They raced around the room, the possessed man spinning in the circle on the outside, the two possessed women spinning too, the women in white interspersed with the torchbearers. In the center of the room stood the proud *pai de santo*, arms crossed, a smile lighting his features. He led everyone in an incantatory moan, not a chant, not a verse, not a prayer; merely a moan, long, sustained and ultimately mad.

They circled and circled till Sam thought he'd fall over with vertigo. Each time he looked across at Mother Beloved, she was more into it than the last time. Her eyes were wild. Her hair, matted on her temples with perspiration, flew about her head as she whirled and writhed, shoulders rocking, hips swinging, one arm waving above her head. Perspiration rolled down her cheeks and dripped off her chin onto her cleavage. Her mouth was slightly parted. Her hand on the salver quavered.

Sam himself was drenched in sweat. Bored, aware of the absurdity of the situation yet determined to tough it out and pull off the hit, he persevered, convinced every few minutes that Mother Beloved had had enough, only to look across and see her disappearing further and further into this madness.

Then finally it happened.

She turned to him, possessed, and said, "Sam, I must have you. Now."

27

THAT VOODOO YOU DO

Valhalla Ranch
October 11

"I hope you won't think I'm kinky."

"No. Of course not," Sam Borne said. He was at pains to relax Mother Beloved with whatever it was she wanted to get into. He could handle anything, so long as he could keep her in the mood she had been in all evening. From Dom Perignon before dinner to a stunning Montrachet with it, to Courvoisier afterward, and then to the heady ritual of the *candomble*, from all of it she appeared to be reeling, very near to being out of her mind. She was exhilarated and slightly drunk. And now sexually charged. She was right where Sam wanted her. She could make all the requests she wanted, kinky or otherwise.

"I knew a man of your sophistication wouldn't mind," she said, and smiled. The smile was lopsided and malevolent. She was enjoying something that she was not about to share with him. She raised a forefinger and wagged it at him. "I will disappear for a short while. After about ten minutes, I want you to rise and go through that door." She pointed to a door at the end of the big living room. "When you do, you'll find yourself in a small room with a chair." She paused and smiled, then blew him a kiss on her fingertips. "Just strip. Completely. Then sit. You'll hear me beckon to you from the next room. When I do, rise and walk through the other door in the room. After that, everything will be self-explanatory." She winked at him, then leered, swaying ever so slowly on her feet, crooking her neck. She was trying to be sexy, seductive, even vampish. And she was succeeding. Sam felt his sap start to rise. He forced himself to remain in control, to concentrate. He was on ready alert, every nerve in his body fixed on receiving information and processing it accurately, assessing it, analyzing it; and, ultimately, preparing to act on it.

"I can't wait," he said, then cut her a look nine parts lust and one part longing. It worked. She put down her glass of Scotch and turned without another word. At the doorway leading from the living room, she turned and whispered, "Ten minutes, that's all. Don't keep me waiting." She delivered this last in her best imitation of Marlene Dietrich's gravelly whisper. Then she disappeared. Sam heard her heels clicking on the floor of the corridor, then a door opening and closing. Then all was silent.

Alone in the sitting room, the big fireplace behind him, Sam decided quickly how he would play this: straight, for as long as it took. He would enter into her fantasy, play his part, relax her, then kill her. Once he'd accomplished that, he could concentrate on whatever else the night would bring. He felt fairly certain he could get out of the house and away from the ranch without too much trouble. Once in the jungle he was a match for anyone, and with luck it wouldn't take him long to reach Manaus and get out of the country. He felt a thrill ripple through him, a charge, a rush, the kind of rush he got when the target was in his sights and ready to go.

He picked up his Scotch and took a swallow. All night he had appeared to drink more than he actually had, creating the impression for Mother Beloved that he was as frolicsome as she. In fact, he had been monitoring himself, pacing his alcohol intake. After dinner, he neutralized the effects of the Dom Perignon and the Montrachet with two stiff espressos. Now he was clear-headed. He put down the Scotch and stood. He looked around the large room. It was empty. So far as he knew, the only other people in the house, besides Mother Beloved and him, were the guard in the scanning room and Erika. He stepped off down the room toward the door, wondering what lay in store for him.

In the small room he slowly stripped. The room was bare except for an armchair in one corner. He draped his clothes over the chair, then sat on its edge, waiting. He looked toward the room's other door, the one opposite the one he'd entered. It gave no clue to what lay beyond. In the silence he briefly closed his eyes, then drew several long, slow breaths, clearing his head, poising his system. He opened his eyes and looked around. When he'd entered, without being obvious he had whipped his eyes around the room, looking for detectors, for mirrors, for anything that would give away the fact that he was under surveillance. He found none. Still, there was a possibility he was, so he sat perfectly still, waiting.

He didn't wait long. In moments he heard, clearly and distinctly, Mother Beloved's voice calling him from the next room. He rose and walked to the door, opened it slowly and took one step into the room.

It was dazzling. An army of naked men stared at

him, all the same, all reflections of him. The room was mirrored, ceiling, floor and walls. In addition to his own image, the room held only white. Everything was white, reflected from a huge white bed in its center. Then something white moved—Mother Beloved. Dressed in a flared white wedding dress, her hair topped with a glittering diamond tiara, she stood perfectly still, a maniacal smile lighting her radiant face, her blond hair tumbling on either side of it, her piercing blue eyes shining, her mouth bright with lipstick, her cheeks rosy with rouge. She looked like a fairy godmother, even to the silver wand in her right hand.

She was beautiful. There was no denying it. And desirable. Sam felt a wave of lust roll through him. He fought it, concentrating on what he'd come here to accomplish. Still, his mind had certain ideas, his body others. She noticed.

"I see you want me almost as much as I want you, Sam," she said in her hoarse whisper. She smiled.

"I've wanted you since I laid eyes on you."

"Likewise."

"Then we're both in luck." Sam stepped farther into the room, closing the door behind him. He smiled, then took a step toward her.

"Stop where you are, Sam. We don't want to spoil this."

He stopped. And watched. And thought. Mother Beloved slowly twirled the wand in her hand, looking him over from head to toe. He was eager to get his hands on her. He could only kill her quietly if he could snuff the life out of her. He could not risk killing her in such a way that she could get off a scream or set up a ruckus. He would have to be careful. He would have to wait. He would have to let her control things.

"I know what you think," she said softly.

"You don't have to be a mind reader."

"I don't mean just now. I know what you've thought since you've been here. And I know for sure what you were thinking tonight at the *candomble* ceremony. You were not moved. You considered yourself beyond it. You allowed no spirit to enter you."

"The spirit is in me now. Let's concentrate on that."

"It's a different kind of spirit. I was hoping you would respond to a higher calling when given the chance."

"I thought I did a good job of entering the spirit of the ceremony."

"You merely went through the motions. I could tell. Your body danced, but not your spirit."

"I tried."

"You are a suave man, Sam Borne, but not a sophisticated one. A more sophisticated man would have responded positively to the spirits, would have let a spirit enter him. Yours is a cold mind, a snobbish mind. It's impervious to magic. That's a fatal flaw."

"Why don't you reserve judgment on how sophisticated I am till morning? You'll find out shortly whether I'm capable of magic."

"Yes. But you will do so unprotected by any spirit. No *encantados* entered you tonight, therefore none will aid you now."

She reached behind her. Instantly the dress fell from her. She stepped out of its wide skirt and full bodice. Sam's blood jumped. She was magnificent. Her long legs were encased in white stockings clipped to a frilly white garter belt above spiked white heels. Her torso was covered by a lacy camisole, against which her full breasts pushed. She crooked one leg in front of the other. Sam's throat tightened. If he were not to be lost, he would have to concentrate. His body pulled hard in one direction even as his mind pushed hard in another. He took a small step toward her.

"Don't."

He stopped.

"I don't want to spoil this," she hissed, "so play it as it lays." She unfastened the camisole, and her breasts swung free. They were perfect, full, round, firm. She let Sam feast his eyes, then stepped languidly out of one high heel, then the other. She walked slowly to the edge of the bed and sat down. She reached for the clips on the stockings and unsnapped two.

"I think you should allow me to do that."

"No."

"Please." He wanted to soften her control, to regain some ascendancy, to relax her.

"You will do as I say."

"Yes, ma'am."

She unsnapped the remaining clasps, then rolled one stocking down the length of her leg, slowly, oh so slowly; then she rolled the other, just as slowly, looking up as she did so to monitor Sam's reaction, which was as expected. She was pleased. Laying the silver wand beside her, she made a moue of her mouth, lifted one leg, then the other, sliding her white satin panties from under her. She flicked them at Sam. They hit him in the chest and dropped to the floor at his feet. She picked up the shiny wand and beckoned him with it. She was irresistible, her beauty as radiant as the sun. Her eyes held Sam's like magnets.

"Now, lover man. No preliminaries."

She hitched her legs up on the bed and lay back. Sam moved forward, taut with sexual tension, his mind spinning. He wanted to seize control, and quickly. But his body, all aquiver, ached for her. When he reached the bed, she extended her arms and took him firmly by the shoulders. She was alert, her eyes open and staring up, her right hand clutching the wand, cold against his shoulder. Arching herself, she guided him home. He followed through.

Life's sweetest sensation flooded him. His body went into riot, his mind right with it, blanking completely. Below him Mother Beloved moved, playing him like a string, controlling him. Her arms went behind him. He felt the cold wand hit the center of his back. Despite himself, he felt his will loosen. His legs started to thrust madly. From the soles of his feet, a rush started forward, unstoppable, on its own, self-propelled, moving without thought or volition. His body tightened. It stiffened, it quivered, it shook. Above it all, his mind fought for clarity. Mother Beloved pulled him to her and kissed him hard. Eyes closed, Sam sensed a movement. To his left, behind him, her arm pulled back.

Then it happened. Simultaneously his body exploded and his mind snapped. In a blinding rush, still in the midst of a spasm, he spread his arms quickly, pinning her upper arms against the mattress, sensing danger, aware in some recess of his mind that he had failed but that he wouldn't fail. Without compunction he reached down and clutched her on either side of her throat, lowering his weight against her in such a way as to keep her upper arms pinned down, his elbows jutting painfully into them. She emitted a screech. Then her wind was completely cut off. Focusing all his energy in his hands, Sam pressed his thumbs steadily and mightily into her throat on either side, cutting off her oxygen. She gurgled. He pressed. There came a whooshing sound as her windpipe collapsed. Her face blue, her eyes bulging, Mother Beloved lost all control.

Cold steel landed on Sam's back, then tumbled down it and clattered to the mirrored floor. He ignored it. He held fast to her throat, her body twitching. In moments the twitching ceased. Beneath him she lay perfectly still, her beautiful face spoiled in death, twisted and discolored.

Sam wished he felt nothing, but that was not the case. This was a hit that would haunt him. He had never mixed the ugly with the beautiful so starkly. As he looked at her, disgust washed over him. Disgust with himself. Disgust with the Committee. He felt rage at the Committee for forcing him to eliminate such a stunning creature.

Then he rose and stepped back. His foot touched steel. When he looked down, his feelings clarified themselves, declared themselves. Never would he give what he'd done a second thought. He moved his foot off the cold steel.

On the mirrored floor lay the wand in two sections. From one a stiletto jutted, gleaming brightly, diamond points of light reflecting from it and from the mirrored floor.

He was alive. It was magic.

28

INTO THE NIGHT

Valhalla Ranch
October 11

Sam's ears rang with silence. The clatter made by the falling wand had drawn no one. There were no footsteps, no stirrings at all. He listened for a minute, thinking, evaluating. The house held only the guard in the scanning room and Erika. It was well past midnight. She could be presumed to be sleeping. And it wouldn't be unheard of if the guard were nodding off as well. For now Sam had to move. The first thing was to get dressed.

He left the mirrored room with the big white bed and reentered the small antechamber where he'd disrobed. Quickly he threw his clothes back on. When he was fully dressed, he opened the door leading back to the large sitting room and listened again. Nothing. The house was perfectly still. He stepped out into the sitting room and started across it naturally, not hugging the walls or acting stealthy in any way. In the unlikely event he was being monitored in the scanning room, he wanted to appear as though all were in order. He reached the fireplace without incident and looked out past the veranda. All he saw was the lighted outbuildings. No one moved about. The ranch was empty, everyone sleeping, with the possible exception of the guard in the scanning room and those stationed at the entrance to the ranch and on the waterfront.

It was a safe assumption from what Mercedes had been able to tell him that the scanning room generally monitored only the outer grounds of the ranch house, the gate entrance and the waterfront. There was, to her knowledge, no regular internal monitoring of the house itself. That meant Sam had probably already penetrated the inner sanctum with impunity. His concern now was how to get out of it undetected. The best way to leave, he thought, was to get to the waterfront and escape via the river, one of the many wide tributaries leading to the Amazon. Now all he had to do was leave the house successfully.

To do so safely, he had to take out the guard in the scanning room. So far, on his visits to the house, he had been unable to locate it exactly. But from what Mercedes had told him, he knew that it lay down the corridor beyond the master bedroom where Mother Beloved slept. Thinking logically, he surmised that the mirrored chamber where she now lay dead must be adjacent to the master bedroom. That meant he should start investigating down that corridor.

There was also another option available to him, one he couldn't be sure he wasn't inventing. He could wake Erika and take her with him, enlisting her to show him the scanning room, maybe even using her as a diversion in taking out its guard. She could also serve as a guide to the waterfront; and perhaps there again he might use her as a diversion and get the drop on the guards. There was more than spurious justification for waking Erika and enlisting her in his escape.

He moved off down the corridor, thinking that if he found the master bedroom, one of the bedrooms nearby was sure to hold Erika. He came to a door and opened it. Beyond lay what had to be the master bedroom. In its center it had a king-sized bed with an entertainment unit at its foot. Along one wall was a built-in wardrobe. This was no doubt Mother Beloved's room. Quickly he entered and walked to a small door in one wall. He opened it. It led to a bathroom. He moved to the door beside it, opened it and found himself staring at the dead figure on the white bed, reflected all around in the mirrors. He closed the door.

Retracing his steps, he found himself again in the corridor. He moved down it to the next door. He opened it and found an empty bedroom, one about a third the size of the master bedroom. He closed the door and moved quickly to the next one. Opening it slowly, he heard the soft breathing of someone sleeping. He slipped inside and closed the door behind him. Standing perfectly still, he allowed his eyes to adjust to the darkness. Then he tiptoed across the rug to the side of the bed.

Erika lay before him, her face angelic, her hair splayed out around her on the pillow. She sensed a presence, and opened her eyes. Sam clamped a hand over her mouth and pushed down firmly on her shoulder. Coming out of sleep this way, she naturally panicked, suspecting the worst. Holding her down, his hand suppressing any possibility of a scream, he said softly, "Erika, it's me, Sam Borne. I've decided to leave and I'm willing to take you with me, so long as you agree to do exactly as I say. Is it a deal?"

Her eyes wide, Erika attempted to answer, but Sam still clamped his hand hard on her mouth, making it impossible for her to do so. "Just nod if yes, shake your head if no." It dawned on Sam suddenly that if she should have a change of heart and elect to stay, he would have to kill her to ensure the success of his escape. It was a paralyzing thought, one he hadn't considered. Yet he was sure she would elect to go.

She did. Nodding her head vigorously, she reached up and touched him on the forearm. Relief flooded over him. "I'm going to remove my hand from your mouth," he whispered. "Whatever you do, don't make noise. And tell me right away how close we are to the scanning room and how easy it is to be heard from there." He removed his hand. Erika smiled at him, a smile warm enough to smelt iron.

"The scanning room is at the end of the hall," she whispered. "It's very close, and if we speak in normal tones the guard will hear us. I can dress quickly in the bathroom"—she pointed behind Sam—"and be ready to go while you sit here quietly."

"We won't be able to get away from the house undetected," he whispered. "So it is necessary to overcome the guard. Can you help me?"

"Yes. I know him. He is always making lewd remarks to me. I will lure him in here."

This was perfect. Sam could not have ordered it any better. He smiled at her and touched her affectionately on the shoulder. "Okay," he whispered. "That will do the trick. Just walk him in here. I'll do the rest."

Then she did something that electrified him. She reached out, took his hand and kissed it tenderly. "Thank you," she whispered. "This is like a dream come true for me. I'll do whatever you want."

"Then just do this, and be strong, no matter what happens. You understand it won't be pleasant?"

"Yes." Sam moved back on the bed and she swung the sheet off her. Sam's blood quickened. Dressed in a red baby doll with spaghetti straps, she was incredibly alluring; she looked like every man's fantasy of blond beauty. The skirt on the baby doll barely covered the tops of her thighs. She pushed off the bed and strode across the room, silent on the deep pile rug. Sam swallowed hard and thought of duty. He rose and went to the door and positioned himself behind it. Outside he could hear a low murmur, then footsteps in the corridor.

The door opened and Erika stepped into the room. Behind her came the short, stocky form of the guard. He was fixated on her. He never saw the lightning chop that cut into his throat from the side, paralyzing him, knocking him in a heap to the rug. He landed with a thud. Sam stepped to him quickly, planted a knee firmly in the back of his neck and, slipping both locked hands under his chin, snapped his neck. Looking up quickly, he saw that Erika was horrified. "It couldn't be helped. We'll never make it out of here any other way. You understand, don't you?"

"Yes." She was shaken, though trying hard to be strong. Sam felt for her, wished that it could have been otherwise, then ordered himself to think like someone who wanted to get out of the jungle alive.

"Get dressed."

Erika stood rooted. She had a strange look on her face, a look different from the one of shock she'd had at the killing of the guard. Her look now was filled with relief, but with misgiving; a strange confusion came over her features, reflecting some inner turmoil. Her lower lip trembled. Sam was about to order her again to get dressed when she spoke.

"She's dead, isn't she?"

Sam had not intended to tell her that her mother was no longer among the living, but now he had either to do it or to lie. A lot hung in the balance. There was always the possibility that knowing the truth she would turn against him. But he thought now, as he'd thought since their talk that evening in his room, that she had meant it when she said she could kill her own mother.

"Yes."

For a long interval her face reflected nothing but confusion; then she spoke one word: "Good."

"Get dressed."

"I knew she was dead. You could never have come to me with her alive in this house. None of this could have happened without her knowing it." She paused. "I'm glad."

"Get dressed."

"I will. But I knew from the beginning you were not what you seemed. You aren't, are you?"

"No. Now get dressed. We'll talk when we get out of here."

She moved off quickly to the bathroom. In moments she was back, tucking in a khaki shirt over a pair of blue jeans. She moved to a closet and took out a pair of boots. Pulling these on, she looked toward Sam.

"What's the best way to make it to the waterfront? I know there are two guards there. We have to get there fast. What's best?"

"I think we should slip into the barn, saddle two horses and walk them out of earshot of the bunkhouse. Then mount up and take the bridle path down to the waterfront."

"Could we walk it? Won't the guards hear the horses coming?"

"It's a long walk. The horses will save time in the long run. And when we get near the waterfront, we can dismount, tie the horses and sneak up and overcome the guards."

Everything she said confirmed what Sam had doped

out for himself. The waterfront was a good distance off. The longer they lingered, the more chance of discovery. The best thing would be to clear the ranch proper as quickly as possible, overcome the guards and sail away. It irked Sam that he couldn't just rev up the Rallye and fly out of here, but that would entail too much risk. There was no way they could start the plane without alerting the whole compound. And no matter how fast he was, there was more than a fifty-fifty chance that the plane would be crippled with gunfire while still on the ground or knocked cleanly out of the air. Escape with the Rallye, though feasible, would be daring but foolish. Instead, they would slip off into the night, overcome the guards at the waterfront, disable all but one craft and sail out of here. Mercedes had said there was a good launch at the waterfront, one capable of taking them to Manaus in less than a day. With any luck, they would be so far down the river that Aldo and his forces would have no chance of overtaking them. In the morning, when Mother Beloved was discovered, there would be confusion, maybe panic, and by then they would be in the clear. All they needed was a little luck.

Fully dressed, Erika stood in front of Sam. Her face now wore a smile, the smile the long oppressed have when they're about to realize their freedom. "I'm ready," she said.

"Let's go."

They moved out of the room, out of the house, into the night.

29

ON THE WATERFRONT

Valhalla Ranch
October 11

In the darkness they led the horses slowly, Erika Álvarez walking slightly in front of Sam Borne. When they cleared the buildings of the ranch, they mounted their horses and cantered to the edge of the jungle, where Erika was familiar with the bridle path leading to the waterfront some two kilometers away. Once on the path, they rode steadily, slipping through the dark jungle, the night sounds all around them. They heard the cries of birds and the rustling noises as animals scurried away in the underbrush on either side of the gravel path. During the whole five minutes they rode, they were silent, each alone with his thoughts. Sam had told Erika to rein in when she thought they were close enough to be heard by the sentries at the waterfront, so when she stopped abruptly ahead of him, he knew they were near. He rode up beside her and came to a halt.

"The waterfront is around the bend and down an incline," Erika said softly, her eyes intent, Sam could see, even in the darkness. She had told him in the barn that the two guards rested in a little kiosk at the entrance to the pier built out into the river. They usually

289

lounged there during the night, the nights being nearly always uneventful. Along the pier a number of boats were docked. There were two runabouts and a big launch as well as a handful of canoes.

"Let's dismount and leave the horses here. I'd like to get a look at this layout," Sam said. He did not like the feel of this. It would be no easy thing to overcome two armed guards without some kind of ruse. To try to overpower them would be foolish. He needed a plan, and in order to hatch one, he wanted to look the situation over. On the way down, he had considered using Erika as a lure, but he did not want to endanger her. She had told him back in the barn that she had never had occasion to come here at this hour of the night, some two hours before daybreak.

They tied the reins of their horses to a tree, and Sam followed Erika to the bend in the path. As they rounded it he saw the lights of the pierworks. There were two of them, on stanchions, and they illuminated only a small area. The dark forms of the boats could be seen clearly in silhouette, and in front of them, at the junction of the pierworks and the bank of the river, there sat a small kiosk. This was where the guards would be. The kiosk had two small windows, from which light fell onto the bank and the pierworks. Seeing this setup, Sam liked the situation even less. It was not a good fit. He would have to think of something. Quickly he reviewed his options.

And quickly he decided. He would have to lure the guards out of the kiosk. It would be tempting fate to try to jump them in the kiosk, especially knowing they were in radio contact with the ranch. Even though there was no one in the scanning room back at the main house, there was always the chance that the guards had some emergency option open to them.

Maybe they had a means of rousing the bunkhouse. There was no way Sam could know, and, not knowing, no way he could chance an alarm. To pull this off, he knew he would need Erika's assistance.

From where the horses were tied, if they whinnied it would clearly be heard at the kiosk. If Erika could go back and cause the horses to nicker, the guards would be forced to investigate. Ideally, one would be drawn out, the other remaining behind. Separated, they would be easier to deal with. In that situation, Sam would be able to pick them off individually. In the event they didn't separate but both investigated, he would at least have the advantage of not trying to overcome them in the confined space of the kiosk. He turned to Erika.

"I'll need your help," he said.

"Anything."

Sam felt a great rush for her. Taking her with him was proving more a wise move than an indulgent one. She was paying real dividends. Now if she could only hold up and not panic. It was easy to volunteer for rough assignments, not realizing fully what was involved; it was quite another thing to hold up well when the fur started to fly, and she was extremely young and completely inexperienced at this kind of thing. Still, such courage was always welcome and always gave Sam a warm feeling for anyone who possessed it.

"Do you think you can manage to rile the horses enough to draw the guards' attention?" he asked.

"Sure."

"Good. When you do, I want you to get out of the way. Let's go back now and figure out where you can hide. Once you create the diversion, I want you to get out of the way and *stay* out of the way, is that clear?"

"Yes."

"Let's go."

They started back down the bridle path, their feet crunching on the spalls of gravel. Around them the jungle was alive with sounds, intermittently piercing the silence. Looking up, Sam saw the sky was jet black, with silver stars glinting all over it. With any kind of luck, they would soon be sailing down the river under it, free and easy. But for now there was the problem of the guards.

When they reached the horses, Erika patted them, then turned to him. "I'll have no trouble getting them to nicker. Then I'll just dive into the underbrush here." She indicated the thick plants and trees that grew right to the edge of the gravel.

"No. That won't do." Sam knew that guards were sometimes jumpy. There was no guarantee that, seeing the two horses, they wouldn't panic and spray the brush at hand with gunfire. The suggestion showed Erika's inexperience. "Let's walk back down here and make sure you can duck into the brush on the opposite side of the path." He flicked his hand down the path, and they walked off thirty yards or so. Turning, he looked back to where the horses were tethered. "Okay, this is about right. Make sure you put at least this much distance between you and the horses, and make sure you duck in on this side." He indicated the side away from the side the horses were tied on. "Whatever you do, don't tarry once you've got the horses riled. And don't run or mark up the path. Even in the dark, you can leave tracks if you do this wrong. Just get the horses to nicker, then walk quickly back here." He paused. "Get deep enough that you're not reachable with a poking rifle barrel. Try to get in about ten yards or so."

"Okay," she said.

"I know the prospect of burrowing in a night jungle is not pleasant, but I don't want you exposed."

"Don't be a mother hen."

"Got ya."

As they retraced their steps, Sam ran down what he wanted Erika to do. Since she had no watch, she was to count slowly to sixty fifteen times, allowing him fifteen minutes to position himself where he wanted to be. He did not reveal to her how he intended to handle himself once he walked back down the path and disappeared around the bend. The less she knew the better. He wanted her to execute exactly what he had instructed, and then to stay clear, no matter what happened, no matter what she heard. He would handle everything. She was not to come out of cover until he walked back and instructed her to do so. When he'd told her all he had to tell, he looked at her in the darkness. Her face showed worry for the first time. When she reached out and touched his hand, he realized it was not concern for herself that worried her but concern for him.

"Don't fret," he said. "All will go well. Just remember: Follow my instructions and don't take any chances or come out of hiding no matter what you hear. Got it?"

"Yes."

"Chin up." He touched her on the cheek with the back of his hand, then turned and walked off down the path, weighing his next move, ticking off his options, psyching himself to take out two armed guards with as much dispatch and as little ruckus as possible.

He crouched in the thick underbrush on the bank of the river just to the side of the kiosk. From there he could see clearly the small door to the kiosk, and through one window he could even see into it, though now it revealed nothing. He listened, waiting for Erika to rouse the horses, hearing only the lapping of the river water against the hulls of the moored boats. The chirping of night animals filled the air, and occasionally out in the river a fish would break the surface and fall back with a splash. Otherwise all was still. He was unable to hear any voices at all from the kiosk. It would not have surprised him if the guards were dozing in their chairs, or sitting quietly playing cards or reading. Against his arms the high grass prickled, and occasionally, when he shifted, the leaves of a plant would brush against his back. He crouched low, waiting, realizing that Erika was counting slowly, maximizing the time allowed for him to position himself correctly.

Minutes passed. Sam started to wonder what was keeping her. He had a stab of panic as he thought that perhaps something had gone wrong; someone had discovered Mother Beloved, or had just wandered down to the waterfront and come upon Erika. Then he put such thoughts from his mind, realizing their unlikelihood. No, she was just being cautious, doing it by the book, taking his instructions for law. He told himself to wait, that patience was a virtue.

Then he heard it. The horses nickered high and clear. There was silence. Then they nickered again. Silence followed. After a few seconds he heard voices in the kiosk, followed by the sound of a chair scraping on a wooden floor. A door pushed open, squeaking on its hinges.

Through the foliage Sam saw a square of light fall onto the riverbank beyond the pierworks. Then came a quick exchange in Portuguese. Sam understood enough to know that one guard had volunteered to check out the horses while the other stayed put. This was perfect. Sam could not have scripted it better himself. As he watched, crouching lower, he saw a pair of battered boots walk by, with the barrel of a shotgun dangling ankle high. He listened carefully and heard the footsteps on the gravel as the guard started up the path. Then he heard the other guard go back inside.

There was nothing to do for a minute but steel himself. He did not want to spring out and overtake the remaining guard until he was sure the guard checking the horses was out of earshot. He bided his seconds, listening to the fading footsteps of the guard climbing the gravel path. He counted quickly to ten, for good measure, and was about to slip along the bank, still in the foliage, when his luck got good. The guard came out of the kiosk and stood in front of it.

This was what Sam had hoped for but was not foolish enough to rely on. Still, he'd prepared himself, and now that the opportunity was here, he was ready to capitalize on it. Raising his right fist carefully, he threw a preselected stone the size of a golf ball out onto the path, to the right, up in the direction of the horses. The guard started, the stone alerting all his senses for survival. Through the foliage Sam could see that he'd raised his shotgun to his shoulder and crouched immediately, ready to fire. When nothing happened, he spoke into the darkness. Sam understood he was warning whoever was there to present himself. When again nothing happened, he started to walk forward slowly, the gun still raised and ready to fire. Sam could see his feet approach, draw parallel to him, then pass.

About four feet of brush separated Sam from the gravel path. When the guard had moved past him two steps he sprang forward. In two quick strides he reached the path and hurled himself onto the guard. Grabbing him about the shoulder with his left arm,

Sam chopped brutally into his neck with his right hand, open and flat and slicing down at a steep angle with tremendous force. The blow caught the guard solidly, dropping him to his knees. Sam jammed his own knee into the center of his back and landed on him with all his weight. The shotgun clattered to the ground, scraping against the gravel, but, luckily, not going off. The guard lay unconscious. Sam thrust his knee into the center of the man's nape and snapped back cleanly with both hands under his chin. His neck snapped like dry kindling.

Sam rose and snatched the body off the ground. Holding it under both arms, he dragged it into the brush on the riverbank and heaved as hard as he could. It thudded into the brush and rolled down. A tiny splash told him it had reached the water's edge.

Quickly he reversed himself and climbed out of the brush. On the path, he stooped down and spotted the black shape of the shotgun against the dark gravel. He snared it and stood up straight, listening. There wasn't a sound. Now he had to calculate, and gamble. Assuming Erika had stayed put, by now the other guard would have found only the horses. In all likelihood he would have left them and scouted the area briefly. Finding nothing, he would report back to his partner. That would mean he'd be coming back now.

At a sprint Sam tore up the gravel path until he reached its crest. There, at the bend where the path led off in a direct line to where the horses were tethered, he stepped as quietly as he could into the brush at the side. The guard could be ten steps away or thirty yards, he had no way of knowing. Crouching into the underbrush, he heard nothing. Cradling the shotgun across his chest, he listened. Soon he heard a hand slap hard on horseflesh; then he heard the hooves of the horses crunching on the gravel. Listening intently, he could just discern the sound of human footsteps. The guard was leading the horses back toward the waterfront.

Crouching about five feet in from the corner of the path, Sam could squint through the foliage and make out a good ten-yard portion of the path on the side leading down to where the horses were tethered. In the other direction, he could see the apex of the corner and then another ten yards of the path as it led down to the waterfront. He would time this perfectly. Crouching, he waited, the crunching of the hooves on the gravel growing louder.

In seconds the first dark shape appeared on the path. It was the guard. He was holding the reins of the horses in his right hand, the shotgun dangling in his left. Behind him the huge dark shapes of the horses loomed into sight. The guard drew parallel to Sam, then turned the corner and started down the incline to the waterfront. While the horses were just starting to turn, Sam catapulted himself out of his crouch and leaped out of the brush, adjusting his grip on the shotgun as he came. It all happened too fast for the guard to properly compensate. Hearing the rustle of the brush above the crunching of the hooves, he swung around, dropping the reins, swinging his shotgun from left hand to right. He never made it.

Sam caught him across the face with the barrel of his shotgun before the guard could swing his own weapon into place to fire. The barrel crashed across the guard's eyes and nose with maximum force, sending shock waves up Sam's arms, knocking the guard's head back and loosening his grip on his shotgun, which went sprawling as he fell over backward. Sam was on him instantly, beating down on him with the barrel of the shotgun, the metal slamming into his skull with a sickening thud. Driving blow after blow onto him, Sam pulled up only when he was certain the man was unconscious. Winded, Sam stood for a moment catching his breath, feeling the sweat run down his arms and off his wrists. The exertion and tension had drained him, and in the afterwash he was grateful that things had gone so smoothly, that he had created scarcely a sound. He could have used the shotgun, but at two kilometers in the jungle night there was a small chance that the shot would have been heard. This way was safer.

Bending down, he checked the guard. His face was a mash of blood and tissue, his breathing irregular. There was little chance the man would make it, but since he was no longer a threat to Sam or Erika, there was no point eliminating that small chance. Hitching a hand under each of the guard's arms, Sam dragged him to the side of the path. Then he went back, picked up the other shotgun and led the horses back up the path toward Erika. In the dark he estimated the distance to where she crouched hidden.

"Erika," he called. "It's me, Sam." There was a rustle some fifteen yards ahead; then Erika hopped out of the underbrush. She hit the gravel with a crunch, then walked rapidly to him. Spontaneously she threw her arms around him and pressed him to her. A sweet sensation rolled through him, but he put a hand on her shoulder and pushed her gently back. "Let's move," he said. "We have a clear path out of here, but let's not take anything for granted."

"I can't believe this is happening," Erika whispered, almost to herself.

"It is. And we have to move. Take the horses." Handing her the reins, Sam turned and started back toward the waterfront. When they turned the corner, Erika heard the moans of the guard and started to go to him, but Sam cut her short. They tethered the horses beside the kiosk, and Sam waited while Erika ducked inside and picked out the ignition keys to the launch. When she came out, Sam had a sudden inspiration, stepped inside and took two boxes of shotgun shells from a small shelf, plus an Ingram M-10 submachine gun and an extra thirty-round magazine for it. It didn't hurt to be armed in the Amazon. For good measure, he pulled the wires out of the radio set. Stepping back outside, he told her to set the canoes adrift with a hard push toward the center of the river. While she did this he unhitched the outboards from the two runabouts and heaved them onto the open back of the launch. When they were well out on the river, he would toss the outboards off the back of the launch. In minutes he was ready and Erika joined him in the launch, a thirty-five-footer with twin inboard engines.

In the darkness he inserted the ignition key, then looked around one last time. To his right, at the far end of the pierworks, a dark shape loomed in the shadows, about the size of a two-car garage. He looked back at Erika, behind him on a bench seat. "What's that?" he asked, pointing.

"No one knows. Mother kept it locked at all times. She had the only key. I think Aldo knows, but he's the only one."

For a minute Sam hesitated, an uneasy feeling creeping over him. Then he realized there was nothing for it but to go. He would like to have breached the building, checked it out, made sure he was secure, but it wasn't on. Daybreak was only an hour or so away. Time was precious now. The launch was ready, the moment ripe. He hit the ignition. The big engines sprang to life. He turned on the running lights and the night spot on the bow. The dark river ahead was illuminated, swift, brown and muddy.

"Throw off the lines," he said over his shoulder. When Erika had, he eased the launch out into the river and they were gone, the night air over the windscreen whipping a small breeze into his face. Sam stood at the wheel, calculating cautiously that if they got an hour's free running time, they would be in the clear. Squinting ahead into the dark and treacherous river, he kept a sharp eye for floating logs. He couldn't open the launch up. He would have to feather it until daybreak, but even so, with any kind of luck, they could put Valhalla behind them.

With any kind of luck, in an hour they'd have it made.

30

BY DAWN'S EARLY LIGHT

Amazon Basin
October 11

On the water the light was silver. It started as a glow, grew to an illumination, then settled itself as a silver sheen. Before them, over the bow of the launch, somewhere lost in the mist rising from the river, the sun was trying to break through. In minutes it would rise high enough to burn color back into the jungle; to put green back on the trees overhanging the distant banks; to angle down on the river hard enough to restore its natural muddy color; to paint the plumage pink on the large herons standing at water's edge; to fix the white and black coloration of the *jaburus*, the legendary five-foot storks of the Amazon. But now it was just a presence, the sun, a fiery orb at horizon's end obscured behind a mist the color of old pearls.

At the helm, the morning breeze whipping against his face, Sam Borne let go a sigh of relief. Everything was suddenly good. They were now, he figured, downriver some thirty miles from Valhalla. At the ranch, the cowboys would just be stirring in the bunkhouse. The maids would just be getting to the kitchen in the main house. The guards who took over on the waterfront would just be getting dressed for breakfast. It would

301

be another hour before anyone would discover the havoc he had raised. By then he and Erika would be better than another forty miles downriver. As soon as the mist burned off he intended to open the big launch up, to let it eat up the river. By evening they would be sailing into Manaus. Before they reached the famous floating dock, he would ditch the launch along the river, near the city, preferably in the suburbs. From there they would make their way swiftly, but cautiously, to the airport. They'd book a flight, they'd board it, they'd be in the air, Brazil and Mother Beloved behind them, the assignment complete. To contemplate all of this was sweet, standing at the helm, the morning breeze in your face, a beautiful young woman napping behind you on the cushions lining the rear well.

Suddenly a hand landed on his shoulder. "Sam." The single word hung in his ear like a symphony. It was Erika, awake, alive, and free. The thought gave him a thrill, especially knowing he was responsible for her newfound condition. Slowly her hand curled up from his shoulder, grazed the side of his neck, raked the hair behind his ear. The softness of her hand, the gentleness of her touch, sent shivers down his spine. Cupping his chin, she slowly tugged his head about. Before he knew it, her lips were firmly on his, pressing, probing, her tongue suddenly parting his lips, searching, exploring. With his right hand, he reached out and encircled her waist. He felt flesh. Pulling away, he looked at her.

In the pearly dawn light she stood revealed in all her glory, completely nude. From crown to soles, she was every man's idea of feminine perfection. Her hourglass figure needed no support, no sculpting, no adjustment. It was superlative. Her golden hair, loose now, cascaded down both cheeks and broke against her shoulders, hanging down almost to the tips of her breasts, which, full and firm, were taut in the chill morning air.

Sam took her arm and pushed her back a step. He wanted to view her like a great painting. Indeed, she looked, on the river, like Venus rising. Her hips were full and rounded, her legs slender and shapely, a curve of muscle at the calves tapering to delicate ankles. Her stomach was flat, her waist tiny. At the base of her stomach was a wisp of tawny golden hair. He had never seen a more beautiful woman. He felt snared by the most powerful dream known to man. And he was.

Stepping forward again, Erika pressed against him, curling her body into his, molding her shape to his. Half turned from the wheel, Sam took her in his right arm and kissed her long and deeply. She responded with strength, moving against him, pressing into him, seemingly more hungry for him than woman had ever been for man. He touched her hair, played his hand across her back, caressed her shoulder.

He had a decision to make. He had to decide whether to pursue this was fortune or folly. He pulled away from her kiss, looked at the river over his shoulder. It was turning now from silver to brown. The sun had burned off much of the mist, and away in the distance he could see the green of the shoreline peeking through the wispy air. He checked behind him as far as he could see. There was nothing but brown river, mist swirling off it. He listened. There was nothing but the daybreak singing of birds. Below him the boat swayed slightly, rocking on the wash as the bow sliced through the water. Turning, he looked ahead.

With the mist disappearing, he could see farther now than at any time before. The night light was no longer necessary. He hit a switch and doused it. Ahead the river flowed endlessly, with nothing in the way. There was always the chance they'd hit a floating log, but that was unlikely. By now they were some forty miles from Valhalla, a Valhalla with its boats wrecked. It was likely they were safe. Still, he wavered. He remembered Oscar Wilde's line that the best way to handle temptation was to give in to it.

He felt Erika's long fingers on the buttons of his shirt. He considered. While he considered, her fingers went to his belt buckle. When they did, he reached down and tied the wheel firmly with a hank of rope. They would hold a straight course. Fuck the logs. If they hit one, it would only give the launch a good jolt. Stooping down, he scooped Erika up in his arms and carried her back to the wide bench at the side of the rear well. Laying her down gently, he looked at her again for a second, then knelt beside her as he unfastened his shoes. She was truly incredible. Alive with anticipation, he stood and shucked off his shirt, stepped out of his trousers and briefs. Kneeling again, he kissed her on the lips while his hand caressed her breast, teasing the nipple. She moaned, reached out and swirled her hand across his lower abdomen.

Kissing her throat, Sam lowered his hand. He felt the silken hair at the base of her stomach and caressed it gently, his fingers tracing a soft, consistent path along her wet lips, lingering for short intervals at the top. She moaned and took him in her hand.

"Now, Sam, please," she whispered.

He delayed, caressing her, stroking her, teasing her. He wanted to bring her to exactly the right pitch.

Beneath his hands she squirmed once and started to tremble. Bringing up her knees, her chest heaving, she sighed and moaned. A tremor shook her, then another.

Between short breaths, she pleaded, "Please."

Arching her back, she pulled hard on his upper arms, then more urgently.

Sam rose and lowered himself gently onto her. She reached out and guided him, arching and twisting, trembling and gasping.

Dipping, he entered her. And hit resistance. He thrust forward. A sharp intake of breath followed, and a little whimper. Then he felt something warm and sticky. He knew what it was.

Gripping him hard about the shoulders, Erika gasped, "I wanted you to be the one, the first." Then she moved against him, gyrating hard, swinging her hips. Sam rode her, matching her stroke for stroke till she let him take over, setting the rhythm. Pushing against him mightily, the muscles in her neck and throat drawn tight, she whimpered, then loosed a long string of yelps, trying as she did to free her body from his. He pursued her, pinning her against the bench, propelling her up and up and over the top, taking himself along for the ride. A thousand stars burst in his head, his body quaked, and he emptied himself with a shudder.

She ran her hands along the back of his neck, pinching and grinding, her head thrown back, a long sigh playing out on her lips. Raising her one leg, she ran it along the back of Sam's, then clasped his buttocks in her hands and pulled him hard against her. "It was wonderful," she sighed. "Just wonderful. Thank you."

Above her Sam heard in his head the driving

rhythms of Madonna. Erika was a virgin, touched for the very first time. He had been privileged to do the touching, and had been thanked for it.

His assignment over, this was the perfect conclusion.

31

FLAGRANTE DELICTO

Amazon Basin
October 11

Sam Borne luxuriated in the afterglow, a low buzz filling his ears. He lay on his side, facing Erika, the tips of her breasts brushing enticingly against his chest. She faced him, on her side, her eyes half closed. She stroked the hair at his temple with her index finger, then swirled it around his ear before trailing it across his chin to outline his lips. Propped on his elbow, cradling his head in his left hand, Sam enjoyed every minute of it, her attention like a warm balm on a battered sensibility; killing Mother Beloved, no matter how despicable she was, had not been easy. Though it hadn't disconcerted him, it had unsettled him, and it helped to be enjoying intimacy with another beautiful woman. Beneath them the blue mats of the bench squeaked from time to time. Otherwise the only sound was the soothing music of a jungle dawn. And the buzz in his ear.

The buzz grew louder. In a flash Sam came alert. Leaping off the bench, he scrambled to his feet and stared behind him. At the edge of the horizon, a small red-and-white dot appeared on the muddy surface of the river. As he watched, the dot grew rapidly larger.

His heart kicked in like an afterburner. Snatching his pants from the well, he shouted for Erika to rise and dress. She sat up languidly, eyeing him. Then she said, "Don't be such a prude."

"Get dressed," he said over his shoulder as he pulled on his shirt and went forward to the cockpit. As soon as he reached the wheel he untied the rope he'd used to hold the launch on course. Then he hit the throttle. The launch shot forward, the bow bobbing under the sudden acceleration. In seconds he had the launch under full throttle. Looking behind him, he saw beyond the stern that the red-and-white dot had grown enormously. Watching intently over his shoulder, the launch now cutting through the water at nearly forty knots, the bow up, spray fanning over the sides, Sam saw the red-and-white dot grow distinct. It was a speedboat, a very fast speedboat, one gaining on them rapidly.

"What's wrong, Sam?" Erika asked. She was behind him. She'd pulled on her slacks but was still topless. Instinctively she leaned against his back, still in the mellow mood of their lovemaking. When she started to massage his shoulders, he pushed her gently away and continued to look past her at the speedboat, now close enough to be made out as a red-and-white Donzi. It looked like a twenty-two-footer. Sam knew the boat. It was a dazzling speed machine, a custom-crafted number built in Fort Lauderdale and capable of reaching a speed of sixty-five miles per hour. He had once bobbed around Long Island Sound in one, annoying the serious Connecticut sailors. He knew the deep-down muscle of its 360-horsepower Mercruiser engine, not to mention its lightning maneuverability. He knew he was no match for it.

308

"Get down," he said, leaning hard on Erika's shoulder, forcing her to the floor of the well.

"What's wrong?" she protested. "I can go topless if I want."

Just then, over the sound of his engines and the roar of the Donzi, Sam heard the unmistakable sound of an airplane engine. Looking up, he saw the Rallye. It was bearing down on them rapidly, coming in over the Donzi.

Erika started to rise.

"Stay down," Sam snapped, pushing on her shoulder. With his right hand, he reached out and grabbed the Ingram.

Erika kicked him. "I don't have to take this," she said. Sam ignored her. She punched him in the thigh. He ignored it. The Donzi lay just off his stern on the starboard side at a forty-five-degree angle. He could see the five men in its cockpit, four armed with submachine guns leaning over the gunwale. He cut the launch hard to port. The Donzi sliced in behind them.

Instantly it was on them.

Yelling "Get down," Sam flung Erika, who'd half risen, against the forward bulkhead, shielding her with his body, the Ingram still in his right hand.

Machine-gun fire raked the launch, splintering fiberglass, sending shards of it flying through the air, mixing with the flying lead in a deadly maelstrom. Above them the windshield shattered, raining plexiglass down on them. Then the firing stopped. The launch rolled in the Donzi's wake, listing and pitching in the huge swells. Sam wondered when the Rallye would strike. Immediately he started to count, timing the interval for the Donzi. It would have to swing around to come back at them again. He needed to know how long that would take.

309

Just then machine-gun fire stitched the well and bisected the cockpit, narrowly missing them. Sam had pinned Erika as hard as he could against the forward bulkhead and the floor, balling them together in a tight knot, pulling in limbs, making as small a target as possible. The Rallye roared overhead and Sam continued to count, trying to estimate both the interval for the Donzi and the approximate amount of time it would take for the Rallye to strike again.

Bracing Erika as hard as he could, he felt her tremble. Face to face with death, she was no longer strong. The siege had reduced her to putty. He felt her shoulders shaking even as she tried to say something and failed. Sam could only guess where the next attack would come from, but his strong hunch told him the Donzi would strike next from the opposite side, from the port side. He adjusted his position slightly, and that of Erika. Still clutching the Ingram, he realized he would have no chance to use it yet. It would be suicidal to try to return fire now, not knowing if he would expose himself to the brunt of the next firestorm at exactly the wrong time. He continued to count.

He got nearly to the two-minute point when machine-gun fire exploded over them from the port side, ripping at the fiberglass, tearing it and sending pieces of it flying. It mixed with the flying bullets, some ricocheting off the gunwales, the floor and the bulkhead. Sam felt a snick in his left shoulder and knew instantly he'd been hit by a shard or a bullet. He felt the sticky wetness of blood ooze onto his shirt.

In a corner of his mind, Sam indicted himself for not sabotaging the Rallye, for not investigating the locked boathouse that had obviously held the Donzi. He heard again Mercedes telling him that Mother Beloved had promised never to be captured at Valhalla, and it all made sense: the plane, the secret speedboat, the whole setup. But self-recrimination wouldn't wash. He couldn't have tarried at the ranch, making sure the Rallye wouldn't fly. He had killed its only bona fide pilot, yet it was clear now that Aldo's boast on the flight back from Manaus was not an idle one. He could fly the plane, and was doing it now, trying his best to kill him, Sam Borne. And as for the boat-house, it had been still better to get off the waterfront fast. He could never have risked going back to the house, looking for a key. And breaking in, he was sure, would have caused a ruckus, or even set off an alarm, besides wasting precious time. No, recrimination was all bullshit. If Sam had pulled the short straw this time, so be it. He would live with it—or die with it.

Right now he would avail himself of his only chance. Leaping up when the Donzi passed and spinning the wheel around farther to port, he made a run for the riverbank, about a mile and a half away. He would let the chips fall where they might. If they could make it to land, they would have at least the sliver of a chance at survival. On the river, they were out of the running, sitting ducks. But on land they might make it.

As he thought this, water washed into the boat. It spilled into the cockpit, slowly filling it. The launch was riddled with holes. They were taking on water everywhere.

They were at full throttle. The Donzi wouldn't be back for another minute and a half. Sam had it within his power to do one other thing that would give them a fighting chance. Rolling again in the swells from the speedboat, pitching and listing, the launch struggled to maintain speed. His left hand steady on the wheel, holding them on a sharp course for the riverbank, Sam shifted to the gunwale and crouched there, exposing as little of himself as possible, cradling the Ingram.

Above the rumble of the launch's engines, Sam listened for the Rallye. If his calculation were right, it would return before the Donzi. He glanced back at Erika. She was crouched against the bulkhead as he'd left her, in a tight ball.

Sam figured the Rallye would angle in on them from the port side, ready to unleash another salvo. From the sound of the engine and the accuracy of the gunfire last time, Sam estimated the Rallye would be in slowflight.

Here was his other chance to reduce the odds against them.

Sweating, he fingered the Ingram.

32

BESIEGED

He heard it before he saw it. The Rallye flashed white in the corner of his eye, coming in at an angle on the port side. It came from Sam's right as he crouched against the gunwale, the Ingram M-10 cradled against his right forearm. He could see Aldo clearly in the cockpit, leaning over the side, his submachine gun ready to unleash a fusillade at the launch. There was no time to think, no time to play marksman. There was only time to do one thing, and Sam did it. Bracing the Ingram up against his shoulder, he swung it out a few inches over the gunwale, cocked at an upward angle. Then he raised it higher, at the same time crouching behind it and sighting. He led the Rallye slightly. Then he opened up.

Sam had only thirty rounds. He didn't want to waste them. Holding the Ingram in a tight lead, he watched the Rallye fly right into the line of fire. As close as he was able to, Sam held his fire on the engine. Aldo returned fire, spraying the water in front of the launch, then shattering its side, splintering fiberglass and forcing Sam to flinch.

Too fast to comprehend, Sam's plan worked. Holding the Ingram steady on the engine, hoping to sever a fuel line or nail a carburetor, he succeeded. It burst into flames. Instinctively Sam raked the cockpit, forcing Aldo back, shattering the plexiglass of the canopy. Without pause, Sam swung the Ingram out and blasted the wing, holding his fire as near as possible to the tanks. Flames burst from the wing. Yawing violently, the Rallye veered to the left, passing over the launch in a fiery ball.

Swiveling around, Sam saw the Rallye dip violently, then convulse in a small explosion, pieces of the flaming wing dropping off. It swung around ninety degrees, dipped violently, then plummeted into the river, its flames sending up an eerie hiss as they interfaced with the water. In seconds its tail stood straight up, then slipped down and disappeared beneath the surface. The water sizzled and the Rallye, and Aldo, were gone.

But the Donzi wasn't. The roar of the Donzi's engine filling his ears, Sam looked beyond the steaming point where the Rallye had disappeared. Coming in fast on its flank was the red-and-white speedboat. Pivoting, still in a crouch, he threw himself on Erika, pinning her tighter against the intersection of the bulkhead and the deck. A withering fusillade ripped into the launch, the tearing sound of fiberglass again counterpointing the chatter of automatic fire, the whirring sound of the bullets flying overhead and ricocheting around the well and the cockpit. More plexiglass shattered, pouring down on Sam's back as he lay prone against the deck, his left arm pressing down on Erika, his right hand still clutching the Ingram. Bullets still tore into the cockpit from the direction of the bow when the launch started to roll, dipping and cresting, in the wake of the big speedboat. The water in the cockpit washed from side to side, soaking Sam and Erika. Flipping quickly onto his back, Sam held the Ingram on his stomach, keeping it out of the water. He had made a decision.

As soon as the fire trailed off from the Donzi, Sam leaped up and spun the wheel hard to port. Through the shattered windshield he could see that the river-bank was something more than half a mile off. The throttle still at full bore, the launch was riding erratically in the water, a great deal of drag caused by its nearly shattered hull. It was taking on water rapidly. Glancing to starboard, Sam saw that the Donzi was swinging around for another pass. Holding the wheel hard to port, Sam realized that their chances were next to none. But he couldn't forestall the hope that if he could force the Donzi to cut back on the port side, between the launch and the riverbank, provided the launch could survive one more barrage from the sub-machine guns, he would have the slimmest of chances at reaching the bank and getting them both off the river. Once on the bank, he could use his jungle skills, and the Ingram and the shotguns, to at least make it interesting. As he thought this the launch started to list to port, losing speed. It was going to be close.

Watching the Donzi swing around, Sam reached out and snatched a new magazine from the dash. He extracted the partially spent magazine and rammed the new one in. This would give him thirty more rounds, no match for the firepower on the Donzi, but at least a cushion if they did succeed in reaching the riverbank and had to engage in a firefight, either there or in the jungle. Then it dawned on him that Erika had not made a sound, not even a whimper, for some time. He looked down at her.

The muddy brown water around her head and

upper torso was marbled with pink. Checking quickly, Sam saw that the Donzi had made its turn and was coming back, not yet declaring itself. It would strike either to starboard or to port, he couldn't tell which. He had maybe half a minute. Stooping down, he shook Erika by the shoulders. She didn't respond. A lump leaped into his throat. Shaking her harder, he yelled her name. There was no response. Her body lay listless in the muddy water. Anger tore through him. Rising again, he saw the Donzi bearing down on him, cutting in to the port side, moving at tremendous speed. Enraged, realizing he would die on this stinking tributary of the Amazon, the death of so beautiful a young woman weighing on him forever, he opened fire.

And immediately realized his mistake. The return fire from the Donzi, tearing first into the bow of the launch, kicked in Sam's finest instincts for survival. Flinging his legs out from under him, he threw himself to the deck and lay there as tight as possible, his body prone, the brown water washing over it, the Ingram held above it as much as he dared, which was little. The bullets tore into the launch, their high whine mixing again with the sounds of shattering fiberglass.

Over this Sam heard the roar of the Donzi's big Mercruiser engine. Then he heard a thud. Suddenly the sound of the engine changed. It roared higher, surging. Sam had heard this sound before. The propeller was out of the water. Raising his head slightly, enough to peer through a hole torn in the side of the launch, he saw the Donzi standing on its stern, out of the water. Then it flipped sideways, spinning, hurling the gunmen from the cockpit, the pilot clinging to the wheel, suspended, before losing his grip and plunging into the water beneath the upturned speedboat, which hit the river with a plop, its big propeller spinning free above it in the air until, with a deep groaning sound, the Mercruiser cut out, water having flooded it.

The Donzi floated. Sam stood. The men from the boat surfaced and clung to its side. Sam raised the Ingram. In a sharp burst he raked the side of the boat, drilling each of the men where he clung, watching as they jerked with the impact of the bullets, lost their grips and slipped below the surface.

The launch listed harder to port, the engines changing pitch. Awash in river water up to his calves, Sam looked down and saw the still form of Erika. Bending down, he turned her over. She was beautiful still, even in death. Her forehead had a hole in it right below the hairline. It occurred to Sam that if she hadn't been in the way of the bullet, shielding him, it would have killed him. He felt cold and empty. The deck lurched beneath his feet, the launch listing harder to port. Behind him the engines sputtered. He was now maybe two hundred yards from shore. The engines coughed and kicked. Listing, the launch bucked. Instinctively he put his hand on the throttle, ready to coax it, to nurse it somehow so it held together for another two hundred, now a hundred and fifty, now a hundred yards. It coughed, it sputtered.

Then it cut out. The launch moved forward on momentum, its bow down, no longer high and slicing through the water. The riverbank was some eighty yards off. The launch slowed. With luck it would make it. Without luck Sam Borne was going to have to brave a large tributary of the world's most treacherous river, the Amazon. It was a prospect that gave him pause.

Low in the water, moving slowly, the launch took on water like the *Titanic*. Erika's body was now a good six inches under water, its features still clear, her breasts

317

bobbing in the current, her hair fanned out in the brown liquid like Sir John Everett Millais's painting of Ophelia Sam had studied so often in the basement of the Tate Gallery in his student days at RADA. Her blood still marbled the muddy water. Standing in the water almost up to his knees, Sam had an unpleasant thought.

He stepped up onto the blue matting of the bench, now riddled with bullet holes, its foam-rubber interior sticking out in places, badly nicked by the bullets. He turned and studied the shoreline, now only some forty yards away. At the rate the launch was drifting, it would take only a minute or two for him to reach the safety of the bank. Behind him he heard the water churn. His heart caught in his chest, pounding arrhythmically, unsteadily, racing. He forced himself to look, his instincts telling him to keep it to a glance.

What he feared had happened. Above Erika's body the muddy water churned with a yellow foam. Her blood had attracted a school of piranha. Slithering into the cockpit through the gaping holes in the hull of the launch, they attacked her beautiful body with avidity, lost in a feeding frenzy. In a glimpse Sam saw all he needed to; all he had feared was there in a glance. His stomach churned. His head reeled. Grasping the Ingram hard, by reflex he moved back a step along the bench. A wave of dizziness passed over him. Bending at the waist, he vomited into the well of the boat. Beneath him the bench lurched. Unbalanced, he nearly fell backward into the river. Bucking, the launch shifted lower in the water. Now the well and the cockpit were full nearly to the gunwales.

Looking to shore, Sam saw that he had only twenty yards to go. Yet the launch was nearly still in the water, sinking, the river's current the only thing pushing it along at this point. The bow settled lower in the water, and Sam shimmied along the bench till he reached the transom, now the highest part on the boat.

He had fifteen yards to go. In front of him the water still foamed yellow above Erika's body, the piranha tearing into it, stripping it clean. Frenzied by blood, they would allow Sam no chance if he attempted to reach shore by entering the water. Sweating, fighting wave after wave of nausea, he balanced himself on the transom.

Beneath him the launch settled again. It would not make it to shore, but would sink here, some five yards out.

About three yards ahead, the branch of an over-hanging tree jutted out above the river. The launch listed, sinking, yet drifted slightly. With just a little more drift, Sam would be able to reach the branch. He offered a silent prayer to the seven lucky gods of Japan, concentrating on Ebisu, the god of sailors.

The launch continued to drift slowly, settling lower in the water all the while, sinking. The branch was some five feet away, off to Sam's left. The launch shifted again, the bow disappearing beneath the muddy surface. Water surged over Sam's feet. He hurled the Ingram as far as he could. It hit the river-bank with a thud.

He leaped and caught the branch with his left hand. Pulling himself around, he stretched out his right hand. The branch broke. Grabbing desperately with his right hand, Sam latched onto the branch behind the break. Swinging out, his feet hit the water. Quickly he pulled them upward, straining them forward, and looped them over the branch, farther down, nearer to shore. Upside down, hanging by his arms and legs, he shinnied down the branch. When he was near enough, he flipped himself upright, stood on the branch and leaped for the bank. He hit its soft, muddy flank, then rolled upright on his hands and knees. The Ingram lay in a patch of fern some three feet away.

It was Sam Borne against the jungle.

33

NOT FOR NOTHING

Dorado Beach
November 1

"Hit him."

The deep silky voice came from over his shoulder. The dealer hit the shoe, and a five of diamonds hopped out. That gave Sam Borne the magical number of twenty-one. The dealer flipped him a chip, and he turned to see who belonged to the voice. She was stunning: tall, dark and ravishing. Dressed in a black sheath, with a single strand of pearls around her scooped neck, her breasts swelling against them, she was enough to give him a quick case of romance in all the right places.

"Thanks for the advice. I usually hold on sixteen," he said.

"Sometimes it doesn't pay to be too conservative."

"If you say so."

"I say so."

"Care to play a hand or two yourself?"

"Delighted."

Sam rose from his stool and graciously assisted her onto it. As she adjusted herself, constricted by her tight skirt, his pulse rose. She played ten hands, won

321

eight, and started to draw a crowd. Sam had never been in a casino yet where a woman on a hot streak didn't draw one. Crowds accumulated around a woman winning with twice the speed and in double the numbers as those around a winning man. There was a tension, a thrill, an almost sexual charge around a woman winning at gambling that drew people like sharks to blood. After three more hands, two of which she won, the woman turned to Sam and said, "I've won enough for dinner for two at El Convento. Care to join me?"

"Delighted to."

"Let's call a cab."

"Not necessary. I have a car."

"Let's go then."

Sam helped her down from the stool. They cashed their chips and headed out through the lobby. Sam handed the carhop the chit and turned to his dark-eyed companion. "Where did you learn to gamble like that?"

"Around."

Sam smiled and she smiled too. Her smile was radiant, shining from a wide, sensuous mouth full of dazzlingly white teeth, and from large oval eyes the color and depth of well-polished mahogany. Her whole face lit up when she smiled.

"My name's Sam."

"Mine's Adina."

"Is this your first time here?"

"No. I've come here for years, even with my parents years ago. How about you, this your first time?"

"No. I've been here a few times before."

"It's good for a long weekend now and then, even a week if you can squeeze it in."

"How long are you here for?"

"Just a few days. I have to be back in New York for an important client meeting on Tuesday."

"That gives you three whole days."

"How about you? Judging from that tan, I'd say you've been here awhile."

"A little more than a week," Sam lied. In fact, he'd been here over two weeks. He'd spent the time till now recuperating from the shoulder wound he'd received in the Amazon, and brooding over the death of Erika Álvarez. It was a sore point with him, losing her. Otherwise, he would have executed the perfect assignment. Of course, he'd had a lot of luck. The floating log that had wrecked the Donzi was pure good fortune, but then Sam had forced the speedboat closer to shore, closer in to where debris would float on the big river, so maybe it wasn't all luck. At any rate, it was a big break, one that enabled him to be standing here, dressed in an ivory wool tropical suit from Ralph Lauren over a blue-and-red-striped Turnbull and Asser shirt and a subtly patterned red tie by Ungaro Uomo. With a Patek Philippe watch and light brown alligator loafers completing the look, he might well have passed for a young investment banker on holiday.

"You're lucky to get so much time off. What do you do?" She was definitely from New York; nowhere were people so direct as they were in New York.

"I'm an investment banker."

"In New York?"

"No. London."

"And you can get that kind of time off?"

"My partners thought I was near to burnout, so they suggested I take a fortnight out of the country."

"You don't sound British except for that fortnight business."

"I'm not. I'm working over there for a firm run by Americans."

"New Yorkers?"

"Texans."

"Oh."

"In any event, I got the time off and came here again."

A silver Lotus Turbo Esprit pulled into the circular driveway. Sam stepped up and opened the passenger side. Adina gave an appreciative look, then slid into the sculpted bucket seat, flashing just enough leg to quicken Sam's pulse. Closing the door, he handed the carhop two dollars, then walked around and climbed into the driver's seat. Slipping the Lotus into gear, he moved out of the driveway. Down the long access road, overshadowed by stately palms, they drove in quiet. When they got out onto the public road, Sam let the Lotus out a little and the spunky 910 engine responded quickly. They were through the town and out on the wide expressway to San Juan before he really opened it up, letting the Lotus range up to ninety miles per hour before cutting it back. At fifty thousand dollars a pop, Sam found the Lotus to be good value for the price. Responsive as a cat, it handled well, cornered well, had great lateral acceleration and held the road like a Formula One racer, from which, of course, it was developed. The Brits were taking a lot of hard knocks these days, but they were a people who still had a feel for the best, and how to build it; at least at the Lotus works in Hethel, Norwich, they knew.

As they drove toward San Juan the sun set behind them. Adina said little, and Sam followed her lead. As they passed the housing projects with the garish murals, Adina said that she found them reminiscent of subway graffiti in New York, but Sam thought they showed more structure, if less feel for design and color. "Are you interested in art at all?" she asked.

"Yes. All kinds, everything from typefaces to Julian Schnabel."

"Then you really should live in New York."

"London does all right, and in my job I travel a lot."

"Do you get to New York often?"

"Not enough. It's hard to get enough of New York, but I manage to hit it about three or four times a year."

"That's not enough."

"Agreed."

They drove along again in silence. When they reached the outskirts of San Juan, Adina stirred in her seat. "Do you know," she said, "I once saw the most fabulous sight right about here. A double rainbow, the two of them arching into the sky, one above the other. I've never forgotten it, and I never will."

"Puerto Rico is full of surprises. Its natural beauty is underrated."

"Not by my cleaning lady. She's always homesick."

"You'd be too if you'd grown up here." Sam smiled across at her, his face lit by the glow of the recessed instrument panel. She was hunched back into the seat, sidesaddle, gazing at him. She smiled back, but somehow her face didn't respond the way it had back at the casino.

When they hit the cobbled streets of old San Juan, it wasn't long before they drew up to the famous restaurant in the converted convent. They got out, entered and were seated at a lovely table in minutes, its white linen tablecloth and shining silverware warm and inviting. They hadn't been seated long when, over vodka Gibsons, Adina asked Sam why he'd been reading a book as heavy as Turgenev's *Diary of a Superfluous Man* on the beach that day.

"I'm flattered you noticed."

"That doesn't tell me why you were reading it. It's hardly a beach book."

"I like Turgenev, I like literature. And it's a book I've been meaning to read for years."

"Should I read it?"

"Of course. I'll give it to you."

"Thanks."

"Your book was hardly a beach book either."

She flushed, pleased enormously that he had noticed her on the beach. "I've been planning to reread *The Sun Also Rises* for years, ever since I read it in college."

"Any special reason?"

"None, I hope. What do you think of it?"

"It's a remarkable novel, for style at least, but Hemingway must have been an unimaginative lover."

"Hemingway?" She was incredulous.

"Jake, at least."

"I don't understand."

"Think about it."

She did, and in a minute grinned widely. "I see," she said. The waiter came and they ordered. Adina ordered a chicken paillard and Sam a shark steak. On the side they ordered braised bananas and cold asparagus with hollandaise sauce. Then Sam requested a bottle of Batard-Montrachet. The wine came first, the asparagus right after. The cold white wine, so full-bodied and dry, offset and complemented the cold vegetables exquisitely. When their entrées came, it held up as well against the shark and the chicken. They settled back over *poires* and Adina's face flashed distraction. It was not the first time he'd noticed it.

"What's bothering you?" he asked gently.

"I have a meeting Tuesday with our biggest client,

the franchise for my agency, and I don't have a slogan
for them yet. They're the biggest and the best auto
dealer in the New York market, but a lot of newcomers
are making chopped liver of them and I can't think
how to stem it."

"They're bigger and better?"

"By far, but they're losing customers to flashier
dealers. And I don't seem capable of stopping it. I'm
afraid I'm going to lose them." Adina's face, so young
and vibrant, coiled with worry. Over dinner, she had
told Sam how her father had built his advertising
agency since the late forties, then brought her into the
business after college. He'd had no sons. Adina had
worked her way up, but she hadn't been sure she could
handle things when her father died suddenly of a coro-
nary a year ago. Now she was beset by doubts even
more severe.

"You should go with your strengths," Sam said.

"That's easier said than done. This New York auto
dealer war is a small-scale version of the burger wars.
Everybody's playing for keeps."

"Still, your client is the biggest and the best. Does
it have that tradition behind it?"

"Yes."

"Then go with it."

"How?"

"You need one line, I take it. A sell line like 'We try
harder' or 'Only her hairdresser knows for sure'?"

"Right."

"Why not 'Not for Nothing Number One'?"

Her face lit up like Las Vegas. She smiled the deepest smile Sam would see till Christmas. "I think that's
it. I think that could do it. We'll keep it simple. Just the
one sell line."

Sam smiled. "Always keep it simple." He raised his

right hand and scribbled on the air. The waiter brought the bill but, before he could pay it, Adina snatched it away. "Remember," she said, "this was my treat. We're eating my gambling profits." They both laughed.

Outside, they retrieved the Lotus quickly and set off in the moonlight for Dorado beach. On the way, Adina was quiet, so quiet Sam popped a tape into the deck and filled the cockpit with music. Glancing over at her, he wondered again if she were troubled, if maybe she were having second thoughts about the sell line.

"What's got you so quiet again?" he asked.

"I'm wondering what to do on Tuesday."

"I thought we'd put that problem to bed."

She laughed. "Oh, we did. I mean the problem of the election. Who to vote for. I don't know whether to vote for Reagan or Mondale. I don't know whether to vote my conscience or my pocketbook. What are you going to vote?"

"My ear."

She hesitated. "Your ear?"

Sam nodded toward the tape deck. "Wynton Marsalis. I'm sponsoring him as a write-in candidate."

"Not a bad idea."

"Why don't you do it too? That way I won't feel so lonely and you won't be so troubled. I have a feeling the election is a lockup, anyway."

"No doubt you're right." She giggled and settled in her seat, her head back, staring up at the moon. When they reached the Dorado beach, Sam pulled up in front of the pavilion and hopped out. He gave the kid two dollars and went around to Adina. "What now?" she said, with more than a hint of challenge in it.

"Why don't you come back with me and get *The Diary of a Superfluous Man?*"

"Good idea. I'll also have a nightcap, if you don't mind."

"Not at all."

They walked along the lighted path to Sam's second-story beachfront room, the moonlight raining down on them, the chirping of the legendary *coquis* filling their ears. When they reached the room, Sam quickly broke out an old bottle of Haut-Médoc. He poured two goblets and handed one to Adina. "To a great copywriter," she said, clinking her glass off his. They took a sip, smiling.

"Would you like some music?" Sam asked.

"I'd love some."

He went to the stereo and slipped on *The Best of Bird*. Soon the sounds of the Charlie Parker Quintet filled the room. They swung into "Dexterity." Sam picked up the Turgenev and turned back to Adina. She had climbed onto the bed, her shoes off.

"Bring it over," she said.

He did. When he sat on the bed beside her, she reached up and pulled him to her. They embraced, kissing deeply. For a long time they were motionless, then Sam dropped the book and climbed onto the bed.

Bird soared.

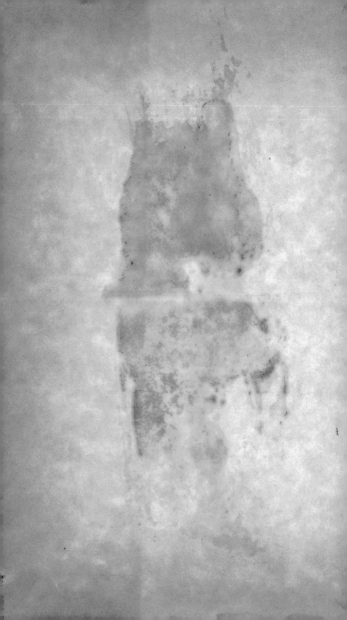